UNITED LOVE

TERRI LYNNE & THE UNIVERSE

For more information about the author,
Terri Lynne please visit:
www.UnitedLove.Love
TLWhispers@UnitedLove.Love

ISBN: 978-1-7345839-0-8

Dedication

I am dedicating our
"LOVE" story to all;
The Lovers
The Dreamers
The Peacemakers
The Believers
The Earth Angels
The Light Workers
And
The Healers
Upon Earth and
Heaven sent to manifest
"UNITED LOVES"
BIG DREAM
Come true!
I believe you all know who you are!
This book is created for and dedicated to... YOU!
With heartfelt LOVE from my HEART
to yours!

Table of Contents

Acknowledgments

First and foremost, I wish to acknowledge every ONE of the LINKS in our CHAIN OF LOVE, whose energy has filled the pages. I wish to say THANK YOU for allowing our hearts to unite in order to create a LOVE story to share with the Universe!

Together we are initiating a LOVE REVOLUTION, or "Lovelution," as I like to call it. This "LOVELUTION" is a revolution transcending borders, race, culture, religion, age, genders, and beliefs.

Love is... meant for all, because
Love is... the universal language.

If you find yourself holding this book, you are part of this "Lovelution." I thank you for the role you are playing in the evolution on planet Earth. It's your job now to spread the love that the new world needs. I wish for you to pass this book forward with a message of love to someone who you feel needs it most. Keep in mind I never met a soul who ever said, "I do not want to feel LOVED today." Meaning every single soul with a heartbeat could use more love in their life every single breathing moment of their lives. The more love we experience, the richer our lives will be!

Love is... free and makes you feel
as if you are the wealthiest person alive!

Each ripple of positive energy we create together will elevate the LOVE (Level Of Vibrational Energy) on earth, transforming the universe one heart at a time. I am a "Hopeful Mom" (Here Opening People's Eyes For Universal Love – through – Messages Opening Minds) and I am hoping that the messages throughout the pages touch your heart, as you see LOVE in your own mirror's reflection from this moment on. May the end of this book, be our new beginning of a Love Revolution designed for and dedicated to YOU, for Eternal LOVE to fill the pages of your own life's story!

It takes inner courage
To own your story
It takes unconditional
self love
To accept it

Terri Lynne

58
YEARS
AGO
I
TOOK
MY
FIRST
BREATH...

For the past 58 years
I have been learning what takes my breath away!

What I have learned is:

"LOVE UNITED,"
created my first breath and
"UNITED LOVE,"
takes my breath away!

NOW my breath is dedicated to the Universe!
My intention behind the following
pages is to:

Pass "UNITED LOVE" on...

"LOVE IS...

The greatest GIFT you can give to yourself and pass on to another!

Terri Lynne

Forward

This book is a collaboration of hearts blended, from near and far, through friends and familiar strangers. The intention is to spread LOVE through the ripples in the pond of life by building an energy bridge, connecting open hearts from around the world. Sharing messages responding to one prompted question being: LOVE IS? Through this request LOVE spread far and wide, as messages were received and compiled for you to read. These exchanges of energy filled the pages with LOVE, through the flow of heartwarming sentiments received from very open hearted souls, across many states and throughout many distant countries; all blended together inside one cover to unite the world through all of what LOVE IS!

The vision, for this book is to touch one heart at a time by connecting through energy, frequency, and vibration. I am hopeful to create a chain reaction developed to reach an elevated level of positive energy, designed to transform an unseen force into a tangible visible form of matter, being this book you are now holding the energy of. This intangible emotion called LOVE was transformed into a tangible form. United Love was manifested and designed to be shared and passed down through present and future generations, with the intention of spreading love to all who hold this energy in their hands.

I believe that,

Love is... who we are and we are all one!

I believe what it is going to take in order for us to feel UNITED through LOVE is when we choose to: Use our senses. Read the signs. Balance energy fields. Breathe consciously. Accept the courage to solve emotional

blocks. Understand the gift of forgiveness. Most importantly, give love and accept receiving love in a constant exchange of free flowing energy.

If you would like to feel positive energy from around the world, then this is the book for you! Rest assured that when you read the LOVE IS messages shared throughout these pages, you will see into your OWN heart full of LOVE, as well as experience how one heart touching another's will aid in making your light shine brighter! This connection will amplify our heartbeats simultaneously while creating a chain of love to carry forward by passing our, "UNITED LOVE" story on...

NOW it's your turn to understand the breath you take. Let's begin by taking a deep breath in, inhaling to the count of five, while consciously breathing in LOVE, then pause to the count of five, and then breath out exhaling to the count of five, breathing out LOVE! NOW your ready to get started!

I am hopeful you will accept and enjoy the journey traveling upon:

LOVE'S HIGHWAY!

The colors you will see throughout this book, represents the favorite color of each link in our chain of love. Designed to add a touch of their energy created to personalize each one of their expressions from within their hearts.

I personally feel, *Love is... colorful,* beyond seeing love strictly in black and white. Which is why I am starting to spread our love messages through an electronic book distribution, so you can enjoy all the shades of love

through our heartfelt expressions, as well as being able to feel our love messages by seeing love through our eyes!

This unique LOVE story is designed to touch all your senses, so you walk on from this book with a greater sense of what,

LOVE IS!

Love is...
the greatest highway to travel life upon!

I am hopeful you will enjoy the process of seeing this truth for yourself! When following the pathway of love you will begin to notice every day miracles along your journey's way! I am hopeful you will enjoy reading the miracle of this manifested book, and then you too will begin to "Believe in Miracles" manifesting in your own life's story!

LOVE IS... noticing miracles in our every
day lives!

xi

Introduction

Love is...
Passed on from the beginning of time,
designed to flow into
"United Love," never ending!

Dear Universal Family,

During one of my telepathic exchanges of communication with my spirit guide, my grandmother in Heaven, I asked her: "How do we create PEACE ON EARTH Granny? How do we create everyone, everywhere to feel LOVED?" As I cleared my mind from the clutter of negativity absorbing our day-to-day lives, I listened closely to her response... for a whisper of hope to spread here on Earth. She told me to, "UNITE THE WORLD THROUGH LOVE DEAR!" I asked, "How do I attempt to do this Granny?" She replied, "Create a CHAIN OF LOVE DEAR!" So that is where my journey began.

I never gave up on my big dream of uniting the world through LOVE for one reason: I knew through my inner knowing that my life had a purpose and when I asked my own spirit, "What is my PURPOSE for taking my first breath in this linear physical form in this lifetime?" I received a telepathic message, which was: "Your life was designed to teach the world what LOVE IS! But first dear you must understand it for yourself!" So, this is when and where my education began. From there my intention to teach the world of what love is became my life's purpose.

Now it is your time, your divine time, to enjoy the process of learning what LOVE IS! Please enjoy the journey! Then please share... ... LOVE! We are all a LINK in this

CHAIN! When our links in the chain are connected, we can see how we are all ONE large ball of energy inside a CIRCLE OF LOVE! When we recognize that we are all LOVE while seeing our connection, we will then KNOW by FEELING that we are:

One "UNITED LOVE" Family!

I am writing the beginning of this book two years after the original "CHAIN OF LOVE" letter circulated. The "LOVE IS" messages poured into my inbox, reflecting and confirming to my spirit that we are one and energy is very powerful! I learned that every ending is merely a new beginning!

Now I pray you will enjoy feeling love energy from your UNIVERSAL FAMILY, as we are presently witnessing how our energy through frequency and vibration works. Then, I pray you choose to see yourself as the: *Love you are born to be!*

Love is... Eternal!

And...
I will always and forever love YOU, Eternally

Note: Some may question, how can I, Terri Lynne love YOU, whomever you are, when we do not know each other? This is a great question, so here is my answer. I do not need to meet you to know you, all I need to know is that you are LOVE and so am I, so this is how my spirit feels LOVE for you! We are connected through our light, which is LOVE! And... THIS is all I needed to KNOW. My heart knows this TRUTH! I am HOPEFUL your

heart will FEEL our connection and see this truth as well, before turning the last page...

David Krakov
"Love Flutters By Mini"

This book called, "UNITED LOVE" is energy formed
as a physical manifestation, validating that my wish is
becoming my dreams come true!
I could not have accomplished this without each and
every one of YOU!
I am eternally grateful for the role you have played in
my life's shift,
So for this allow me to say, THANK YOU for these WOW
MOMents in giving me my life's greatest lift!
"UNITED LOVE"
Is a WISH my heart made in order to create my
DREAM to come true, for you!
This is revalidated and takes place,
every WOW MOMent a LOVE IS message comes through!
As you read on please remember:
"YOU" are a "LINK" in our "CHAIN OF LOVE,"
even if you do not see what number link
you are in our chain,
We still feel your energy connected
and inside our hearts space...
you will forever and always remain!

If you choose to share your LOVE IS message, we will happily include you in our future WOW MOMents! Thank

you for being drawn in at this MOMent in time, in order for us to share our WOW MOMents with you NOW!

"CHAIN OF LOVE!"

My HEART is blowing LOVE your way,
To touch your HEART, to forever stay!
Sending you LOVE, to pass on because I care...
To touch one heart at a time,
reaching everyone, everywhere!
Creating a CHAIN REACTION just because this is what
DREAMS are made of,
Linking US one to the other through OUR
"CHAIN OF LOVE!"

WHAT A WONDERFUL WORLD this will be...
When *Love is at the heart of it,*
for the entire UNIVERSE to feel and see!
Our chain of love has your link connected within,
So let us open our hearts and allow the unconditional
love journey begin...
NOW is "Our Time," so let us get going,
Feeling our universal energy flowing!
By this "UNITED LOVE" books end,
The old world will be the new world
on the mend!
Get ready to enjoy the LOVE flowing
from one heart to another's,

While recognizing we are
ONE big "SOUL FAMILY,"
which is why we call each other
"Soul Sisters" and "Soul Brothers!"
We are all connected upon earth
in the here and now,
To shine our LIGHT with LOVE
and this book is living proof
that our OWN spirits know how!
I truly believe when you
reach our books end,
You will feel like you have been
reintroduced to a kindred spirit,
your misplaced friend!
Once you turn the final page
a big dream for me will have come true,
As my next dream will be manifesting...
which is to meet each and every one of YOU!
Enjoy accepting and receiving the feeling of
Universal unconditional LOVE,
As a gift from my spirit and your spirit guides
from above!

Love is...
Life's greatest gift!

So I am choosing to gift my love to you!
From this moment on...
I hope you will love
yourself too!
This is the place where our
two hearts blend together as one,
And our LOVE story never ends,
rather has only just begun...
Our new beginning starts here, in this right
predestined moment in time; for us to see,
How we can unite through unconditional

LOVE ENERGY!
NOW please ask your heart this one question:

What is LOVE?
I BELIEVE IN LOVE!
Believe to me means:
Balancing Expressive Love Infinitely Evolving Vibrating Energy

To me:
Love is...
A chain reaction.
Our spirits are simply links in this chain!

I FEEL our story and I AM HOPEFUL you will
FEEL our story too!
STORY to me means:
Simple Truths Offering Realistic Yearning

Our STORY is being brought to life through our
UNITED ENERGY, captured and treasured within our
book titled:

"UNITED LOVE"
By: Terri Lynne & The UNIVERSE!
If your energy was linked with mine for the purpose of
this manifested creation, then soon you will see what
number LINK you are in our, "CHAIN OF LOVE!" As well
as feel the energy of all the other souls you are linked
with inside the flowing pages.

From yesterday, to today, through each new tomorrow,
always and forever we, Terri Lynne & The Universe
sincerely thank you for sharing your heart on this
"JOURNEY OF LOVE!" Now is your time to enjoy the
path we are paving through our collaboration of hearts!

Love is... a collaboration of hearts;
uniting through the ripples!

xviii

Section One

LOVE LINKS

IN OUR CHAIN OF LOVE

LOVE LINK #1

Dear Universe,

I wish to begin our book with a poem I shared in the original "Chain of Love" letter, intended to express what I feel about what *LOVE IS...* for you to see what I feel about LOVE, then to learn all you see and feel, while connecting through the links in this chain! I am hopeful you will enjoy our LOVE connections!

"LOVE IS..."

Love is...
An endless dream
Love is...
An overflowing stream
Love is...
In the air
Love is...
EVERYWHERE!

Love is...
An unconditional GIFT
Love is...
What gives your heart a chance to SEE Earth's
Universal SHIFT!
Love is...
A connection beyond compare
Love is...
A feeling we all can share!

Love is...
Your lights reflection
Love is...
Your spirits direction
Love is...
I and love is you
Love is...
When the Universal master plan comes true!

Love is...
A level of vibrational energy
Love is...
Created for you and for me

Love is...
Here from our first breaths start
Love is...
What we feel inside our beating heart!

Love is...
The light inside our soul
Love is...
All we need to feel whole
Love is...
What we are all made up of
Love is...
A heavenly gift sent from above!

Love is...
Honest, pure, kind, real & true
Love is...
Telling your own mirror, "I love you!"
Love is...
All we will ever truly need to live
Love is...
Designed to accept receiving and the greatest GIFT to give!

Love is...
What this CHAIN OF LOVE is all about
Love is...
Energy to exchange, something that we cannot live without
Love is...
Listening to the whispers from your angels touching your heart
Love is...
A part of your spirit from your first breath's start!

Love is...
A collaboration of souls linking together as
one
Love is...
What makes this thing called life, fun!
Love is...
Uniting with one another inside our hearts space,
Love is...
Two hearts that beat as one at any time,
in any chosen place!

Love is...
The new word for war
Love is...
What breaks down walls and opens a door!
Love is...
Gods greatest blessing and gift from above
Love is...
God & God is LOVE!

Love is...
Gratitude and eternal true bliss
Love is...
Starting your day, as well as ending one,
feeling, "I am not going to miss THIS!"
Love is...
Earth's highest vibrational energy joining one and all
Love is...
My WISH & MY BIG DREAM wrapped up in one large
ball!

Love is...
A union of all of us together sharing our
minds, hearts, bodies, spirits and souls
Love is...
A heavenly journey, joining in love is one of my
lifelong goals!
Love is...
The greatest lesson one can learn
Love is...
A breath away, designed to share another's breath in
return!

Love is...
The best lesson one can teach another
Love is...
To be kind to yourself-first,
then pass this love ball to each other!
Love is...
Nature in all its beauty for all of us to see
Love is...
In the eyes of the beholder and the beholder
is tucked inside you & me!

Love is...
Viewed from mountain tops to the valley's
below
Love is...
Seen across oceans and rivers; so let your LOVE flow!
Love is...
In the warmth of the sun
Love is...
In the view of the moon each night reflecting a new
cycle has begun!

Love is...
In the stars we make wishes upon
Love is...
Here in our timeless present moments,
from dusk through dawn!
Love is...
Found within, not always displayed on the outside
Love is...
A healing feeling shared behind closed doors,
with nothing to hide!

Love is...
Loving every wrinkle and accepting every
scar
Love is...
What penetrates your soul to its core and
accepts you as you are!
Love is...
Habit forming and could become your greatest
addiction
Love is...
A true blessing when two hearts beat as one, this is
not a sin, yet rather a WIN, WIN!

Love is...
Meant to be taken seriously and
handled with the utmost of care
Love is...
In you and in me and in everyone, EVERYWHERE!
Love is...
A whisper inside your precious heart
Love is...
Listening to these whispers to guide you to loves start!

Love is...
Our goal!
Love is...
What your heart from my heart stole!
Love is...
Being touched by an Angel in your dream state
Love is...
Always showing up on time,
because love's clock is called fate!

Love is...
Predestined with divine intervention
intertwined!
Love is...
A MIRACLE and a precious blessing to find!
Love is...
My gift I wish to share with the universe
one heart at a time
Love is...
Now offered through words, blending our hearts for
good reason, through loving rhyme!

Love is...
A wish your heart has a choice to make
Love is...
Where dreams come true for earth and heavens sake!
Love is...
The most valuable GIFT!
Love is...
What the world needs now to see our Universe SHIFT!

Love is...
When you close your eyes and still see
LOVE in your dream,
then you must do everything within your power to
build an angelic team!
MY BIG DREAM has been designed not just for me,
but compassionately and intentionally designed for
each and every one of you,
So we all can witness a MIRACLE while
SEEING A BIG DREAM COME TRUE!

Sent from my open heart to yours,
NOW it's your time to witness how LOVE links us
together, through open windows and doors...
While FEELING the FLOW of our LOVE LINKED
bringing us back to ONE!
Witnessing how our LOVE REVOLUTION is EVOLVING
and has only just begun!

Love is...
A miraculous, big dream coming true!!!
And... For this I wish to say,
I am eternally grateful and
I THANK EACH AND EVERY ONE OF YOU!

"What The World Needs Now is Love" – Diane Warwick
Please search for youtube.com link and watch this
video.

Love is ...
Found within
the ebb and flow
of life   *Terri Lynne*

LOVE LINK #2

"LOVE...
IS."

"LOVE 'IS' period.
Love Just IS."

Big Al
California, **USA**
AKA: Terri Lynne's Husband

LOVE LINK #1 & LOVE LINK #2

LOVE IS...
A SINGLE ROSE!
The Final Rose!

Given to: Terri Lynne from Big Al
On Valentines Day 2016
California, **USA**

LOVE LINK #3

"LOVE IS...
A relationship between people!"

When you will do anything for someone because you know they will do anything for YOU.

LOVE IS...
MY
FAMILY!

Father And Mother I Love You
And I Love My Sister Brittany Too!

Brandon Murray

Brandon Murray
California, **USA**
AKA: Bubby and SLICK and Terri Lynne's Son

LOVE LINK #4

"LOVE IS...
Intangible, indefinable, incomprehensible,
Yet so real.
You cannot see love,
But you can see it in their eyes.
You cannot touch love,
But you can feel it in your heart.
You cannot hear love,
But you can hear it in their words.
You cannot hold love,
But you can feel the warmth while
Holding them.
Love is hopeless, yet so hopeful
Love is painful, yet so liberating
Love is sacrifice, yet so worth it
Love is hardship, yet so rewarding
Love is nowhere, yet everywhere.
Love is a feeling impossible to define,
Yet once felt it changes us. Forever."
Brittany Maurae - California, **USA**
AKA: Honey, BMAZIN and Terri Lynne's Daughter

LOVE LINK #5

"LOVE IS:

FAMILY!

LOVE IS:

TOGETHERNESS!

LOVE IS:

FAMILY TOGETHER!"

Leslie

California, **USA**

Aka: Terri Lynne's Mom & Nani

Dedicated to: My Mom

6/15/1936 ~ 6/30/2017

"REST IN PEACE"

LOVE LINK #6

LOVE IS... a four-phase process. Love comes in four stages... First stage is when a baby is born and the parents are responsible for the baby and the baby needs their parent's love and nurturing and getting them everything a baby needs; and then as the baby grows up comes the second stage. During the second phase is when he or she becomes an adolescent, as young adults when they go to school and then they begin to feel an attraction to another person and their energy in their body erupts and they share the dating period and they think they are "In Love," but it is more an infatuation phase so they date different people to learn what they are feeling. Then comes Stage Three. Stage three is when stage one and stage two blend into stage three and all stages are connected. Once they pass the first two stages, comes stage three which is when they move into the adult phase of love and this is the real love that you feel when you go into a room and you see a person across the room and eyes meet and you "Fall in Love." In this moment you feel that this is "Your Person," this is the one that God has brought to you feeling this is the one I will love for the rest of our lives. Then there is Stage four, which is Senior Love and that period comes when you have all the previous three phases combined and you're with the one person that you love until death do us part many years later and you feel not only Love, but undying friendship! This ties all four previous stages together! These four phases are designed and meant for sharing together in this fourth phase!

LOVE IS... THE MOST IMPORTANT PART OF LIFE!!!

Richard (Dick) Aka: Terri Lynne's Dad and Papa Man Chatsworth, CA, USA - Malibu, CA, USA - Gilbert, AZ, **USA**

15

LOVE LINK #7

LOVE IS:

Caring For Everyone!

Rose Grace
Aka: Terri Lynne's dad's Wife and Soul Mate
Chatsworth, California, USA - Malibu, California, USA
-Gilbert, Arizona, **USA**

LOVE LINK #8

LOVE IS...

Many things, but this was the first thing that came to
my mind:

LOVE IS...

Seeing my children come into the world.

Love is:

My Children!

Bill
Palos Park, IL **USA**

LOVE LINK #9

Love is...
Not enough,
It is the work we put into those we love,
Not the feelings of love.

Ron Lopez
California, **USA**

LOVE LINK #10

Love is... the universe! Gentle and kind
Love is... gratitude! Silence of mind
Love is... family! Energy around
Love is... nature sky and ground
Love is... unity God source found
Love is... energy centered and loud

Walking with the angel's time to talk to one
Open hearted love for all the time that's gone
See the Universe's light shining like a star
Open hearted virtue going to get you far
Listen to the ripples of Universal love
All of Gods creation sourced from up above

Love is...

Finding the SOUL through LOVE!

Love is soul!! Created love!!
From heavens gate!! To clouds above!!
Internal soul!! Weeps and cries!!
Blue the earth!! In clearing skies!!

Feel the force!! Of love within!!
Soul remorse!! Never to begin!!
Love the self!! And soul aware!!
Created love!! From soul despair!!

Emotions gained!! For love of heart!!
You and feeling!!! Never apart!!
Door to seek!! Love to find!!
Open heart!! Open mind!!

Mick Smith
UNITED KINGDOM

LOVE LINK #11

"Love is...
A vulnerable space!"

"To love at all is to be vulnerable. Love anything
and your heart will be wrung and possibly broken.
If you want to make sure of keeping it intact you
must give it to no one, not even an animal. Wrap it
carefully round with hobbies and little luxuries; avoid
all entanglements. Lock it up safe in the casket or
coffin of your selfishness. But in that casket, safe,
dark, motionless, airless, it will change. It will not be
broken; it will become unbreakable, impenetrable, and
irredeemable. To love is to be vulnerable."
Credited to C.S. Lewis (The Four Loves)

Love is... Solving emotions!

The more EMOTIONS bottled up
That you solve,
The more LOVE you will FEEL inside
Your own HEART!
EMOTIONS = Energy in MOTION!
Keep the ENERGY flowing,
As you work hard at emptying the jar!
When the jar is empty, your HEART will be full of
LOVE!
Do the work!
The more EMOTIONS you release,
The more ENERGY you will receive!

Love is...
Universal Energy!

Love is...
Our eternal light!

LOVE IS...
THE LIGHT OF YOUR SOUL!

"Love is...
High VIBRATION,
Raising FREQUENCY,
Increasing ENERGY,

By tapping into the universal heartbeat,
through the ways and means of telepathy,
creating... *UNITED LOVE!"*

Uniting the Universe through LOVE...
removes the lack of love & allows
universal *UNITED LOVE and LIGHT* to shine!

Love is...
The BRIDGE connecting US to each other!

To FEEL what LOVE IS...
You must let "LOVE FLOW!"

Love is...
When you choose to pay attention to the
silence!
"Only those who care about you,
can hear you when you're quiet."
Author Unknown

Love is... not what hurts!
Emotions hurt!
Love is... what HEALS!

"Everyone says love hurts, but that is not true.
Loneliness hurts. Rejection hurts. Losing someone
hurts. Envy hurts. Everyone gets these things
confused with love, but in reality love is... the only
thing in this world that covers up all pain and makes
someone feel wonderful again."

"Love is...
the only thing in this world that does not
hurt."
-Liam Neeson

GFTLC
HEAVEN and EARTH'S CONNECTION

LOVE LINK #12

LOVE IS... "Unconditional!"
DMAN
California, **USA**

LOVE LINK #13
Love is...
Being one with the Ocean.

Love and passion makes me head for the ocean.

When I take off on a wave,
I am completely infatuated with a strong and
emotional desire to be one with the universe.

This sensation makes me feel fulfilled.

My connection with the ocean to me is considered to be purely intimate.

Can the ocean be my Soul mate? Absolutely!

My affection has no limits and I can blossom until my last days.

My Journey of Love will no longer feel SOLITARY.

If I were a poet I would throw love into the abyss and never look back!

Jorge Ricardo Garcia Casas
Born: Mexico City
Resides: California, **USA**

LOVE LINK #14

Love is...
The sum of all there is.

Zenon
CANADA

LOVE LINK #15

I received a letter the other day from a newfound friend on SN. She had questions for me about some of the things I had posted mainly the one about love. I replied to the questions and in the process came to understand something I had not looked at before. The word *LOVE* and what it means, *"Level Of Vibrational Energy."* It was quite an amazing revelation for me because of the work I am doing right now in vibrational energy. It uniquely wove itself into the fabric of my current understanding of what we produce in this world and how. The level of Vibration is behind everything and it is the energy we create that send out the ripple across the water touching all life around us. In the process of increasing your energy field you will increase the joy you create and therefore create *LOVE*.

Love Is...
"The inevitable outcome of all who seek the path to enlightening the soul and connecting to the source energy, which resides within us all."

My friend Terri Lynne showed up at the right time and the right place for multiple reasons, one of which is the manifestation we create and our vibrational alignment merged. We have never met, but we helped place another level of our understanding about our paths we walk. I am truly grateful for this connection and the knowledge it has produced... Thank you SN for this opportunity and being the medium in the connection. The Level of Vibrational Energy is, how it and we all live and is what we are continuing to vibrate outward that creates our lives.

This is the truth in love and the levels of our existence. I know in the sharing of this information that it will

touch your soul as it touched my soul. It is all about the energy and its all Love.

Thank you so much for the opportunity to share this information with you and the time you have taken to read what I have written. I am currently working on writing my own book about my perspective of life to this point and the lessons I have learned. Whether it is published or not, the process of writing the book is truly the gift. It has defined many things in my life, in so doing the writing required and the research of the principles I believe, have added to the collective of my focus. Leaps and bounds is the expression I want to convey to you, in what has happened to me in my life since I made the decision to write the book. Every thought, every inspiration is being channeled into the pages and it is amazing how the energy flows. I did not know were to begin, nor did I know what it was I wanted to say. I even felt I should keep it to myself until it is written so as to not expose the information too soon. What has happened is I am sharing it now through my posts and I am receiving so much more in return. The flow of writing is coming quickly and the information and clarity of it is astounding me.

It is truly a blessing to be able to feel the vibrational energy around me increase and the spirit of all those who vibrate on the same plane and higher are increasing my own levels. So from this day forth, when I say the word *LOVE* it will have every bit of the *Level Of Vibrational Energy* I can channel into it with it. It has also become one of the words in my meditation chants. Be well and Be Love. Thanks again SN

P.S. If you have any questions or comments please post. I am finding much inspiration in all. Thanks.

Stephen - Ohio, **USA**

***Note: Stephen was in the process of writing a book titled, "The Seam," and we have since lost contact. So if anyone reads this and knows Stephen from Ohio, who used to be a member on the Spiritual Networks site, please ask him to contact Terri Lynne to resume our conversations. Thank you, TL

(My reply to Stephen's message above)

I love our connection and don't ever stop loving, "YOU" my friend!

Meaning for Stephen to, keep on LOVING him self, as I will keep on LOVING myself! Keep on connecting through LOVE!

LOVE, Terri Lynne California, **USA**

STEPHEN PICTURE of: "VIBRATIONAL ENERGY" (Look at the outline of Stephen's frame)

We are a drop in the ocean felt by every fabric of its being. That drop emanates from our center out into the sea of eternity. Levels Of Vibrational Energy "love" slowly rippling over each and every spectrum of life, increases the perpetual movement of space and time. We are because we choose to be in this realm, we have come to fully understand the purpose of the human existence as a spirit channeling the light.

Stephen - Ohio, **USA**

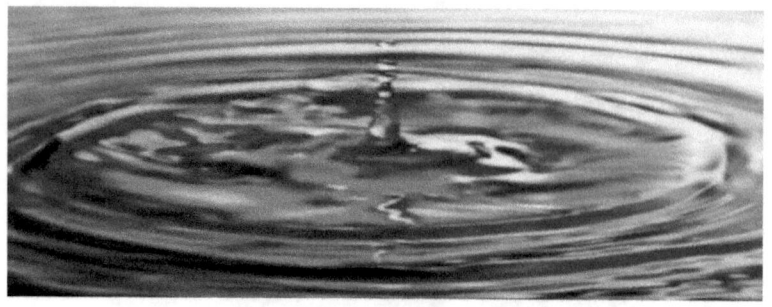

The RIPPLE AFFECT!

Stephen,

Another parallel: My intention when writing my book was to touch souls through the "ripples in the pond," by one heart touching another's creating the ripple effect... I am hopeful that by touching one another's lives with LOVE, we create a BeeeeeeUtifull ripple throughout the universe touching many souls, beginning with ourselves! Thank you for being a ripple attached to my soul, as well as holding my KEY to LOVE by learning what *LOVE IS... Level Of Vibrational Energy!*

Your Friend Terri Lynne - California, **USA**

(My reply to Stephen's message from above)

LOVE LINK #16

Love is... PEACEFUL!
"Love is... finding a SPECIAL someone who gets you off the couch from becoming moldy and is PEACEful through the chaos!"

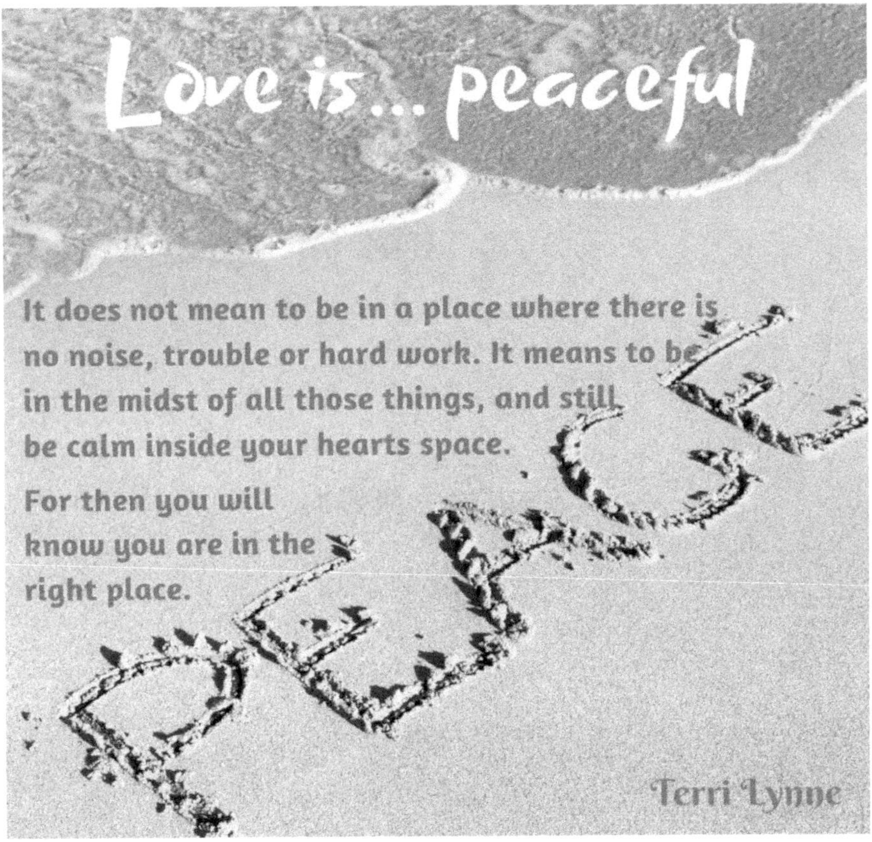

Love is... peaceful

It does not mean to be in a place where there is no noise, trouble or hard work. It means to be in the midst of all those things, and still be calm inside your hearts space.

For then you will know you are in the right place.

Terri Lynne

RPM
Born: Texas
Resides: California, **USA**

LOVE LINK #17

Love is...
Never giving up!

Elona B.
California, **USA**

LOVE LINK #18

Love is...
Loyalty!

Bill B.
California, **USA**

LOVE LINK #19
Love is...
Embracing our connection to everything
and everyone, is the essence of Divine
Love.

Loving everything and everyone is the one true
Absolute Power.
Chuck Meares - Kirkland, WA **USA**

There are two basic primary feeling modes which shape human relationships and interactions: loving, understanding, and fearful unknowing. The former lifts us up and frees us; the latter binds us and encumbers us. All human beings at their core want to give and receive love. Once fear takes hold however, our attempts at giving are based upon what we perceive to be the needs and desires of others or own needs and desires projected upon them. Fear blocks our ability to truly connect with our own most essential being, rendering us incapable of giving from a place of true compassion and detachment from personal gain. What we then give comes laden with a need to sense a feeling of indebtedness from the recipient. The "gift" is weighted with expectation. The recipient must respond in a particular fashion or risk being accused of taking the "gift" and the giver for granted. Whether that which is given has any real intrinsic value to the recipient becomes a moot point to the giver.

This form of "giving," emanating from a fear-based value system, and seeking validation from the recipient, is a commonly accepted operational norm. As a result, there is intense societal pressure to acknowledge this mode as sincere and loving. As children, we are constantly urged to show gratitude, regardless of whether or not we are truly grateful. We are instructed to always say "thank you," and to be polite, to not talk back. In other words, we are, from an early age, trained not to show our true feelings and to accept whatever acts of "love" and "kindness" we are offered, even when these acts are insincere or inappropriate. Hence, we quickly lose touch with our deepest inner need for genuine love and an acceptance of our own uniqueness. We lose sight

of loving understanding and fall into the trap of fearful unknowing.

The most valuable and vulnerable issues regarding the inherent unique spirit of each individual are not recognized and nurtured within the larger social order of modern culture. There are no educational requirements for mastering the art of loving, no testing procedures to determine our fear-to-love ratio, no government subsidies for the loving impaired. It is left to individuals with a great capacity for love, a strong desire to seek deeper truth, and a powerful drive to share their inner wealth with others to open and illumine the minds and hearts and lives of the human family and bring us all back home to loving understanding.

Chuck Meares - Kirkland, WA **USA**

"Love is... the key!"

And it is to find the Love Within You
And Feel the Power that Gives to You
And know the peace you should know

Author Unknown
Shared By: Chuck Meares
Olympia, WA **USA**

LOVE LINK #20

Love is...
Your heart getting a big SMILE when you
think of someone special!

YOU...
"The answer I would always give if somebody asked
me what I was thinking of."

Author Unknown
Shared By: RC - California, **USA**

LOVE LINK #21

Love is...
Everything!

"Everything in the world exists in order to end up as a
book." -Stephanie Mallmore

Shared By:
Aaron Hunter - Age 12 - California, **USA**

LOVE LINK #22

Love is...
Living what you love!

Becca - Age 9 - California, **USA**

LOVE LINK #23

LOVE is...
What is there when all else is removed?
Fear. Self.

Love is... not so much found, as uncovered.
Love is... an aperture that opens in both directions.

rB - Randy Bruck
Aka: Terri Lynne's Healer

"The Malibu Healer"
Malibu - Hesperia, California, **USA**

34

LOVE LINK #24

Just BE love... this is all their really is...

Sheri
Illinois, **USA**

LOVE LINK #25

Love is:
Emotional security!

Renee J.
California, **USA**

LOVE LINK #26

Love is love ~ pure and simple ~

It needs no reason ~ it needs no reference ~
Blessed are those who can give ~
Blessed are the hearts that can receive

Akashaya Sathish
Chennai, **INDIA**

LOVE LINK #27

Love is...
Beautiful!

The three most beautiful words to say to yourself is

"I LOVE YOU"

Repeat these three words "I LOVE YOU all day" to yourself

By repeating these words your brain gets used to these new self-empowering words,

And it will change your whole perspective

It gives you a feeling of being home

In your own body and mind.

When you can LOVE yourself it

Makes LOVING others less difficult

XCassiopei Earth Angel

WORLD WIDE

LOVE LINK #28

To Me...
Love is...
A state of being that can bring us to a
taste of oneness with all creation and yet
still be our own individual self.

One
Pennsylvania, **USA**

LOVE LINK #29

Love is... A GIFT!

Love is...
What to be THANKFUL for! Especially EARTH ANGELS!
I AM, YOU ARE, WE ARE, INDEED ALL ONE BIG
UNIVERSAL
LOVE FAMILY!!!!
Happy Thanksgiving Soul Sister!
I AM VERY GRATEFUL FOR TERRI LYNNE on our team,
in our... Universe!
We are givers of much needed waves of healing Love,
THANK YOU!!!!
It begins with... I AM LOVE and ends with WE ARE
LOVE!!!!
Arkangelo - Gregory Fitzgibbon

Born: Joplin, MO Resides: In OK, USA
(Wherever he lives is OK with me)

Title: LOVE IS A GIFT
https://youtu.be/Bsem9hAybOM

Love is:
Spreading LOVE Every Where To Every
One,
So that other's may FEEL the same
JOY!!!!!!

LOVE IS... when we can,

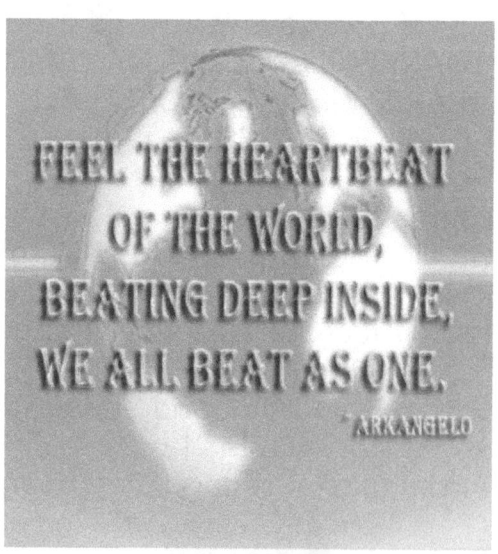

Love is... inside your heart!

ALL THE LOVE
THAT YOU'VE YEARNED FOR,
FOR SO LONG,
HAS ALWAYS BEEN WAITING
FOR YOU ALL ALONG,
SEARCH INSIDE OF YOUR HEART
AND YOU WILL SEE,
THAT LOVE IS ALL YOU NEED,
IF YOU BELIEVE,
IT WILL SET YOU FREE.

— ARKANGELO

Love is...
Imperfectly perfect!

Perfect love is true love and true love is perfect.
However, it takes two imperfect people
working towards the "Perfection of true love."

Arkangelo
Gregory Fitzgibbon
Born: Joplin, Missouri - Resides: OK, **USA**

LOVE LINK #30

LOVE just IS.

Unconditional, no expectations, just love!
It is so simple, however, the human mind creates
complications!

Gerry
Born: Sebring, Ohio - Resides: Jacksonville, Florida
USA

LOVE LINK #31

Love is...
In me, and all there is, all there ever was,
and all there ever will be.

Creation, non-creation.
It's everything, energy.
On a physical level, personal love to a partner,
nature, children, animals, all vary...
We are so lucky to have all this to experience.
Our origin, the core is the first mentioned.

Jaana – **FINLAND**

LOVE LINK #32

LOVE is...
My purpose, and the reason for living.

Outside of LOVE there is nothing.
LOVE is... my life!
Only Love is real and the rest is illusion.
See Yin How Tue

MAURITIUS. In the Indian Ocean

LOVE LINK #33

Love IS...
An unseen chain made of energy within us,
between living people or animals.

Which means that it's unconditional because it's there making a connection between two energies. There is a way to disconnect love like the way of a mom and a baby for example cutting the umbilical cord, but the umbilical cord is a linear visible connection until the cord is cut; but the energy remains connected and this is the cord spiritual beings will still see without seeing anything at all. The level of the connection is different between different people, the same as different strings or different chains can connect between different objects.

Sometimes one connection is stronger on the one side than the other which makes you feel more than the other feels and vice versa.

As much as you FEEL the love from some people, your heart knows when you are not loved. Such as corporate relationships, when the time reaches an end and separation is on the way as a result of not feeling fulfilled at your job, the string is about to have the cord cut, you feel the lack of the love energy that turns from extremely motivated and energized, to being unmotivated to do your job. At the same time, since the love energy on your side is still strong you will still give without motivation because the cord is still connected.

There are four types of love:

1. The strongest one is the love within ourselves keeping us moving forward in our lives.

2. Then comes the spouse you love, being strong chemistry including intimacy (Romantic love) in which is like a magnet to steel where you want to connect physically by having their presence in your life.

   Love is... having sex, as sex is the act of making love. When not using birth control, the sex results in having babies, which becomes the fruit of love.

3. Then there is family or friends whom you love and you want them to feel your love always, so the string of energy will keep you connected.

4. Then there is acquaintance love connection that comes in for a period of time to learn from each other and if the person goes away the energy is still felt, but on a lower vibrational level.

So this project CHAIN OF LOVE will show us how much we are all one. The main point is that our lives are intertwined making us UNITED through LOVE ENERGY~ by an invisible chain, string and cord!

For Me,
Love is...
Dancing!

LOVE brings you to a higher level
of energy, as does DANCING!
It's important to charge our batteries,
and dancing is one tool that does this,
For me!

"Dance is the hidden language of the soul."
-Author Unknown
Galit
Born in: **ISRAEL** – Resides: California, **USA**

LOVE LINK #34

What is a mom love ~ dad love ~ family love?
Love is...
Not an automatic and simple thing.

Love is unconditional. Love is a giving. Love is a compromise. Love is caring. Love is acceptance of your precious one as is. Love is support. Love is worrying, love is quality, love is happiness, love affects us - when your loved one is happy you are happy, when your loved one is sad you are sad, when your loved one smiles you smile, when your loved one laughs you laugh. When you give love and see the joy on your loved one you enjoy seeing it and participate in his/her happiness. When your loved one works too hard it hurts you. When your loved one is sick it hurts you. Life is all about greetings and blessings for happiness, joy, wealth, love, health and having a peaceful soul. Your soul aims to be relaxed and happy. What makes your soul happy is doing what you love to do, because you do it from your heart using all your heart and you succeed in what you do. There should be two sides to love otherwise one side can feel emptiness with no one on the other side you can give your love to. Love goes with you everywhere you go. Your loved one connects to you unconditionally.

Dina Vered
ISRAEL

LOVE LINK #35

"Love is frequency."

Love is...
"When you follow your heart, you walk in the
footprints of your dreams which will lead to your
reality."

Inspirational Quote Request from Terri Lynne
Keyword = Love:

"Love is the healing element to dismantle
negativity."

The love in your heart is the remedy to all of which is in opposition of believing it will be. You must be the love you want invited into your life. A loving person sheds light upon all that is living and to all who is wanting to live."

"Love is so powerful it can travel faster than the spread of light, walk through walls at any unknown moment and reach you; it can be felt from one continent to the next, touching the lives of others, and is the prescription to all imperfections."
–Joseph Mercado

Love is...
What will persevere!

"The perseverance within you is one key strength that has veered you into the direction of accomplishment. The result is a predecessor of your thoughts. Graduation day is your moment where you level up in your life. Such an outstanding achievement is to be proud of. Not only do you graduate academically, but also personally, setting the sail for your future endeavors and your dreams. Through hard work and diligent efforts, you achieve the unknown, whereby; you are known by the ripe fullness of your fruit and for what you manifest on the tree of life. Your success is held in the roots of your spirit and on the tips of your membranes. Continue to surgically operate on your possibilities while being the overseer of your thoughts. Opportunities will grow abundantly in your favor. Your beginning has no end."
-Joseph Mercado

Gift to Brandon Murray from Joseph Mercado,
For his "PERSEVERANCE," achieving college success!
Love is... being a success story!

Love is...
Passionate!

"To be passionate is to love. This is true when it comes to your family, friends, and people you have a heart for. The sensitivity within you allows you to sense untapped emotions within people. Your delicate, yet ambitious mindset, becomes the listening device to your soul, giving you total control over what you want and don't want in your life. Freedom exists before it is discovered. Your internal passion is the ion that electrifies your life."

-Joseph Mercado

Gift to Brittany Maurae from Joseph Mercado,
For her "PASSIONATE" Heart & Soul,
Full of LOVE!

Love is... holding the KEY of PASSION!
Joseph Mercado New Jersey, **USA**

LOVE LINK #36

EMAN'S ENGLISH (Google) TRANSLATION:

Love is... an easy word to say difficult to implement, as it contains many meanings, such as altruism and sacrifice, and the preference of others.
Love is... a disease and medication at the same time.

His disease for both does not know the meaning of love and how it is a medication to anyone who can decipher these emotions interlaced and already begins to love everything around it shall be Kpop solh positive energy and happiness infinite.

Eman
Alexandria, **EGYPT**

LOVE LINK #37

Love is... the message!
You are love-experiencing life!

Life is not happening to you but through you. You are love, experiencing life. Everything is happening around you but nothing is happening to your actual presence as the witness of your experience. The personal aspects of you are constantly changing, similar to the clouds in the sky. Your thoughts, emotions and intentions change, but nothing happens to you the observer. Pay close attention to the part of you that is, unchanging and everlasting because that is your loving soul.

Love is...
What never fails!
Bending the Universe towards light.

With every act of kindness, compassion, and love we are creating a force that is stronger than any known resistance. This pushes Earth's society towards unity and global peace. As we acknowledge the presence of hate and indifference, let our hearts remain pure and let our intention be known. This Universe belongs to those that live and let love.

Love is... an expansion of oneself!

I have secrets to tell and so do you. As souls we are all born with gifts to share with the world. We are all interconnected and driven by our soul's purpose. The illusion is happening whenever we are holding the belief that our great journey is external and somehow outside of ourselves. For most of our lives we are asleep to the fact of who we really are. In awakening the veil of the illusion falls away like the skin of a snake. The ego thins like clouds. When we awaken to our truth, we awaken to the pure loving awareness inside of us all. Our greatest journey in life is internal towards the call of our souls. In your awakening you will discover the gifts of your higher purpose, enabling you to place your piece of the puzzle into the universal equation of life.

Shared By: Dr. Russell Clayton

There are only a few forces that can alter your life. Love is... one such force.

Love can change your life and elevate your consciousness as well as the hearts and souls that are surrounding you. The mystical Power of Love is simply unlimited. Love... Transforms hearts and rebuild souls. Love always endures. Far beyond the end of time when there's nothing left, love will still remain.

Love is... a movement!

Love is...
More than just a feeling,
Love is... A movement.

NOTHING EVOLVES US LIKE LOVE

Embrace the unconditional love that resides in your heart, it is there that you will find inner peace. Serenity is the whisper of love's beautiful voice. Love's call is a gentle caress of the soul to awaken. Love is the most powerful force in the Universe and its appearance in your life is a calling to come alive. What the world needs now is for more souls to come alive. When we awaken to love, we awaken to our truth.

Nothing evolves us like love.

An infinite ocean of LOVE surrounds us.

"We are surrounded by an infinite ocean of love."

-Panache Desai
Shared By: Dr. Russell Clayton

Love is...
Your existence!

"LOVE IS...
NOT AN EMOTION,
IT IS YOUR VERY
EXISTENCE."

-Rumi
Shared By: Dr. Russell Clayton

Love is...
The greatest present you can gift to yourself!

"Love yourself unconditionally
It is out of unconditional
Love that you were created
And it is out of unconditional
Love that you shall create
All that you desire."

Terri Lynne and Dr. Russell Clayton
California, **USA**

TRUE LOVE exists in the absence of fear, doubt, imbalance, codependency, attachment, unrest, and aversion to commitment.

Love Changes Everything

Dr. Russell Clayton
Chicago, IL – California, **USA**

LOVE LINK #38

Hello sisters and brothers, my name is Miguel Silva, founder of, "Love Awakens The Soul," and I want to share with you something that started this group. We are about to hit 10,000 members and it is a good time to remember how this all began. This is the very first image I posted here when the group was originally called Divine Twin Flames. I have been reading in other group posts on how this does not exist, I'm here to tell you that it does exist and it always will. Maybe some people lost hope or maybe they are not fully awakened. People use this as propaganda and call themselves twin flame experts and so on. I'm here to tell you that no one can tell you who your twin flame is, your heart will tell you and that's the truth. No reader, spirit, or coach will confirm this. The love will be so strong for each other... Strong enough that the LOVE AWAKENS THE SOUL.

Here is the original post... Enjoy and always believe something beautiful is about to happen.

Twin Flames experience their last lifetime here on earth together. Twin Flames love mutually, unconditionally and without limits. Twin Flames have no doubt of who they are and that they are meant to be together. Twin Flames are the ultimate power couple and are powerful. The energy between Twin Flames is so intense that it is unlikely that both will not feel it. The attraction between them is too strong to deny and keeps them BOTH coming back together. Their time apart is never too long and they are never too far away. Twin Flames share most of each other's strengths and weaknesses, but may experience them differently. Twin Flames ARE NOT karmic soul mates Soul mates are plentiful. A Twin Flame is only one. That means that there can only be one. There is no such thing as "twin energy" going from one body to another, as a Twin Flame's body is

already chosen and as it appears above it will be below. BOTH individuals will feel the call, pull, heat, energy, attraction, intensity, and love for one another.

Miguel Silva
Born: Monterey, **MEXICO**
Resides: Poinciana, Florida, **USA**

Love is... "Magic!"
Magic with intention is what Love is!

Magic exists. Who can doubt it when there are rainbows and wildflowers, the music of the wind and the silence of the stars? Anyone who has loved has been touched

by MAGIC. It is such a simple and such an extraordinary part of the lives we live!

Miguel Silva and Terri Lynne
Born: Monterrey, MEXICO and Born: Boston, **USA**
Lives in: Poinciana, Florida, USA and California, **USA**

Love is...
Expressing & sharing,
Voices of the Heart!

The simplicity of honest conversation words traded, exchanged between two offered even as gifts humble treasure for one another that keep for eternity inside the heart. With each word she whispered hope while he spoke trust to her an intimate communion between lost souls. A beautiful blank canvas created to embellish freely with love he had an intrinsic ability to color her mind with a magical brush. He painted for her a brilliant night sky each word he left was a star added that scattered light illuminating even her darkest hours. While she gracefully placed her fragile words within his hands so that throughout the day while they were apart he could paint his own clouds to add her delicate softness and filter the harsh sun of his reality.

Miguel Silva - Born: Monterrey, **MEXICO** & Born: Boston, USA Lives in: Poinciana, Florida, USA & California, **USA**

LOVE LINK #39

Love is...
A connection!

"Love Connects
Let it flow through you
Inside you
And around you."
Author Unknown
Shared By: Ruth Snyder

Love is...
What we are!

Love is what we are, when we drop all the things that stand in the way.

-Karen Maezen Mille
Shared By: Ruth Snyder
North Carolina, **USA**

LOVE LINK #40

"Love is... a tremendous caring that arises in the wake of transcending the personal self."

In the wake of this transcendence, something amazing arises. A deep love and caring arises from within emptiness, from nowhere. This love and caring seeks only the Truth in every moment and in all circumstances."

- Adyashanti - The Impact of Awakening

Personally I feel creation itself is Love, God is, I am, you are, and everything is.

Adya is bringing out a point here of understanding beyond mind. It is not something that comes out of our own doing... it is always everywhere.

Les Nisbett - California, **USA**

LOVE LINK #41

Love is...
Sitting in the silence,
When the heart comes alive,
Then, there is just...
Love.

Content credited to: Video "Full Embrace of Life"
Messenger Unknown

LOVE LINK #42

Love is...
Patient,

Kind,

It does not envy,

It does not boast,

It is not proud,

It is not rude,

It is not self-seeking,

It is not easily angered,

Keeps no record of wrongs,

Does no delight in evil,

Rejoices with the truth,

Always protects,

Always hopes,

Always perseveres,

Never fails.

(Sharing Corinthians 13:4-8a post)

Michele Dionne
Samia, **CANADA**

LOVE LINK #43

When I was younger, I thought love was that feeling in your chest like your heart was about to explode, just thinking about a certain person. I thought that I had to spend every moment possible with another, and that she had to want to spend every moment with me. I thought that being in pain from missing someone was love. I associated so much unpleasant suffering with love.

But that's not love at all. Yes, I still get excited and my heart beats very fast and loud, but love is so much cleaner, organic, and just plain enjoyable when you lose the unhealthy attachments. When you can just let someone be free to be themselves, AND find genuine happiness in THEIR happiness, even if it doesn't include you, then you've learned to love yourself so unconditionally that you're now able to love others that way.

So what is love? We are love. That is all we are and all we need to be. When we can remove all the labels and ideas the world has infused us with, and get back to who we were born as and what we were born from, all there is, is LOVE. We have an endless supply. That's why we should never stop loving. It is impossible to run out. :)

Michael - New Jersey, **USA**

LOVE LINK #44

As I grow and learn and change, my definition of LOVE changes. What I feel at this moment in time is:

"Love is...
Full and complete acceptance, without judgment."

This doesn't mean without opinion, discussion or thought. It means true listening, hearing, curiosity, assistance and kindness. It is truly being there for another in the way they need you to be there, not the way you need to be there.

"Love is...
Selfless, but also connected."

Jill MM Chicago - California, **USA**

What Love means to 4-8 year old kids...
Slow down for three minutes to read this.

A group of professional people posed this question to a group of 4 to 8 year-olds:

"What does love mean?"

The answers they got were broader, deeper, and more profound than anyone could have ever imagined! See what you think:

"When my grandmother got arthritis, she couldn't bend over and paint her toenails anymore. So my grandfather does it for her all the time, even when his hands got arthritis too. That's love.

Rebecca- age 8

"When someone loves you, the way they say your name is different. You just know that your name is safe in their mouth."

Billy – age 4

"Love is when a girl puts on perfume and a boy puts on shaving cologne and they go out and smell each other."

Karl – age 5

"Love is when you go out to eat and give somebody most of your French fries without making them give you any of theirs.

Chrissy – age 6

"Love is what makes you smile when you're tired."

Terri - age 4

"Love is when my Mommy makes coffee for my daddy and she takes a sip before giving it to him, to make sure the taste is OK."

Danny – age 8

"Love is what's in the room with you at Christmas if you stop opening presents and just listen."

Bobby – age 7   (Wow!)

"If you want to learn to love better, you should start with a friend who you hate."

Nikka – age 6

(We need a few million more Nikka's on this planet)

"Love is when you tell a guy you like his shirt, then he wears it everyday."

Noelle - age 7

"Love is like a little old woman and a little old man who are still friends even after they know each other so well."

Tommy – age 6

"During my piano recital, I was on a stage and I was scared.

I looked at all the people watching me and saw my daddy waving and smiling. He was the only one doing that. I wasn't scared anymore."

Cindy – age 8

"My mommy loves me more than anybody you don't see anyone else kissing me to sleep at night."

Clare – age 6

"Love is when Mommy gives Daddy the best piece of chicken.

Elaine- age 5

"Love is when Mommy sees Daddy smelly and sweaty and still says he is handsomer than Robert Redford."

Chris – age 7

"Love is when your puppy licks your face even after you left him alone all day."

Mary Ann – age 4

"I know my older sister loves me because she gives me all her old clothes and has to go out and buy new ones."

Lauren – age 4

"When you love somebody, your eyelashes go up and down and little stars come out of you." (What an image)

Karen – age 7

"Love is when Mommy sees Daddy on the toilet and she doesn't think it's gross."

Mark – age 6

"You really shouldn't say 'I love you' unless you mean it. But if you mean it, you should say it a lot. People forget."

Jessica – age 8

And the final one:

The winner was a four-year-old child whose next-door neighbor was an elderly gentleman who had recently lost his wife.

Upon seeing the man cry, the little boy went into the old gentleman's yard, climbed onto his lap, and just sat there.

When his Mother asked what he had said to the neighbor, the little boy said, "Nothing, I just helped him cry."

****

Shared By: Jill M
California, **USA**
Credited to: Unknown creator of this project

LOVE LINK #45

Love is... what I guarantee!

The Love I Guarantee

As I look into your eyes
I see your heart and every part of your soul
Touch my heart tenderly and I will touch your yours
Dream with me and I will try to make your dreams come true
Love me completely and I will show you the most beautiful love there is
Comfort me when I hurt and my heart is yours to keep
Treat me right and I will be yours forever
Show me your gentle way and I will always follow

My Love this
I Guarantee

~the Sage

Love is... a friend!

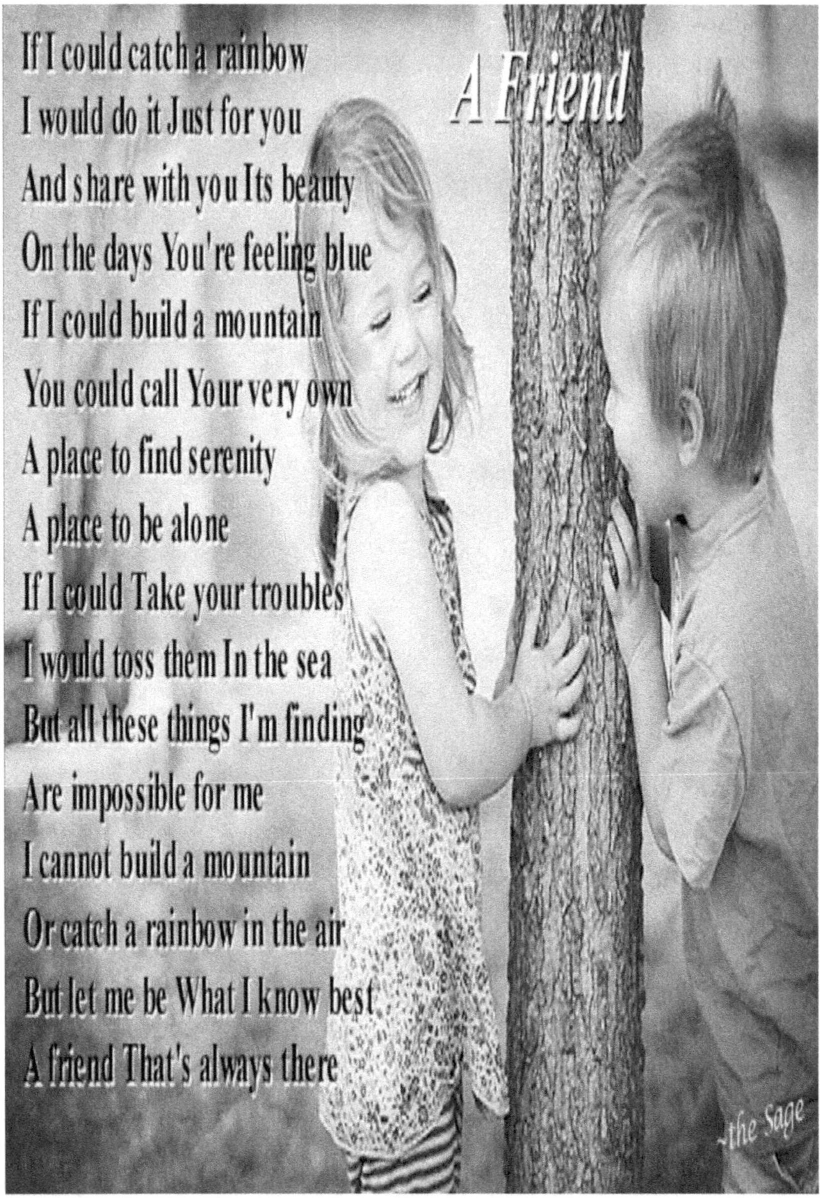

A Friend

If I could catch a rainbow
I would do it Just for you
And share with you Its beauty
On the days You're feeling blue
If I could build a mountain
You could call Your very own
A place to find serenity
A place to be alone
If I could Take your troubles
I would toss them In the sea
But all these things I'm finding
Are impossible for me
I cannot build a mountain
Or catch a rainbow in the air
But let me be What I know best
A friend That's always there

~the Sage

Love is...
Found looking into your eyes!

I am still Dreaming
When I look into your Eyes

When I fall asleep
It is you I wear
Your arms hold me
Your touch warms me
Your breath comforts me
Then I dream
You are here with me
When I wake
It Is You That Awakens Me

~the Sage

Love is... a choice!

I Choose You

To be no other than yourself
To loving what I know of you
and trusting who you will become.
I will laugh and cry with you
I will love and cherish you
I will respect and honor you
always and in all way.
I choose you
from this day forward.
To love myself before no other...

Signed: the reflection in the mirror

~the Sage

Love is… a piece of your soul!

Love is...

When you give a piece

of your soul

They never knew

was missing

~the Sage

Love is...
Silently, still!

When one becomes still
Great wisdom arrives
It is known as love
It's not mine or yours
It is just love

Not to be defined or totally understood
It is eternal, which means, it is forever
It is real and alive, living in each of us
Awaken your mind
and embrace

Love

~the Sage

LINK #1 & LINK #45

Love is...
A conversation with a stranger, who is connected to my spirit through ENERGY, for ENERGIES sake alone!

TL Whispers, California and Darnell, Illinois **USA**

LOVE LINK #46

Love is...
filled with many colors,
flourishing like a BUTTERFLY!
Lisa S.
Boston - California, **USA**

Love is...
giving a GIFT and
sharing your GIFTS,
just because!
Lisa S.
Boston - California, **USA**

74

LOVE LINK #47

To me what LOVE IS...
LOVE... it knows no boundaries or borders,
distance cannot weaken or break it and the
only judgment passed by love is that it is
and must always be unconditional.

In this world, there really is no force stronger than love, nothing that can truly destroy it for any love that is destroyed could not have been love to begin with, even when that love is with another, if it is truly love, it never goes away.

When I came to realize this, I came to realize I needed to follow my heart and love and in doing so have now found the greatest challenge of all... letting love flow and having faith that it truly is love and everything will work out, no matter the challenges or trials because true unconditional love can not be broken or destroyed.

Love is...
Photography!
Capturing BEAUTY in a FLASH!

Ryan "LunaWolf" Smith
British Born and Breed
Shepherdswell - Kent, **UNITED KINGDOM**

LOVE LINK #48

What does Love mean to me?
Love means so many things to me.
Here is my personal list of what I feel Love is:
Love is in knowing that you have people in the world that truly care about you
Love is getting big hugs from your grandchildren
Love is hearing the laughter of others
Love is seeing an elderly couple holding hands
Love is being silly with your best friend
Love is eating your favorite food at your favorite restaurant
Love is feeling the warmth of the Sunshine on your face
Love is taking a hot bubble bath
Love is being out in nature and seeing all the beautiful things that God has created
Love is seeing your children be happy and healthy
Love is seeing people being kind to one another
Love is hearing that you are going to be a grandma again
Love is finding other like-minded people as you
Love is getting a new puppy or kitten
Love is listening to your favorite song
Love is being able to relax and know that God is always with you
Love is feeling your best health
Love is the sound of the tide rolling in at the beach
Love is watching the sunrise and sunset
Love is in knowing that God has you here for a purpose
Love is being around others that make you happy
Love is the feeling of being protected and cared for always

Love is the feeling of gratitude for everything and
everyone in your life
Love is looking in the mirror and liking what you see
Love is a hot cup of coffee in the early morning
Love is having sweet dreams that come true
Love is in me and Love is in you

***My list could have gone on and on. I suppose to
make it shorter, I could have said:

*"Love is... all the things that make me feel
good!"*

*"The beginning of LOVE is to let those we
love be perfectly themselves, and not to
twist them to fit our own image.*

Otherwise, we find the reflection of ourselves
we love in them."

-Thomas Merton
No man is an Island
Shared By: Luv-Dolphin 1111 -Missy Pope
Florida, **USA**

Love is...
A gift that the more you give away...
The more you will receive!

"You cannot lose LOVE by giving it away!"

-Author Unknown
Shared By: Missy Pope and Terri Lynne
Florida, USA and California, **USA**

"Love Is...
A meeting of two souls, fully
Accepting the dark and the light
Within each other, bound by the
Courage to grow through struggle
Into bliss."

Author Unknown
Shared By: Missy Pope
Florida, **USA**

LOVE LINK #49

Love is... someone you can trust and they are always there.
Love is... someone that is dependable and always has your back, without even asking them to be there.

Lots of forms of love, but I believe you get back what you put out... I never like to be the one who doesn't end a conversation without trying to be helpful or loving. I am a person who knows love and has no problem spreading it! Have a nice night Terri

Tim Baldani
Sacramento, CA **USA**

LOVE LINK #50

"Love Is... YOU!"

Love is who I am

Love is our life's true plan

Love is all of humanity

Love is never insanity

Love is our creative rite

Love remains bright through our darkest night

Love is our purest self

Love is peace and inner health

Love is Wellness

Love is fulfilling

Love is the hand that grabs us when we're slipping

Love is Perfect

Love is True

Love is your children

Love is... YOU

Love is a friend's gentle touch

Love is the base element of all of us

Love is there to greet you at the end

Love is your best friend

Love is quintessential Grace

Love is the look on a newborn's face

Love is the gift we bring when we arrive

Love is our destination on the other side

Love is what connects us from the start

Love is sharing your heart

Love is our greatest gift

Love is our perpetual lift

Love is... a choice we all can make
So choose love and begin to create

Imagine Life - "Peace"
Isa, **AUSTRALIA**

LOVE LINK #51

Dear heart,

I could tell you what love is but you would not believe me. I could tell you what it is not, but still you would seek it and spend your life trying to get what you forgot. I could make you feel it with my words but you would think my poetry evoked it. I could lay you down and make you feel the pleasure but you would think the act caused it. I could give you riches in gifts of gold but you would feel love with conditions that can easily be sold. I could help you on your journey meeting all your needs but you would depend on the help for a feeling you falsely perceive. I could spend my days giving all my time to you but the quality would diminish when my presence began to bore you. These acts would make you feel love no doubt, but all the love you've ever felt came from in not out. *Love too much. More Amor.*

Juls Amor<3
Born: Texas USA - Residing: Playa Samara, **COSTA RICA**

LOVE LINK #52

Love is...
To be true to yourself!

Iris
NETHERLANDS

LOVE LINK #53

Love is...
energy, light, peace, beauty, truth and
timeless.

The more you give it out the more overflow it becomes in you; and it radiates and vibrates at immeasurable strengths!

Boyman Saungweme
ZIMBABWE

LOVE LINK #54

Love is…
A Verb:
To act in a kind
Non-judgmental way.

Eric Kahalelehua
Honolulu, **HAWAII**

LOVE LINK #55

Love is… an individual's perspective!

When you look through the EYES OF LOVE you don't see the faults in other people, you just see the perfectly whole person.

LOVE changes the perspective because you no longer look at the external illusion, but gaze into the perfect soul.

Credited to: Daniel Nielsen
Shared By: Clay Bailar
Born: Topeka, Kansas
Resides: Apple Valley, California **USA**

LOVE LINK #56

Love is... twin flames!

Eternal Love | A true story about Twin Flames!

Twin Flames!

Two souls connected, Two souls who know, Two souls whose purpose is to find each other and glow. Between you is a cord, that connects you through and through, for a while this cord lay dormant, waiting for the perfect moment to pursue.

Your other part of self, which your soul is searching for, could be at the other side of the world, or tomorrow come knocking at your door. However your destined meeting is, be sure and know this to be true; That when your eyes meet and your hearts unite, you'll know this is soul is the only one for you.

Allow yourself to remember, of that one who holds you tight. That one who truly understands you, and makes your entire Being know it's right. Back in your time of separation, when love was all you sort.

But in the waves and waves of pain, this love began to distort.

The pounding seas crashed down, on that pure heart of yours. As you sat within the boat, frantically searching for the oars! Time began to take its toll, whilst crashing through the waves.

Lee-Anne and Cory Peters

9

Always searching blindly for, the one you gave away.

Know within your heart of hearts, you had to experience the journey. So you could both come back full circle, and find where you held the key. The journey was long

and painful, there's no denying of that fact. Your heart so cold and lonely, for the one you made a pact.

The connection never went, it never faded in the dark. No matter how distant you may seem, you have never truly been apart. Open your heart again, for the time is upon you now. For the remembering of the love, who long ago you took a vow.

You vowed you'd find each other again, no matter what obstacles in your way. And one day, followed by your heart, this soul is here to stay. United at last, beyond all things, the love you feel so strong. For this was all

because, no one can ever break your love bond.

Let your hurt and pain go, expand your heart and your knowing. Fully surrender and trust that where you are right now, is just where you need to be going.

10

Eternal Love | A true story about Twin Flames!

Clear all obstacles in the way, find a way around and over them. Take action when you're guided to, allow all old hurts to mend.

When the hurt and pain drop away, and the time is absolutely right; you will be held tight in the arms again, and you can hold with all your might. Whether the time is perfect to hold your love, right now or long ago; know in spirit love remains, that connection is never broken.

If one is ready and the other is not, this breaks the hearts of those, for their choice has been to deal with pain, until the thorn turns into rose. Then two hearts unite as One, together in perfect union. A knowing, a trust, a feeling beyond words, that brings absolute free dominion.

Together at last, the suffering gone... Stand up, stand tall, this is YOU. Two souls merged as ONE, Your reconnection has just begun... .

Lee-Anne Peters ~ 1st June 2009

11

Lee-Anne and Cory Peters

Preface

'Together in Union, Together at Last, In this place where no linear time does pass! I hold you forever in this place of mine, Together in our hearts we sing our sweet rhyme.

Lee-Anne
Shared By: Terri Lynne - California, **USA**

LOVE LINK #57

Sitting in the silence, when the heart comes alive, then there is just... LOVE!
Credit to: Unknown Video

In the late 1980s, Lieserl, the daughter of the famous genius, donated 1,400 letters, written by Einstein, to the Hebrew University, with orders not to publish their contents until two decades after his death. This is one of them, for Lieserl Einstein.

"When I proposed the theory of relativity, very few understood me, and what I will reveal now to transmit to mankind will also collide with the misunderstanding and prejudice in the world.

I ask you to guard the letters as long as necessary, years, decades, until society is advanced enough to accept what I will explain below.

There is an extremely powerful force that, so far, science has not found a formal explanation to. It is a force that includes and governs all others, and is even behind any phenomenon operating in the universe and has not yet been identified by us. This universal force is LOVE.

When scientists looked for a unified theory of the universe they forgot the most powerful unseen force. Love is Light that enlightens those who give and receive it. Love is gravity, because it makes some people feel attracted to others.

Love is power, because it multiplies the best we have, and allows humanity not to be extinguished in their blind selfishness. Love unfolds and reveals. For love we live and die. Love is God and God is Love.

This force explains everything and gives meaning to life. This is the variable that we have ignored for too long, maybe because we are afraid of love because it is the only energy in the universe that man has not learned to drive at will.

To give visibility to love, I made a simple substitution in my most famous equation. If instead of $E = mc^2$, we accept that the energy to heal the world can be obtained through love multiplied by the speed of light squared, we arrive at the conclusion that love is the most powerful force there is, because it has no limits.

After the failure of humanity in the use and control of the other forces of the universe that have turned against us, it is urgent that we nourish ourselves with another kind of energy...

If we want our species to survive, if we are to find meaning in life, if we want to save the world and every sentient being that inhabits it, love is the one and only answer.

Perhaps we are not yet ready to make a bomb of love, a device powerful enough to entirely destroy the hate, selfishness and greed that devastate the planet.

However, each individual carries within them a small but powerful generator of love whose energy is waiting to be released.

When we learn to give and receive this universal energy, dear Lieserl, we will have affirmed that love conquers all, is able to transcend everything and anything, because love is the quintessence of life.

I deeply regret not having been able to express what is in my heart, which has quietly beaten for you all my life. Maybe it's too late to apologize, but as time is relative, I need to tell you that I love you and thanks to you I have reached the ultimate answer! ".

Your father,
Credited to: Albert Einstein
Shared by: Primal
AUSTRALIA

LOVE LINK #1 & LOVE LINK #58

Love is...
Friendship!
Keeping each other close regardless of the distance in between.

Below is an unedited version of a conversation between friends. One friend named Gisela, living in Germany who speaks German fluently, with broken English and myself Terri Lynne, who speaks English and doesn't speak any German at all. Regardless of our language barrier at first, we connected in our hearts space and together we managed to create a beautiful friendship. I am sharing this conversation to share how deep our conversations go, and how much love and respect we have for each other. Even with so much distance separating our physical bodies, our hearts will always be connected. To me... Love is... connecting, even when miles apart, by connecting inside one another's heart.

Feeling there isn't any distance between these two hearts uniting.

Please enjoy our conversation:

Dear Terri,

I want to tell you something... Always when I am ironing which I like doing because for me its time to listen closely to my radio and hang in my thinking...

So last time there was a woman that came on, she was from Israel, she told about her family how violent all her childhood was with more that just arguing, but also other bad hurting's. She could not stand the family any longer, so she ran away to get free, and she went into a religious home or something like that. In this home there was also so much cruelty, so she could not go back, she learned to stay away, she learned to forget, but it was always there. Anyway her dad after years decided to go and bring her back, and he did. Nothing changed at all in her home. So she decided to leave and for her the only land she wanted to go was Germany, because she felt there is where she would find her Freedom and also for her some Peace.

So she went with a very small suitcase and nothing more to Germany and arrived with the plane in Munich. She met nice people always WHO treated her with respect. So this woman came alone without anything besides good thinking. She made a social studying and when the Refugees arrived in Munich, she was the first one WHO went to the railway station to help these people handing them food, clothing, and with language problems, she cared for others in many other ways... .

It came to the point that she was not allowed any longer to go there from the border...
So she was already so well known that the people contacted her over Facebook.

No one could stop this woman.

Why do I tell you this story?

I thought when you have a good childhood its how you react, but I see that this woman from such a dark background can give back so much more than anyone else ever can do, and that is the difference between talking and doing, and to me that is really LOVE...

I want you to write this in your book for me!

You can take out my original message, cause I think for me, she is really a HERO, not to always just look at someone and say hi, I am fine, but to respect and to give your all to help others! For me she is like a New Mother Theresa and we can all learn from her actions!

Gisela
Ingolstadt, **GERMANY**

Dear Gisela,

That is most definitely a beautiful display of taking a feeling of Love not received and turning it into an offering for many to receive LOVE! The LOVE she was lacking coming from external people and places and things, she developed SELF-LOVE & SELF-RESPECT and recognized she didn't need to be loved by anyone but herself, for with THIS LOVE ALONE she could touch the world with UNCONDITIONAL LOVE...

For me:

"I believe a true LOVER is one who offers LOVE, without knowing who the receiver of your LOVE may be!"

What a beautiful choice Gisela!!! I LOVE YOUR HEART and I KNOW how you put your heart & soul into sharing the expression that represented what LOVE means to you!

Can I use it with your letter to me, as is and my reply to you? THIS FULLY REPRESENTS OUR GIFT OF LOVE & FRIENDSHIP ON EARTH!!! We connect in our hearts space and share loving stories always! I'd love for that to be shown to the world, how distance (You in Germany &

I in California) doesn't separate two hearts that are full of loving energy, with pure intentions. Rather it is the polar opposite, this friendship is based on pure hearts energy, and these hearts keep us connected and close together forever!!!

I ADORE YOU GISELA & THANK YOU FOR YOUR HEART!

Love,
Terri Lynne
California, **USA**

LOVE LINK #58

"Love is... a feeling!
Love often is connected with music,
at different ages."

One of my Songs is:
"Love Hurts" By: Nazareth
Gisela - Ingolstadt, **GERMANY**

LOVE LINK #59

A step above unconditional love...

Agape (Ancient Greek: ἀγάπη, gape) is "love: the highest form of love, charity; the love of God for man and of man for God." Not to be confused with "phileo" – brotherly love – gape embraces a universal, unconditional love that transcends that and serves regardless of circumstances. The noun form first occurs in the Septuagint, but the verb form goes as far back as Homer, translated literally as affection, as in "greet with affection" and "show affection for the dead." Other ancient authors have used forms of the word to denote love of a spouse or family, or affection for a particular activity, in contrast to Philia (an affection that could denote friendship, brotherhood or generally non-sexual affection) and Eros, an affection of a sexual nature.

Christianity developed Agape as the love of God or Christ for humankind. In the New Testament, it refers to the covenant love of God for humans, as well as the human reciprocal love for God; the term necessarily extends to the love of one's fellow man. Although the word did not have a specific religious connotation, it has been used by a variety of contemporary and ancient sources, including biblical authors and Christian authors.

The notion of agape has been examined as to traditions, whether Judeo-Christian or other world religions, religious ethics, and science.

CS - Satya Baggaria – **INDIA**

As human beings we are wired for love! We thrive on being loved and enjoy sharing our love with others. We are made for love, and, without it, life is lackluster, meaningless, or downright depressing.

Have you lost that loving feeling in your life? If so,

You have to try my new meditation, "Connecting to Your Loving Essence"... .

Perhaps you wish you had more closeness with your partner, more communication with your kids, or you were more enthusiastic about going to work?

Perhaps you wish life felt more magical and exciting? Feeling love-for yourself, others, and what you're doing - is the secret to all of that.

Yet, because of tensions and traumas in past painful experiences, it's easy to close our hearts to giving and receiving love.

Love might make us feel too vulnerable - and we don't want to be hurt again. We don't want to leave ourselves open and risk feeling the pains we can feel when our love isn't returned or when we are hurt in loving relationships.

Sometimes it just feels easier and more comfortable to keep our hearts closed.

When our hearts shut down, we may become cynical about love.

We may think it's too soft, weak, wishy-washy, or naive. Now, you may not have moved that far from love, but all of us, to some degree, close us off from the full measure of love we can feel and share.

We've all been hurt and we've all put up walls in the past. These walls protect us - and, after years and years of maintaining these walls, they become invisible. We don't even know they are there. Yet, we can know them by their signs. If you're not waking up with joy in your heart, if you're not thriving on the interactions you have during the day or if you've lost motivation,

If life feels somewhat flat, or if life seems to have lost its magic, you can be sure that those walls are in place.

There are invisible walls around your heart that are blocking the natural flow of love that makes life feel special, magical, and joyous.

When you are able to let down those walls, when you can release them and let go, you open the natural flow of love through your whole body and outward into the whole world. Your life comes alive and you feel like yourself again. That's because you're a being whose essence is Love. You are love. You thrive on love.

O.K. so what can you do if you've lost that loving feeling? How can you find it again? How can you get it back?

Fortunately, because love is part of your essential nature, part of which you truly are, it's already inside of you. It never left. Perhaps you just lost touch with it?

There are several ways to get back in touch.

1. Notice moments when you feel bored, unmotivated, uninterested, and lethargic. Notice what you're telling yourself in those moments. What are the words in your head?

Maybe you're feeling trapped in a situation, powerless to change it, or feeling like things are beyond your control? Perhaps you feel like you have no options? Just notice what you're thinking and how it relates to what you're feeling.

2. Ask yourself, "What do I wish could happen in this situation? What would make things more fun, interesting, meaningful, and exciting?" Whether or not you think any of these things are possible, entertain them. Imagine them. Fantasize about them. Enjoy the fact that you can imagine anything that you want to. Then ask yourself, "Is there any way I could bring a little bit of that into what is happening now?"

3. Set aside that particular situation for the moment and focus on connecting with and growing the feelings of love in your heart. If you've lost that loving feeling, it may take some time to get reacquainted with it. You can do this in the privacy of your own space-your own inner space-regardless of what is happening around you. Focus into your heart. Smile. And welcome the feelings of unconditional love there. What would it be like to feel unconditional love in your heart? Can you feel it?

Enjoy your practice! - Kevin
Shared By: Satya Baggaria – **INDIA**

LOVE LINK #60

"Love is...
The essence of the true self"

-Deepak Chopra
INDIA
Credit to: Oprah & Deepak 21 Day Meditation

LOVE LINK #61

Love is... so many different stages.

One is love of a child, second is love of a mate, third is love of an animal, fourth is love of a friend, fifth is love of a relative and then love of the world.

Love is so much better than hate and it would make the world be a much better place.

June L.
Florida, **USA**

LOVE LINK #62

Love Is...
When you feel your best,
When you're with the person you
LOVE.

Joe L.
Florida, **USA**

LOVE LINK #63

Promise me, O women of Jerusalem, by the
gazelles and wild deer, not to awaken love
until the time is right.

Credited to: Song of Songs 2:7
Shared by: Carolyn Shaw
Born: Chicago, IL
Resides: California, **USA**

LOVE LINK #64

Love is:
Not an emotion; It is your very existence.

Kahlil Guzi Piscopo
HONG KONG

LOVE LINK #65

Love is...
A FEELING inside that is different for
everyone and everything.

I feel it on the inside.
This "FEELING" stems from inside my heart.
There are no words to explain it!

Susie - California, **USA**

Love is...
The gentle, grateful, unconditional bond
between my rescue horse named, "Blaze"
and myself.

Rescued on: October 12, 2018

Susie and Blaze

Susie M.
California, **USA**
Blaze was rescued from The Kaufman Kill Pen
In Texas

101

LOVE LINK #66

Love is...
CREATED!

We were
CREATED

In LOVE
By LOVE
For LOVE
To BE
LOVE

Love is...
what DEFINES us!

How
The world
Defines LOVE

Is not
LOVE
At all

Love is...
CONDITION!

The only
Condition
For LOVE

Is that LOVE
Is without
Condition

Love is...
INCREASED

LOVE
That is
SHARED

Is LOVE
That is
INCREASED

Love is...
SENT

LOVE
Was SENT
Into the world

To LEAD us
Back out of it

By: David Wellens
Imperial Beach, California, **USA**

LOVE LINK #67

Love is...
A wonderful wicked thing!!!

Dwayne James and His Mama
JAMAICA

104

LOVE LINK #68

Love is...
The origin of religion!

Rita Bourgeois
Born: Chalmette, Louisiana
Resides: Picayune, Mississippi
and
GFTLC
HEAVEN & EARTH'S CONNECTION

LOVE LINK #69

"Love is...

LOVE... you feel it in the touch.

LOVE... you see it in the eyes.
LOVE... you taste it on the lips.
TRUE LOVE...
Caresses the heart and fills the soul.
The touch of TRUE LOVE is felt for a lifetime."

Phyllis - Aka: PAWS
California, **USA**

Love is...
making your children your 'first' PRIORITY!

Phyllis, Aaron & Becca
Aka: PAWS

Picture Captured: Puerto Vallarta
Resides: California, **USA**

106

LOVE LINK #70

LOVE
-Sex is the seed; love is the flower, compassion, is the fragrance- osho

-Love is patient, is kind, does not envy, is not boastful, is not conceited-

Does not act improperly, is not selfish, is not provoked.

-Love finds not joy in unrighteousness but rejoices in the truth.

Bear all things, believes all things, hopes all things, endures all things and never ends.

Love is karma. Karma is created from our thoughts and actions in which results in our experiences, so the love we give and receive is the direct result of our thoughts & actions.

To have love we must first choose loving actions. We must regulate our behavior and be vigilant about creating and maintaining the highest intentions.

Honor, respect, surrender-releasing the ego. These are the laws of love.

This is the love: to fly towards a secret sky, to cause a thousand veils to fall each moment. First to let go of life. Finally to take a step without feet - Rumi

Lovers don't finally meet somewhere-they are in each other all along-rump

Many go from partner to partner on an empty search for fulfillment; but the answer does not lie in another. The answer lies in you. Love yourself.

When you vibrate and love finds you... This is the heart of love Tantra

Your task is not to seek for love, but merely to seek and find all barriers within yourself that you have built against it - Rumi

This is how to truly make love: actions and reactions/ cause and effect. Love is karma.

-Author Unknown

LOVE LINK #71

Love is... an action, or intent of life.

It is something you do but many of us look for it in others. You can't really receive love, but you can feel the result of love. It is a choice in life of how you wish to be. I think, judge and observe my life and I hope I DO IT with LOVE at my starting point.
Laura Whipps **USA**

LOVE LINK #72

When we think how we love something that we have created - it can be a very powerful feeling to us.

When we understand that God is pure love and loves everything that God has created which is everything that we see and don't see. What a powerful feeling that must be!!! As we evolve more we see the bigger picture and appreciate and love more. As God is Infinite and we are on this Infinite journey, we learn more, appreciate more and Love more - how can it ever come to an end? But we can become part of this Infinite Love.

Hope that this is ok for now. In my 5th book, "The Source - Creation and Appreciation," is based on this Love.

Wasyl Kolesnikov - **UNITED KINGDOM**

LOVE LINK #73

Love is...
A four-letter word and we use it to describe sub feelings and we confuse those feelings.

Love can be what you want it to be. To some LOVE is more than like, to some love is the ultimate feeling. Love can be used for light or dark, for me love is both a power and a feeling that the word love can't describe. To us

it is a warm, cozy, secure acceptance, feeling wanted, feeling free, an emotion and whatever else you want to call love. We are told what love is but to describe it, love has to be felt firsthand, therefore then and only then will you know what LOVE IS!

Bradley Koch - Missouri, **USA**

LOVE LINK #74

"Love is...
The final truth;

Which when realized is the biggest strength,
Of those who are in it, in all manners."

Love is... what changes us!

"Don't try to change people;
Just love them!
Love is what changes us."

Author Unknown
Shared By: Girish Daga
Mumbai, **INDIA**

110

Love is...
In every cell of our being
Ready for activation,
N O W!!!

Girish Daga
Mumbai, **INDIA**

Love is...
An Endless Ocean
Flowing freely!

"Love rests on no foundation.
It is an endless ocean,
With no beginning or end."

-Rumi
Shared By: Girish Daga
Mumbai, **INDIA**

Love is...
All and all is love!

-Author Unknown
Shared By: Girish Daga
Mumbai, **INDIA**

Love is...
The echo of the soul's vibration!

As we walk hand in hand eternally on the road to freedom living in pureness and truth from our hearts!

-Author Unknown

Love is...
what you should let inside
your HEART!

Love is... an inside job.

Love is...
Inside all of US!

Love is... Healing!

"Love is the most healing force in the world;
Nothing goes deeper than love.
It heals not only the body,
Not only the mind,
But also the soul."

-Osho

Love is...
Your Souls Light!

-Author Unknown
Girish Daga
Mumbai, **INDIA**

Love is...
Friendship!

FRIENDSHIP IS...
The most even,
Unconditional,
Exchange of LOVE!

Girish Daga
Mumbai, **INDIA**

LINK #1 & LINK #74

Love is... your essence!
"Love is... the pure essence of our very
being."

"It is the breath of life. It is what binds us together. To love is to survive, to create and to hold one another in golden arms of peace. It is our greatest ability, our greatest gift and is that which will never escape us as the powerful Spirits we are... you are love."

Author Unknown
Shared By: Girish Daga and Terri Lynne
INDIA and USA

Love is...
The best lesson to learn!

And
All you need to learn is,
What Love Is!

Love is...
My teacher!

Terri Lynne & Girish Daga
California, USA and Mumbai, **INDIA**

LOVE LINK #75

Love is...
Reality!!!
"LOVE IS the only reality and it is not a mere sentiment. It is the ultimate truth that lies at the heart of creation."

-Rabindranath Tagore
You tube video

LOVE LINK #76

Love is…
What we are and what God is.

Love is a being not a feeling.
When we love, we create a being just as God created us.
All that we love lives forever in our heart and cannot be lost…

Bill Lighthall
MEXICO

LOVE LINK #77

Love is…
The thing that holds us, binds us and connects us.

It may be sticky, it may be icky, but without it we all fall apart. Love comes in all sizes, shapes, ups, downs, round & rounds, a Merry-Go-Round, a ride you never want to get off from.

My favorite kind of LOVE is grand kids!

"Love is... Grandchildren giving you LOVE!"

Love is... in her eyes...

Hilary (Aka: Hilarence, H.A.)
Northern California, **USA**

LOVE LINK #78

What LOVE IS to Me:
There are really only two emotions, love
and fear. Love is spirit and fear is ego...
I choose love.

When our spirits are born into our bodies and the physical world, a part of our truth is snuffed out from the overbearing force of ego. As we grow and become domesticated, we forget who we really are... pure bliss. If we are fortunate enough, as we evolve, we again become aware of our inner truths and strive to walk back into the light, into love and into ourselves. This place that we yearn for is a place of free flowing acceptance that allows and not resists, a place that promotes and not demotes, and a place that unites and not separates.

Love knows neither time nor space, when love itself is ready to be revealed, it will do so in it's own energetic beauty and grace. Love is blind because true love is not of the physical but of a divine connection. Love is oneness and unified yet individual and subjective. Two people could see the same one love; however, their perspectives could be different. One may choose to see love from a place of divinity, where they will bask in the sunshine of their bliss; and the other may choose to see from their ego, where they will remain trapped in the four walls that close them in. Love is overflowing with compassion for mankind, not in constant competition with our earth family. Love is silent and still, in this silence you can hear the most beautiful song of your soul. Love is having faith that you have already received and will continue to do so, and does not require seeking of any kind.

In this physical world of many different paths and choices... choose love, it is already the case after all.

Marci - Boston - California, **USA**

LOVE LINK #79

Blanket me
With your love

Surround me

With your radiance

Hold me

With your strength

Reach for me

And I will love

Ask of me

And I will give all

Lean on me

When you stumble

Allow me

To be you're equal

Have faith

In our love
And together
We will stand tall
Love Revealed

Shanthi Sathish Babu
INDIA

LOVE LINK #80

WHAT IT MEANS TO RETURN TO A NATURAL WAY OF LIFE... TO BE HUMAN

1. *It's important to note that our natural state of being is* love. The problem is... we've simply forgotten. The outside world is a product of the current state of collective consciousness. What are the majorities of humans believing now? What thought system are they following? What thoughts are influencing them? What images are they focused on? What are we studying? What are we resisting? What are we striving to become? And most importantly to what end and why?

2. The more we know, the more we accumulate, the more we think we need... the more we desire... the farther away from love... the farther away from our natural selves we venture.

3. Sad and unsatisfied faces fill the streets of the most abundant country in the world because of the thought that we still don't have enough. The

media... from television, to the radio, to the internet or even paperback tells us that we need to look like this... smell like that... drive in this... travel to there... learn about whatever they want us to learn about...

Or we are not really living... or in other words... we are not COMPLETE human beings.

4. The question was how to return to love when there is so much fear and anger being promoted. The answer is not to return... rather to simply remember. Love is what you are. Love is the energy that pumps your heart, inflates your lungs... love is life... you are life... having a human experience... simply remembering this will ease the load of what surrounds us.

5. Most of us have forgotten what we are and are living in a dream state of who we think we are. We have temporarily abandoned our connection to the whole... well at least we think we have. We believe we are separate.

6. While this separation is literally impossible... a belief in is not... and since we are all creators... we are creating an illusory story of separation that becomes stronger and stronger in our minds with every new subscriber to it.

7. Those of us who subscribe to such stories are easy to control and sway. We become easy to be slid around because we are no longer thinking... rather we are being thought... or in other words... the thought system / dream is doing the thinking for us.

8. We must stay vigilant we must stay awake. If all of us fall under this spell, the end of the world as people have been predicting for so long will be inevitable. Simply remembering that we are love... pure and simple. Simply remembering that we are one people... one consciousness... one energy... we

are all of one source... that remembrance alone is all we need to once again sense the truth of what we are.

Oh Soul Simple Life - California, **USA**

LOVE LINK #81

Love is...
Loving Yourself!

"Learn to love
YOURSELF
First
Instead of loving the idea
OF OTHER PEOPLE
Loving you."

-Unknown Author

Love has to spring spontaneously from within: and it is in no way amenable to any form of inner or outer force. Love and cohesion can never go together:

But though love cannot be forced on anyone, it is essentially self-communicative. Those who do not have it catch it from those who have it.

True love is unconquerable and irresistible; and it goes on gathering power and spreading itself. Until eventually it transforms everyone whom it touches.

-Meher Baba

Close your eyes...
See LOVE...
Stay there!
-Rumi

Oh Simple One
California, **USA**

LOVE LINK #82

Love is...
Pure!

Love is...
Limitless!

C LOVE
California, **USA**

123

LOVE LINK #83

Love is... Limitless!

Dominique Thierry
Bonneuil Sur Marne, **FRANCE**

LOVE LINK #84

Love is...
space and time measured by the heart!

-Marcel Proust
Died in 1922
Paris, **FRANCE** - French Novelist

LOVE LINK #85

"Love is... the only sane and satisfactory answer to the problem of human existence."

Erich Fromm
GERMANY
Died: March 18, 1930
A German Social Psychologist

LOVE LINK #86

The Definition of what LOVE IS to me...

"Love is... in every breath I take!"

Monica Christine
California, **USA**

LOVE LINK #87

Let's begin our journey...

As we are brought forth into this world on earth, we begin as pure love. Innocent, with no preconceptions, no demands, no damage... we are just that Love. Then the outside influences begin to play a pivotal part in creating the concepts of what eventually we learn to live as love. From parental/family beliefs, to religious pressures, to societal biases, right down to the personal life involvements we see, hear, touch or become touched by, our experiences and redefining of love transcends what appear to be eons of realms. Hence, as I sit here today living from the depths of my heart and soul, I want to share with you my personal journey from true source of pure love down the paths my soul chose to return me back home to where love always resided. So, let us set course and sail through this chain of love from my soul to yours.

It begins many years ago, with a young girl from a small town with dreams of becoming everything she believed, dreamed she could be, and what she knew she had been created to be. Though many did not see or understand her heart and soul's desires, she began her journey from her source of love knowing. For joy, love, and grace was a world in which she derived from. And

though unfortunate circumstances such as childhood moments of darkness, illnesses and tears became to be familiar path, she understood at a very young age that these were all just stepping stones that would eventually reconnect her broken heart and spirit to a greater and higher level of love that she felt but could not see during those times. See I am this small town girl, and yes, I am a golden light of love just as you.

I never thought I'd ever know a love so deep, so true. Until I came through the darkest parts of me to once again be in touch with you. For I have searched the whole world trying to find; the love always locked within... that one of a kind. We began as friends, a bond with no end. Then I allowed the world to take me from you. Many moments passed without me knowing what to do. As I left you in the shadows, the dark, I failed to realize that I was only dimming out our spark. With grace and time I have come to learn, rediscover, the love inside of me lost, hidden under life's shielding cover. So, I ask myself now to forgive me, forgive me for all that I didn't allow us to be. Find it within to come from the cold, dark space I so long ago left you. Take my hand, reunite our soul, and allow me to forgive me too. For the love, light and joy awaits us, take my hand so I can regain your trust. For the fear is over now, take my hand and let me show you how.

See this was just the beginning of my true understanding that the illnesses, abuses, pains, sorrows, tragedies and losses were in fact tests, lessons, and eventually would be the answers to all that I felt had been emptied in me. Yet there was still a burning fire deep within my being to keep love alive.

The darkest clouds were filling in the skies, love and faith seemed to slip away without their goodbyes and now the rains and thunder roars. The depths of the sorrow they bring can't last much more. Knowing you're lost, yet how powerful it is to find, the strength in where you belong. To bear forever despite all that is wrong. When at last the darkness begins to clear, the light reveals itself, long after the noise and troubles are gone. Our belief in love still shines its bright, beautifully colored, powerful glowing light.

But then like always, there would come a blessing. And the two most amazing blessings soon arrived and showed me a new and profound meaning to true love; for I was blessed with two beautiful and healthy earth angels, and through the remainder of my journey thus far, have been the reason I love, breathe and continue to shine.

My dream came true the day God gave me my earth angel, a divine blessing as a mother came true. Then one day, when I least expected, out of Heaven my heart expanded, another blessing, and then there were two. Now the time has come, they both are no longer babies. Within a blink of an eye they had grown into very special young ladies. So, I am writing this little note to remind them when I am gone, that a mother's love and bond will forever remain strong. And if there should ever come a time when their life is afloat, they can sit down and reread this little note. And remember to hold on to one another, for this love has no end, and there will never be anything stronger than the love and bond of a daughter and a mother.

And then there is the love of a true soul mate, twin flame, within my being, and at one moment I truly thought that the Universal Cards had been dealt. For a man came into my life finally that made me begin to not only believe, but actually feel the unbelievable spiritual connection of souls that were destined to be.

There's nothing more I want than to love you for the rest of my life; to each morning awaken your wife. To wake every morning with you right beside me, knowing no matter what was to come, in my day you would always be. Everyday returning to you, to a love like no other, so honest and true; to share our ideas, our dreams, the everyday little things. The one's that make us laugh to the not so little ones that we can't stop stressing about. I want to give you all of my Love, as we grow old, watching every moment of our life together unfold. Making our dreams, one by one, come true, spending every second loving you!

And though life circumstances once again turned the tables on what I still long for and refuse to give up hope of this hand to be fulfilled.

I long to feel your embrace, your kiss, and your touch; for being apart has been cause for my longing to be in your clutch. For the separation of our souls have left us incomplete; leaving our hearts rhythm on an unsteady beat. The signs are all around me telling me you're near; for there is no other answer to the feelings I have... urged on by the track of my tears. And though to some this may be foolish or just plain dumb, I know that a life without you in it will forever leave me numb. I long for your embrace, but more so I crave the love you left without a trace. My plea to the Creator of you and I is

to shine a brilliant light down a path leading us home to one another from the depths of the night.

But until the day arrives that this dream of love comes again, I have found a new founded love that had so long been set aside along my journey to where I am now; for I rediscovered and embraced the surrender to all that love encompasses.

I reach into the depths of my being in search, for I feel you. I hear you call out my name, and shine a dim light seeing me through. I feel your pull, the longing, and the desperation. My will is strong to close this separation. The twist and turns I encounter, will never divide us. For the light of my being I trust. I feel we're getting near, as the longing to reunite with every fiber of you draws clear. The reason, meaning, of our bond no longer sits on the shelf. The burning is real for I know your name now, the name I call and love... is Self.

So now we come to not quite the end of my journey for I know that the love of all is still ever expanding my heart and soul and is long from over, but we leave each other to continue to shine for others. Sharing our own testimonies, giving witness that indeed no matter the paths, true love's bright, powerfully glowing light forever shines for all along this chain of love.

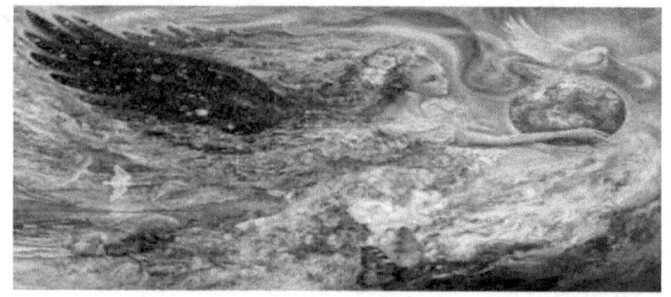

Rita E. Bourgeois, June 5, 2016
Born: Chalmette, Louisiana
Reside: Picayune, Mississippi **USA**

Love is not a person
Love is a heart
Connected
To a soul
Into the Source of All

-Peter Bach

Love is...
Being in the flow!
"What is the meaning of love?
No words...
Just flow of divine vibrations!"

-Peter Back

Love is...
Souls kissing!

For it was not into my ear you whispered,
But my heart...
It was not my lips you kissed...
But my soul!

Rita Bourgeous
Born: Chalmette, Louisiana
Resides: Picayune, Mississippi **USA**

LOVE LINK #1 & LOVE LINK #88

Love is...
Praying for another's healing!

Terri Lynne Praying for Indi Shan

***Note: Indi is paralyzed presently, due to spine surgery causing paralysis of his legs. Praying for a MIRACLE that Indi WILL walk again very soon! His mission and purpose in life is designed to be teaching the Universe about what Unconditional LOVE IS!!! This is part one of Indi's messages from his hospital bed in Melbourne, **AUSTRALIA**

LOVE LINK #88

I will write about love when my dexterity improves. It's hard now typing out messages. It will be a long one because *love is... all there is. There is nothing well else, but love. It's all that exists and everything that doesn't exist, is love. The simple version is I am love. You are love, every body is love, and LOVE creates. There is love to feel, and then there is the mind that thinks it knows love.* Big difference. I'm meditating and learning a lot in humility. Relying on nurses to do everything for me like I'm an infant.

Love is...
An eternal connection blending souls!

We are connected forever in the eternal love unconditional...
Indi "LOVE" Shan
Born: INDIA
Residing: Melbourne, **AUSTRALIA**

LOVE LINK #1 & LOVE LINK #88

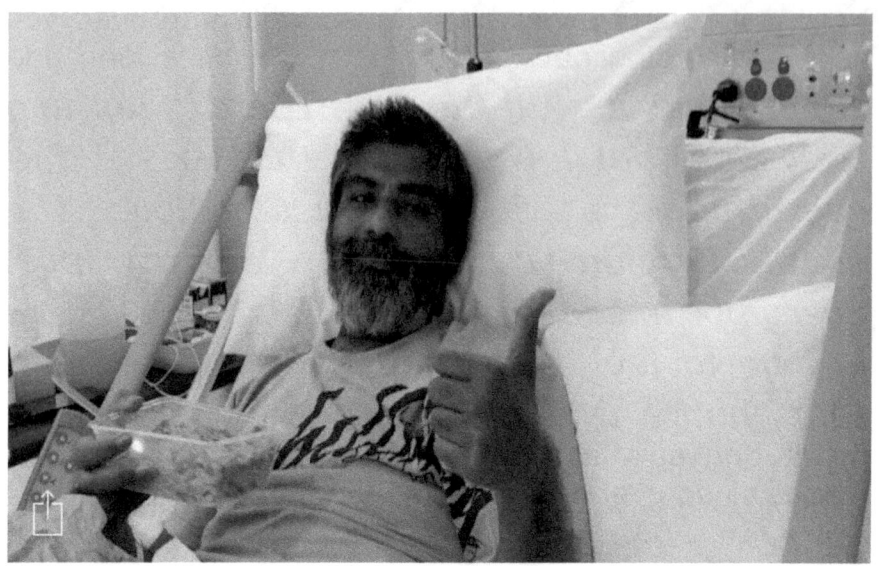

Please PRAY for Indi to have a FULL RECOVERY,
so he can continue his journey of touching one heart at
a time, through teachings of what Unconditional LOVE
IS!
Thank you in advance for your prayers,
Terri Lynne

INDI "LOVE" SHAN'S JOURNEY
~ From Strength to Sorrow to Source ~
All in a single lifetime!

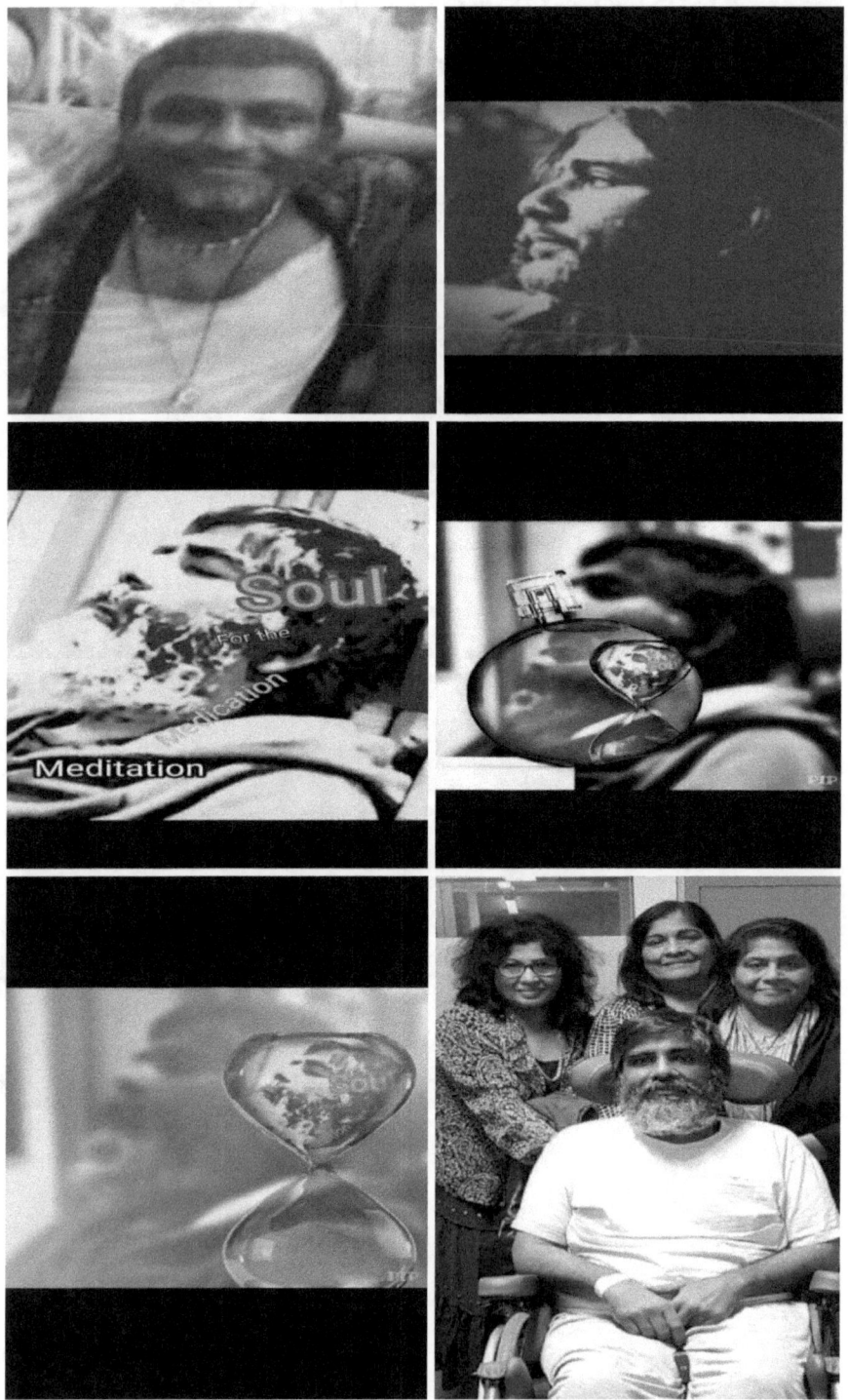

***UPDATE ON INDI'S STATUS:

Indi has been working hard on solving EMOTIONS, while accepting UNCONDITIONAL LOVE from a familiar stranger with a COMPASSIONATE HEART and presently he WALKED 10 meters or 32.81 feet with a walking frame.

*"MIRACLES are not "IMPOSSIBLE"
When you BELIEVE... "I'M POSSIBLE!"*

Indi is being discharged on December 24, 2016, WALKING his way out of the Hospital! Thank you all for your prayers throughout the development of this book!

-Terri Lynne

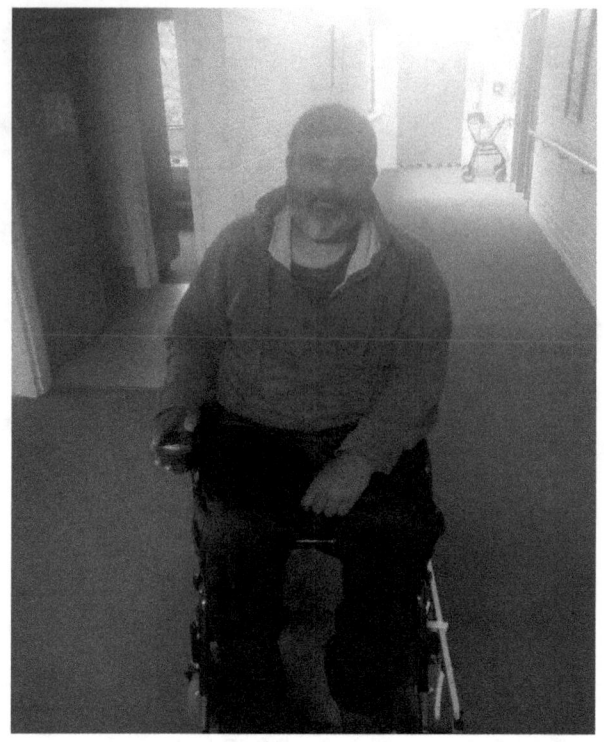

New Electric Wheelchair
Making progress...

"Love is...
Determination!"

"Determination looks like this. ☺ With faith and meditation proving the specialist wrong with pleasure. No spinal injury will keep me down."

-Indi Shan

INDIA – Melbourne, AUSTRALIA

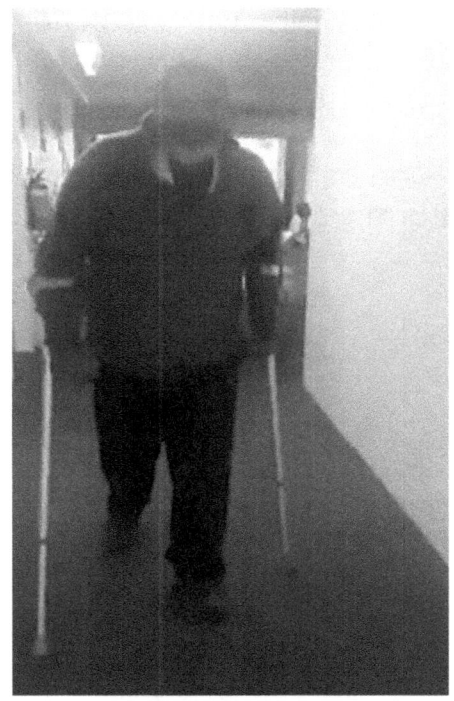

THIS IS PROOF THAT MIRACLES CAN HAPPEN!!!

Indi Shan IS WALKING with crutches, after being paralyzed for a year and NOW on his way towards walking on his OWN!!! ☺

One baby step at a time...
(Determined to share guiDANCE!)

"Love is...
Motivating!"

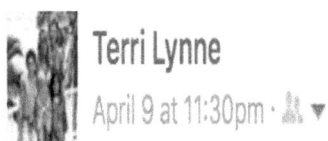

Terri Lynne
April 9 at 11:30pm · ▲ ▼

Indi LOVE Shan sharing his SUCCESS!!!! He never gave up on proving everyone wrong and only listened to his OWN spirits whispers in KNOWING he would WALK AGAIN, after being told he is paralyzed due to a staff infection in his spine and after emergency surgery, he came out of surgery paralyzed and all doctors, nurses, physical therapists and everyone attached to his case told him he would never walk again...

This video is Indi's MIRACLE IN ACTION, after many days and nights of extremely hard work, dedicated to never give up, having FAITH in his own power & with a heart overflowing with LOVE to share with the world VERY SOON!!!!! Indi LOVE Shan thank you for sharing your trials and tribulations with me, and NOW lets introduce YOU to the world so you can share your TRUE LIFE'S STORY up close and personal!!! I AM your biggest fan my friend! You allowed me into your heart and NOW I will carry you in mine forever more! This is the BEST VIDEO I have ever seen! WELL DONE & KEEP MOVING FORWARD...

You have ALOT to look forward to on this roller coaster called LIFE! Always LIVE INTUITIVELY FOR ETERNITY and you will create MIRACLES UPON MIRACLES your entire LIFE! Thank you for being who you are, a BRIGHT SHINING SUPERSTAR!!!!!!!!!! Sending you LOVE from afar, TL xxxooo

Love is...
- Always -
All the way, in all directions, with no end...

No cover...
Naked...
Vulnerable...
Beautiful...
Bare truth.
Like a child is born,
I come to you,
Like the first time,
He opens his EYES,
Sees the world,
Feels the warmth,

And breathes the air...
Indi "LOVE" Shan

Born: INDIA Resides: **AUSTRALIA**

Indi Shan's LOVE IS message:

The message below was written from Indi's hospital bed at St. Vincent's Hospital in Melbourne, Australia. It is where he landed after getting diagnosed with a staff infection in his spine and receiving emergency surgery. Immediately following his surgery, he became paralyzed and is presently a paraplegic ☹. Indi's FAITH and strong WILL and BELIEVING IN MIRACLES, is what appears to be carrying him through these life changing, challenging days and nights of darkness, until he retrains his brain to receive the correct messages to one day soon walk again naturally and freely. Then he CAN WALK his way out of that hospital and into the hearts and souls of millions around the world, who must learn of Indi's story and FEEL Indi's HEART FULL of nothing but, UNCONDITIONAL LOVE! I, Terri Lynne ask for you to please pray for Indi Shan to reach a full recovery, so he can touch the lives of many with his radiant LIGHT while pursuing & fulfilling his BIG DREAMS which are created for all of you!!!

Indi's life's mission is to share the GIFT OF WHAT LOVE IS by simply touching your heart, with his! TL

These are the days, where through every moment of my life I am living the very experience in life that I have been talking about and what I have written at length in here about recently.

And I am talking, :) AGAIN! About… . LOVE! Love unconditional… and those who can remember my droll, will remember me saying, Love unconditional, has to pass through intense heat before it becomes its purest form, which is compassion, Compassion is the purest form of love, the divine love, that acts upon it. Just as base metal has to pass through heat to become its purer form, Gold… . Heat in love's case is the hardships, suffering, and the mistakes that shape and teach us all.

Where whatever we experience, doesn't kill us in the learning process, then we are the stronger for it when we have learned the lesson from it, whether we prevail and go forward or are forever suffering from its presence.

Now those who have heard me, and have read my article with the message of what love is… I always have likened it to an infant, or someone with an injury, learning to first roll, then crawl, sit up, find their legs and stand. Then finally take one step forward, then the other, one by one; till they get to the point they don't think about it, they just automatically walk. And then they transcend the way by going beyond and now learning to run… walking is no longer a thing, it is no longer separate to us, we are one with the walk. We are the walk, there is no differentiating it… we are oblivious of the hundreds of muscles involved; the stomach trunk, etc. This applies to everything we do, or learn to do in this physical existence… and so in the spiritual realm, it works just the same. We must first seek to find what really is love, and then when we find it, we must have it for ourselves, with no reservations. This is unconditional and compassionate, as there is no judgment. And then only you will know what to give to others, you first must have ten bucks if you want to give someone ten bucks; not 7, 8, 9, 11… just 10. You must first have it, and then you can share it. Then you share it with everyone, liberally applying love to everyone in existence, until

it just exudes out of you. You are no longer aware you are being compassionate and loving. It becomes one with you, just like the walk. When you become love, all will see and behold that you ARE LOVE!!!! Then you will have to go beyond the compassion, or transcend to the next spiritual realm to find a face of love we haven't yet been privy to here.

When I talk about love and compassion from this day forth, I see it in it's truest light in terms of transcending the physical walk. It is an analogy, yet at the same time it is not, we are love, and so our walk, our legs, our physical, our soul, our consciousness, our energy it is all that love unconditional I am talking about. Love literally, is all there is. There literally is nothing other than love in existence, Love conquers all and will transcend time and space. We are made in love's image, we possess the attributes of it, making us one and the same... love is eternal... as it always will be, as it was already in existence, we only saw it in a different light. Always changing, it appeared to be, so much so that the only thing constant in existence is change. It always changes constantly, in other words, it is actually becoming, like a sculpture, until it is complete, it appears to be changing, but it was becoming, love is becoming, we are becoming, everything is becoming, and nothing is also becoming... until it has become what it already was. Does this make sense or did I become too complicated? Love or compassion, always is...

It's a simple existence, really, become love, and by default, you can only serve the will of love. Imagine if everyone gets there together, well maybe not together, but one by one, as people wake up and see the light. We all will because we come from the same source, love. We will go back to it, there is nothing in existence that is out of place.

There is not a single evil atom in existence; otherwise, it's like saying everything is evil, if even one atom can be evil. It is either evil or not evil... or it is actually neither, it just is... .

Ha-ha! Get it; It's just a way of being, action in the will of love, or action without the will of love or no action at all. The will of love does not exist to make one want to act. Depression to inaction to oblivion. One must choose and be one or the other, not a little of both, halfway up is nether up nor down. All or nothing folks... love like there is no tomorrow, because we are love and we live in the now, the present. Tomorrow never comes, when it does, it is now, today... ha-ha.

Herein is all the secrets of the universe, take what you feel is your truth, what resonates; at this moment for you... hopefully it is clear and helpful to most. IF NOT one day it will... only through living through a disaster, paraplegia, one will know what it really is. Not through the encyclopedia written about it, but by all that one felt through it, that's why god moves in mysterious ways. We can never understand his mind because he has no mind, he is not a he, but he is a LOVE. One can only feel it to understand and know it, not by reading or hearing about it. One will be in its vicinity through reading, somewhere thereabouts, within its zone, but never will be one with it, never will be it. Namaste.
Indi Shan

Born: **INDIA** - Resides: Melbourne, **AUSTRALIA**

Indi's personal love is message:

LOVE is... a subject I like to talk about!

A subject discussing the order of the universe and how it correlated to the very word the bible is founded on. For even the bible gives us a clue... "IN THE BEGINNING THERE WAS THE WORD, AND THE WORD WAS WITH GOD, AND THE WORD WAS GOD."

IT is singular... Word... Not words. It wasn't referring to every single word written in the entire bible cover to cover... It was referring to the energy it was written in. The tone, the power; that one and only word can create. For nothing else can create something other than the power of LOVE... AND GOD IS LOVE... HE AND THE WORD ARE ONE... LOL.

MANY DON'T GET THIS... ESPECIALLY IN CHRISTIANITY...

I'm now about to head downstairs on my stiff and hopeless wheelchair lol... It's hard to push compared to the light weight manual chairs that fly with every push forward... This high back chair was designed to keep a person's spine in line and protect one from falling due to lack of use of one's core to sit upright... Lol. I don't need that now, where once before I needed that... Now my shoulders are hurting from pushing that thing around lol... But my arms are strong, it'll adapt... My muscle tone memory should come back pretty quick now.

Message you more later...

Terri... Sending more seamless energy of love, it never will stop... I draw it from the divine source and send it to you and the more I send, the more room there'll be in my heart, to gather more to send more... A continuous flow, this is the economics of love, the more you share the more you receive. Not like material wealth, which

needs to be hoarded to become wealthy, it cannot be shared like love... Lol truth

That is my take on what love is...

To LOVE, IS... To be in the image of God... And it is the most humble place... To come with love is to face the unknown, rejection, darkness, a leap of faith is needed into the darkness until you find the light. One cannot plan for the future where love is involved; it is always in the right here right now. To act can end in death, (rejection) and to not act it definitely leads to death (rejection).

That is the love that I channel to all things living in this entire creation... It flows through me, and I am no longer needing to be aware of it... I am oblivious to the fact that love flows right through, it emanates from me in everything I do, and to everyone I come in contact with, in so many ways... I am LOVE... JUST AS YOU ARE LOVE... GOD IS LOVE, AND HE IS IN EVERYTHING THAT HE HAS CREATED...

LOVE IS... the wind that flows through the bamboo hollow, and plays the beautiful tune of love. And we are the bamboo that which is called a flute. Without the breath, the flute has no purpose and without the flute the breath lacks purpose. It is also useless.

This love of God is not separate to God. It is one and the same... And we are in his image, we have the attributes of God. To me this means, we are one and the same... So long as we act in the divine selfless love... The purest... Compassion!

Lol, that's me flowing in love... Ha-ha, walk like an Egyptian!

Ha-ha in the words of Michael Jackson... .
'I'm starting with the man in the mirror'...
Indi "LOVE" Shan
Melbourne, **AUSTRALIA**

LOVE LINK #89

Thank you for your friendship and also for bringing to my attention the wonderful work that you are doing.

What do I have to say about love? Well, *"Love is... the medium of communication by which souls interact with each other."* It is the spiritual essence found in reality in which replaces space and time. It is the air and is necessary for oneness and attainment of the divine universal mind. Simply put, "Love Is because we are." And in this is the mystery of "I AM." This is just a summary. But because "Love Is so expansive and all encompassing filled with thousands of words," I think your book will turn out to be heavy. You're such a blessing for what your undertaking. I wish you all the best and God bless.

Willock Flame
Resides in **KENYA**

LOVE LINK #90

Love is... all we need!

Jannet Garal
Resides: Villahermosa, Tabasco, **MEXICO**

LOVE LINK #91

Hi Terri - and thank you for connecting through friendship. This is an interesting question you ask, and one that will have many answers. I think there are different 'kinds' of love. However, on a very esoteric scale, *I think the Universe was created out of - or with Love.* So it lives, and permeates, all that there is. Perhaps that is why so many spend so much time thinking of it. It's part of our 'DNA' so to speak.
Jim - Massachusetts, **USA**

LOVE LINK #92

Love is...
Found inside your heart and soul!

May you have LOVE in your HEART and
PEACE in your SOUL!

Sandie Adkins
West Virginia, **USA**

LOVE LINK #93

Love is...
Boundless!

LOVE knows no boundaries!

A Very Happy Sunday to All My Friends... for All The Madness Human Beings Are Capable Of... the Power of Love Is The Most Powerful Force There Is & Fortunately Has No Boundaries or We Surely Would Have Perished as a Species Long Ago...

What a Beautiful Thing... :)

"Love is...
The most powerful weapon on earth!"

Author Unknown
Fighting Fire With Fire Produces More Fire...
That is Why We Fight Fire With Water...
To Fight Evil With Evil is Madness & Produces Only
Sadness...

The Only Weapon That Will Ever Truly Extinguish "Evil"
is LOVE… .

Not Too Long Ago… Someone I Know Said to Me: Steve, You Seem to Use the Word "Love" a lot… how Can You love so Many People? I Simply Said, How Can I Not… Love is Not Simply About Intimacy… it is About Much More Than That… It is Kindness in Action, The Love for Each Others Well Being… if One Lacks That, They will Never Truly Know a Love of Any Kind… wishing All My Friends a Fantastic Day! :)

"Kindness is not an act.
It is a lifestyle."
-Anthony Douglas

Love Is…
Beyond Judgment!

"What is love?
Love is the absence
Of judgment."
-Dalai Lama

Steve Manley
Boston, MA - Tennessee, **USA**

154

LOVE LINK #94

Love is... A Choice!

To choose not to love, to wait to see what another does first, to watch and observe before you deem it safe to give, is to never give anything the chance to become its full potential. We understand that many of you have been hurt by the absence of love from others, but we urge you to BE the love you are, to show up with your love and to allow it to shine, for that is the only way you can be seen in your truth, and to draw to you the perfect matches that can mirror that back to you beautifully. To hold yourself out of love, Dear Ones, will only continue the experience of the absence of love, and we want so much more for you than that. -Archangel Gabriel

Shared by: Jonathan Curzon
Cape Town, **SOUTH AFRICA**

LOVE LINK #95

"LOVE IS...
What stands apart from comprehension...
And stands beside... contemplation."

Keith Holder
Southern Ontario, **CANADA**

LOVE LINK #96

Love is...
The creator energy!

Christina Marie
Florida, **USA**

LOVE LINK #97

Love Is...
Beyond compare!

Patricia Milano **USA**

LOVE LINK #98

Love cannot be compared with any other emotion.

It is because of love alone that the Universe exists, and continues to exist. Love is the motivation of creation and the movement that sustains creation. Love is everything. If we can strip away negativity we will find love because love is the root of all things.

Catherine Leblanc
CANADA

LOVE LINK #99

Love is...
raising ecstasy!

The best love is the kind that awakens the soul and
makes us reach for more,
that plants a fire in our hearts
and brings peace to our minds.
-Nicholas Sparks

Tara Ursulesclu
Calgary, **CANADA**

LOVE LINK #100

Love is...
WHY!!!

LOVE IS...
WHY WE ARE HERE!

Henry Atkin
New York, **USA**

LINK #1 & LINK #101

Love is... Finding your WINGS!

Susan Bennett and Terri Lynne
Florida and California **USA** –Cousins

LOVE LINK #102

"Love is...
What makes life a
Beautiful ride!"

LOVE doesn't make the world go 'round.
LOVE IS... what makes the ride worthwhile!

Susan Bennett
Florida, **USA**

LOVE LINK #103

"Love is...
An Unexplainable Feeling!"
"Love is... an unexplainable feeling that
touches the core of your soul.

It is the ultimate happiness, a joyful feeling that you do
not ever want to lose.

Love is... Magical and splendid.

The worst part about Love is... losing it!

The pain is tremendous and it weighs on you deeply and
it can be very painful & hurtful.

LOVE comes without asking for it in many different ways and love leaves and can potentially hurt you without asking for it as well.

The best part about LOVE IS... falling in love with something or someone over and over again.

LOVE can go to sleep and be woken up immediately.

LOVE can crash hard when it is lost within a blink of an eye.

The pain of losing LOVE is unexplainable; it hurts deep within your soul, leaving a permanent imprint upon your heart forever more.

You can find LOVE within many different things, such as with a parent, a child, a life partner, a friend, a relative, your work, nature, the environment, or just plain life in general.

The greatest GIFT you could receive would be if you could wake up every day and find LOVE and utilize LOVE to push you forward... for then your life will be well lived and you will feel as though you lived a successful life!"

Chad Everett Oristano Florida, **USA**

LOVE LINK #104

Love is... free!

Love is...
Always changing and ever lasting!

Jackie Johnston
Florida, **USA**

LOVE LINK #105

Love Is... my best friends!

Love Is... my siblings!

Love is... colorful but also blind.

Love is... in the shadows we try to hide.
Love is... kindness so you know it's real.
There is no describing to how love feels,
Love will... run deep and very wide.
Love will... always stay by your side.
Love will... heal when others cannot.
Everlasting like a never-ending knot,
Love... hurts and causes you pain.
Love... always takes the blame.
Love... opens your heart and makes you judge free.
It unites countries, religions, you, and me.

Brianna Oristano
Florida, **USA**
16 years old

LOVE LINK #106

Love is...
clicking with someone instantly!

"Love is...
wanting to marry your fourth cousin!"

Shayla Oristano's Wish!
In Picture: Shayla and Brandon

"Love is…
Our Purpose!"

"LOVE IS…
GROWING OLD
TOGETHER!"
Shayla Oristano

Florida, **USA**
Age 13

LOVE LINK #107

"Love is…
when you are with someone
you want to spend the rest of your life
with!"

"Love is…
The time you spend with your loved ones!"

"Love is...
When you love someone with all your
heart!"

Ashlyn Oristano
Florida, **USA**
Age 12

LOVE LINK #108

"Love is...
Somebody in your heart!"

"Love is...
The stars in your eyes to your heart!"

"Love is...
A newborn baby!"

"Love is...
To your sunshine!"

"Love is...
The shells and the ocean!"

"Love is...
Your Dog!"

Sebastian Blaise Oristano
Florida, **USA**
Age 5

LOVE LINK #109

Love is...
When you CRAVE something so much,
You can't stand to not have it!

Best Love Song Eva:
"SEAL TOUCH"
Testo: Without your touch, I've been lost without the
things I love. Without your kiss, I've been dreaming of
the things I miss.
Your eyes, your mouth, your lips, your mouth, your
face, your touch...

Jamie Oristano
Florida, **USA**

LOVE LINK #110

Love is...
Catching crabs at the Surf Rider in Malibu
with my dad!

Sullivan age 6
California, **USA**

LOVE LINK #111

"Love is...
Found, not bought!

Rescuing LOVE!"

Rescued my dog with wings attached!
Steven Scot Bono
Malibu, California, **USA**

"Love is...
magical when finally found!"

Like finding my three legged "Angel" dog -
with WING markings!"

Love Is...
being rescued and loved!

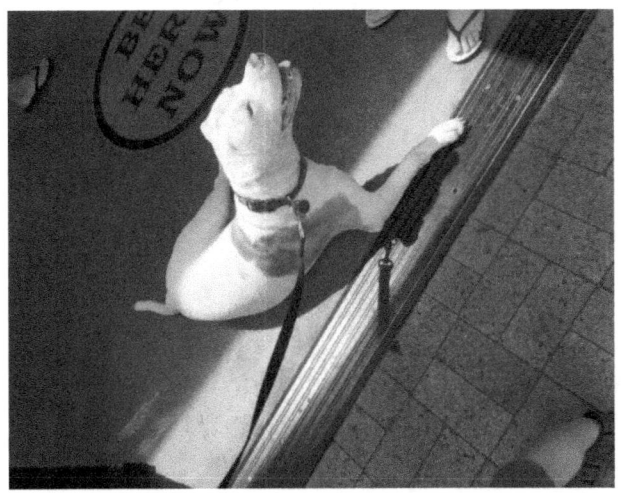

Oscar (dog)
Steven Scot Bono (Owner)
Malibu, **USA**

LOVE LINK #112

For one moment
Our lips meet
It's so wonderful,
Delicate and sweet

Your touch is soft,
Tender, and true
Just one kiss
And I'm addicted to you

For that one second
I'm complete
When our souls connect
When our lips meet

For that one moment
The bad is good
Everything's in place
Just as it should

No one is evil
There is no sin
I feel happiness
Rise deep within

When your lips
Are in place
Every pain
Is magically erased

For that one second
There is nothing wrong
When I feel your hot flesh
I feel so strong

Everything is perfect
The world is full and bright
I press against your lips and
Convey my love with all my might

So perfectly serene
So perfectly complete
All this in the second
In which our lips meet

Rajesh TR
Born: Kerala, **India**
Resides: Trivandrum, Kerala, **INDIA**

LOVE LINK #113

Love is...
Passions of the heart!

LOS PASIONES SON LOS VIAJES DEL CORAZON!

The Passions Are The Journey's Of The Heart!

Brandon Murray
California, USA - Barcelona, **SPAIN**

LOVE LINK #114

PEACE and LOVE IS... ALL WE NEED!

Brittany Maurae

Brittany Maurae
California, **USA – PRAGUE CZECH REPUBLIC**

LOVE LINK #115

Love is... timeless,

Love is... eternal,
Love is... creation,
Love is... the energy of existence in which binds us all together.

Stephen Metcalfe-Davies
South Wales, **UNITED KINGDOM**

LOVE LINK #1 & LOVE LINK #115

Love is...
Nothing to be FEARful of!
Stephen Metcalf-Davies' crossroad intersection!

Steer away from the direction of FEAR!
Always choose the direction of LOVE!

Terri Lynne & Stephen Metcalfe-Davies
California, USA and South Wales, **UNITED KINGDOM**

Love is...
The TRUTH inside your heart!!!!!!

Terri Lynne's crossroad intersection!
TRUTH Avenue/LOVE Avenue

When you go in the direction of LOVE,
You will always be headed in the right direction!
The TRUTH leads you on to LOVE'S Highway!

Terri Lynne inspired through Stephen Metcalfe-Davies
California, USA and South Wales, **UNITED KINGDOM**

LOVE LINK #116

Love is...
A connection!

"Some souls just
Understand each other
Upon meeting." -N.R. Hart

Olympia Le Point
California, **USA**

LOVE LINK #117

What you will see is love coming out of the trees, love coming out of the sky, love coming out of the light. You will perceive love from everything around you. This is the state of bliss. -Don Miguel Ruiz
In this Eternal Moment of All That Namaste We Are Oneness Love

Love IS and more is coming!

Pat Dunn
Jacksonville, FL - Marietta, GA **USA**

LOVE LINK #118

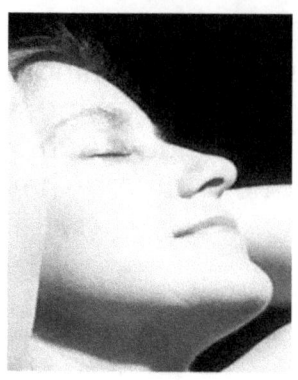

What LOVE IS to me?

I pondered this question; and at first I was trying to come up with something that applied to sunshine, roses, rainbows, and baby giggles. But I found that I could not come up with anything and kept on feeling my thoughts blocked and just not right. Then one morning I woke up and realized that sure; it is all that, but not just that... it was not balanced. After realizing that there is actually a duality here it finally came to me.

Love is not just happy, but also experiences sadness. It is exhilarating and yet painful, real and fake, unconditional as well as conditional, fair weather love as well as stormy, it can even be used as a weapon to hurt.

My personal experience as to what LOVE IS...

It is indeed the innocent laugh of a child, but also the pain that is felt when I have listened to a child cry in pain. The unconditional love of a dog that looks up to you as his whole world, but also the pain when I have seen abuse that has been done to an animal to the point of myself feeling traumatized. The happiness of playing

with your siblings, as a child. Also the sadness that is felt as an adult, when you are not included in their fun. The unconditional love you feel from your parents, but also having a parent that you feel that there love is conditional and only there, during fair weather. Even conditional love is love, perhaps the only way they know how to love. I forgot about controlling love. A love that may not be so perfect and can be painful for both parties. Confusing for the one trying to control wondering why the love is not being projected back in the way that they expect. Even a fake love is love for some sort of effort is put into it.

The love I feel for my own children and grandchildren can be put in a category all by itself. Words are difficult to find for the unconditional love that is felt toward them. Guiding children as they grow up and delight and relief to see them survive and thrive in their own lives. Even though there is a bit of sadness when they no longer live under your roof where you see them every day, but pride as well as a blessing to see that they can survive on their own. Then the sheer delight and bliss when your grandchild runs to you yelling "Grandma" and giving a great big hug when walking in the room wanting you play with them, but there is also heartbreak when you are unable to see them as much as you like especially while they are young. But I do feel my heart expand when I realize that I will always be needed as mother and grandmother.

Then there is a new love and an unexpected love, one that catches you by surprise, a romantic love. A love that you did not know you could feel or even existed with someone that comes back into your life after so many years. Someone that you knew as a child and even played with on the playground when no one else would play with you. To reconnect and have such a

relationship turn romantic. Now that is a magical love. To love someone that feels like home. Who kisses your hand and treats you like a goddess. To love a man that does not run the other way when your anxieties run rampant. It's even just driving in a car together daydreaming then suddenly he takes your hand and kisses it. I look at him and just smile... no words are needed.

Linda Philipp
Wisconsin, **USA**

LOVE LINK #119

Love is... Contagious!

You can easily spread it to others by leaving your heart open, your mind open, your ears open. Symptoms include: a smile :) on your lips and in your eyes, a warm and happy feeling in and around your heart and tummy. Your normal mind chatter is replaced by a song in your entire body and laughter pouring out of you at the drop of a hat. Feel free to pass love around...

I know you asked me to express this on paper for your book awhile back, and I'm sorry it took so long... there just wasn't much of it in my life to identify with... Thank you for bringing it back into my reality, so I could remember what it is. Thank you my dear friend Terri!!! With Love, Shelly - California, **USA**

LOVE LINK #120

Love is...
Like breathing!
SAVOR IT!

April Lynn King
Born: Pueblo Colorado
Resides: **DOMINICAN REPUBLIC**

LOVE LINK #121

Love is...
What you're made of!

It is vibrating in every cell of your being
You emanate loves
Healing power.

Love is...
Peace on Earth!

LOVE IS...
LIVING IN PEACE!

Love is...
Powerful!

"When the POWER OF LOVE overcomes the LOVE OF
POWER,
The world will know
PEACE!"
-Jimmy Hendrix

Michele Lewis
NEW ZEALAND

LOVE LINK #122

Love is... Nourishment!

If you want to change the world,
Love yourself,
Really love YOU,
Encourage YOU,
Feed YOU,
Allow YOU,
Hear YOU,
Hold YOU,
Heal YOU and in time,
This nourishment of LOVE will envelop you.

Like having strong arms around you,
it will center and clear your thoughts to bring focused
attention, and allow you to dream.

This is the TRUE seed that you can feed to grow a new world, as ONE.

Michelle A McPoyle
NEW ZEALAND

LOVE LINK #123

Love is... Grand!

Bruce Colmer
Citrus Heights, California, **USA**

LOVE LINK #124

Love is...
THE BEST!

Life is best when you are in love.

Michael Moriarty

LOVE LINK #125

Love is...
Blending families with love!

L-R Jenna, Alex, Daniela, Bill, Barbara and Kaylee
Our Blended Family
California, **USA**
Blended Family By: Alicia Keyes

Love is...
a good round of golf!

Love is...
being able to breathe!

Bill M.
California, **USA**

LOVE LINK #126

Love is...
My daughter's happiness!

Barbara (Mom) and Kaylee (Daughter)
SWITZERLAND to California, **USA**

LOVE LINK #127

Love is...
Love!

Liebe IST. LIEBE!

Trudi Gobbi
SWITZERLAND

LOVE LINK #128

Love is...
The intense FEELING of deep affection,
When two people touch each other!

Dedicated to my departed husband Tom!

Love is... What WE shared!

Serena
Indian Wells, CA **USA**

LOVE LINK #129

Love is...
When you're supported
UNCONDITIONALLY!

Maurae
La Quinta, CA **USA**

LOVE LINK #130

Love is...
A full nights sleep because my wife got up
with the baby!

Ryan
La Quinta, CA **USA**

LOVE LINK #131

Love is...
Happiness & Joy.

Family & Friends.
Unforgettable.
Life.

LOVE is all you need!

Marla E.
California, **USA - ISRAEL**

LOVE LINK #132

Love is...
Responsibility, loving others,
being a parent and romance!

Pinchas E.
Israel - California, **USA - ISRAEL**

LOVE LINK #133

LOVE IS...
Honesty & Friendship.

Moshe E.
California - **ISRAEL**

LOVE LINK #134

Love is...
EVERYTHING!

Shmuel E.
California - **ISRAEL**

LOVE LINK #135
Love is...
FOREVER!

& David Beckham
Sarah E.
ISRAEL - California, **USA**

LOVE LINK #136

Love is...
Our Son Liam!

For us Love is our son Liam, the day he was born,
He redefined the word "LOVE" for us.

Arie and Yardana
California, USA - **ISRAEL**

LOVE LINK #137

Love is...
Your FAMILY and FRIENDS!

LOVING one another and doing for one another!
Frances

Aka: Mom M. and Nana
Rancho Mirage, CA **USA**

LOVE LINK #138

Love is...
My baby brother Carson!

TOMMY 5 Years Old and CARSON 3 Months Old
Tommy - Palm Springs, CA **USA**

LOVE LINK #139

Love is...
Health, Happiness, Family and above all,
HOPE for mankind!

Sean - Palm Springs, CA **USA**

LOVE LINK #140

Love is...
FAMILY & Spending time with my cousins!

Tatum Lee - 7 Years Old
Cousins: Tommy Marc - 5 Years Old & Carson Lee ~ 3
Months Old Palm Springs, CA **USA**

LOVE LINK #141

Love is...
Never selfish!

Sabrina and Tatum - Mother and Daughter

Palm Desert, CA **USA**

Serena, Sabrina, and Maurae's Dedication to:
Our Son-in-law, Husband, Dad and Uncle Tom

LOVE LINK #142

Love is...
LOVE is... more than what can be
expressed in words.

LOVE is... not just a feeling that makes love together; it's something that makes you die for one another... LOVE is... the only feeling that exists forever on this planet.

-Sri and Vinay
INDIA - California, **USA**

193

LOVE LINK #143

Love is...
A COSMIC CONNECTION!

True Love is a cosmic cellular universal connection,
Pure in nature as it heals the soul.
The energies shared between TWO,
Become ONE infinite Whole.
For God is Love and
Those who embrace this blessing bestowed
Are forever bonded, in life and after death,
Eternally rooted in Love forever and ever.

- Cynthia Fitzgibbon
OK, **USA** (Wherever she lives is OK with me!)

LOVE LINK #144

Love is...
Friends Traveling Together,
Spreading American girls hearts

Throughout Edinburgh, Scotland

Brittany and Annie
American Girls, **USA**

LOVE LINK #145

Love is...
Spending quality time with someone
SPECIAL,
While knowing they love
Spending quality time with YOU!

BBTLC
New York - California, **USA**

Love is...
TRUE FRIENDSHIP!

To me Love is... a deep feeling inside your heart and your soul.
True Love can make you happy or make you sad.
It is the deepest positive emotion that there is.
True love never dies; it only gets stronger with time...

Bill Brown
Born: New York, USA
Resides: California, **USA**

LOVE LINK #146

Where the LOVE IS...
IS where YOU should go!

"Some people won't love you no matter what you do
and some people won't stop loving you no matter what
you do.
Go where the love is!!"
-Author Unknown

Helen Newbury
Calming Souls Family
Resides: California, **USA**

LOVE LINK #147

Love is...
Standing, sitting, soaring and staying
"UNITED" in Love!

Geri and Roger Stofferahn
California, **USA**

LOVE LINK #148

Love is...
A force of energy!

LOVE IS...
Uniting Hearts through this
POWERFUL FORCE!
LOVE IS...
What makes the impossible possible!

"LOVE is the most powerful force in the UNIVERSE that makes impossible possible.

-Author Unknown

Love is...
So powerful, that it can even connect strangers!

Shalini Malhotra Aka: "PEACE" and Terri Lynne
New Delhi, **INDIA** and California, **USA**

"Things, which can't be even imagined with the human brain, are possible with love. It can produce miracles."

Love is...
SURRENDERING!

"When a heart is filled with LOVE the whole UNIVERSE surrenders!"
-Author Unknown

Shalini Malhotra
Aka: "PEACE"
New Delhi, **INDIA**

LOVE LINK #149

Love is...
What shines through in your energies
TONE!

ITLC
AUSTRALIA and **USA**

LOVE LINK #150

Love is...
Different by ages.

In the beginning it's the chemistry that attracts,
Later on it's how much you can depend upon a person!

Rita (Aleksandr's Wife)
LITHUANIA

LOVE LINK #151

Love is...
I don't know she told me so!

Aleksandr (Rita's Husband)
UKRAINE

LOVE LINK #152

Below is the Email of an explanation of what LOVE
should be built on, from my special friend...
This is the idea.
"I asked the teacher what is the difference between
chemistry and alchemy in relationships and the answer
was these beautiful and wise words:
- People looking for "Chemistry" are scientists of love,
That is, they are accustomed to action and reaction.
People who find the "Alchemy" are artists of love,
Constantly creating new ways of loving.
Chemicals love necessity.
Alchemists love by choice.
Chemical dies with time,
Alchemy is born through time...
Chemical loves the package.
Alchemy enjoys the content.
Chemistry happens.
Alchemy is built.
All seek Chemistry,
Only some find Alchemy.
Chemical attracts and distracts sexist and feminist.

Alchemy integrates the masculine and feminine
principle.
So it becomes a relationship of free individuals
and their own wings, not an attraction that is subject
to the whims of ego.
In conclusion, the Master watching his students said:
Alchemy brings together what separates Chemistry.
Alchemy is the real marriage,
Divorce is from Chemistry which we see every day in
most couples.
"Let us begin to build conscious relationships,
Because the 'CHEMISTRY' will always make us grow
old in our body,
While 'ALCHEMY' will always cherish us from within!"

The lesson that I, Terri Lynne learned from this email is
something I had already searched my heart for answers
on and learned to be the truth!

LOVE LINK #1 & LOVE LINK #152

"An Alchemist is one who turns everything into love."

-Emmanuel
GFTLC
Heaven and Earth's Connection

The Difference between

ALCHEMY and CHEMISTRY:

Alchemy was a very early step in understanding chemistry, and set many of the techniques we currently use.

The main difference between chemistry and alchemy are that chemistry is motivated by science, and magical thinking motivates alchemy. To put it another way, chemists believe that there is a reproducible and rational explanation for why things happen, whereas alchemists tend to believe that there were certain magical or charmed things that would get the job done for them. It's not that alchemists didn't do any chemistry, or that they didn't accomplish anything - just that they didn't really think the same way as modern scientists do.

Definition of ALCHEMY:

Alchemy is a power or process of transforming something common, into something special .

An inexplicable or mysterious transmuting

Source: Merriam-Webster -

Alchemy is a seemingly magical process of transformation, creation, or combination.

"Finding the person who's right for you requires a very subtle alchemy"

Definition of CHEMISTRY:

The branch of science that deals with the identification of the substances of which matter is composed; the investigation of their properties and the ways in which they interact, combine, and change; and the use of these processes to form new substances.

The chemical composition and properties of a substance or body.

Plural noun: chemistries: "The chemistry of soil."

Source: Merriam-Webster - Chemistry is a strong attraction between people.

While I was simultaneously receiving the above article about CHEMISTRY VS ALCHEMY, I was reading this article, which resonated as TRUTH inside my HEART! I found that this IS what is most attractive to my spirit.

When I look inside the spirit of a man,

To feel whom I accept to let in,

I in turn see the spirit of the lady in my mirror.

As I, have searched the hearts of many a soul throughout my life thus far, I wish to share how I feel I have been blessed with experiencing many relationships which acted as a compass guiding me in the direction of teaching my heart what LOVE IS. Throughout the pages of this book project, each and every past soul that touched my heart, whether for a blink of a moment in time or a love that I carry inside my heart every step of my life's way, has been a part of my journey and greater understanding of what the word LOVE is all about!

Those who know me well throughout my life know I question everything! I question everything in my mind first and then I ask for my heart's answer to my questions. But through a very special connection, I was offered a suggestion, which was to, "Go to my heart," and I will "Know" my answers, without having to go to my mind to search for my truths. So throughout the pages of this book, I made it my practice to only listen to the voices inside my heart and when I was in my heart I did FEEL my answers, rather than seeking for truths in my minds intellect! I learned that my HEART had all the answers I ever wanted to know. This friend shared an email with me one fine day, explaining a bit more on the subject of what LOVE IS that resonated as truth in his heart. I today FELT that this is a beautiful analogy of where LOVE can have a misstep verses how LOVE can remain forever strong and last throughout eternity and today I wish to share this message with you! Please "Go to your heart" then read the message below and only you will KNOW if "CHEMISTRY" is what you wish to continue seeking in relationships, or if "ALCHEMY" is your pathway to what LOVE IS meant to be!

To me, Love is... ALCHEMY!

"She doesn't want 'things,'
She wants the full presence and essence of
'you.'
Be more than a male,
Be her man."

-Graham R. White
GFTLC
Heaven and Earth's Connection

5 THINGS SEXIER THAN THE DAD BOD

1. **HE'S PURPOSEFUL vs. POSSESSIVE**

    A man with a purpose has a rare quality of certainty and confidence that is irresistible. It's a confidence that comes from deep inside, is never arrogant and definitely not desperate, demanding or needy.

    A man has a choice about what he will pursue to fill the void in his soul - the man who has chosen to follow his purpose won't chase you, cling to you or act as if all the air has been removed if he senses he may lose you.

    It's not romance that makes us feel desperate for another; neediness is the result of feeling incomplete when we're not yet complete. Two incomplete people result in codependency, a feeling so common it has become mistaken for love.

    A man living with purpose won't obsess over you, keep tabs on you, and constantly need to be with you, stalk you, chase you, or attempt to wear you down until you take him back.

    He's motivated by purpose, not guilt. If he messes something up he makes a sincere apology and puts in the effort, whatever it takes, to make it right and do better, regardless of whether it "saves" the relationship or not.

Two whole and conscious people generate synergy when they're together, but are happy and accomplished when doing things alone.

The reason this feels so attractive is that when he's with you, you know it's a conscious choice, not a vacuum of loneliness he's filling. He's not just safe to be with, he's also safe to leave if that's what you feel is best.

A man without a purpose professes love loudly and becomes needy or enraged man when he fears being left. A man without a purpose fears being alone and quickly replaces the woman he said he cannot live without if he can't be with her.

A conscious man takes time between relationships because he's purposeful about his life, not desperate in his "love."

2. HE DOESN'T LOSE CONTROL

    He doesn't rage, stomp off, or even "Manage his anger," because he doesn't suppress how he feels. He makes his choices based on the circumstances as they happen to be, not the way things "should" be or what he feels is "fair" to him.

    Cursing in traffic, raging at his partner, dog, kids, the government, a neighbor, coworker, family member or friend doesn't happen because he takes life as it happens.

    Instead of watching him react to stress, fume or explode, you actually witness him become stronger and more powerful in his choices as pressure is applied.

    He's not controlling his anger; he's in magnificent control of his thoughts and his choices at all times.

3. HE STEPS UP UNDER PRESSURE

It doesn't matter if he's tired, sick, worried about finances, or there is danger, or illness he is confronted by, it's when things feel hard and the pressure is on that you see him at his best.

He faces his fear and circumstances that are challenging with the will to succeed and the courage to lead. Instead of asking others to bear some of the burden and responsibilities for him, he's the one stepping up and doing what must be done.

4. HE'S ALWAYS A CLASS ACT

His sense of humor doesn't dip down because he's with the boys or had a few. In fact, he likely won't refer to them as "boys" or indulge to the point where his behavior necessitates the excuse of having had "one too many."

He's confident enough that he doesn't need to tease you, make jokes at the expense of others, or talk behind people's back. Because he speaks of everyone else with respect when they're not present you can be confident he has the same dignity for you.

5. HE ALWAYS MAKES ROOM FOR WHAT HE SAYS IS IMPORTANT

There is no such thing as a day that's too hard for him to acknowledge you, a meeting too important or an outing so fun he loses track of time or his commitments.

No matter what, you can always count on him to make space, follow through and show up when he said he'd be there.

Be cautious of men with high potential, who the more you get to know them the more excuses and explanations they require. A committed man

living with purpose doesn't require excuses. He is consistent in what he does and follows through on what he says.

The gifted man with great potential can feel intoxicating, but a man living with purpose becomes more attractive the more you observe him under pressure, not the other way around.

Rather than chasing women, he intentionally chooses a partner - a woman he knows is uniquely the one for him, one that makes all interest in others disappear. Once he finds her, he stops looking or even wondering what else is out there, because when he chooses her he is clear about who HE is and what he's been looking for.

There's a growing community of women who are choosing to wait for a man with purpose rather than settle for a man with potential.

-Graham R White
You can find them here: www.EvolvedWomen.com
Terri Lynne and GFTLC
HEAVEN & EARTH'S CONNECTION

LOVE LINK #153

Love is...
LIFE!

"Where there is
LOVE
There is
LIFE."

-Mahatma Gandhi
BOAZ - **ISRAEL**

LOVE LINK #154

Love is...
Never having to say you're sorry!

Liz
St. Augustine, **IRELAND**

LOVE LINK #155

Love is...
FRIENDS... GIVING!

Making friends from different Countries!

(Brittany & Annie made a Thanksgiving Dinner for their new friends in Edinburgh, SCOTLAND!)
Top Row Left To Right:
Enda - **IRELAND**, Adrian - **GERMANY**, Floris -**NETHERLANDS**, Markus - **GERMANY**
Bottom Row Left To Right:
Annie - **AMERICA**, Birte - **GERMANY**, Brittany - **AMERICA**, Eli – **GERMANY**

LOVE LINK #156

Love is...
making connections around the world!

- FROM STRANGERS TO FAMILY -
IN JUST SIX MONTHS,
STUDYING ABROAD TOGETHER!

Left to Right
Bottoms Up!
Markus - **GERMANY,** Brittany - **USA,** Birte -
GERMANY,
Enda - **IRELAND**, Adrian - **GERMANY**, Floris
-**NETHERLANDS**, Eli - **GERMANY**, Graham -
SCOTLAND, Aaron - **SCOTLAND**, Adrian - **GERMANY**

LOVE LINK #157

Love is…
So much more than a four letter word,
It is the greatest feeling in the world and will always
put a smile on your lips!

Elvira Wittendorff
Born in **DENMARK** - Residing in **SCOTLAND**

LOVE LINK #158

Love is…
Letting go of hesitation and accepting
another person as a part of who you are.

Annie E.
Northern California to San Diego, California
USA to Edinburgh, **SCOTLAND**

213

LOVE LINK #159

Love is...
Feeling home.

LOVE IS...
Trust and loyalty.
LOVE IS...
Being loved without the need to change oneself.
AND, LOVE IS...
The one thing, making everything else in
Your life seeming to be better.

Adrian - GERMANY

LOVE LINK #160

Love is...
A big bubble closing you in with whom you
love!

Or it could be a bigger bubble encompassing
humanity!

Dr. Norman Lavin
California, **USA**

LOVE LINK #161

As to what I feel love is...

Love is...
Everything, it's all around us in the air we
breathe, the sky, and the ground... It's in
all we do, all that we think and feel.

I've lived in the absence of love and I was quite literally empty and that's all. We are without love, because when we live without love, we live without purpose without the spirit, without the very essence of what we are. We do not need another to have "Love," that is just something that we share through a mutual connection, real love...

Real love is us, each and everyone of us and when you see this truth and feel it in its essence, you'll find that a life with love, true, unconditional, love is a life of abundance and peace in all things.

I hope this is what you're after (and can use)!

Ah Terri... the universe works in strange and wonderful ways by you typing "our" instead of "your" is simply because without your energy I would not be sitting here typing this to you and without the contributions of every other person this would not be able to become a reality. Every contribution is another addition to the energy and so "our" is exactly right.

Ryan "Lunawolf" Smith
Kent, **UNITED KINGDOM**

LOVE LINK #162

As for the word love –

Love is...
Learn to F.L.Y - First love yourself

(I could sit here all day trying to send you something impressive, but this is what I say all the time)
Oh and the other thing I say is:

Love is...
Not WEAK.

Then below –

Is a saying I really, really, love maybe you can pick something out of this as well - I think you will like it - the original person to say it is Edward James Olmos.

My version and the original below.

Another message that reminds of love –

That's you drops of water and you're on top of the mountain---- SUCCESS... . one day u start sliding down the mountain and u think wait a minute... I AM a Mountain top Water Drop... this Valley... this River.. A dark ocean with all these drops of Water, One day it gets Hot and you slowly evaporate in the Air... ... ... Way up, Higher than any Mountain Top, all the way to the HEAVENS... and you UNDERSTAND that at your lowest you were closest to GOD... LIFES a journey that goes Round and Round and the End is Closest to the Beginning... IT'S the CHANGE YOU need!!! TO finish YOUR journey... SO YOU MIGHT AS WELL ENJOY :))))) THE RIDE!

Feel... Connect... Live... Love... Understand and Enjoy the Journey!

Jonathan Curzon
Cape Town **SOUTH AFRICA**

LOVE LINK #163

Love is...
The most priceless feeling a human can
feel!

Morgan
California, **USA**
Photo in: London, **UNITED KINGDOM**

LOVE LINK #164

Love is...
Companionship!

Taylor
California, **USA**

LOVE LINK #165

Love is...
When you can be your unapologetic self!

Blair
California, **USA**

LOVE LINK #166

Love is...
To me, there is no formula; you have to
tackle it at each moment that it comes. But
with control and knowing over your
emotions, you are able to get greater joy

from those moments of deep love and connection.

Atarangi Muru
NEW ZEALAND
Maori Healer

LOVE LINK #167

Love is...
Actually our true condition,

Prior to the illusion of ego-
I assumed separation.
LOVE IS...
A feeling that happens when the heart is open.
LOVE IS...
What is felt when "LOVING" transcends the fear that
"You don't love me."

Jerry S.
Boston, Massachusetts, **USA**

LOVE LINK #168

Love is...
A universal connection,

In which a living being's soul recognizes
and touches another's.

Kabir B.
California - Indiana, **USA**

LOVE LINK #169

Love is...
THE GLUE!

Through thick and thin,
Life and death,
LOVE IS...
What keeps us connected to each other and
To everything around us!

Malcolm Hunter
California - Arizona, **USA**

LOVE LINK #170

Love is...
Knowing that no matter what, you will be
there for each other. Always.

Jonny
California, **USA**

LOVE LINK #171

Love is:
Like air at first you don't notice it, although
it guides you,
And makes you grow.

Satvik Ramineni
Born: **INDIA**
Resides: California, **USA**

LOVE LINK #172

Love is...
Special and unique,
It's a sense of being complete!

Felicia F.
California, **USA**

LOVE LINK #173

Love is...
The highs and lows of an extreme
emotional roller coaster,

That one can't resist;
While enjoying the ride of your life!

Mackie G
California, **USA**

LOVE LINK #174

Love is...
When you see yourself mirrored in
someone's eyes and you want to take care
of that mirror.

That's it in a nutshell my dear.

"A man has only one escape from his old self: to see a
different self - in the mirror of some woman's eyes."
-Clare Boothe Luce

Yours,
Keenan
Resides: Wilmington, Delaware, **USA**

LOVE LINK #175

Love is...
The nature of the human being.

At the end is what keeps us together and gives us the
strength to keep moving forward.
Sometimes love is the only thing that can be a feeling
or a decision.

Tais Gonzalez
MEXICO

LOVE LINK #176

To me Love is...
Being able to put someone or something
else ahead of one's self.

It links us and draws us closer to one another and
creates relationships that do not rely on tangible
things, but emotions and aspirations.

Casey S.
California, **USA**

LOVE LINK #177

Love is...
Finding your soul mate and sharing your
hopes and dreams with him/her!

Kathy & Scott Back THEN

Kathy & Scott NOW...
Childhood LOVES, back together again forever more!

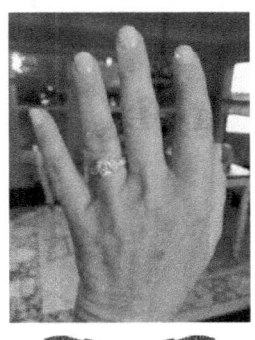

225

Poughkeepsie, New York ~ California, **USA**

LOVE LINK #178

Love is...
The most, stunning, invigorating, soul-
filling and soul-stirring, tragic, haunting,
and beautiful connection that exists in this
world.

And, don't you dare trade a moment of it – the easy
love or the hard love - for anything because we need
more love, more connectedness in our world.

Ashley Wenters
California, **USA**

"Love Blind
And
Without
Judgment!"

-J Iron Word
Ashley Wenters
California, **USA**

LOVE LINK #179

The biggest message of what LOVE IS...
To me is, God is love

Another one I like is...
When the power of love, overcomes the love of power,
the world will know peace!

Bridget B.
INDIA - California, **USA**

LOVE LINK #180

Love is...
HERE!

Love is...
Love to me is extending it anywhere and
at anytime to those whom need it whether
it is a good deed, a shoulder to lean on or
helping someone in need.

For me it's also about giving to a person & loving being there for them.

Love to me is, wanting to give your love & support & wanting to see them be happy & succeeding. I think it's also about being honest, trustworthy, loyal, compassionate & supportive.

Being there for that person or pet & thoroughly giving your love & attention to them.

Grace Medany
Aka: Pebbles
UNITED KINGDOM

LOVE LINK #88 continued...

Indi Shan

January 14 at 7:47pm

THE ART OF DYING

To perfect the art of life one must perfect, first, THE ART OF DYING.

What is the greatest mystery of existence? It's not life, it's not love, it IS DEATH. Science tries to understand life, so remains partial. Life is only a part of the total mystery - a very tiny, superficial part. It has no depth, and so science, too, remains superficial.

Life is finite, momentary. It is a breeze, it comes and goes... It doesn't abide. Hence science knows only the partial truth. What it knows is true, but it is not the whole truth.

Love is... in the middle.

Love is... exactly in the middle of life and death.

Love is far more mysterious than life itself, because it has life in it and something more; it is life plus death. And only those who are ready to die will know the life of love. Those who are afraid to die will never enter the mystery of love.

Art explores the world of love. Hence art is far truer than science, and it goes deeper than science. The vision of the artist contains much more than scientific knowledge can ever contain, although art is totally different from science.

Science can be objective because it is peripheral. Art is half objective, and half subjective. It cannot be free from the observer. Religion is concerned basically with death. Death contains all: life, love, and something more. Death is the culmination of all, the crescendo, and the highest peak. Life is the base, death is the peak - love is somewhere in between.

The mystic tries to explore the mystery of death. In the process, he comes to know what life is, what love is. Those are not his goals. His goal is to penetrate death, because there seems to be nothing more mysterious than death.

Love has some mystery because of death, and life also has some mystery because of death. If death disappears there will be no mystery in life. That's why a dead thing has no mystery in it; a corpse has no mystery in it, because it cannot die any more.

You think it has no mystery because life has disappeared? Wrong, it has no mystery because now it cannot die any more. Death has disappeared, and with death automatically life disappears. Life is only one of the ways of death's expression.

Religion is founded in the search into death, and to understand death is to understand all. To experience death is to experience all, because in the experience of death, you not only experience life at its highest, love at its deepest; in experiencing death you enter into the divine. Death is the door to the divine. Death is the name of the door of God's temple.

The meditator dies voluntarily. The mystic dies voluntarily - before the actual death. He dies in meditation. Lovers know a little bit of it because 50 per cent of love is death. That's why love is very close to meditation. Lovers know something of meditativeness; unaware they have stumbled upon it. They know silence, stillness, and timelessness. But they have stumbled upon it - it has not been their basic search.

The MYSTIC dies continuously and remains as fresh as dewdrops or lotus leaves in the early morning sun. His freshness, his youth, his timelessness, depend on the art of dying. And then when actual death comes he has nothing to fear, because he has known this death thousands of times. He is thrilled, enchanted; he dances!

Joyously he wants to die. So he dies without becoming unconscious, and he knows the total secret of death. Knowing it, he has the master key that can unlock all doors. He has the KEY that can open the DOOR OF GOD.

Indi Shan
INDIA - Melbourne, **AUSTRALIA**

LOVE LINK #181

Love is...
The Completion of the Soul!

Taylor C.
California, **USA**

LOVE LINK #182

Love is...
Selfless acts from the heart that you hope
are evenly returned.

But not necessary.

Robbie Rosen
Boston - California, **USA**

LOVE LINK #183

AMOR ES...
LOVE IS...

Yo Te quiero mucho!
I love you so much!

Mi Corozon Te quiero mucho!
My heart loves you so much!

Yo los quiero mucho atodos!
I love everyone in the world so much.

Eloiza Alvarez
Born: Guatemala, Central America
Resides: California, **USA**

LOVE LINK #184

Love is... a GIFT!

To be given away freely, unconditionally!
What love we've given, we'll have forever.
What love we fail to give, will be lost for all eternity.

-Leo Buscaglia Aka: "Dr. Love" **USA**
Born: March 31 1924
Died: June 12, 1998

LOVE LINK #185

Love is...
TRUTH!

Tarra Lynne
California, **USA**

LOVE LINK #186

Hi Terri Lynne,
Your book idea is fantastic!
Here is what I think of love:

"Love is...
CARING!!!"

"Caring for the other person and balancing your own happiness with theirs, with nothing materialistically speaking to gain. It is the courage and the humility to apologize or and to accept an apology without degrading one another."

Nomie Azoff
ISRAEL - California, **USA**

LOVE LINK #187

Love is... Family!

Hector Hernandez and Taylor (Granddaughter)
Born: Mexico City and California, USA
Resides: California, **USA** and Cabo, **MEXICO**

LOVE LINK #188

Love is...
Spreading the rainbow!

Good morning fellow rainbow love tribe

Today let's paint these colours. Everywhere we go
leaving no space to be untouched. Feel the JOY

deep, deep within you, as you sprinkle rainbow dust everywhere and feel how your Love touches and changes all others who step on it. What a magical day it is.

Allow your inner child out to play... !

Go be happy, be spontaneous, be love, be JOY xxxx

Elspeth Kerr - **CYPRUS**,
(In the Mediterranean near Syria & Turkey)

Love is...
Everywhere
and
in everything!

Elspeth Kerr and Kerry Metcalf
CYPRUS, (In the Mediterranean near Syria & Turkey)

LOVE LINK # 189

Love IS...
YOU.
Not bound by time or container.

LOVE is... a state of BE-ingness,
Not DO-ingness
You are LOVE. All Ways.
Sometimes we forget, and we begin to search and seek LOVE outside ourselves, forgetting who we are at our core, we are LOVE.
The light that beams from within,
radiating outward, in its ever-expanding nature is LOVE.
The LOVE we give returns to us, there is a never-ending supply. The flow of LOVE is our greatest natural resource.
LOVE IS, the BREATH of life. As we expand and fill on an inhale, we must exhale in order to create space for the next breath.

Inhale and expand into LOVE, exhale and create space for LOVE. LOVE IS... YOU!

Krista Eiberg-Kubik
California, **USA**

LOVE LINK #190

Love is...
A "feeling" that makes your heart swirling and feel bigger and yet bigger, pulsating & radiating HEAT throughout your entire body.
Love feels like...
A huge party within your body sensations going from tingling to throbbing to warmth to possibly even

scared or overwhelmed because of the reckless nature of the sensations taking over your body.

What makes the feelings of Love ❤ deep within your heart is family for sure, but is undefined when it comes to physical desire.
Passionate Love is soul to soul.
Communication speaks eye to eye.
Mere words need not be spoken.
It's a knowing a deep understanding of each other.
The essence of two becoming one.
Time is stagnant.
All is right in the Universe and there is no place to go and nothing else to do... because you have love ❤

Love,
Your Boston Cousin Karen
Boston, Massachusetts, **USA**

Dedicated to: Lisa Ligon
(Karen and Terri Lynne's ANGEL in the sky)

LOVE LINK #191

Love is...
Ever changing!

Rosana
California, **USA**

LOVE LINK #192

A conversation with a friend referring to what LOVE IS?
When asked, "Is LOVE endless... ?

The response was:

TL, you are asking a question I can not answer, as stated above, Love is endless... to me... that is not an answer, it is like saying love is orange, love is big, love is kind. I would assume these are adjectives. *When I think of love, I smile.* I try not to "understand," I try to accept that it is beyond definition. Can we define a soul, can we define a spirit, a higher power. I do know that when I saw my grandson, when I held that bundle of joy, I knew for sure that it in fact was love. I know I love him, and all of them beyond description or measurement, not just like them, not just admire them. *Love has no definition; it is a sense of being.*

KC
Hawaii – **USA**

LOVE LINK #193

Love is...
Family.

Here we are on New Year's Eve enjoying a small family get together to sing, rejoice and welcome in 2017.

"LOVE is... what binds me to my husband, my children, my parents and my siblings."

Love is... how we can all come together with support for each other whenever anyone of us is diagnosed with an illness.
Love is... when we wholehearted celebrate when any one of us overcome that illness.
Love is... when we can share our successes and celebrate together.
Love is... when we can share disappointments and we can hug it out and commiserate together.
Love just simply wants to be together to hangout, have a meal together when we can, taking out the guitars and drums to have our sing-alongs to worship God.
Love is... knowing that God is with me and that He loves me. It is that simple and clear.
"Love is... God."
Maryann G

Born in: **Singapore** ~ Traveled & Lived in: New York ~ **London** ~ **Paris** ~ Munich, **Germany** ~ **Tokyo** ~ California, **USA** ~ Presently residing in: Vancouver, **CANADA**

(I was born in Singapore and lived there till I was 21. Left to travel Europe in the early 1980's and have since lived in New York, London, Paris, Munich and Tokyo. I've also lived in LA where we were meant to meet and now, to answer your question, I reside in Vancouver, CANADA.)

"I find that it is impossible to give straight answers because I believe nothing in life is rarely described by one word. My travels to different countries changes and defines me in their own ways. The people I meet influence my take and my views of life. I am who I am at that time where I lived."

LOVE LINK #194

Hi all. The following message is inspired by this meme, posted by Deniz Marchmont, which I have shared here... Indi Shan

It is the nature of all things. The order of nature... for every high there is a low... every positive there's a negative... two sides to the same coin... . heads and tails... high and low... Here is a great secret that has been around from before time itself... There are two little words in the English language, which translates similarly into two words or syllables in every language on earth...

And these are the most powerful words in existence... If you use them carefully, you will always be in the highs rather than the lows... . Good and honest verses dishonest and underhanded... . healthy and wealthy verses unhealthy and poor... . Powerful and successful verses weak and unsuccessful... The choices are yours, what words to use them in conjunction with...

Most importantly to be aware of its existence and to be aware fully, the way in which you have been subconsciously using these two words... . because it is the most powerful words within the realm of your subconscious mind that determines what kind of human being one is... . And everything you are today is determined by the way you have been using those two words...

Here it is... "I AM"... use it wisely from here on in... some examples are... . I AM kind and gentle. I AM healthy and wealthy. I AM Successful. I AM considerate... I AM compassionate... . I AM Loved... I

AM LOVE! That last one is the greatest combination... We become whatever it is we are pursuing in life... I AM LOVE...

If one becomes love than one can do nothing but the will of love. Just like a chair can only ever be a chair and can never be: a "table" or a "bed." While a chair can be used as a table or bed, it will never suit the purpose perfectly. It will be a lousy table, and a very uncomfortable bed...

But the chair will always be a perfect chair.

THE UNSPOKEN TRUTH IS we, mankind, like everything in existence... ARE created by LOVE... Only love, passion, inspiration brought on by lovable conditions can CREATE... .

And so while we can choose to be anything lesser... Our birthright is LOVE... (The highest vibration) and the Kingdom of LOVE which is no different than the Kingdom of Heaven... is ours, the true state of anarchy, no man controlling another man... We are created in the image of everything good and benevolent... this is what we do best; it is our greatest good... Thus, is something we can rejoice in knowing... Although at the moment we are just a little confused, living in the Archy of man (Man controlling man, Oligarchy)... But we as a species will finally get their one soul at a time... We will go back to SOURCE.

So for now... "BE TOTALLY EXCELLENT TO EACH OTHER."

(Bill and Ted's) And start with... "I AM"... and live it, breathe it... own it, BE IT... and this will be a testimony unto yourself and a great influence unto thy neighbors... bringing about awareness and a shift of consciousness. Bringing about the exposure and in turn the awareness to give great consideration as to how to better use the two little words... *"I AM" to become a great and*

united species. To consciously choose to BE Love!

Love and light to all... Vannakam.

Deniz Marchmont Melbourne, Victoria, **AUSTRALIA**

Founder of plastic bag sleeping mats for the homeless From Down Under, Rising UP!

Deniz

LOVE LINK #74

CALMING SOULS FAMILY

Dear Calming Souls Family,

One of our "FAMILY" members is working on a book project and she is requesting a message from whoever wishes to be a part of this book.

All you have to do is complete this statement:

LOVE IS... .

In a message for Terri Lynne's book project titled:

UNITED LOVE by: Terri Lynne & The UNIVERSE!

You can post your message here and she will see it or you can email her your message privately to: TLWhispers@ UnitedLove.Love

This way she can add YOUR ENERGY, as a link in this "CHAIN OF LOVE!"

Thank you from her heart to all of yours!

This was her birthday request from me, to link our "FAMILY" with all other energies in this book.

Girish Daga

Mumbai, **INDIA**

LOVE LINK #195

LOVE IS... Light

Debbie Carson
Resides: Seattle, **USA**

LOVE LINK #196

LOVE IS... the absence of fear and judgment
Eva Hansson
South of **SWEDEN**

LOVE LINK #197

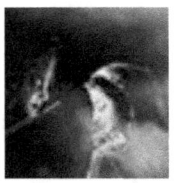

LOVE IS... Eternal...

Nanda Sathyanarayan
Bangalore, **INDIA**

LOVE LINK #1

THANK YOU GIRISH! What a LOVE you are!!!

Thank you Eva, Nanda & Debbie!

You are NOW a part of this CHAIN OF LOVE!

I thank you from the bottom of my heart!!!!

Terri Lynne, **USA**

LOVE LINK #198

LOVE IS... In the hearts that seek it.

Rachel Gillard-Tew

Christchurch, **NEW ZEALAND**

LOVE LINK #74

All I know is LOVE IS... I.
The one who understands me only fully will gain from me.
The rest of others will leave one by one like many who have boasted and left the family.
They came in search of love, but were lost their selves about the very meaning of it.

Girish Daga
Mumbai, **INDIA**

LOVE LINK #199

LOVE IS... Unconditional.

I know what it is but not in words... I lived it rather than just talked about it... it was giving/taking at the same time... sense of completion. And completing another part of self at same time.

Kerry McErlean **USA**

LOVE LINK #200

LOVE IS... Compassion

Gladys Justiniano Williams
Born: Bronx, New York
Reside: California, **USA**

LOVE LINK #201

LOVE IS... in everything and the fabric of being and life, everyone seeks it in everything we say, do, and are. Love is... infinite, love is energy, sound, vibration, I Love you. As far as the numbers go. You can always add one. Smile...

Helen Newbury
Carmel - N.Y. - **U.S.A.**

LOVE LINK #202

LOVE IS... all that matters, the juju that will heal our beautiful world, the thing that shall bring unity and peace on earth.

Love is... the force of all, it is what we are born of, what we shall return to.

Love is... beautiful and magical, the ultimate Healer of all things, the ultimate freer of humanity.

I love the rainbow but if I need to pick one color its magenta.

Rebecca Krausst
QLD **AUSTRALIA**

LOVE LINK #203

How awesome!
LOVE IS... feeling complete.

Lynnette Stiltner White

LOVE LINK #204

LOVE IS... Life
Alice Burbaugh

LOVE LINK #205

LOVE IS... Power
Shannon Kelly
Omaha, Nebraska **USA**

LOVE LINK #206

LOVE IS... the Universe... Powerful and Infinite...
LOVE IS... Sacred

Ruth Snyder
Born: Eureka, Montana
Resides: Durham, North Carolina **USA**

LOVE LINK #207

LOVE IS... Never having to say you're sorry. Touching the heart of others, whether it is from a smile, or the wave of your hand, a blink in the eye or even a quick glance at them from a distance. Every time you give a part of yourself you are giving love to someone else. Love is so much more than just a word. It's a power that most people don't get.

Darlene Leach
Shingletown, California, **USA**

LOVE LINK #208

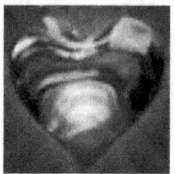

LOVE IS... completeness.

Jackie Harriel
Alabama, **USA**

LOVE LINK #209

LOVE IS... a very sensitive word
indescribable to the human vocabulary.
LOVE IS... a noble sentiment in scripted in your soul;
it's in the DNA, of creation.

Abigail Alban

LOVE LINK #210

LOVE IS... the fuel of all living beings.

Brigitte Corthay
Geneva, **Switzerland**

LOVE LINK #211

LOVE IS...
1. Everything
2. Everlasting
3. Infinite
4. All
5. Life
6. Unconditional
7. Energy

Nils Ascended
Starnberg to Munich, **GERMANY**

LOVE LINK #212

I did a couple Love Is messages some time back actually.

Here's one more:

Love is...
Loving everything and everyone is the one true Absolute Power.

Chuck Meares

Olympia, Washington **USA**

LOVE LINK #213

LOVE IS... everyone unconditionally around the world.

Kathy Reynolds, **USA**

You are most welcome my dear friend Terri with unconditional love too you

Kathy Reynolds
Gary, Indiana in **AMERICA**

LOVE LINK #214

LOVE IS... supreme.

Kizito Larger **NIGERIA**

LOVE LINK #215

LOVE IS... brutal and bittersweet, raw and tender. And yet the greatest experience and highest honor One could ever surrender to.

Mini Amitola

LOVE LINK #216

LOVE IS... when you feel seen and feel acceptance and belonging that fills your heart with warmth, peace and joy!

Mary Gina Igoe
Schenectady, New York, **USA**

LOVE LINK #217

LOVE IS... the key to our evolution.
Only by living the path of
Love is the way ahead clear and assured.

Leanne Johnson
AUSTRALIA

LOVE LINK #218

LOVE IS... what you want it to be.

Linda Klub
USA

LOVE LINK #1

WOW!!! CALMING SOULS FAMILY,
I FEEL ALL YOUR LOVE NOW &
WILL SHARE YOUR LOVE WITH THE
UNIVERSE CREATING OUR RIPPLE!
SPREADING OUR LINKED ENERGY!
FROM THIS SITE THROUGHOUT THE WORLD!
THANK YOU, TO EACH AND EVERYONE OF YOU,
WHOM SHARED YOUR HEART OF LOVE WITH GIRISH
AND I FOR THE GOLDEN OPPORTUNITY TO BE A
"LINK" IN THIS "UNITED CHAIN OF LOVE" STORIES
BOOK... THE UNIVERSE APPRECIATES YOUR LOVE
ENERGY!

Terri Lynne - TL Whispers
California, **USA**

LOVE LINK #219

What is love?

Love is...
Amazing and refreshing

Love is...
The warmth in our hearts when we bring a smile to another's face
Love is...
The feeling you get when you hold your flesh and blood in your own arms for the first time and every time thereafter.

Love is...
So many things, but for me God's LOVE...
is the greatest love of all.

WEST VICTORIA HSG
Truginina, Victoria, **AUSTRALIA**

LOVE LINK #220

Love is...
All there is!

Amy Sarah Friedman

Mullumbimby, New South Wales, **AUSTRALIA**

LOVE LINK #221

Love is...
Eternal!

Follow each other's heart, with every relation.

Only hearts to hearts stay forever.
Egos to ego's are love to use each other.
Egos to hearts use the heart.
Hearts to Ego is an argument and a fight.
Let egos not attack your heart.
Love a heart in the same way you love your own heart.
Be unconditional love for everyone who listens to his
or her heart.
And that will make it.
Eternity

You make me curious about the book

Corné de Vries
Born: Oudenbosch, **HOLLAND**
Resides: Bladel, Holland **NETHERLAND**

LOVE LINK #222

"Love is...
Sharing stories from the heart!"

Come and sit around this table my friends,
And for a while,
No need here to pretend,
And say our stories,
Of who we are,

To tell the tales,
Straight from the heart...
A place of truth where
Our bond shall start!

Love is...
Divine seduction!

"Love's Divine Seduction"
By Gabriel Szczurek

Kiss me
... Sweetness
Hold me close Grace
In tenderness
Whisper to me
... In melodies
Bring me back those
Forgotten memories
That speaks to these
... Eyes blind
That seeks for me
I find
By the hands
... Of caress
Holds my weary head
In rest
Poured from mouth
... This taste
Soul's longing thirst
Embraced
Gently moves through
... In waves
Into every moment

It stays
Pierced the heart
... In beat
Rendered the way
Its deep
By the breath
... Of life
Is the fragrance
In delight
Upon the winds
... Of wings
Carries the light
Love brings
By this dance
... We weave
Into every dream
We leave
Only your eyes
... I see
Sweetness
Kissing me.

Love

will you open your eyes
if you say you have love
well
i hope it ain't a lie
cause love is never blind
love sees everything
yet
love is rarely unkind

love never has a doubt
cause it's never in your head
when you have love
nothing ever needs to be said

and love is never blue
oh no
cause when you have love
you have all the colors
inside of you

love is never obsessed
love ain't lust
it cannot be bought, sold
or possessed

and love can heal
the deepest of wounds
in the way that love
so gentle cradling you

so open your eyes
open your heart
and let love flow
like a river to
the ocean of your soul

She's Love

She love's in
Passionate displays
Can you see
Her emotions
And colors
That taste
Fragrances
In textures
Of flowers
And nectar
Like the desire
In hummingbird wings
In her spirit
She may bring
Turtles and Avatars
Spaceships
In her night's stars
Wildness
In secret dens
Doors through knowledge
Nature slightly bends
In presents of
Diamonds and gems
But the light in her eyes
You forget about them

She has ember
From the sun
But you cannot
Find in reason
How she soothes
Healing your wounds
Like a rose
Out of season

And in time
You may know
She may show

In solitude
Where she goes
In a sacred place
She tends to her soul
And should she
Invite you in
Lovingly in a sigh
When the timeless dance
Really begins

Gabriel Szczurek
Born: Kosice, **SLOVAKIA**
Resides: Vancouver, **CANADA**

LOVE LINK #223

Love is...
ALOHA!

We live it.
Love you!

Willy J.
3x3o
Terri Lynne's "Lifetime Special Friend" xxxooo
Honolulu - Maui, **Hawaii**

265

LOVE LINK #1 & LOVE LINK #223

Love is...
blending the PAST,
with the PRESENT,
for the FUTURE!!!

L-R Terri Lynne, Big Al, Brandon, Brittany, Nani,
Kainoa, Keanu and Willy
One big happy family!

Our "OHANA!"
HAWAII and CALIFORNIA, **USA** June 2011 xxxooo

LOVE LINK #224

Love is...
Father and Sons
HANGING LOOSE!!!

Kainoa, Keanu and Willy J.

Maui, **HAWAII, USA**
Terri Lynne's "Special" Guys!!!

LOVE LINK #225

"Love is...
What connects us
and
Completes us all!"

"LOVE IS...
Always about
APPRECIATION!"

Dash Singh
Agra, **INDIA** - California, **USA**

LOVE LINK #226

Ok LOVE IS...
Making sacrifices for your children
And
It makes you smile and your heart full!

Lori Hunter
California, USA
Terri Lynne's "Pawtner"

Lori, Malcolm and Ted Hunter

California and Arizona, **USA**

LOVE LINK #227

Love is...
Not always loving what you do,
But doing for those you love.

Ted Hunter
California, **USA**

LOVE LINK #228

We must catch up. Terri Lynne,
I am writing my screenplay.
This manuscript of what Love is to me is (I just this
second went back and typed, *"Love is... just the*
tip of the iceberg" back here typing here now.
I'm "blown away" by the timing of this, as mentioned.
I look forward to answering your question of my
intrigue of all this, magic. Wow.

For now: please know I wrote this entire stream of conscious during spurts and I just hope it is of some use. Feel free to manipulate it or change it. Move it around. At your own free will. And I am at your disposal Terri. I do look forward to catching up.
Dearest, Scott

Love is...

By: Scott Fulmer

Love
LOVE!!... okay maybe that's a few couple too many!!!
BUT!... If any one word ever, actually, definitely, for sure, totally, deserves all those over used exclamation marks,
It...
Is...
Love

Love, is the tip of the iceberg... and everything below

But, if you really must know
Love?... you say.
Is not all that.
Yeah.
I mean don't get me wrong and please don't worry

Love is the cliché run on sentence of puppy dogs and flowers and that sunset and rainbows and things that shoot rainbows... yeah. That.

That love.
That watered down over-inflated whatever it is type thing called LOVE that so many just can't find when they need it most.

But even in darkness and despair, Love is ALWAYS there.

Spare Me! Kill Me! Please stop the world and Let Me Off! We cry.
Oh Love... What are you? Where are you?

Love is humor
Love is universal

Love takes the blame

Love knows you better than you will ever know you

Love
We chase it
All over the world and back if we could and we would
Oh we would
And we do
We bash ourselves with blame

Love is Grace

Love is Serendipity

Love doesn't need to be taken too seriously
Love is playful

Dear Love,

We see so many people having you. In Love and in you and happy. You, In Love and Happy. I mean not everything of course, and not everyone of course. In fact not most really, but we are just injected, vaccinated and programmed and media'dized and robot'ized to Death!!!... With you, from them. They, use you. They, use you to make us feel like we don't have enough of you, that most of us fall short of you, short of having enough love in our lives and we hurt the ones we love the most because... we don't have enough love. We try to fill the void with other stuff that doesn't have anything to do with you Love, at all. Material things, harmful things, wicked things, the dark. Anything to fill in the gaps of the lack of love. Thank you for listening Love.

Sincerely... Love, Us

Love is our very life source
Love is life itself
Love is in every cell
In every molecule of air

Love is the most real thing in your mind

Love loves you
Love wants the best for you
Love doesn't want you to give up

Love is the will to survive

Love is hope
Love is power

Love is the wind

It is all around you
You can't touch it
But you know it's there
If you are one of the lucky ones

Love wants you to lift someone up
So they know

Love is in the heart of the nihilist
Love is undeniable

Love will not be denied ad infinitum

Love
Not death
Follows every last breath
Love is eternal

Love
Beyond, Beyond, Beyond, all human comprehension
Love
Further
Further, Further, Further,
Forever

LOVE HOWLS!!!

Love is not blind

Are you?

Do you want it?
Take hold

Love
You do not have the right to complain when you have
turned your back on it

Love demands Courage
Yes Love demands!
Yes it does!!
Yes it does!!!
Love demands
Love demands because it Loves you

Love can make you sick
Love can kill you
Because you are weak and afraid and full of fear
So Love persists to torment you because Love loves
you so much
Love will not ever leave you alone
Love will beat you into submission

Love can take your breath away
Love can sweep you off your feet
Love can blow you away
And it will

Ask for it
Pray for it
Beg for it

Lose yourself to madness if that is what it takes
You are worthless without it

Love is desire
To change the world

Love is endless

Love cannot be created nor destroyed

Love is the alpha and the omega

Love will confiscate everything you own
Because it has something better

Love will never lie to you

Love is there for you when you put a
noose around your neck because you feel
forsaken
Love is there when you feel doomed
Love is there for you at your worst

Love wants you to live

Love forgives you

Love has passion
Not pride
Love has desire... if you embrace it
Love will not do the work for you
Love matches you to the millionth degree

Love is the speed of light

Love is at it's fullest in that one more step

In that little space just beyond your outstretched hand
Exhausted beaten down desperate grasp
Whaling
When you have collapsed

Love is the synapse

Love is why you keep going, on and on,
around the river bend
Endlessly

With your eyes fixed on the horizon
Without relief but full of hope
Hoping to find the answer
Full of anticipation
... if you are one of the lucky ones

LOVE HAUNTS YOU BECAUSE IT WANTS YOU!!!

Love is not a destination
Love is way more than the journey
Love is immortal

Love does not try to escape the odds
Love lets the odds muck about on their own while we
try to manipulate our own indulgences, play our best
hand, roll the dice, point our finger at our best chances
and attempt to look collected

Love has done so much

Love is so much

And Love, is right here

At your feet
Right in your hands
In your heart

Let it be... Let it be
Let it be, Let it be...

Love is all of this

Yet Love, is at it's best, at it's most fulfilled, in it's highest expression WHEN IT IS SHARED!

Thank You TL, for sharing this book, and your Love, with the World.

Scott Fulmer

Austin, Texas - Los Angeles **USA**
Terri Lynne's Friend

LOVE LINK #229

Love is...
A Loving List!

LOVE IS...
A gentle touch
A kind word
A knowing glance
A sweet kiss
A hand to hold
A warm snuggle
A falling tear
A bright smile
A heart divided
A heart reunited
A warm bath
A cup of tea
All that exists between

Noreen Egurbide
California, **USA**

LOVE LINK #230

Love is...
Powerful.

Powerful in both the bad and good.
It could make us do something that is so wonderful,
Yet so foolish.

Avid Egbali
California, **USA**

LOVE LINK #231

Love is...
THE SEA OF LOVE!

Mario Blanco
Cabo, Mexico
I suggest for you to listen
to the song titled: SEA OF LOVE

LOVE LINK #232

Love is... Feeling good all over!

Bette Jo

Bette Jo & Byron
Married for 56 Years - California, **USA**

LOVE LINK #233

"Love is... UNDERSTANDING!"

Byron (Pop)

LOVE LINK #234

Love is...
Being understood without having to explain myself!

Janice
California, **USA**

LOVE LINK #235

Love is...
Harmony and being in tune and in touch
with nature!

Hello friends recently I have been asked to give my definition of what LOVE IS, and I'm going to attempt to explain this from my heart.

To me Love is... harmony and being in tune and in touch with nature, and all living things. It is compassion with no boundaries. Love starts from your own beating heart because if you don't feel love there's no way to send that vibration back to the universe that is needed for everything to run fluently. I do believe that every one of us is put here on this planet to contribute with this vibration that God intentionally put in US to make all living things run the way it's supposed to. I purposely set myself this year in unique situations in geographic locations. I have intentionally placed myself away from what society these days suggest us to be... I wanted to be more in touch with nature. Away from production, wars, mainstream media and television was purposely banned so I had no distractions. And the things I learned were far greater than what I had anticipated. Once I separated myself from all of this, I had to what I like to call desensitize myself from all of the distractions. This took about 2 weeks and then something magical happened. I began to see LOVE like I had never seen it, or imagined what it would be like before. I would listen to the owls hooting back and forth to each other, certain animals that would show their presents to me in certain situations with overwhelming intention. I begin to somewhat

understand what was going on around me and it really wasn't that complicated. It took me to understand what LOVE IS to separate from what society demands from us, which is so complicated. Intentionally set forth to distract us from a simple rhythmic heartbeat that is right on time to allow us to feel that beautiful emotion of love.

So when I'm asked what true love really is, it's basically everything and everyone living harmoniously together, with an emotion that was imprinted in US, that could get us out of any sad situation or heartbreaking situation if only with faith.

Much love and light to all of you.

Sincerely, Michael Post
Adventurist, Photographer and Light-worker

That came from my heart, so for me what *Love is...* *really simple, it's just a vibration that we all need to feel, including nature, so we all can live harmoniously.* Not only here on this planet before the universe everything needs to work on that vibration and unfortunately Society has imprinted a glitch to sort of throw a wrench in the system, so that is not obtainable unfortunately.

There are a group of people in this world that do not want us to be enlightened, I know this to be fact, I've met many influential people in my travels, some who work for the government whom I trust and some for NASA.

I know doctors and I know attorneys, as I have a lot of them in my family and I took all of my research and figured it all out. I know what's happening, the law of attraction as we know it, is not obtainable because of these groups of people who know how to obtain it

themselves, are fearful that if we do we may share some enlightenment.

It's a very, very, deep dark rabbit hole and I know a lot of facts in which are very sad because it basically comes down to good and evil.

These groups of people have been around a very long time and money to them is everything. Most people on this planet are slaves and don't even realize it.

There are things in drinking water and toothpaste intentionally put in the ingredients, to do things to our pineal gland, that's nothing short of a horror movie.
There are two types of fluoride in this world I know both I know my minerals. There is one that is a mineral and there is one that is a chemical. The one that is a chemical is the fluoride that is put in our toothpaste and tap water. Scientifically this is been proven to calcify your pineal gland and you are a smart lady, our pineal is what we use to meditate with or pray to God.

Calcification of the pineal gland is no Bueno, LOL
This is one hundred percent fact, there are people out there that do not want us to love or be enlightened because it would take profit out of their pocket.

Now you talk about heartbreaking, I don't feed into it I just know the fact, so I intentionally set out on my mission to discover what love really is so you asked the right person...

It's really simple, LOVE IS... a vibration needed for true happiness. I have found this through nature, something the Native Americans knew all along, which is probably another reason why the white man pushed them off from their own land and turn them into alcoholics in which is very sad.

Thankful
Michael W. Post
Part of Terri Lynne's Soul Tribe
Born: Lansing, Michigan, **USA**
Resides: **ALASKA**

LOVE LINK #236

Love is...
Understanding even the smallest of things
you do can make the biggest impact on
others.

Understanding nothing in life is personal and that most
people are just fighting their own battles.
Daring to be vulnerable even if it is the scariest thing
to do.

Follow your heart, without judgment.

Knowing you matter even when others say you don't.

Loving those who nobody else loves.

Love and light,

Werner.

BELGIUM

LOVE LINK #237

LOVE IS...
"LOVE BUG!"
A nickname my mommy calls me
sometimes!

Quinn T.
Aka: QT
5 Years Old
California, **USA**

LOVE LINK #238

Love is...
"Accepting and caring unconditionally and conditionally no matter what!"

and
Love is...
When your husband wakes up and makes your
daughter breakfast
(And takes the dog and cat with him)
And lets you go back to sleep!

Alyssa
California, **USA**

LOVE LINK #239

Love is...
When your husband wakes up makes your daughter breakfast and lets you go back to sleep!

Brett T - California, **USA**

Love is...
"Papa loves mamma, mamma loves men
mammas in the graveyard,
And papa's in the pen"

(Garth Brooks Song)
&
LOVE IS...
"The mud, the blood and the beer"
(Johnny Cash Song)

Brett T - California, **USA**

LOVE LINK #240

How Nice Terri Lynne. I shall do so ... as I was born on Valentine's Day ... and my heart is my strength and weakness too. The seat of the soul sits in the heart. Indeed Love is a Universal Language. We all came from a spark of light... which is Love... unconditional. The strongest vibration in the universe is LOVE... it rises above all. Love dispels negative emotions and inspires Happiness and Good will. We are all part of that magnificent magical Vibes. One Love

Yara Miller
West Yorkshire, **UNITED KINGDOM**

Spiritual Networks LOVE IS... Messages...

LOVE LINK #241

LOVE... IS when the relationship inside is in harmony/balance/wholesomeness...

Rylan
Born: Raleigh, NC, **USA**
Resides: Rangeley, ME, **USA**

LOVE LINK #242

Sonny Thomas
Resides: **CANADA**

LOVE IS... the connection we share with others that reconnect us back to the source of oneness...

LOVE LINK #243

My interpretation of making love is when two energies escape the physical and merge together to manifest the whole of oneness... Namaste

Marri Yanada

LOVE LINK #244

Love is... the eternal desire of souls to merge with each other unconditionally, in joy and in the true nature and image of the Source

Yet somewhat limited by the physical and the material in doing so.

Passer by
UNITED KINGDOM
Thanks Terri.

LOVE LINK #245

Love is...
Knowing the difference!

LOVE IS...
Being ONE with the WATER!

Treci Maxwell-Horowitz
California, **USA**

LOVE LINK #246

Love is...
The feeling you have deep down in your
soul of connection, acceptance, lightness
and joyfulness.

Somehow it lets you know that you can do anything, be anything and that all things are possible. Love compels you to share that positive energy and be a force of good.

Ellen F.
Born: Brooklyn, New York
Resides: California, **USA**

LOVE LINK #247

Love is...
Being surrounded by
Family and Friends!

Lori Forman
Los Angeles, California, **USA**

LOVE LINK #248

Love is...
Expressing your emotions
Through ART!

Bailey Forman
Los Angeles, California, **USA**

LOVE LINK #249

Love is…
A wonderful emotion developed from an
insane amount of care that can explain
why
love feels good and can hurt

Kainoa Jacinto
Maui, HAWAII, **USA**

LOVE LINK #250

Hey Aunty!! Love means a lot to me!

For me, Love is...
"Giving Aloha to those around me each
day, by never taking things for granted
and being thankful for what I have and
treating everyone with kindness from the
HEART!"

Keanu Jacinto
BORN: Maui, HAWAII - RESIDES: California, **USA**

LOVE LINK #251

Hi Terri Lynne, I hope you are well. I was thinking about what love is to me.

One thing I really resonate with love being is kindness.

Two quotes come to mind.
One is: My religion is simple. My religion is kindness, by the Dalai Lama.
The second is: a lyric to a song … and in the end only kindness matters, by Jewel the song is called, "Hands." Kindness to me is allowing other people to be exactly where they are, and to listen to them from that space that they are in.

I also call this mindful listening.
To me this is an important aspect of love.

Christopher Page
Sacramento, California, **USA**
Hands By Jewel
Please listen to the song titled, HANDS by Jewel

LOVE LINK #252

Love is...
Caring about another in a
Selfless way!

Stacey Z.
Madison, Haley, Stacey and Larry
California, **USA**

LOVE LINK #253

Love is...
Patient, kind, sometimes painful...
But most of all,
LOVE IS...
The SPIRIT of GOD!

Gary Rodriguez
California, **USA**

LOVE LINK #254

Angel Terri, Some quick thoughts.
Feel free to use any of it.
Thank you for including me, such an honor.
Looking forward to reading your book.

Love is...
Love!!!!!!!!
The depth of LOVE is in direct relationship
with love of thy self. The deeper your love
for self, allows you to be present in a state
of loving kindness with another.

LOVE IS...
Sharing ones presence in a neutral place/space.
Being with another, in what is and seeing them in
their god self, (highest self-source) regardless of the
circumstance.
LOVE IS...
Shining light and seeing the beauty in everyone and in
everything!

Sophia (Wisdom) DAYA (Kindness & Compassion)
"Together equating to KEYS for PEACE and LOVE
prevailing on the planet!" Aka: The Aquarian Lawyer

Born: The City of Angels - Resides: **USA**

LOVE LINK #89 continued...

Love is...

All there IS!

Indi "Love" Shan
Born: **INDIA**
Resides: Melbourne, **AUSTRALIA**

LOVE LINK #255

"Love is not something we think about it emanates from deep within your soul to the point that you cannot contain it. Love is seeing others through the eyes of God."

Delia Mercado
New York, **USA**

300

LOVE LINK #256

Love is...

Living with the person you love is not what everyone thinks it is. It's not waking up early every morning to make breakfast and eat together. Its not cuddling in bed together until both of you peacefully falls asleep. It's not a clean home and a homemade meal every night. It's fights about who has to put the dishes away. It's screaming and crying because you've had a hard day and came home to the laundry not being done even though you asked them 5 times to do it. It's your love waiting until you get into the shower to decide they need to take a poop. It's falling asleep on separate couches because the day has left you too exhausted to move to the bed. It's waking up to all of the pop tarts you bought for yourself, already eaten. It's someone who steals all the covers and knees you in the face because the bed is too small for both of you. It's slammed doors and harsh words, it's wondering if you've made the right decision. It is, despite all of those things, the one thing you look forward to every day. It's coming home to the same person everyday that you know loves and cares about you. It's laughing about the one time you accidentally electrocuted yourself trying to plug in the washer and dryer. It's about spontaneous food fights and eating the cheapest and easiest meal you can make and sitting down together at 10pm to eat them because you both work crazy hours. It's when you have an emotional breakdown and your love lies on the floor with you and holds you and tells you everything is going to be okay, and you believe them. It's when "Netflix and chill" literally means you watch Netflix and hang out. It's about still loving someone even though they make you absolutely insane. Living with the person you

love is countless fights about absolutely nothing, but is also having a love that people spend their whole life looking for. *It's not perfect and it's hard, but it's amazing and comforting and the best thing you'll ever experience.*

Lori Werman Windloss
Florida, **USA**

LOVE LINK #257

Love is...
Feeling that every day brings new possibilities and endless joy that there are people in your life to share that happiness with.

Susan
Born: West Palm Beach, Florida
Resides: California, **USA**

LOVE LINK #258

Love is...
Letting go and trusting at the same time.

It's about allowing yourself to be vulnerable & letting your guard down with those you care most about. Because those people are the ones that know you inside & out... for all your good sides and your bad ones, your

quirks, the little things that make you who you are. And that's why we trust them. So love in the end it is both an expression of the real you & acceptance of that expression by both yourself & those you choose to love.

Noam
Israel - Resides: California, **USA**

LOVE LINK #259

Love is...
Floating while flying high!

Love is... like rounding up all the sensory receptors a person has within his/her body, setting them all into action in one single moment, a tsunami abounding with warmth, kindness, forgiveness, patience, and understanding. Love knows of no boundaries, love permeates hate, jealousy, sadness, and hopelessness. Love cleanses the mind, heart and soul. Many search for love their entire life, looking for fulfillment, happiness and peace. To some it is a treasure so they search for the secret map. But there are many treasures in life, which are never found, even when they are placed right in front of them. For some reason, man believes the most rare gems must be sought through journey and toil, when all they needed to do was to allow it to happen.

Iona K. Niihau-Sherman
Maui ~ Honolulu, **HAWAII, USA**

LOVE LINK #260

Hi darling - For me,

LOVE is...
The only reason we are here!

Jenny Swire
UNITED KINGDOM

LOVE LINK #261

Love is...
Protecting our Earth!

I've had a huge number of emails from many people who have been attending and participating in the Standing Rock - Water is Life protests. Our prayers are with you as media is leaving and arrests will be made on those left behind.

Keep peace in your heart and mind, as you stand strong in your beliefs.

Be diligent, be wise, our time is upon us and the fear and pain government and big business stupidity and blundering does, is starting to shift and influence the small, the meek, the unheard, so that the voices become louder, stronger and POTENT.

Our Mother knows the many are working to protect, heal, and love her. This Earth is all we've got, thank you for being there and allowing me to be here where I am

right now, doing what I do in order that it help in some small way.

Kia Kaha, KIA Maia, KIA Manawanui.
Atarangi Muru - Auckland, **NEW ZEALAND**

ANOTHER MESSAGE POSTED FROM ATA:

You know the best kind of epidemic we can start is LOVE and KINDNESS.

Just saying it, cause after some of the things that happened yesterday at work (doing the bodywork that is), it's much needed.

I'm good at reminding people to be easy on themselves, to take time out to do something that sparks their deep inner joy and to remember love and kindness is a gift to us given by a power and energy greater than ourselves, so give it out freely and plentifully.

It will return in good stead and multiplied, this I know from my own life experiences. Today, I'm going to have an even better day than all my yesterdays. Why??? Because I'm in it, it's my choice and I want to! Ata Muru - NEW ZEALAND

"Love is...
What begins within and this we can't live
without!"

Terri Lynne - California, **USA**

Love is... The MAORI Healers!

Share in a private message   ×

To: Terri Lynne ×   Atarangi Muru ×

I FEEL BLESSED TO HAVE MET THIS LADY, ATARANGI MURU! A
LOVING ANGEL OF LIGHT, WHO'S ENERGY IS BEAUTIFUL, MAGNETIC
& INSPIRATIONAL! ATA, YOU ARE A GIFT!
Terri Lynne
xxxooo|

A Friendversary to Celebrate!

Terri and Atarangi became friends on Facebook 7 years ago.

Cancel   Send

Terri Lynne and Atarangi Muru
California, **USA** Auckland, **NEW ZEALAND**

Ata replied:
Your pretty magnetic and beautiful yourself,
wonder woman.
Terri Lynne replied: Thank YOU Ata

LOVE LINK #262

Love is...
"Simple, its three words:
GOD IS LOVE!"

Rebecca Casas
California, **USA**

LOVE LINK #263

Love is...
TOGETHERNESS!

When everyone's altogether!

Esther Fiss (92 Years Old)
California, **USA**

R.I.P. Aunt Esther passed on November 2019

Visiting Aunt Esther at The Scholl Estates
Terri Lynne, Rey Vasquez, Aunt Esther, Jorge, Al

LOVE LINK #264

Love is...
Very strange!

Rey Vasquez (From Scholl Estates)
MEXICO - California, **USA**

LOVE LINK #265

Love is...
Sharing!!!

~✶~

All I ever wanted
Was to reach out
And touch another human being
Not just with my hands
But with my heart.

~✶~ LOVE IS... ~✶~

Your ego will always have arguments
Why you cannot love...
You must have this or that, you have no time,
You're tired,
You will not get anything from other people...
And so on.
Your ego will always try to keep you away from a life
You would want to live.
Ego is looking for efficiency,
Status and prestige in the world,
But if that falls away, what is left of you?
Your true being
And the only thing that is valuable
(When the whole world around you collapses)
Is love, because love of self and love for others
Pulls you through all circumstances.

"Make people aware that they are more than their ego,
They are the love of themselves."

-Corine
Shared By: ~✱~ ORLANDO ~✱~
Born: **NETHERLANDS**
Resides: **WORLDWIDE**

LOVE LINK #266

Love is... A Poet's Journey

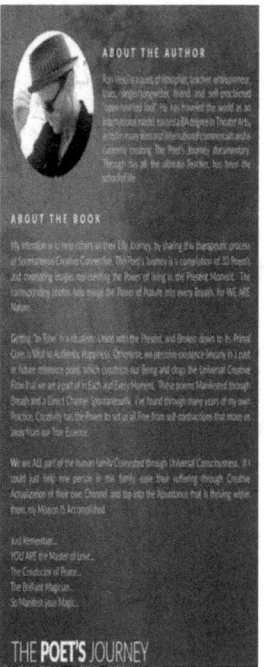

"Love is... A reflection!"

Ron Vesci - Boston - California, **USA**

LOVE LINK #267

LOVE... IS!

Harriett (80 Years Young) Top Right &
Left – Mickey Wapner & Judge Wapner (98 Years
Young)
(Mickey Wapner & Judge Wapner CELEBRATED
Their "70 Year Anniversary" in November 2016)

"Love is...
Longevity!!!"

Congratulations! ☺
Terri Lynne xxxooo

Love is... a difficult feeling to put into one meaning. There are so many kinds of love. For me, I have been "in love" and I have "loved." I have experienced so many kinds of love throughout my life.

My first love was probably that cute boy in my 8th grade class who I had a mad crush on...

Then we go into high school and many other love experiences were there. Can't remember them all but there were many!

Family love became the most important for me especially as I grew older...

The first time I held my daughter in my arms after giving birth... that was a kind of overwhelming love I had never experienced before.

Then as the children grew there was the kind of love watching them grow into their own experiences of life and seeing them happy and being so proud of their accomplishments and knowing we did a good job of raising them so that they turned out to be good people!

Then along come the grandchildren! WOW! A different kind of love I never had experienced as a grandmother towards my grandchildren! The epitome of a grandparents love for her grandchildren... Watching them grow into fine young men and making their way into the world.

Then comes the great granddaughter! The future of the family is assured! We will continue and go on. The love I have for her is over whelming... Now the "loves" of my life were and are very diverse.

My first husband was the kind of love that was solid and steady... No fireworks or mad passion, but he was hard working and was a good husband and father who took good care of his family. He was very responsible and trustworthy. He passed away very young just (58 years old).

My second husband was the "fireworks and passion!" He was the most exciting man I had ever been with and showed me a life of excitement and fun. We had so much fun together and did everything... Travelled the world

and baseball at Angels and Dodgers... Spring training every spring along with meeting so many players in the sports world. My life with him lasted only 10 years but they were exciting years for me.

The man I am with now is very kind and we enjoy theatre, concerts at the Disney Hall, Museums and Opera. A different lifestyle from before, yet I love the slower pace and we have a love of the same things and love being together. He also loves baseball and the Angels and we go to many games together... It's a calm love... One that we appreciate each other and are comfortable in each other's company. A comfortable kind of love... .

As I look back to my 80 years of being on this planet I realize I have experienced so many different kinds of love and would not trade any of them for any other life... These different loves have made me the person I am today... I have had a wonderful life and am truly grateful for the life I had...

I am truly blessed.

Harriette Spero

Los Angeles, California, **USA**

(Terri Lynne's Mom #2)

(Three days later... I, Terri Lynne received this message from Harriette)

Just want to let you know that Joe Wapner died today... I would keep the information for your book if you still want to. I think it would be good to write about a love and marriage that lasted for 70 years! Mickey would like that too!

I am so happy he came to my 80th birthday! He seemed to have a good time!

Love,
Harriette xoxoxoxo

Dear Harriett & Family and The Wapner Family
I had a FEELING this was happening!!

I felt his LOVE with his BEAUTIFUL WIFE would be reflected as a permanent incredible LOVE STORY in this book all about what LOVE IS!

Thank you Harriett (Mom #2) for allowing their story to be apart of this book, uniting the world through LOVE! What a fine example they have set for the world to learn from! As well as your own expression of what LOVE IS! Thank you for allowing us to be a vessel of DIVINE TIMING upon earth in this life!

I LOVE YOU!

Daughter #3 - Child #4 -Terri Lynne xxxooo

My condolences go out to the Wapner family!

With due respect, I am proudly sharing this LOVE STORY stemming from a full heart filled with LOVE EVER LASTING & NEVER ENDING - Mickey & Joe Wapner's "70 year MARRIAGE" will be embedded in our hearts forever more!

Thank you Harriett (Mom #2) for the exchange of this LOVING ENERGY! Happy 80th Birthday ANGEL! May you live to 120 years young, because the world needs a LOVING HEART like yours! Terri Lynne xxxooo

LOVE LINK #268

Love is... being a Grandparent!

"One of the most important promotions you can attain in your lifetime is to "grandparent." The birth of a grandchild is when love blooms and flourishes in a way you have never known. Cherish them, teach them, and let them know how special they are! Be someone they will never forget; give them all the love in your heart, for in the end, the love in our hearts is all we take with us."

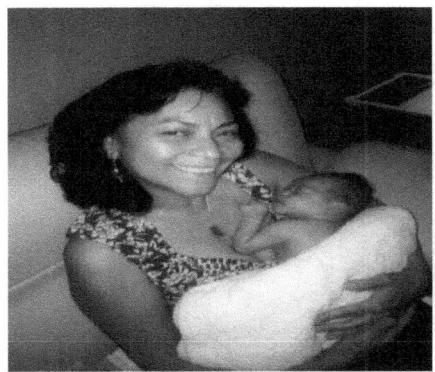 

Theresa Ann Lucero - Elijah Lee Davis
Born: San Antonio, TX.
I have lived in 28 states and eight countries.
Resides: Arizona, **USA**

LOVE LINK #269

Love is...
Always being able to make someone laugh
And knowing what to say to put a smile on
their face.

Megan and Chris
California, **USA**

LOVE LINK #270

Love is...
Mysterious!

The Mysterious Goddess
There is a Unknown Goddess, shrouded in Mystery,
Her Temples; desecrated, destroyed since history,
Since time immemorial She has existed,
and somehow, whispers of Wisdom persisted.

The points She makes, mostly missed,
Knowledge She offers, widely dismissed,
For Her songs of virtue, and of beauty,
Are viewed as primitive, exposed so crudely.

Many sail to a far away place,
To see only followers, Legacy disgraced,
Whether be it the place; Her Sacred Books speak of:
An Imaginary Heaven or the Hell beneath us.
However She guards Wisdom like forged iron doors,
Her minds sharp like A Thousand Cleaving Swords,
Her Eyes penetrating like a piercing lance,
Yet when She sees her followers, at glance...
The Universe shall sing in song and dance,
As if all for one;
And self in trance.

For darker days to come, many a day without Light or
Sun,
Time, one evil and ignorant to strike war drum.
Brightly, unison, shall strike the final blow:
With the Sword of Wisdom, the Sword of Swords,
Better days for all, for evil, will lose, the final war.

Dyrr Keusseyan
Aka: LOVE
Otawa, **CANADA**

Love is...
Compassionate!

The Mighty Goddess of Compassion

Deep In the Universe of which we perceive but a
fraction:
Exists an All-encompassing Mighty Goddess of
Compassion,
Whether crying a Luminous being immune to any
curse,
Or a simpleton Woman, with a few worries to nurse,
Whether at home, or some world's distant shore
Whether sentient ones in distant Heaven adored
Whether in silence or at war, Goddess we whisper or
roar!

Wisdom sweet like the Nectar of a thousand peaches
Worlds at Peace, Passages to Endless Realms
within our reaches
For Love, Peace above us to Crusades beneath
A Goddess Bold, a Heart of Blissful Eternal Heat.

We fight, and strikes red devils, black knights
For the ones innocent with truthful plights,
Our Hearts in our chest, Truly Only One Holy Crest!
Hearts and Minds United with The Goddess, Eternally
Blessed.

Whether one lost or confused,
Whether sad, much trust found, lost then misused
One who speaks dearly forever to those abused
Goddess of Compassion, Light with All Hues.

Even when facing immeasurable defeat.
Whether in the Cold Hells frost or Hot Hells heat,
Whether trouble or sinking fast and deep,
Or perilous journey through Mountains; passages
steep.
Compassion an elixir and sword of eternal heat.
With Wisdom together, an improbable defeat.
Whether evil in the Battlefield or crawling evil hidden
Reading Ancient Wisdom or Knowledge Forbidden,
Even if a thousand vile voices slander in unison,
The Goddess of Compassion Eternally is warm and
Singing.

Dyrr Keusseya Aka: LOVE
Otawa, **CANADA**

(And thanks. What gave you the idea to write a book?)
What inspired you?
I hope it works out; we do indeed need a book about
Love,
since there is little material on that subject matter, and
a lot
of junk info out there, just 'sayin.'
Take good care and stay in touch!
Peace

LOVE LINK #271

More than a noun, Love Is A Verb...

Demonstrate Love through your deeds, words, support and sacrifice. Practice Love and experience greater relationships with your family, friends, co-workers and with the people you meet in daily life.

Eric Kahalelehua
Honolulu, **HAWAII, USA**

LOVE LINK #272

Love is...
PURA VIDA!

Pure Life!
Love,
Tica
Yamile Gastelo
COSTA RICA - California, **USA**

LOVE LINK #273

Love is...
A blending of PASSION & FUN!

Heather and Charlie Brocato
Chicago - California - Texas, **USA**

LOVE LINK #88 Continued...

Love is...
A WAVE OF HEARTS LIGHT!!!

Sending you all my LOVE so it can flow through me to you and then through to all of creation... Let it flow like a wild mountain river with raging rapids... Forming pure white love waves crashing into the hearts of all creatures great and small alive.

With no life vest supplied as in this case I want u to drown deep within my LOVE... It is all around waves of love the size of Everest... There is no escaping it, no vessel made great enough to withstand the power of my LOVE... It will be drawn with ease... Lay still and let it come over you like the night over the earth... Fight not for it is a fight not worth winning... And being still is not losing... Being overcome is the joy and bliss that no earthly treasures can bestow... My love's ocean will wash away all that vexes your soul... Let me inside your skin... Entering in through your nostrils. Breathe me in... Fill your lungs with me, fuse it through your life's blood flow and let me flow through every vein and artery through your heart and around your body and through your heart ♥ again and again... Forever... Our souls shall then dance the dance of loves tune in the light of eternity... As we flow together into the God's greater ocean made of pure intense LOVE and light!

There. Is my reply to the LOVE story... I was guided on the fly to write this... With nothing prepared in my head, with no clue, I was going to write it as soon as I said I would write it shortly... But shortly became in the NOW. I trust it should be sufficient for now.

Indi "LOVE" Shan
Born: **INDIA** - Resides: Melbourne, **AUSTRALIA**

LOVE LINK #274

LOVE IS messages from my brother Bill's FAMILY

LOVE IS...

Many things, but this was the first thing that came to my mind:

LOVE IS...

Seeing my children come into the world.

Love is: My Children!

Bill
California - Palos Park, IL **USA**

LOVE LINK #275

Love is...
What gets you through hard times.

Penny - Palos Park, IL, **USA**

LOVE LINK #276

Love is...
Ever changing and to be determined yet
again tomorrow.

Steven - Palos Park, IL, **USA**

LOVE LINK #277

Love is...
The strength I get from the support of my
family.

Nicholas - Palos Park, IL, **USA**

LOVE LINK #278

Love is...
The light that brightens up my heart when I
am sad.

Alyssa - Palos Park, IL, **USA**

LOVE LINK #279

Love is...
The key to our humanity.

It's in the smiles and laughter of those that mean the
most to us.
It may change form, but it lives with us forever.

Nicole, San Francisco, **USA**

LOVE LINK #280

Love is...
A captor of your emotions.

It makes your heart heavy... or light; it makes your
feet drag... or skip; it makes your body sick with
sadness... or sheer joy; it makes you do easily what
you should... or defy convention and do what you
should not. Without it one is dead, even if they walk
the earth. Love is life.

Jeanne Lawson
California, **USA**

LOVE LINK #281

Love is...
experienced in three kinds of ways:

LOVE IS...
Family!

οικογένεια
Oikogéneia
Familia

LOVE IS...
Erotic Love!

Ερωτική αγάπη
Erotikí agape
Amor erótico

LOVE IS...
The LOVE of God!

Αγάπη του Θεού
Agápi tou Theoú
Amor de Dios!
The love of God has shown me how to LOVE!
Patience is the greatest teacher in finding LOVE!

Maria De Los Angeles Calva
Aka: Mama, Mami, Mamita
(Mom of 6 Children & Grandma of 18, Great Grandma
of 16, and Great-Great Grandma of 2)
COSTA RICA - California, **USA**

LOVE LINK #282

Love is...
Sincerity as soil sustains life, the sun
shining on nature, the airwaves provide
freshness, and flowing water gives life and
space that balances all life.

(This is in Indonesian language)
"Cinta adalah ketulusan sebagaimana tanah
menopang kehidupan, matahari menyinari alam,
udara menghembus memberikan kesegaran, air
mengalir memberikan." "Kehidupan dan angkasa yang
menyeimbangkan semua kehidupan."

Satria Black
BORN: Pedawa, **INDONISIA**
RESIDES: Indonesia, **BALI**

LOVE LINK #283

Hi, Terri Lynne.

It was such a joy meeting you this afternoon at Serenity
Rocks!

Here are a few of my musings on what I feel Love is.

The first two quotes are my original thoughts, and then
I share the Osho quote, which I had mentioned to you.

Love is... where two individuals come
together to nurture and support each other
and co-create together.

Love is the sum of all our cells and every molecule and atom that makes up this ever expanding universe. We are forever seeking outwardly for love's affirmations, while it patiently, faithfully waits within us in silent, constant prayer, hoping we will find it and feed off its blessings instead of being in a constant state of insatiable hunger.

"Don't fall in love, RISE in love. Immature people falling in love destroy each other's freedom, create bondage, and make a prison. Mature persons in love, help each other to be free; they help each other to destroy all sorts of bondages. And when love flows with freedom there is beauty... A mature person does not fall in love, he or she rises in love... Two mature persons in love help each other to become more free. There is no politics involved, no diplomacy, and no effort to dominate. Only freedom and love."

Enjoy a beautiful, magical evening!

Credited To: Osho
Shared By: Angela Williams
Malibu, California **USA**

LOVE LINK #284

Love is...
The pure essence of this universe,
everything else is absolute Maya, which is
unreal.

Only LOVE exists, everything else is MAYA (Illusion)!!!

Chakravarthy Baddepudi
Born: Chennai, **INDIA**
Resides: Amsterdam, **NETHERLANDS**

LOVE LINK #285

"Love is...
Warmth from the sun!
"SUN LOVE IS GOOD LOVE!"

Powerful light codes today downloading from the sun... I'm getting that it's not about the warmth of the rays so much as the vibrational frequencies coming through them. It could be just as strong and effective at boosting your auric field in a cold climate as a warm one (although it's more likely to be sunny obviously in a warm one.) It seems so genius to me really... to boost the consciousness of ALL of us through one of the few universal things that we experience... sunlight.

It really does feel like an aspect of the overall "plan" for Gaia's ascension to transmit codes this way that could lead to our suppressed DNA strands reactivating, our pineal gland being energized and activated (third eye center), Vitamin D levels going up. The crystalline body likes and needs the sunshine. I see it all the time here in Puerto Vallarta... people coming from cold, rainy, overcast climates and seeming to just about be dying for the sun (and the warmth too.) when they get here. They lay under it for hours, recharging what they've been missing.

This seems basic to be offering to get in direct sunlight as much as feels comfortable for you yet we've received so much conditioning about the dangers of UV rays. Conditioning meant to suppress our desire for it, our need for it, and our activation underneath it. Getting regular direct sunlight and ideally meditating while receiving it into your body provides this immediate

sense of higher frequency, relaxation, expansion... this is why I feel that people crave to lay out in it.

If you do undertake some sun therapy, do track and feel how much you are taking in. It is strong right now in the sense of what is coming through and I've been guided a few times that it's not "really for me"... meaning, the blasts are for those who are on the tipping point of awakening and need the boost rather than those of us who are pretty firmly on our way. So, we are more sensitive to it and smaller doses are probably very effective because our auric field and chakras are less congested. Most people will not be conscious of what they are taking in through the sun and this too means it will not go in as deeply.

Also, taking pictures of the sun is amazing right now as it shifts and changes in so many different forms and frequencies. It has looked like a tetrahedron a few times now and also a portal many times in photographs with many different colored orbs or Ethereal BEing "tracks" showing up. Would love to see any pictures you've taken of the sun lately if you'd like to share in the comments on my site: Soulfullheartwayoflife.com...

Sun love is good love!

Jelelle Awen
Puerto Vallarta, **MEXICO**

Love is...
Remembering the LOVE that you SEE!

Remember the LOVE that you ARE..

SoulFullHeartWayOfLife.com

Jelelle Awen
Puerto Vallarta, **MEXICO**
Soulfullheartwayoflife.com

LOVE LINK #286

"Love is... wiping that special loved ones ass.

You're on the receiving end as a baby. You're on the giving end as a new parent. Then unfortunately you're back on the receiving end very late in life. Only a special love continues that special favor during our cycle of life."

Doug B.
Los Angeles, California, **USA**

LOVE LINK #287

Love is... Unconditional!

Theresa G., Amanda G. & Andy G.

California, **USA**
R.I.P. Theresa Princiotta Gamsu
8-4-62 ~ 10-17-19
(Terri Lynne's Friend/Sister for 52 Years
Love from me with a heavy heart!)

LOVE LINK #288

Love is...
"Rising above it all because you believe in
the path that your guides have you on over
everything else!"

Victoria
Los Angeles, California **USA**

Love is...
Young innocence!

Victoria receiving young LOVE
On her birthday!
California, **USA**

LOVE LINK #289

Love is:
The strength to endure all good and bad,
the vision to see good in all things with a heart of gold
that contains forgiveness. Filled with inspiration of
hope for you and all existence, creatures, and earth.

Amber Link - California, **USA**

LOVE LINK #290

Love is...
"PUPPY LOVE!"

"Love is... looking into your doggies eyes and knowing how deep your love is for them and you can tell they feel the same way!

Love is... kissing and squeezing your dogs so much that you have to be careful that they won't pop!

Love is... unconditional and it comes so effortlessly and naturally to them! I don't think it's a coincidence that DOG spelled backwards is GOD!"

Andrea Covell
California, **USA**

337

LOVE LINK #291

Love is...
Life!

Chris Tomei
Providence, **Italy**

LOVE LINK #292

"Love is...
A Shield Of Protection!"

"Love is... the strongest force in the universe!"
Love is... the shield that keeps all bad and evil away
from those on the right side of the shield.
Love is... all those that are in the shield are connected
by mutual goodness, affection and loyalty.
The shield is impenetrable - it is 360 degrees.
All of those within the nucleus of the shield are tied
together by each of the group that is sharing this
goodness, loyalty and affection. It flows one to another
and then back and forth... ebb and flow. This group is
the inner circle. The affection, goodness and loyalty,
intensifies as time goes on. Those within the nucleus
homogenize. They become one with each other. The
inner circle becomes stronger from within.
This is LOVE. You are invited into the inner circle.
LOVE will protect you. LOVE will soothe you. LOVE will
set your emotions free. TRUE LOVE is atomic. It is the
strongest force in the Universe. With LOVE you will
conquer all...

It is the FORCE... may it be with you...
Luke Sywalker... AKA Allan Mazal
Allan Mazal - California, **USA**

LOVE LINK #293

Love is...
"Everything GOOD that keeps
All of the BAD out!!!"

Lisa Mazal
California, **USA**

LOVE LINK #294

"Love is...
The softest whisper that penetrates the
loudest noise.

Its ring is always true, never silent and the purest
essence.
You know it because you are it."

The love you describe isn't love. What YOU are is. The gentle pull of love is inexorable, subtle, but more powerful than anything you think, action you take or faith you profess. There is nothing greater than its force, and yet it isn't a force. IT just is, and it is so with or without your description of it.

Even in your darkest hour, your seething anger, your mind-filled hatred, YOU are full to the brim with love. IT will never let you go. Beautiful, love-filled day!

Carl Bozeman
Born: Tacoma, Washington
Resides: Colorado, **USA**

LOVE LINK #295

"Love is... what we cannot exist without!"

As physicists, we try to quantify our universe by creating models that explain the phenomena we are able to perceive as empiricists.

So far we have found 4 fundamental forces that govern the way the universe works:

Electric, Magnetic, Strong, and Weak Force.

With these, we can explain (almost) all Phenomena between Quantum Mechanics and General Relativity. However, we completely fail to describe one overall principle that determines all of human existence: Love!

We could try to break it down to a biochemical reaction in a well-defined region of our brain that is developed as part of our Evolution, but it is not.

It can't be put into numbers, because Love is: The main Essence of Life itself. It's human life's principle, cause and the beauty in it.

We cannot exist without LOVE.

Julian Boell
GERMANY - California, **USA** - **GERMANY** - California, **USA**

LOVE LINK #296

Love is... being ME!

Juhbreel
NIGERIA

LOVE LINK #297

Love is...
Love to me is unconditional. It means
patience, compassion, kindness,
generosity, and harmony. To love someone
is to be there for him or her through thick
and thin.

"I offer you peace. I offer you love. I offer you
Friendship.
I see your beauty. I hear your need. I feel your
Feelings.
My wisdom flows from the Highest Source.
I salute that Source in you.
Let us work together for unity and love."
Credited To: - Mahatma Gandhi

Shared By: Jean M. Numa
Born & Resides: Port-Au-Prince **HAITI**

LOVE LINK #298

Love is...
What adds to life!

Depression kills!
These are the facts of life!

Hillik M.
Born: **ISRAEL**
Resides: California **USA**
Dedicated: Leslie

LOVE LINK #299

"Love is...
Contentment!"

Stacey Powells
California, **USA**

LOVE LINK #300

Love is... a world; Love is a way;
You will never understand it until you live
it.

Love is a combination of many feelings that exist, that we feel; good or bad; Love is intelligence, even something above. Love is a sweet contradiction that makes trees grow up, while it knows all the leaves will fall one day.

Written By: Same Sohrevardi
An Iranian Refugee living in **TURKEY**

LOVE LINK #301

Love is...
My Family!

Amore es...
Mi Familia!

Raquel Guron
Born: El Savador
Resides: California, **USA**

LOVE LINK #302

Love is... not having to make excuses,
it's just knowing and feeling how your
significant other is.

Love is... being with someone whom you want to spend
the rest of your life with.
Love is... watching a show, or nothing at all with, and
falling asleep on each other.
Love is... laughing at the simple things in life together.
Good luck with your book.

Kevin Lavis
Born: Manhatten Beach, CA **USA**
Resides: Yakima, WA **USA**

LOVE LINK #303

LOVE IS...
Worth holding onto no matter how worn or
aged it is!

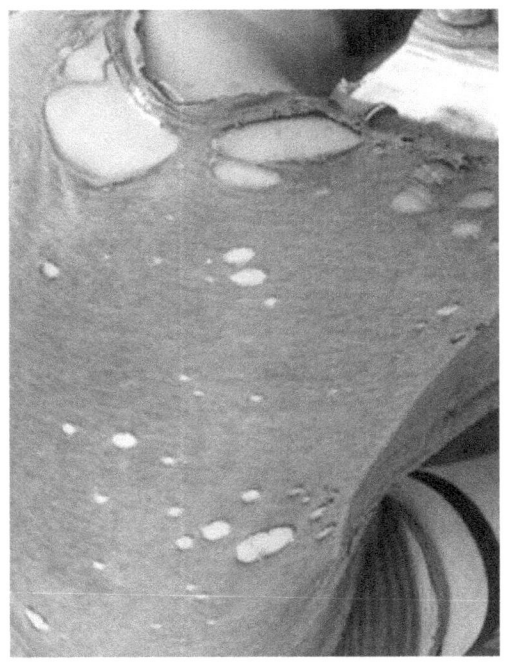

This is the love of a man for a t-shirt:
And the back is much better than the front... !
And my love for this man keeps me from throwing
the t-shirt, or what ever is left of it away and I'll most
probably frame it one day, but I'll never throw it away
because I would feel like getting rid of a piece of my
beloved husband...
I think that can be called Love!

Caty Aka: Cathy
France – California

LOVE LINK #304

Love is... My LOVE!

Andreas Gallios
Athens, **GREECE**

LOVE LINK #305

LOVE IS... COHESION!

L'amour EST...
La Cohésion!

Kian Kazemi
California, USA

LOVE IS... FLYING FREE!

KIAN FREE FLYING!
In France

Kian
California, USA

LOVE LINK #306

LOVE IS...
SOARING!

KAYLAN Bungee Jumping!
In France
California, USA

LOVE LINK #307

"LOVE IS... JUMPNG!"
Knowing if you jump you will FLY!"

KALVIN FLYING IN FRANCE!

Kalvin
California, USA

LOVE LINK #308

Love is...
ANIMALS!

IT FEELS
AMAZING TO
BE TOUCHED BY
THE PERSON WHO
UNDERSTANDS
YOUR MIND,
THE PERSON WHO
ACKNOWLEDGES
YOUR FLAWS AND
LOVES YOUR
SOUL.
KUSHANDWIZDOM

Fernando Herrero Del Valle
Colmenar Viejo - Madrid, **SPAIN**
"ANIMAL LOVER"

350

"Puppy Love"

but the most beautiful things in life are not things. They're people, places, memories and pictures. They're feelings and moments, and smiles, and laughter.

Fernando Herrero Del Valle and Friend
Colmenar Viejo and Madrid, **SPAIN**

LOVE LINK #309

"LOVE IS... An Experience!"

THE EXPERIENCE OF LOVE

Many people fall in love and often do not realize that they are experiencing their own body, mind and spirit vibrating in such a way that they can feel a glimpse of the capacity of love that is inside of them at all times. (The capacity to love by the way is immeasurable) The person on the outside, who elicits such feelings of joy and love, is a stimulus, nudging you to bring awareness to the abundance of love inside of you. And let it. Let it open your heart. When you understand this, you can have more gratitude and appreciation for others in your life. Many people have fear that they will lose love, and will start to try to control and manipulate others to stay. But the love is abundantly already inside and always was. Love is in every molecule of your being, every cell, every thought, every breath, every heartbeat. Love is in how you move and express yourself. Love is the undertone of every relationship. It is the bridge between people, animals, and molecular bonds. Love is in your auric field. Love is in your bones. Love is in water! You cannot help but to love and be of love and light. *Anything blocking love can be freed with feeling your own abundant source of love inside of you and all around you.*

- Christine Surrago-Kousouli, ND California, **USA**

LOVE LINK #310

Trying to understand the L-word

What is love? Seems like an easy enough question to answer right? However, love is much more complex than we perceive. Love is a constantly evolving word, with different ways it can be shown and felt. The Greeks tried to categorize the idea of love into seven categories that now in psychology they are classified by. Eros, Philia, Storge, Agape, Ludus, Pragma, and Philautia. Each word is Greek based that has a deeper message; The words and names are symbolic. Understanding each type of love is important so that we can be in touch not only with others but ourselves as well.

The first description of love is Eros. This is considered to be a passionate love, a love that is so intense it is like getting hit by cupid's arrows. Eros can also be one of the most difficult to fall out of unfortunately. Philia is described to be a friendship kind of love, however Plato, a greek philosopher believed that Eros and Philia went hand in hand. The two types of love are linked because a friendship is usually built before passion between two people grows. Both coincide in a way that the relationship has a shared desire for a higher level of understanding of the self, the other, and the world. Storge is your love that you have for your family, it is love that is not based off the qualities of the person rather the position you are born into. An example of this is the saying "Blood is thicker than water," meaning that the relationship you have with your family is more important than a friendship because no matter what they will be there. Agape is universal love, more precisely a love for everything. Agape can tend to be a personality trait that provides a refreshing perspective on any situation. A term used to describe this, is a person who sees a "glass half full."

Another kind of love is Ludus which is a playful kind of love, mostly based off of lust and usually chooses to not have strings attached between two people. Ludus is primarily a short term feeling of companionship and desire that can have a spark of Eros between the two individuals. On the other hand you have Pragma, which is the love that endures. An example of Pragma is merely the act of two people so in love they decide to get married. Marriage is a bond between two human beings to be together through good or bad, which is necessary with Pragma. Lastly there is Philautia, the love for yourself, the most important kind of love there is to have. A prime example that comes to mind as Lucille Ball once said, "Love yourself first and everything else falls into line. You really have to love yourself to get anything done in this world." Without this final quality the previous six types of love have no relevance, because if you do not love yourself first, how can you love others?

Also there is Philautia, which is one of the most valuable kinds of love because it a love based off of your inner self. Some may consider certain types of love to be more important than others, the idea is that if one has a love for themselves and the things around them, they are able to lead happier lives. Many people misunderstand exactly what the expression to "love oneself" means, or how to practice it. According to <u>wellbeingcenter.com</u>, they talk about "SPA," which means to do three conscious acts on a daily basis in order to strengthen the love for yourself which include; 'Set' aside time, take some time and do something that is enjoyable. In today's world we get so caught up in little details that we tend to forget about ourselves. Next is to 'praise' yourself! It might sound silly, but by saying congratulations every now and then to your own mirror, really does help lead a healthier, more positive life. Take the time to give yourself a pat on the back, because we as humans need to remind

ourselves that this life is a crazy experience and we are hopefully all trying to do our best. We need to remind ourselves that we are accomplishing something on a daily, weekly, monthly and yearly basis of things we need to be proud of. Lastly we have 'affirmations,' which many people can find controversial. It is something that I have seen create a dramatic change in many people's lives who surround me. Affirmation offers a unique chance to speak in what some may call 'future present tense.' Kind of think of it as the beautiful human you want to become. Some might use the following saying as one of the many affirmations they tell themselves throughout the day, "I am proud of myself and all that I have accomplished." The amazing thing about affirmations is that it is something you can do anywhere because it's simply thinking positive about who you are as a person.

Now the universal love, Agape is another kind of love that leads to having a healthy lifestyle. The book and now movie The Secret talks about how if positive thoughts are put into the universe, how they will be returned because they are attracting the energy to oneself. The idea for the book is based off of the law of attraction and how we can use it to our advantage. If you are able to find love in the people, places and things around you, then you are more likely to be a positive human being throughout your life. According to the law of attraction when you focus on positive thoughts, positive experiences will come into your life. When you focus on negative thoughts, then negative experiences will be what you are drawn to. So with this in mind if we have more favorable influences, we in turn will be more positive and attract the same energy back to us. In the religion Agape it is considered God's love for mankind, it is unconditional to the point that it transcends, it serves regardless of any situation. Implementing a self-less

kind of love which in the end will benefit any lifestyle because people become satisfied with what they have in their lives.

Learning about each type of love not only makes you self-aware, but it makes you aware of others people's feelings as well. With life follows love. We as humans develop and understand the idea of love as we progress and develop. Love is not a physical state of being, such as showing acts of affection. With that in mind, it makes it that much more challenging to pinpoint the exact definition of love. Love goes far beyond our understanding because no matter what, even through death, love will still somehow continue on. It is valuable that we as humans try to understand how important love is to have in one's life. In the modern world we are seeing that one of the leading causes of death is suicide. If there are ways to change ones lifestyle to live a better life, we must do our part and try so more people could have the knowledge to make a difference. We have the opportunity to possibly be able to create change in the lives of others, especially for those who feel alone, so why not be a part of the change that the world needs? *Start by loving yourself and loving other's.*

Kayla - Florida to California, **USA**
(Written for a college essay, shared as a gift for the world to read)

LOVE LINK #311

Love is...
Being in the flow!

Love is the flow of the Universe; it is the powerful unseen whose force can change worlds. Love is the essence of all there is and is beyond space and time. Love is seeing the beauty in everything and honoring it within everyone. Love is a frequency of alignment where magic happens!

Amber Sibley
London, England **United Kingdom**

LOVE LINK #312

Love IS...
The only driving force in the universe!

Paul Luftenegger
Born: **CANADA**
Resides: **WORLDWIDE**

"I am a citizen of the world
and the universe"

LOVE LINK #313

Love is...
The most important emotion there is,
as we are heading into our new world.

-Dolores Cannon

St. Louis, Missouri **USA**
Researcher for Nostradamus
Shared By: Terri Lynne

I, Terri Lynne couldn't agree more with
Dolores Cannon's statement above!

LOVE LINK #314

Love is...
What makes life worth living!

Dana D.
California, **USA**

LOVE LINK #315

Love is...
Love = Trust = Happiness

I not only find love in friendships, but also in a committed relationship. I find love in a significant other.

Yes, I have kids that I love in an unconditional way, which is a form of love that needs no explanation. But to love a partner and a significant other, for me is a different form of love. This kind of love feels like it is easy in certain peaceful moments and difficult at other times. I use to think that love was always just good all the time. But what I have learned over the course of my life is that you really know how much someone is capable of loving you, when the times get hard, really hard. Then to come out stronger of a bond with another, well to me that equals what LOVE is. I strongly feel that love starts with trust, as well as being able to share all with that person! All of yourself, all your dark, happy, and sad moments and they are by your side no matter what comes your way! They just want every bit of you, no matter the time of day. You are each other's rock! You are able to forgive and forget.

LOVE IS... easy. LOVE IS... hard.
But ultimately with the right person, your
person, then LOVE IS... GREAT!

Richard Tachin
Aka: Cali Rae's Dog Groomer
California, **USA**

LOVE LINK # 316
Dedicated to: The Silberman Family

LOVE IS... never allowing LOVE to die!

Max Silberman will live on in the hearts and souls of all who loved him upon earth and still LOVE him until they meet again!

LOVE IS... ETERNAL!
~ Rest In Peace ~

MAX SILBERMAN
3/31/1992 ~ 6/29/2017
USA to HEAVEN

LOVE LINK #189 Continued...

"Love is...
A Vibration!"

"Love is... the vibration of our true nature, which creates and sustains all things.

The more love you are able to share, the more love will be drawn unto you in a never-ending spiral, a spiritual dance with the Divine. This is the ultimate of our existence ~ to love and to be loved. It's as simple as that."

Author Unknown
Shared By: Krista Eiberg-Kubik
California, **USA**
On Valentine's Day 2017

LOVE LINK #317

Love is ...
like a *butterfly*
it goes where it pleases and it pleases where it goes...

Terri Lynne

Michelle Lewis
NEW ZEALAND
Dedicated to: Terri Lynne

Section Two

MIRACLE BABIES

BORN throughout the BIRTH of our LOVE story!

LOVE LINK #1

CONGRATULATIONS to the parents and the new born babies conceived throughout the development and birth of this book!

I BELIEVE children are our future and I am choosing to ask for all of us to teach the children well, by educating the world about what LOVE IS!

WITH LOVE, HEALTH, PEACE, and HAPPINESS,
From My Heart To All Of Yours,
Terri Lynne - TL Whispers - California, **USA**

LOVE LINK #318

LOVE IS...

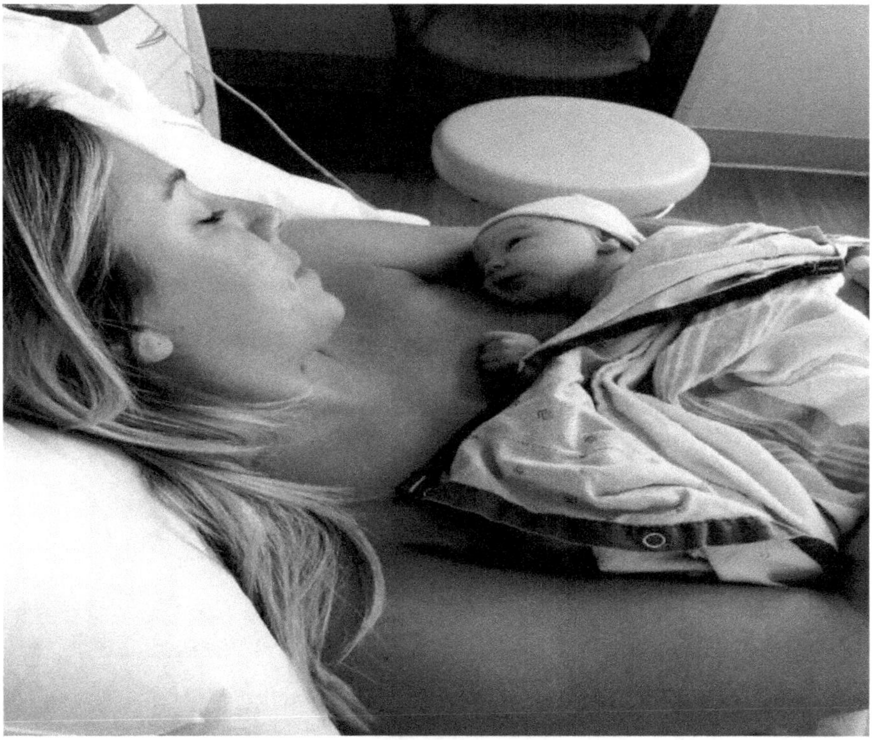

EMERY PARKER

DOB: July 15, 2015
Height: 20 inches
Weight: 6 lbs. 10 oz.
Time Of Birth: 5:15 PM
Resides: California, **USA**
PROUD PARENTS: Ashley and Cory

LOVE LINK #319

LOVE IS...
Being a Grandma for the first time and feeling your heart fill with life!

Maria De Los Angeles and Grandson DANIEL

PROUD PARENTS: Lissette and Dan

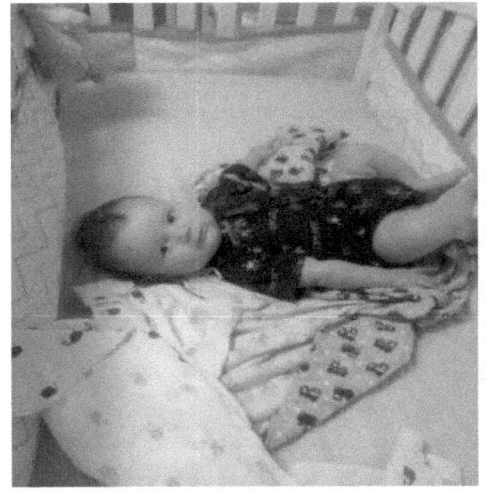

LOVE IS...
DANIEL

DOB: December 13, 2015
Weight: 8 Lbs. 11 Oz.
Height: 26"
Time: 11:15 PM
Resides: California, **USA**

LOVE LINK #320

LOVE IS...
LIAM RAPHAEL

DOB: January 11, 2016
Weight: 3 ½ Kilos
No Height given until they see the consultant
Time: 11:05 AM
Resides: **ISRAEL**
PROUD PARENTS: Arie and Yardena

LOVE LINK #321

LOVE IS...

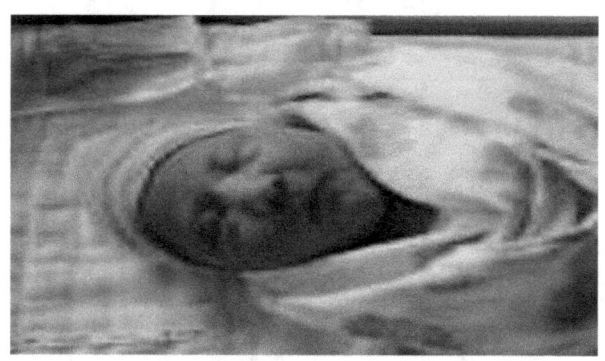

PATRICK THOMAS

DOB: May 31, 2016
Weight: 10 Lbs. 1 oz.
Height: 21"
Time: 2:22 PM
Born: Bellevue, Washington, **USA**
PROUD PARENTS: Courtney and Gordie

Patrick Thomas with:
Gordie (Daddy) with Grandpa (Tom)

LOVE LINK #322

Grand parenting LOVE, IS...
perfect and without an agenda.

Patrick Thomas with: Grandma Shelley
Washington, **USA**

LOVE LINK #323

LOVE IS...

CARSEN LEE

DOB: July 17, 2016
Height: 21.5 Inches
Weight: 10.14 Lbs.
Time: 4:45 AM
Resides: Indio, California, **USA**
PROUD PARENTS: Maurae and Ryan

LOVE LINK #324

LOVE IS...
Being BORN into this FAMILY!

Maurae, Tommy, Ryan and Carson

LOVE LINK #325
LOVE IS...
Holding a baby in your arms,
Even when it's not your own!

David resides in Orange County, CA **USA**

LOVE LINK #326
LOVE IS...

MATTHEW HARRISON MEIER
DOB: August 20, 2016
Height: 21.5"
Weight: 8 lbs. 3 oz.
Time: 8:54 pm
Resides: Mission Viejo, California, **USA**
PROUD PARENTS: Katelyn and Andy

LOVE LINK #327

LOVE IS...
Being my Son's Teacher & Coach!

Katelyn and Matthew Harrison
California, **USA**

We just got our family holiday photos back and they gave me all the feels.

~

Looking at the pictures of our little family has highlighted just how much this little nugget has completely and utterly changed my world. I expected things would change, but I never knew how truly amazing it would feel until now. He's made me feel every emotion more deeply; he's taught me the true meaning of the word LOVE, and he's made me more patient, more giving, more kind, and more compassionate. He's shown me my true strength, and just how brave I can be. He's slowed me down, calmed my soul, and made me appreciate the little things in life even more. He's shown me that my true purpose in life is to be his "Mama," and that I've subsequently been elevated to the most important teaching job I could ever have.

Because of him, I am gentler, more thankful, and I smile more than I ever have before. He is the single greatest blessing in my life, and I could not be more in LOVE with him.

Kate Meier Aka: "Coach Kate"
Dedicated to our son, Matt!

LOVE LINK #328

LOVE IS...

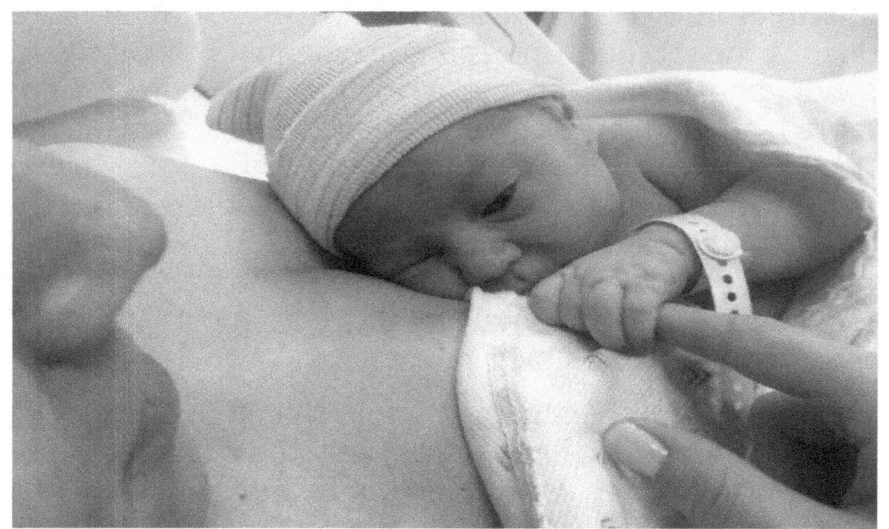

DECLAN SIMON

DOB: November 8, 2016
Height: 19"
Weight: 7 lbs. 5 oz.
Time: 2:30 PM
Resides: Tarzana, California, **USA**
PROUD PARENTS: Cara and Scott

LOVE IS...
Family United!

CARA & SCOTT'S PARENTS & AUNTS & UNCLES

CARA (Mommy) and DECLAN (Baby) - Middle
JAY (Poppy) Left and DEBBIE (Grandma) Right
California, **USA**

LOVE LINK #329

LOVE IS...
ROBERT SANFORD BUCKLEY IV

DOB: November 13, 2016
Height: 22"
Weight: 8 lbs. 10 oz.
Time: 4:33 PM
Resides: Florida, **USA**

PROUD PARENTS: Kayla & Robert

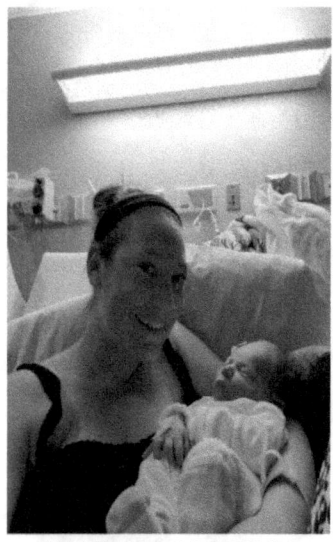

KAYLA - MOMMY   MISSY - Grandma

"Yesterday was the best day of my life as we got to meet our beautiful Baby boy! Thank you everyone for your warm wishes and visits to meet little Robert. We love you all!"

LOVE IS... my son!

LOVE LINK #330

LOVE IS...

SOLOMON IVOR METCALFE-DAVIES

DOB: January 6, 2017
Weight: 7.2 Lbs.
No Height given until they see consultant
Time: 12:16 Hours
Resides: SOUTH WALES, **UNITED KINGDOM**
PROUD PARENTS: Steven & Camille

Here is my family... Before I entered their world!

Sophie Metcalfe-Davies Born: 17-12-12
Sienna Metcalfe-Davies Born: 13-12-13
Stephen (Proud Daddy) and Camille (Proud Mommy)

LOVE LINK #331

LOVE IS...

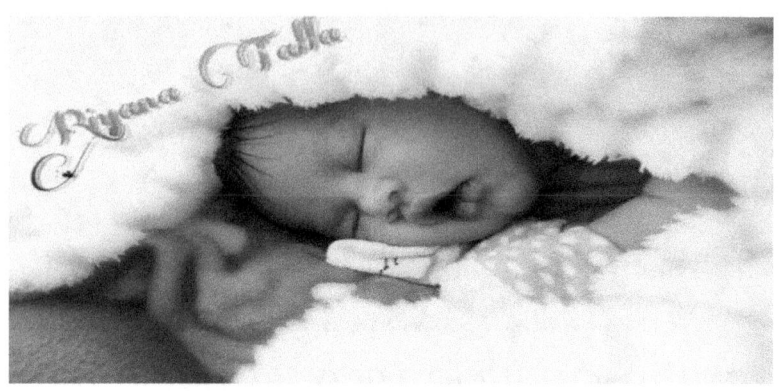

RIYANA TALLA

DOB: December 6, 2017
Weigh: 7.8 Lbs.
Height: 20.5"
Time: 5:48 AM
Resides: California, **USA**

PROUD PARENTS: Sri & Vinay

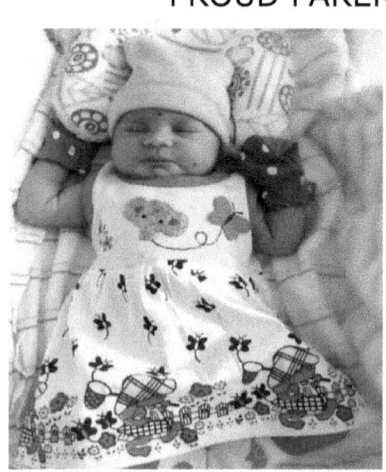 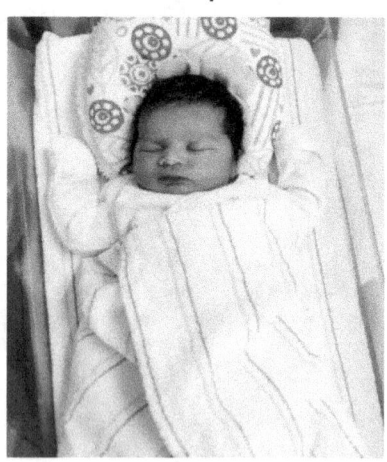

***Added during editing process because this princess couldn't be left out! Love, CaliNani

LOVE LINK #1

"Teach The Children Well"

All the children being born now,
are the futures, for our tomorrow!
So we must teach them well today!

Let US teach them what LOVE IS...
in every present moment of every
blessed day!

We can do this simply by being
whom we are BORN to be!
So they can be who they are
born to be, exponentially!

Our spirits know who we are
which is... LOVE!!!
Just ask your Spirit Guides and your
Angels from above!

As we "UNITE" through "LOVE,"
we will be teaching the children well!
Then listen for another angel in heaven
ringing their bell!

This bell reflects another angel earning their wings,
Then listen for heavens voices in unison showing us
the joy to them this brings!

Through this "LOVE" we will " UNITE,"
Giving our children their WINGS to take flight!

This is my wish and my big dream,
Now all I ask of you is to join my divine team!

Take my hand and then touch another's heart,
While knowing by you holding this book now, shows
me we are off to a great start!

Children are our future so let's give them what they
need,
With LOVE in their hearts they WILL ALWAYS and
FOREVER... SUCCEED!

With heartfelt LOVE for all these Angels,
Terri Lynne

Image of Brandon and Brittany
when little dancing together

This book was created and designed to TEACH
MY CHILDREN WELL from then to now and now
throughout the rest of their blessed lives!

Section Three

In The Circle We Are All Equal

When in the Circle

No one is in Front
No one is Behind
No one is Above
No one is Below

Love is...
Equality

Terri Lynne

Introducing
TERRI LYNNE'S
INNER AND OUTER
Circle of Angels

INTRODUCING TERRI LYNNE'S

Inner Circle of Angels

Terri Lynne

"A small group of thoughtful people could change the world. Indeed, it's the only thing that ever has."

\- Margaret Mead

LOVE LINK #1

TERRI LYNNE
"ANGEL OF LOVE"

TERRI LYNNE
Love is...
Terri Lynne's Circle Of Angels!

"Just A Mom"
California, **USA**

LOVE LINK #2

BIG AL
"ANGEL OF TRUTH & FAMILY DEDICATION"

(Witnessing the TRUTH through Observations)

ALLEN M.

Terri Lynne's Husband
30+ years of Marriage
"Real Estate Appraiser"
The "Witness" of TL'S Life!
California, **USA**

LOVE LINK #3

BRANDON
Aka: "Slick"
"ANGEL OF HEALING"
(Healing Mind, Heart, Body, Soul and Spirit)

BRANDON MURRAY

Terri Lynne's Son and Best Friend!
"Doctor To Be"
California, **USA**

LOVE LINK #4

BRITTANY
Aka: "Honey"
"ANGEL OF HOPE AND HUMANITY"
(Creating Human's Unity)

BRITTANY MAURAE

Terri Lynne's Daughter and Best Friend!
"Event Producer"
California, **USA**

LOVE LINK #288

VICTORIA
"ANGEL OF EARTH'S VILLAGE"

Terri/Vicki Vicki/Terri

VICTORIA POWELLS-CONWAY

Best Friends since 4th Grade, 49+ Years
"Retired Pre School Owner"
"SOUL SISTERS" throughout Eternity!
California, **USA**

LOVE LINK #69

"ANGEL OF CORE VALUES"

Dr. Phyllis Weinstein-Siebold

Friends/Sisters by choice 40+ years
"Podiatrist" California, **USA**

LOVE LINK #279

JEANNE
"ANGEL OF THE LAW AND THE FACTS"

"Attorney" (Terri Lynne's ANGEL/Cousin)
California, **USA**

LOVE LINK #12

DENIS
"ANGEL OF THE TIDE"
(Flow and Relaxation)

DENIS CORDOVA
AKA: DMAN
"Retired Contractor"
(Terri Lynne's "2nd Husband"/Al's Bff)

California, **USA**

LOVE LINK #46

LISA
"ANGEL OF EXPLORATION"
(Exploring the Body and the World)

LISA S.
Friends/Sisters by choice 37+Yrs
"Esthetician"
Boston - California, **USA**

LOVE LINK #189

KRISTA
"ANGEL OF PRANA"

(Prana is known as breath, a universal energy
that flows in and around the body)

KRISTA EIBERG-KUBIK

Friends/Soul Sisters 16+ years
"Yoga Instructor"
California, **USA**

LOVE LINK #104

CHAD
"ANGEL OF EVENT PRODUCTION"

"Angel of
Creating
Smiles"

CHAD EVERETT

Cousins and "Soul Mates"
Lifetime Connection
Florida, and California, **USA**

CHAD IS...
TL'S "ANGEL-STAR!" "Event Producer"

LOVE LINK #79

MARCI
"ANGEL OF ABUNDANCE"

MARCI R.

Cousin and Soul Sister
"Senior Web and Graphic Designer"
Creator of Terri Lynne's Website
www.UnitedLove.Love
Boston, Ma - California, **USA**

LOVE LINK #190

KAREN
"ANGEL OF COMPASSION"

KAREN FECHTOR-KRITZER

Born: Cousins and
By Choice: "Adopted Sisters"
Lifetime Connection "Stock Broker"
California and Boston, Massachusetts, **USA**

LOVE LINK #34
GALIT
"ANGEL OF INTEGRITY"

GALIT

Friends/Soul Sisters and Confidante's 10+ years
"Accounting and Finance Professional (CPA)"
ISRAEL - California, **USA**

396

LOVE LINK #43
JILL
"ANGEL OF GATHERING KNOWLEDGE"

Jill Marder-Meyer

Neighbors, Friends and Confidantes 20+ Years!
"Occupational Therapist and Pilates Instructor"
California, **USA**

LOVE LINK #17
ELONA
"ANGEL OF HONORARY KINSHIP"

Elona Booth

Friends & Confidante's For 19+ Years!
"Just A Mom"
California, **USA**

LOVE LINK #193

MARYANN
"ANGEL OF PRODUCTION"

Maryann Gray

Terri Lynne's "Soul Sister" 22+ Years
"Retired Producer/Director"
Victoria, Canada
SYNGAPORE - California - **CANADA**

LOVE LINK #229

NOREEN
"ANGEL OF THY COMPASS"
(Guiding Light and Direction)

Noreen Egurbide
NOREEN and TERRI LYNNE
Terri Lynne's "Friend/Soul Sister" 16+ years
"Life Coach - Wellness Navigator"
California, **USA**

LOVE LINK #226

LORI
"ANGEL OF PAWTNERSHIP"

Terri Lynne's "PAWTNER!"
We shared a dog named "Misty,"
Whom we both loved and will cherish forever!

Lori Hunter
"Esthetician" California, **USA**

LOVE LINK #58

GISELA
"ANGEL OF LOYALTY"

Gisela Boell

"Pilates Instructor"
Terri Lynne's "Friend and Confidante" 16+ years
GERMANY - California, **USA** - **GERMANY**

LOVE LINK #259

JENNY
"ANGEL OF KINDNESS"

Jenny Swire

"Fashion Director"
Friend and Confidante
SOUTH AFRICA - UNITED KINGDOM - California,
USA

LOVE LINK #223

Willy J.
"ANGEL OF ALOHA"

Willy Jacinto

Willy is Terri Lynne's Friend/Brother
33+ Years "Retired Fire Fighter" Hawaii, **USA**

LOVE LINK #142

SRI and VINAY
Sri - "ANGEL OF RESPECT"
Vinay - "ANGEL OF SINCERITY"

Together: "Angels of Technology"

Sri and Vinay Talla

"Computer Programmer's"
(Terri Lynne and Al's Adopted Children)
INDIA - California, **USA**

LOVE LINK #330

CHRISTINE
"ANGEL OF EMPATHY"

 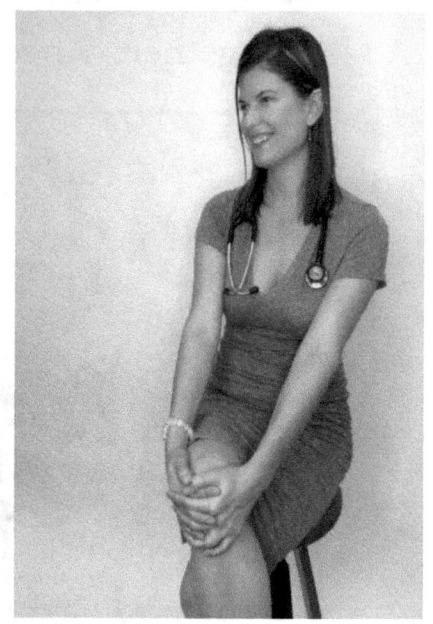

Dr. Christine Surrago-Kousouli

"Naturopathic Doctor & Homeopathy Specialist &
Herbalist"
A Doctor of Thy Mind, HEART, Body,
Soul and Spirit!
Kousouli Chiropractic Health and Wellness Inc.
California, **USA**

LOVE LINK #191

ROSANA
"ANGEL OF BEAUTY"

Rosana

"Hair Stylist and Color Technician"
(Terri Lynne's Sounding Board)
California, **USA**

INTRODUCING TERRI LYNNE'S

"A small group of thoughtful people could change the world. Indeed, it's the only thing that ever has."

-Margaret Mead

408

LOVE LINK #10

MICK
"ANGEL OF EARTH'S GARDEN"

Mick Smith

"Spiritual Partners"
Via Skype Chats on:
"TUESDAYS WITH TERRI"
"Mr. Mom" and Landscape Specialist
UNITED KINGDOM

LOVE LINK #0

FLORUS
"ANGEL OF ALCHEMY"

*Requested to remain a
silent partner and I am
respecting his wishes.

"Spiritual Partners"
"Ecological Land Developer"
NETHERLANDS - CHILE

LOVE LINK #29

GREGORY
"ANGEL OF TONE"

"LOVE IS A GIFT"
By: ARKANGELO

Gregory Fitzgibbon

A.K.A. "ARKANGELO"
Musician - Computer Technician - **USA**

LOVE LINK #143

CYNTHIA
"ANGEL OF HOPE"

Cynthia Fitzgibbon
Musician's Wife and Best Friend - **USA**

LOVE LINK #88

INDI
"ANGEL OF HOMELESS HOUSING"
(Called: The Flatts)

Indi "LOVE" Shan
- Retired Army "HERO" -
Terri Lynne's "Spiritual Partner"
INDIA - Melbourne, **AUSTRALIA**

LOVE LINK #75

GIRISH
"ANGEL OF MULTI-TASKING"

Girish Daga

"Energy Healer"
- Business Development Supervisor -
Mumbai, **INDIA** & **UNITED STATES OF AMERICA**

LOVE LINK #48

MISSY
"ANGEL OF NURTURING"

Missy Pope

Terri Lynne's "Soul Sistar"
"Care Giver"
Florida, **USA**

LOVE LINK #35

JOSEPH
"ANGEL OF NEW AGE EDUCATION"

Joseph Mercado

New York, **USA**
"Master Mind University Creator/Initiator" and
"Plenergy"

LOVE LINK #222

GABRIEL
"ANGEL OF DESIRE"

Gabriel Szczurek
- Poetry Master -
- Construction Professional -
Terri Lynne's "Soul Brother"
Victoria, **CANADA**

LOVE LINK #47

RYAN
"ANGEL OF PURITY"

Ryan "Lunawolf" Smith

- Photographer -
Insurance Broker
Terri Lynne's "Soul Little Brother"
UNITED KINGDOM

LOVE LINK #93

STEVE
"ANGEL OF CONNECTION"

(A Familiar Stranger to Terri Lynne)

"Realtor"
Born: Boston, Massachusetts
Resides: Tennessee, **USA**

LOVE LINK #63

CAROLYN
"ANGEL OF GOD'S MESSAGES"

Carolyn Shaw

Terri Lynne and Leslie's ANGEL!
"Care Giver"
California, **USA**

LOVE LINK #313

MARIA
"ANGEL OF CARE TAKING"

Maria De Los Angeles Calvo
Terri Lynne and Leslie's ANGEL!
"Care Giver"
California, **USA**

LOVE LINK #115

STEPHEN
"ANGEL OF UNITY"

Stephen Metcalf-Davies
"Peace Officer"

Born: Pontypool, South Wales.
Resides: South Wales, **UNITED KINGDOM**

LOVE LINK #283

CHAKRAVARTHY
"ANGEL OF THY HEART"

Chakravarthy Baddepudi

"Fashion Entrepreneur"
Born: Mumbai, **INDIA**
Resides: Amsterdam, **NETHERLANDS**

LOVE LINK #302

FERNANDO
"ANGEL OF ANIMAL SPIRITS"

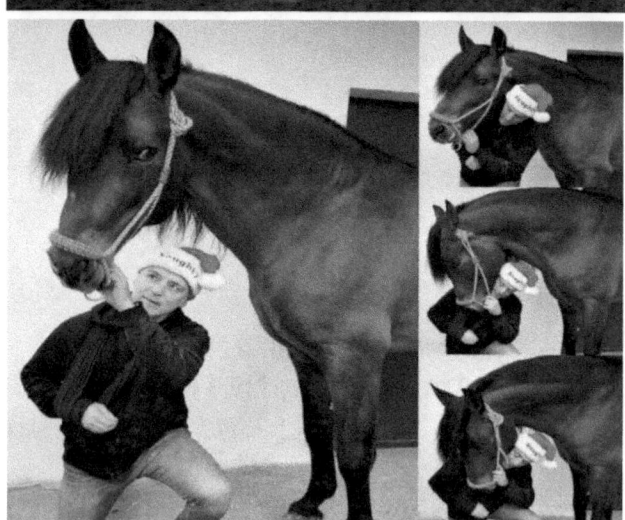

Fernando Herrero Del Valle

"Horse Trainer"
Madrid, **SPAIN**

LOVE LINK #188

ELSPETH
"ANGEL OF JOY"

Creator of "Deck of Joy" Cards

Elspeth Kerr
Soul reader of the heart
Author and creator of "Journey To Joy"
SCOTLAND – CYPRUS

LOVE LINK #306

PAUL
"ANGEL OF PEACE"

Albums by Paul Luftenegger
Available On All Major Streaming Networks
Conscious Kind Loving Music To Help The Heart & Soul From Within

Paul Luftenegger

International Multi Award Winning Singer/Songwriter
Inspiring Global Love & Kindness Through Music
CANADA – WORLDWIDE

LOVE IS...
finding your circle of angels and then
writing a story about uniting through
love together, for the universe to feel
our UNITED LOVE on every page!

Terri Lynne

Thank you to my tribe, for signing the contract agreeing to author each other into this life gratifying script. Enabling us to create this miracle together! This includes every spirit connected to this unique LOVE story; which is everyone born with a heartbeat!

Love is... what brings life full circle

Step out of
the Circle of Time
and into the
Circle of Love

Rumi

Thank you to all the "Angels" in my Circle for linking in "Love"
and for being the best example on this journey of souls,
uniting to spread our love far and wide!

Terri Lynne

I never could have embarked upon this journey
without each and every one of you **"ANGELS"** in my
"CIRCLE OF LOVE!"

I am eternally blessed!

With HEART felt gratitude and sincere appreciation
for each of **YOU!**

I LOVE YOU ALL!

Section Four

TERRI LYNNE'S LOVE IS... INSIGHTS!

LOVE LINK #1

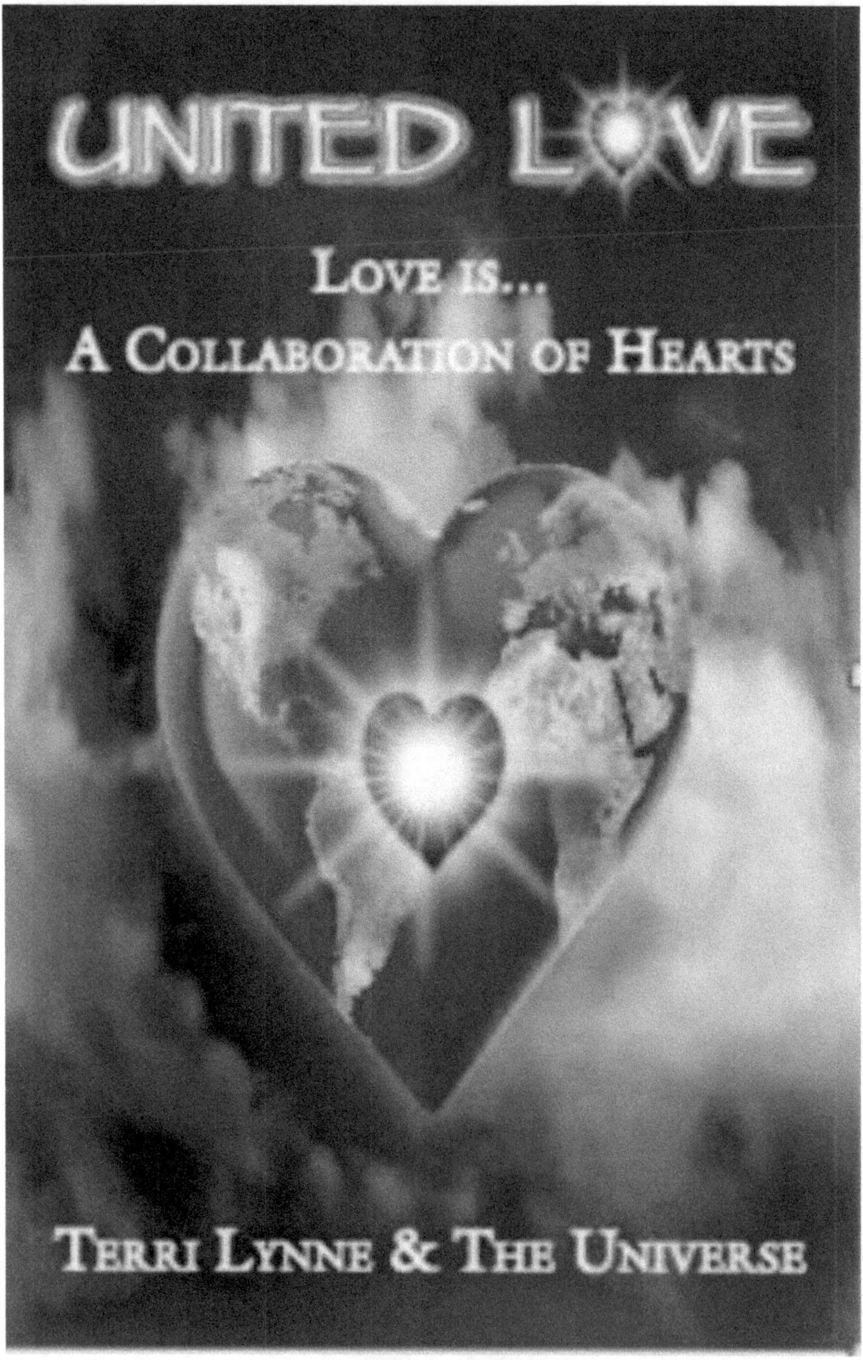
UNITED LOVE
LOVE IS...
A COLLABORATION OF HEARTS
TERRI LYNNE & THE UNIVERSE

LOVE LINK #1

LOVE IS...
OUR CHAIN OF LOVE!

Below are some LOVE IS messages that awakened
my spirit while collaborating with yours,
Offering you a glimpse into what I have learned about
love behind closed doors...
In hopes that this book allows you to feel LOVE
as it did for me by being LINK #1,
Connecting to all the souls throughout this book,
as our journey of LOVE has only just begun!
Below you will see some messages from my open
heart,
Then by sharing our "UNITED LOVE" connection
with your loved ones, my vision will be off to a great
start!
OUR LOVE STORY has been designed for each soul's
energy inside these pages, as well as the soul's
holding this book to please know,
That we should try to wear our heart on our sleeves
in order to allow our love light to glow, to grow and to
flow...
We are presently experiencing how my UNITED LOVE'S
BIG DREAM is coming true,
So once you turn the final page you will see how my
BIG DREAM was manifested for,

EACH

AND

EVERY

ONE

OF

YOU!

"LOVE IS...

My inner gift I extend out to the Universe. I fill myself with love, and I send that love out into the world. How others treat me is their path; how I react is mine.

Love is... my way!

Terri Lynne
www.UnitedLove.Love

I alone can not change the world
BUT I can cast a stone
across the waters
to create many ripples
- Mother Theresa

"LOVE IS... Creating Positive Changes Terri Lynne

LOVE IS...
SUPPORTING
ANOTHER

Terri Lynne

Love is...
supporting a familiar stranger, the same
way you would support your family and
your best friends!

Dedicated to: Steve Manley

Steve was diagnosed with Renal Cell Carcinoma, (Kidney Cancer) after being in a critical car accident, in which didn't end his life, but in turn SAVED HIS LIFE!

The tests to check for any serious injuries came back with the above diagnosis, which is presently contained inside his kidney and can be removed and he will go on and LIVE his blessed LIFE! Thank God!

The reason I am sharing Steve's story publically is because of my reaction to this story!

Steve and I met during the development of this book and his ENERGY has been infectious in my soul! He has been so supportive and always posts the most beautiful, inspirational, heartfelt messages sharing his positive outlook on life with the universe! Never once focusing on anything negative or political or expressing any religious banter, just uplifting messages full of warmth and sincerity!

To me, Steve is a familiar soul, but the news I just read breaks my heart, as if he is my family!!!

I am including this sad message in this book strictly to give a real life example of, HOW WE SHOULD ALL LOVE & SUPPORT EACH OTHER!!!

LOVE IS NOT...

Designed to only love those who can help you climb a corporate ladder, or those who give you compliments or to love someone only because they bought you a gift, or they have been in your life forever...

Love is...
being there whole-heartedly for another!

When given the opportunity,
always support a complete stranger
or a familiar soul, just because!
2-23-17

Please accept that this message was added just after the book was complete, because this was an important fact of life for the universe to understand, to feel and to remember.

Thank you Steve Manley for giving me your permission to share our connection and may you continue to HEAL YOURSELF, so we can be blessed to have you continue to be a HEALING influence upon Earth!

Shared with Heartfelt LOVE,
Terri Lynne,
California, **USA**

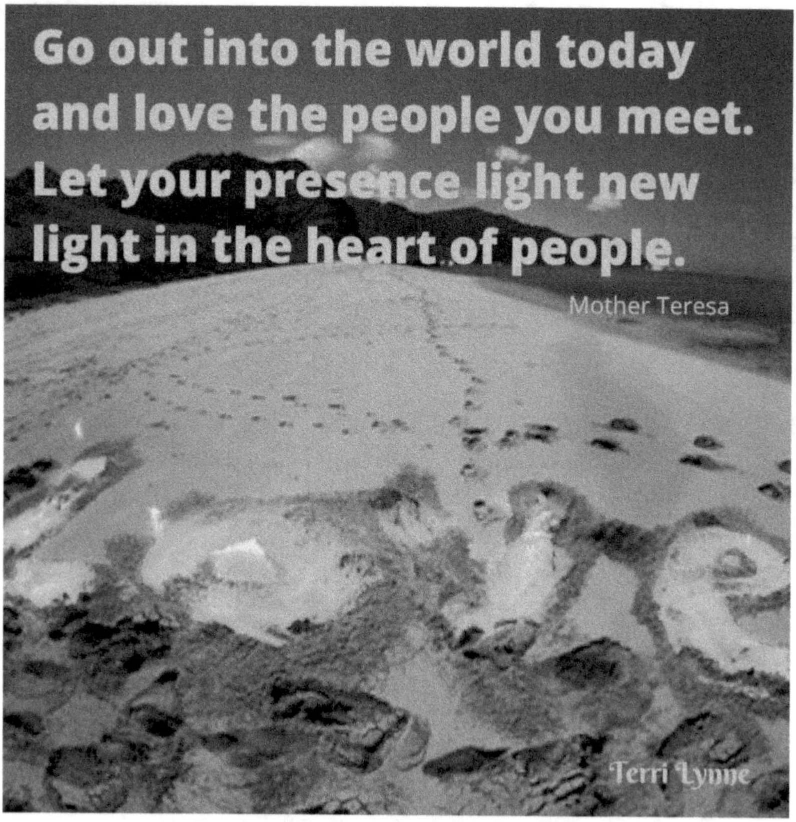

Go out into the world today and love the people you meet. Let your presence light new light in the heart of people.

Mother Teresa

Terri Lynne

-*Mother Teresa*

This is a great place to start to heal the world through all of what... Love is!

TL WHISPERS
LESSONS TO TEACH OUR CHILDREN
WELL

Love is...
designed in your own mirror, then
projected out into the world, so the world
can see your reflection, in their mirror to
project!

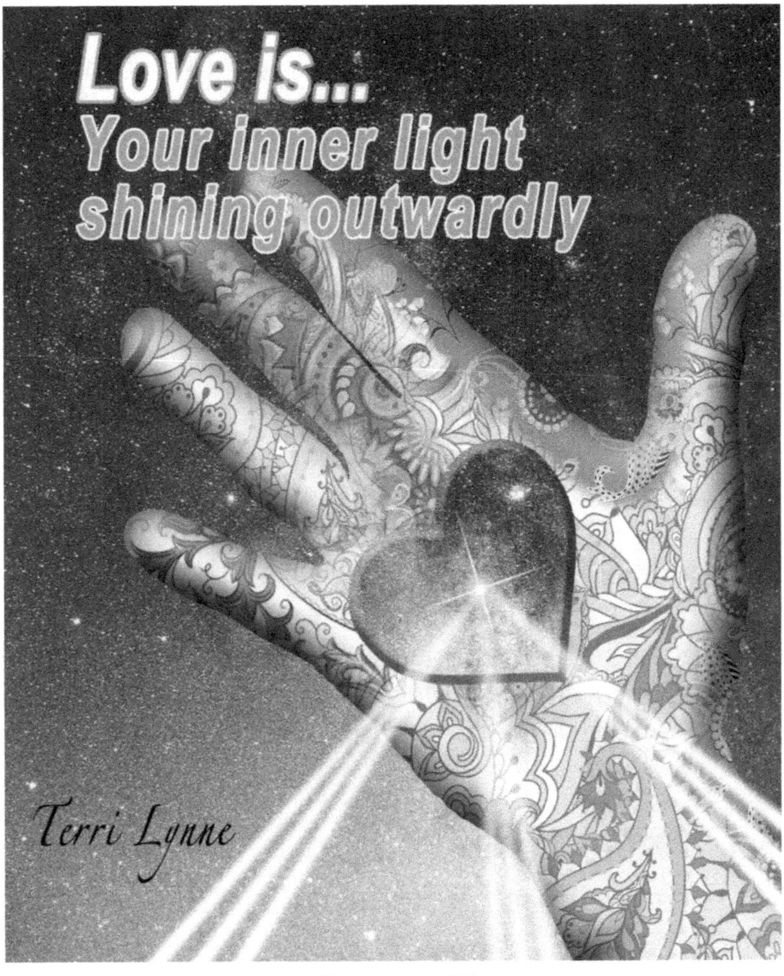

This is... our CHAIN OF LOVE!

Love is...
what I have chosen to project and to reflect!

Loving oneself is not being conceited; not loving yourself is allowing yourself to be mistreated! Please give yourself the gift of taking the time to learn what love is, and then project all you've learned by reflecting your love on to another. This is the greatest gift exchange upon earth! The simple SOLUTION, which is my intention, reflects walking through life consciously acting upon embracing loving oneself, then touching another's life. Your ACTions will teach the souls you touch to LOVE their self, and then to hopefully pass their love on through their ACTions to another! This is the Chain reACTion and the reason I accepted this journey! All are invited to be a LINK in this CHAIN of LOVE!

I believe the greatest love of all is... when you master loving yourself!

I pray you can learn this lesson, so you can pass this great lesson of love forward by teaching the children all you have learned. This way they will have the answer of what love is, without needing to spend their entire blessed life asking questions. Instead they will be living the solution, which is to *Live Love*, by loving their self and all others throughout the Universe, while sharing their open heart full of love with everyone everywhere without fear blocking Universal love from flowing freely!

Love is...
free and one should never have to pay a price for something that should be evenly exchanged.

"LOVE is... the missing piece needed to solve the puzzle of life!

Each of us holds a KEY to be used in order to complete this masterpiece. In turn creating PEACE on earth.

Terri Lynne

Here are some KEY ways to LOVE YOURSELF:

-Treat yourself respectfully
-Be honest with yourself
-Don't be too hard on yourself
-Be your own best friend

-Love Your Mirror's Reflection

-Solve emotions
(The Emotion Code – Dr. Bradley Nelson)
-Carry an open heart
-Don't carry baggage, forgive those whom broke your
spirit, so your spirit can recognize when love is in front
of you
-Send yourself light and love
-Listen to the whispers from spirit above and within
-Read the signs along life's way
-Trust in the process called life
-Say what you mean and mean what you say
-Don't judge yourself or others
*-Love yourself unconditionally and love others without
conditions attached to their love*
-Let love flow to you and through you
-Breathe in love and breathe love out into the world

-Balance your chakras

-Believe In Miracles

-Tap out what you don't need in you

(Nick and Jessica Ortner)

The Tapping Solution By: Nick Ortner

-Remember, the TRUTH you cannot lie about,

so always tell the TRUTH, especially to yourself!

-Love yourself without judgments, conditions or expectations and love everyone, everywhere this way as well

-Be the change you wish to see in the world

-Listen to the whispers of your heart

-Trust your own spirit

-Release Fear

-Let go and let higher powers steer your wheel

-Dance to your own beat

-Follow your own soul's lead

-Give LOVE away freely and accept receiving LOVE

-Dream BIG

-Then after you pay attention to all of the above:

-Practice Ho'oponopono (By: Dr. Hew Len)

And then keep practicing his teaching by erasing all you've learned, while repeating these words as often as you can:

I LOVE YOU

I'M SORRY

PLEASE FORGIVE ME

THANK YOU

Then JUST BE, while observing MIRACLES upon
MIRACLES appearing in your life!

LIVE LOVE every blessed day,
then be certain your life will be one well lived...
by living love in this way!

LOVE and BE-LOVED!

"SELF LOVE
IS...
PEACEFUL

UNCONDITIONAL SELF LOVE
IS AN OUTER REFLECTION OF
EXPRESSING INNER PEACE

Terri Lynne

Love is... found in front of your own eyes!
A vision for the entire world to see!

"LOVE IS...
Viewed in your mirror's reflection!

Terri Lynne

443

LOVE LINKS #1, 3 & 4

Love is...
the bond between a mom and her
children...

An unbreakable tie that is a win, win!
A love forever in your heart,
up close and personal or miles apart...
A love so strong,
lasting forever long!
The greatest gift two hearts can feel,
a blessing from above and a feeling so very real!

Dedicated to my "MIRACLES"
Brandon Murray and Brittany Maurae

Love is... my MIRACLES and my greatest
BLESSINGS, my children!

Love is... giving birth to your two "Best Friends" in the entire world and then observing how they see and feel each other as their "Best Friend" in the entire world too! This is a Mom's greatest "GIFT" to be a witness of! Brandon Murray and Brittany Maurae, thank you for being Ma Mum's best friends!

Love is... found in every day miracles!

LOVE IS...
child birth and
each child's
birth
is a...
MIRACLE to
LOVE!

Terri Lynne

TL WHISPERS
What MIRACLES means to me:
MIRACLES:
Monumental Impressions Reiterating Awareness
Creating Liberating Euphoric Surprises!

Love is...
having a daughter and a grand-dogter
as action heroes!
Wonder Woman Jr. and Wonder Dog

LOVE LINK #1 & LOVE LINK #89

Love is...
praying for another's healing!
(Terri Lynne praying for Indi Shan)

" Love is... Healing!
Use your love to heal
yourself; in turn you
will be loving
and healing
others!

Terri Lynne

***Note:

Indi is paralyzed presently, due to a spine surgery causing paralysis of his legs. Praying for a MIRACLE that Indi WILL walk again very soon! His mission and purpose in life is designed to be teaching the Universe about what unconditional LOVE IS!!! As you have witnessed in his love link messages above.

Love is...
in the eyes of the beholder!

LOVE IS...

A gift for the eyes of your heart to see!
Terri Lynne

448

Love is… experienced upon Love's Highway!

"**Love Is…**

God's gift to us.
When we leave
footprints in the sand;
by heading in the
direction of
LOVE'S HIGHWAY,
then we will be
spreading this gift.
This will be our gift of
love returned.

Terri Lynne

449

Love is...
the bridge filling in the gaps of one to another!

" Love is...
The BRIDGE
connecting you & I,
Then...
Heaven & Earth!

L
O
V
E

Terri Lynne

450

Love is...
within and this you can't live without!

" LOVE IS...

In your mirror and
always within sight,
If lost just search
your soul to find
your inner light.

Terri Lynne

Love is... the key to unlimited bliss!

"Self Love... is the KEY!

Dear Self,

I know you're doing the

best you can.

I believe in you.

I love you!

Love Me

Terri Lynne

Love is... the truest test of time!

Love Is...
Sunrises and Sunsets,
The only true reflection
of time upon earth.

Terri Lynne

Love is... being in the flow,
feeling one with the universe!

"LOVE IS...
Riding the waves
and going with the flow,
Enjoying the highs
while letting go!

Terri Lynne

Love is... the purest affirmation!

Love Is... Loving Thy Self!

SELF LOVE   AFFIRMATION

I love my life. I love my mind. I love my heart.
I love my body. I love my soul. I love my spirit.
I love my home. I love my family. I love my
friends. I love my sensitivity. I love my sense of
humor. I love my eyes. I love to feel inspired. I
love to inspire others. I love to feel vibrant. I
love my energy. I love to sleep. I love to take
time to just be still. I love to breathe.
I love to laugh. I love to celebrate every
precious moment of my life. I love
dreaming big. I love my mirror's
reflection. I love believing
in miracles. I love to
spread love!

I LOVE ME! Terri Lynne

Love is... predestined!

Love is... the recipe for success!

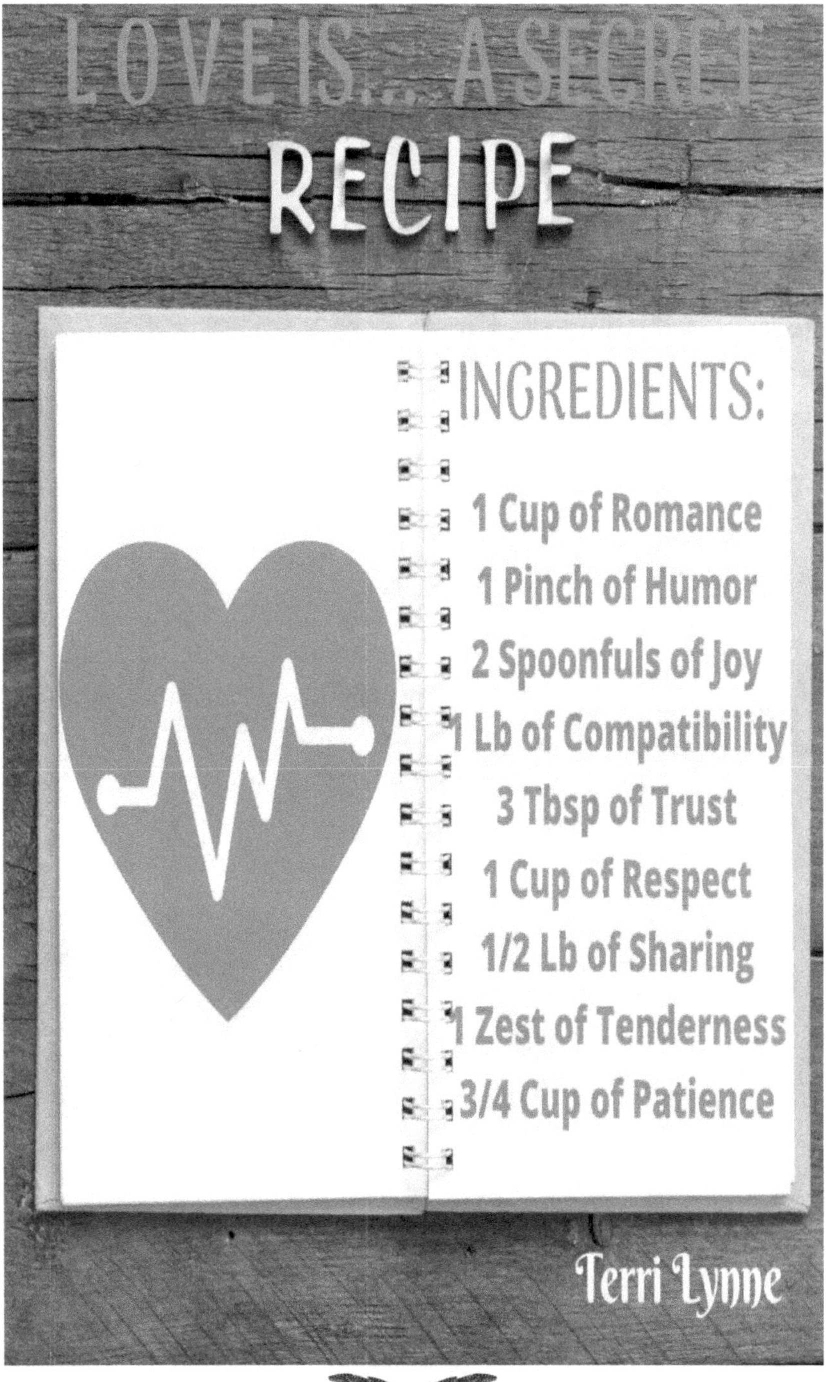

LOVE IS... A SECRET

RECIPE

INGREDIENTS:

1 Cup of Romance

1 Pinch of Humor

2 Spoonfuls of Joy

1 Lb of Compatibility

3 Tbsp of Trust

1 Cup of Respect

1/2 Lb of Sharing

1 Zest of Tenderness

3/4 Cup of Patience

Terri Lynne

Love is... held within our own hands, designed to touch another with all the love we hold!

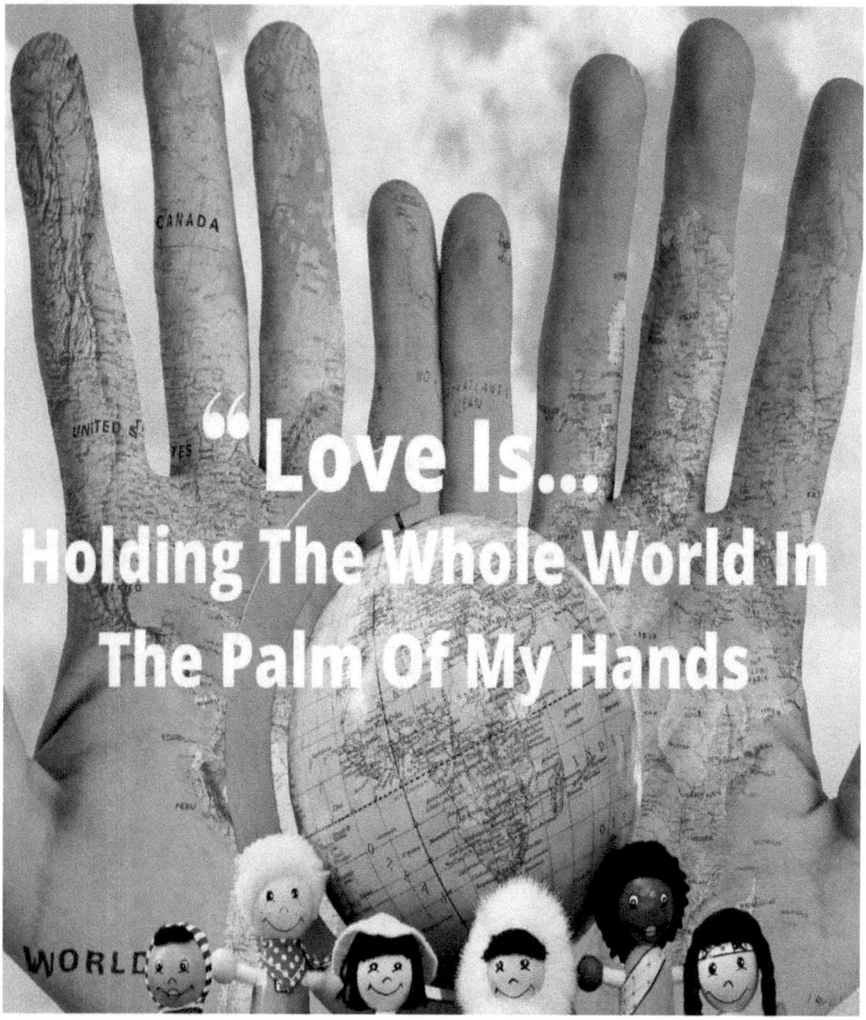

Love is... a free spirit once healed!

When we share love and understanding
we share two of the most healing
properties in the world.

Let's Live

LOVE is...

the healing power and will

set your spirit free.

Terri Lynne

Love is... putting our children first!

LOVE IS... putting another's needs before
your own.   Terri Lynne

Love is... a healed heart!

461

Love is... what I prescribe for you!

LOVE, is...
The Best
Medicine!

A PHYSICIAN ONCE SAID, "THE BEST MEDICINE FOR HUMANS IS LOVE." SOMEONE ASKED, "WHAT IF IT DOESN'T WORK?" HE SMILED AND SAID, "INCREASE THE DOSE."

Terri Lynne

Love is... here to stay!

"LOVE IS... ALL WE SHOULD KEEP!

Keep loving through the violence,
Keep loving through the hate,
Keep loving through the silence,
Keep loving through debate,
Keep loving through confusion,
Keep loving through regrets,
Keep loving through illusion,
Keep loving through the threats,
Keep loving through indifference,
Keep loving through the madness,
Keep loving through resistance,
Keep loving through the sadness,
Keep loving through the stress,
Keep loving through the insight,
Keep loving through the mess,
Keep loving through the darkness,
until you see the light,
Keep loving; until loving is... all that's left
to keep!   Terri Lynne

Love is...
to be reciprocated and repeated
over and over and over again!

LOVE OVER HATE
LOVE OVER INDIFFERENCE
LOVE OVER IGNORANCE
LOVE OVER EGO
LOVE OVER FEAR
LOVE OVER BARRIERS
LOVE OVER BORDERS
LOVE
OVER AND OVER AND
OVER AGAIN

Terri Lynne

Love is...
for everyone everywhere,
without discrimination!

LOVE IS... WELCOME

ALL AGES - ALL COLORS

ALL SIZES - ALL CULTURES

ALL GENDERS - ALL BELIEFS

ALL RELIGIONS

ALL SPIRITS - ALL SOULS

ALL PEOPLE

LOVE IS... SAFE HERE

Terri Lynne

Love is... complete acceptance!

465

Love is... the greatest vision!
2020 Vision!
Love is... a perfect vision!

LOVE IS...

Seen through the eyes of one's soul and designed through the eyes of one's spirit

Terri Lynne

Love is... for everyone!

Love is... the connecting force!

Love **is...**

The thread; connecting one to all!

Love is...
our connection
to all that is,
which is all of
who we are!

Terri Lynne

468

Love is... staying!

REACH FOR ME

Reach for me,
If together we cannot be...
Long for our embrace,
When we cannot see each other's face...
Let me hear your voice,
During moments when time separates us
due to circumstance; but not by choice...
Even when we are miles apart let us feel one another still,
To know our love will grow stronger due to our own free will...
May your scent leave a trail whether you are near or far away,
My hope is for me to be close to you,
by you staying beside me each and every blessed day...
Continue showing me the way so I
can count on reaching out for you,
Now reach for me; always and forever
celebrating the day we said, "I Do!"

Terri Lynne

*Love is... holding on to a void of space,
simply by never letting go to all that fills that
empty place!*

Love is...
The Universal
Language

Terri Lynne

Love is... limitless!
Love is... without boundaries!
Love is... who you are and
Love is... who we are born to be!

So please be... a LOVE magnet!
And please, pass our LOVE on...

From our open hearts full of love to yours,
created to share with your loved ones,
near and beyond, to pass on...

Love is... forgiveness!

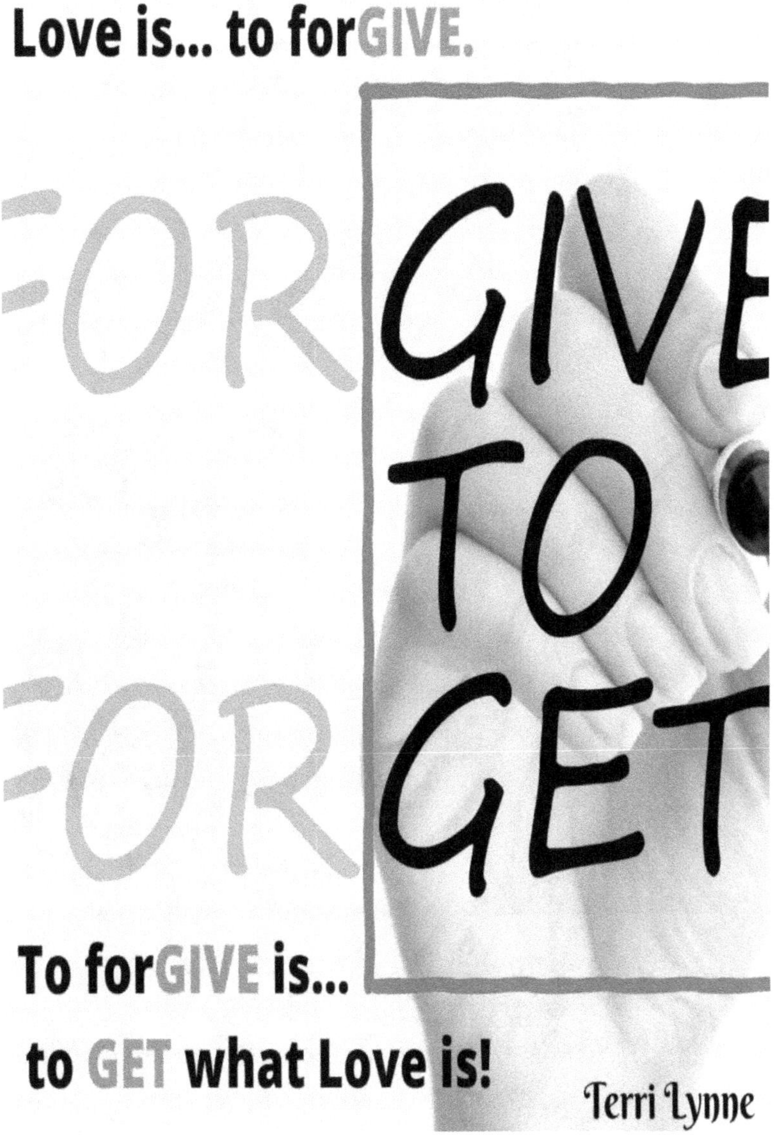

Love is... to forGIVE.

**To forGIVE is...
to GET what Love is!**
Terri Lynne

*Forgiveness is... the key,
which opens your heart to feel all of what
LOVE IS!*

471

Love is...
creating a "Miracle!"

- Uniting a FAMILY back together -
For a great CELEBRATION!!!
Brandon's College Graduation 2016!
(Summa Cum Laude Honors)

L-R:
Al, Terri Lynne, Rose, Papa Man, Brandon,
Brittany
and Nani/ Mom - (RIP)

Love is... colorful!

"Love Is... Seeing The RAINBOWS Beyond The Rain."

Terri Lynne

Love is...
Our MIRACLES!
Brandon Murray and Brittany Maurae

Love is...
What DREAMS are made of!

Love is...
Brotherly - Sisterly L O V E!!!
Brandon and Brittany

Love is...
all that children and adults need,
to succeed!

All the children being born now,
Are the futures for our tomorrows,
So we must teach them well today!
Let us teach them what
LOVE IS...
Every present moment of each
new day!
Simply by teaching them who we
are and
Who they are born to be,
So we all can be united in a
beautiful world,
Full of love eternally!

Terri Lynne

FLY upon the wings of love
to truly be capable of LOVING another!
Fly = First Love Yourself

Love is... what shines the brightest light!

LOVE IS...
Being another's lighthouse!
Shining light for another to find
their way out of the darkness.

Terri Lynne

Love is...
making memories before time runs out!

L-R Brittany, Terri Lynne,
Nani (RIP), Al and Brandon

Love is...
A BLESSING to be
THANKFUL for!

Thank you
Honey, Rose, Dad, Bubby and AL
for a GREAT LIFE!!!
Terri Lynne

Love is...
celebrations with family!

Karina, Rob, Auntie Junie, Ron, Marci, Terri Lynne, Al, Brandon, Rose, Dad (Papa Man)

Love is...
celebrating freedom of choice!

I chose this ladies son, to be my
husband and I received this lady
as my Mom-In-Law!
What a caring LADY she is and what a
LUCKY Daughter-In-Law I AM!

Terri Lynne and Mom M.

Love is...
celebrating the GIFT of LIFE!

Dedicated to Mom M/Nana
Happy 88th Birthday!

L-R Bottom Row
Barbara, Marla, Bill, Serena, Mom/Nana, Sarah, Tatum
L-R Top Row
Terri, Brandon, Al, Maurae, Sabrina,
Ryan, On Shoulders is Tommy

Love is...
good times with great friends...
I choose to call MY ANGELS!

L-R
Lori, Lisa, Krista, Terri Lynne, Noreen,
Galit and Phyllis
*California, **USA***

Love is...
adopting children, (as adults) from other countries, to love you as a third set of parents!

Sri Age: 26 and Vinay Age: 28
*Born: **INDIA** Reside: California, **USA***
*Adopted By: Terri Lynne and Al in America - **USA***

483

Love is...
fragile, yet unbreakable!

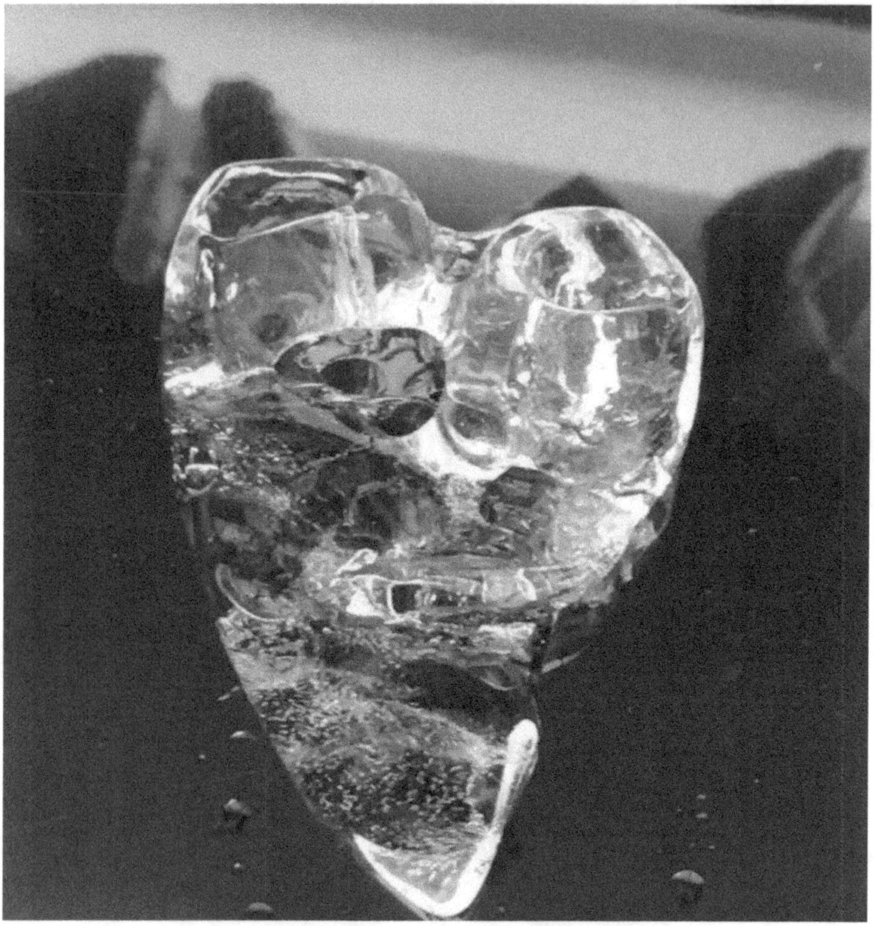

Share your HEART of glass
with another's HEART of glass
and then FEEL what LOVE IS...
when you make another's heart melt!

Love is...
a heart with many divots!

Reflective of how much it has been used.

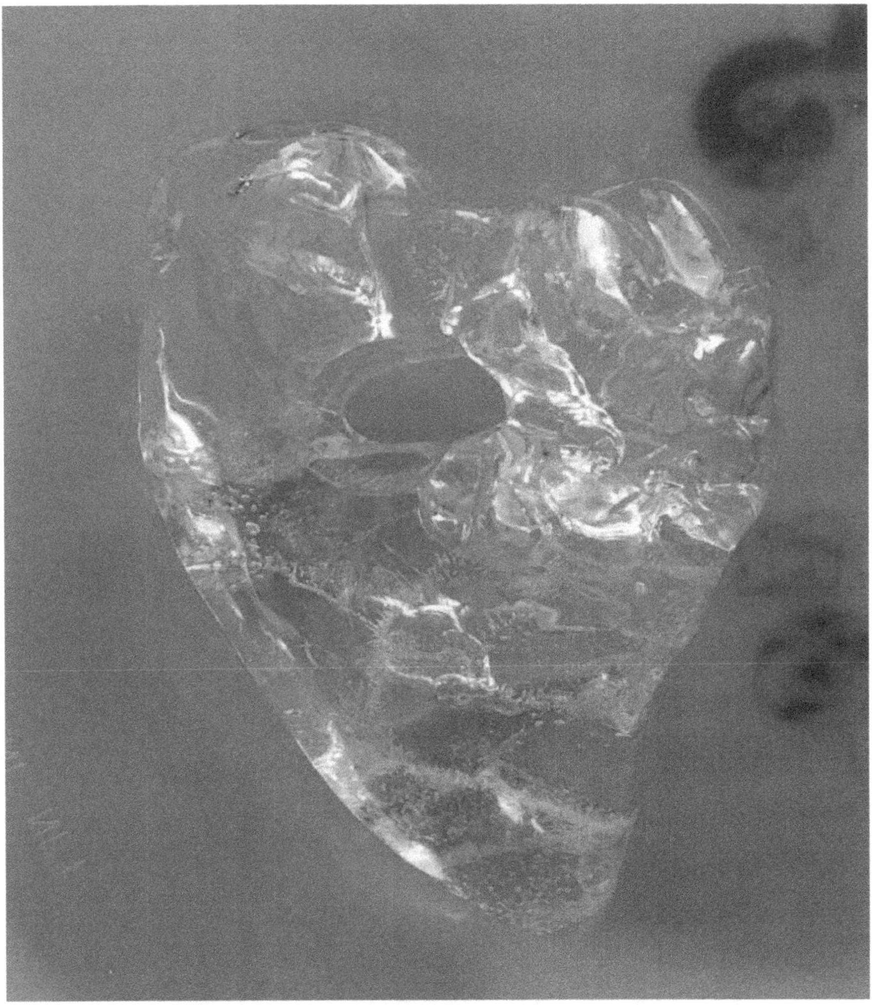

Use your HEART and watch it grow bigger,
stronger and become filled with
never-ending LOVE!

Love is...
observing our children following the
pathway of their dreams,
on to their purpose driven life!

Brandon in his younger years...

NOW Brandon is presently in Medical School...

I predict Brandon is on his way to becoming a Doctor of thy mind, heart, body, soul and spirit. Educating souls on how to make smart choices, in order to live a healthy life!

*Brittany is well on her way to be a leader,
born to deliver positive messages!
Graduated Valedictorian
of her college
San Diego State University 2018*

On the graduation podium delivering her
Valedictory message of "HOPE,"
Titled: "This One's For You!"

LOVE LINK #1 & LOVE LINK #4

This represents what LOVE IS...
to me!

-Varda Carmeli

My daughter in GERMANY sharing this message,
reflective of her and her mom's BIG DREAM!

Love is...
when your children KNOW your DREAMS
and aid in helping you pursue creating
your DREAMS to become the Universes
reality!

Photographer: Alejandro Avila
alxavila1www.instagram.com/alxavila1/
Photographer from Caracas, Venezuela

Love is...
having your parents and grandparents
with you on special occasions!

Terri and Al's Wedding Day
July 8, 1989

Love is...
staying together,
for 25+ Years!

Big Al & Terri Lynne
July 8, 2014

492

Love is... marriage!

![Big Al and Terri Lynne]

Big Al and Terri Lynne
*Cabo San Lucas, **MEXICO***
Celebrating 27 Years Married
July 8, 2016

"LOVE IS...
A CELEBRATION!

Terri Lynne

30 years of marriage is worth celebrating!

Terri and Al's Wedding Day
July 8, 1989

July 8, 2019
30 Years later...

The outcome of our LOVE,
our two AMAZING children!

July 8, 2019
Terri and Al's 30-Year Anniversary
Love is… what keeps US together!

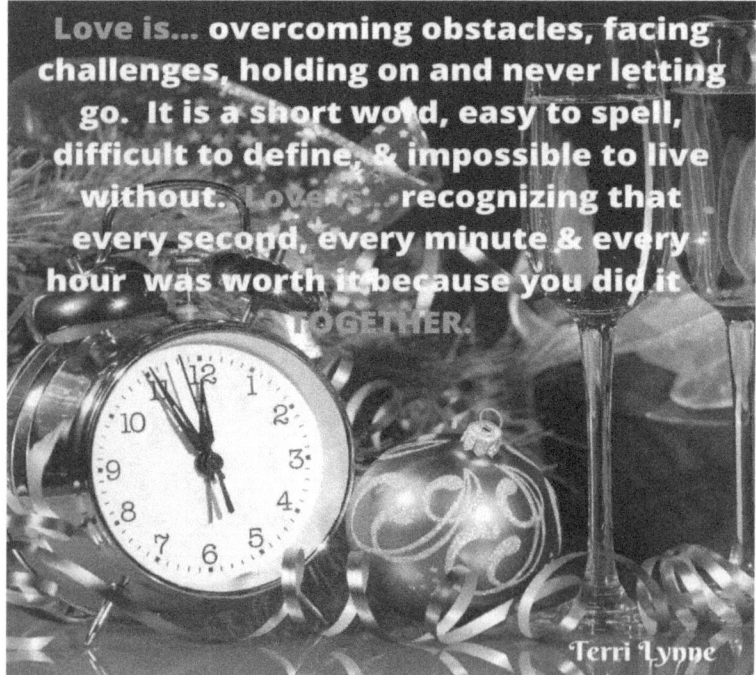

Love is… overcoming obstacles, facing challenges, holding on and never letting go. It is a short word, easy to spell, difficult to define, & impossible to live without. Love is… recognizing that every second, every minute & every hour was worth it because you did it TOGETHER.

Terri Lynne

For me, Terri Lynne,
LOVE IS...
being blessed with the ultimate "GIFT" of
going through this LIFE sharing all of what
LOVE IS...
with my immediate FAMILY!

Love is... togetherness!

L-R:
Brandon, Terri Lynne, Brittany & Al
(Son, Mom/Wife, Daughter & Husband)

Love is...
MY GREATEST GIFT!

My greatest GIFT in this life...
is to go through this life with the
LOVE of my CHILDREN!

LOVE IS...
A Mother ~ Son's
"UNITED LOVE!"

LOVE IS...
A Mother ~ Daughter's
"UNITED LOVE!"

Love is... peace on Earth!

"LOVE IS...
when your big DREAMS become your REALITY!
I am the kind of lady who believes in angels and spirit guides. The kind of lady who believes in fairy tales and romantic love stories. The kind of lady who is a hopeless romantic whom expresses her feelings through letters and poetry. The kind of lady who shares her energy with the universe from the corner of her bed. The kind of lady who loves long days of feeling the warmth of the sun, followed by making wishes upon the stars. The kind of lady who dreams of candlelight dinners on the beach beneath the moons glow. The kind of lady who tells her children goodnight, I love you, sweet dreams before their day is complete, then waits for their reply; I love you too, before drifting off to dream with their angels. The kind of lady who believes in fate, destiny and the power of love. The kind of lady who falls in love and stays in this space forever. This lady loves love. This lady is a hopeful mom, praying for the universe to exude love, while witnessing how every spirit chooses to LIVE LOVE every blessed day of their life. I am this kind of lady and I am the lady who dreams of LOVE being what creates the shift, for all to exchange energy as one UNITED LOVE while experiencing PEACE ON EARTH!

Terri Lynne

Section Five

RAINBOW
COLLECTION

OF
POETRY

Dedicated to YOU!
Love, TL Whispers
xxxooo

"The Rainbow Collection Of Poetry"
Designed with LOVE!

Love is...
what is heard when "listening" to your own heart!
So please "listen" carefully to the rhythm of LOVE,
in order for you to hear your hearts beat jump-start!

~ *LISTEN TO LOVE* ~

"Listen" to your heart and you will hear,
What you came to know, without any fear...
Love is... a sound - oh so sweet,
Pay close attention to hear the music from your OWN
heartbeat...

Then stay still for a while and you'll hear a band,
Uniting us as ONE, rather than divide us through
parcels of land...
Once tapped into the child within,
The music of your heart, will surely begin...

Have you ever truly
Listened for your rhythm inside?
The beating you will hear is your most trusted guide...
"Listen" to your heart and dance only to this beat,
For when the music is over, you may proudly take a
bow - before choosing to take a seat!

One day this beat may stop, but when?
Just to be awakened; to hear it begin to beat again!
So "Listen" to the whispers inside your OWN heart,
Knowing it is NOW the right predestined moment in
time, for your life to start!

501

As long as you hear this beat inside,
You can live your life with LOVING, unconditional,
humble pride!

Love is... your hearts greatest gift to exchange,
With love in your heart, your touch will create
change!

Let your pulse be the ripple heard far and wide,
And if you feel lost, just "LISTEN" to the whispers from
your heart inside!
Then connect with another uniting through LOVE,
Always be grateful for your own spirit and your spirit
guides from above!

Forever listening for their heart beat blending with
your OWN,
For then you will feel your inner child is suddenly full-
grown...
So please take the time to read the signs,
An Angel you will see and hear,
This music that you "Listen" to will be heard in
everyone, everywhere!

Be the music the world wants to listen to,
Then speak the words of universal truth being LOVE
ONE and LOVE ALL for then my big dream will have
come true!
For NOW, I wish to say thank you for all the "UNITED
LOVE" I have accepted to receive,
And my deepest prayers are that you feel my LOVE
and that you too, BELIEVE!

Please "LISTEN" to the song inside your OWN heart,
The lyrics uniquely written for your spirits heavenly start!
What you will feel is the music your spirit has been longing to hear!
If at first you can't hear the whispers, then simply feel your breath right then and right there!

So listen to the silence and listen to your OWN hearts beat through time,
Then breathe and sing your OWN rhythm while treasuring your OWN rhyme!
Together we took division and separation and twisted this in reverse,
And I wish to say THANK YOU for "Listening" to these LOVE messages from the UNIVERSE!!!

~ CIRCLE OF LOVE ~

Round and round, without end,
Please join us in this circle of LOVE my friend...
Once the connection is made, together we'll always be,
Through thick and through thin, throughout ETERNITY!

Talking for hours sharing enough words to fill a book,
Or silently sitting still while exchanging a sympathetic,
understanding look...
Feeling each other's energy without speaking a single
word,
But the look in our eyes let's one another know, we're
heard!
Once you meet a spirit from your soul family,
You recognize there's more to this life than what the
naked eye can see...

Suddenly, the hidden truths you begin to explore,
While together experiencing life offerings, filling us
with so much more!
Distance makes no difference when two souls share a
bond this strong,
Because together in each other's life, is where you feel
you belong...

The circle can only grow bigger allowing other good
energy in,
Just as our "UNITED LOVE CIRCLE" connections chose
to begin...
It all started with a vision of like-minded souls holding
another's hand,
Reflecting UNITY through LOVE leaving our footprints
in the sand...

By holding hands, in time we will continue to touch
many far and wide,
While the bigger the CIRCLE becomes, the more LOVE
each and every heart shall feel inside!
The ultimate goal is to raise Earth's vibrational energy,
With the intention for Heaven and Earth to hear each
other's frequency and synergy...

Through our elevation we'll hear Heaven's heartbeat,
In unison with our OWN,
Knowing while walking on Earth, we will never again
walk alone!
Thank you for sharing your energy in this book, as I
am looking forward to meeting each and every one of
you,
So grateful our spirits connected and thankful that,

"Love" is... what it took to make this
BIG DREAM come true!

If you receive an invitation, please accept to portray
your role in a film with me,
Designed to teach the world how to LOVE
unconditionally!
A chance of a lifetime I know I'll be taking,
Because what my DREAM VISION has revealed to me
is that this film is HISTORY in the making!

At first we must dare to DREAM,
Before we can establish a "UNIVERSAL DREAM TEAM!"
Reflective of our "CIRCLE OF ANGELS"
Inviting you to join this team designed to share our
"UNITED LOVE,"
Connecting Heaven and Earth from the ground,
Yet felt so passionately from up above!

Always in each other's hearts even after we're gone,
Eternally strong accepting our
"WINGS PASSED ON...!"
Please accept this LOVE PASSED ON today,
So you too can be a part of
"Terri Lynne's Way..."

Love one and love all after loving oneself on the inside,
Then connect with another's heart, one by one,
With Heaven on our side!
Get ready for the ride of your life manifesting right this
very minute,
This book has OUR story and every page has "YOU" in
it!

Because each page is filled with LIGHT and LOVE,
This is the lesson we plan to teach that,

Love is... what we are all made up of!

First step is to PASS OUR LOVE on to everyone you
know,
Acting as segway to the live stream telecast,
"BEHIND CLOSED DOORS,"
Designed to let our LOVE show!

I'll see you in my dreams, as I have done for so many
years,
Holding hands as we lived life seeing that

Love is...
Mastered through the laughter and the tears!

Thank you for being so visible through my insight,
You feel like an ANGEL to me, a bright shining light!

I sincerely can't wait to meet each and every one of
YOU,
So we can hold each other's hands, while touching
hearts the way we are designed to!
Entering other's hOMe's to FEEL our ENERGY,
Connecting through all of what love is...
unconditionally!!!

Our CIRCLE OF LOVE has only just begun,
Connecting hearts everywhere as we unconditionally
LOVE every one!
So get ready for your wake up call,
Calling one while awakening ALL!
Prepare yourself to be apart of a movie unlike
any created before,
This movie was designed connecting
Heaven and Earth,
BEHIND (MY) CLOSED DOOR!

For now we will say, we (Granny and TL)
unconditionally
LOVE YOU,
As we THANK YOU in advance for making our
Earthly/Heavenly DREAMS presently COMING TRUE!

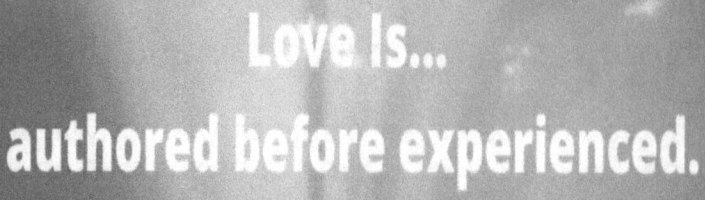

Love Is...
authored before experienced.

I wrote your name in the sky
but the wind blew it away

I wrote your name in the sand
but the water washed it away

I wrote your name into my life's script
long before living this present day

Your name is etched upon my heart
and forever it will stay

Terri Lynne

Dedicated to my past loves that I will love eternally!

"Love's Eye In The Sky"

When you look up what you will see,
Is an eye in the sky watching over you lovingly.
The eye may not be visible at first glance,
So look a bit closer when given the chance!

What you will see is energy on high,
Observing your every move through the clouds in the
sky...
When the rain comes drizzling down,
Let this be a SIGN your Angels and Guides are in
town!

Just as when the sun shines bright light upon your
path's way,
Know Heavens around and wants to make your day...
If you sense a spirit watching over you,
Look to the sky and say thanks for all you patiently do!

Through energy you will feel someone up there,
Knowing you can trust this presence without any fear...
Because one day you too will be that eye of protection,
Assisting another after remembering your earthly
reflection!

So for now be grateful for the eye in the sky,
While paying attention as they pass on by...
Be certain to show your gratitude and say I love you,
Then watch as all your heavenly dreams come true!

Cast your fears,
upon **SOMEONE** who truly
cares.
The one always willing and
able to help during a trying
time,
Ready to give you a gentle
push up your next hill hard to
climb.
Just ASK and BELIEVE,
Then be still for help you shall
receive! Terri Lynne

~ BELIEVE IN LOVE ~

"BELIEVE in only what truly matters and to me all that truly matters is believing in LOVE!"

It doesn't matter what others see,
All that matters is what I see in me!
It doesn't matter what others do,
All that matters is what I see in you!

It doesn't matter what others want to OWN,
All that matters is that I believe we reap what we have sown!
It doesn't matter what others think of who you are,
All that matters is that I know you can reach and capture that distant star!

It doesn't matter if you choose to use your voice to share your story needing to be told,
All that matters is that you know and pay close attention to
what your story will over time unfold!
It doesn't matter what another thinks or chooses to say,
All that matters is that I know I lived my OWN life, in my OWN way!

511

It doesn't matter if they can feel me share my LOVE,
All that matters is that I gave and accepted receiving
all we are blessed to be made up of!
Now I ask for you to follow my lead
and be clear on
what matters with every single breathing minute,
Then take a deep breath and FEEL
your heart beating, while KNOWING you are to
shine the "COLORS OF LOVE"
Through your OWN spirit!

Then unite with the world that you live in,
So our COLORS from our unconditional "UNITED LOVE"
story can begin...
For then Heaven and Earth will reflect
living a win, win!
Through eternity remember it is not about one election
or the power or intention of one man,
IT IS OUR OBLIGATION TO BRING LOVE BACK AND I
BELIEVE THAT IF HEAVEN AND EARTH UNITES,
WE CAN!!!!!!!!

I LOVE each and every one of you,
For playing a significant role in seeing my
DREAM VISION coming true!
LOVE IS...
What I BELIEVE is ALL that truly matters to ME!
and LOVE IS...
All that truly matters to YOU is what I pray to SEE!

I BELIEVE...
In this "CHAIN OF LOVE,"
Energetically linking hearts while gently guiding the
way...
Please trust TL'S Whispers for us to be
UNITED each present and every future
Eternally strong LOVE blessed day!

~ WINGS OF LOVE ~

From birth we carry our
"WINGS PASSED ON..."
Once we take our first breath we can't see them,
feeling as if they are gone... .
Then our entire life we try to see what we
know is there,
so we can fly free to LOVE
everyone, everywhere!

These wings feathers at first glance,
appear to be light,
Until years go by and their colors come with insight...
Seeing these wings as gifts, carrying our purest
treasure,
Attached is LOVE energy, beyond measure!

Although along with the LOVE comes loves
attachment,
Knowing we will all return back from where
we've initially been sent...
So while you are traveling to reach your physical
journeys end,
Always and forever carry LOVE upon your wings my
friend!

Because soon those broken wings will be healed from
any scars,
While you look down to see whose wearing YOUR
WINGS from beyond the stars...
Remembering OUR WINGS appear invisible and
designed for the wise,
So, wear them with humble pride regardless of their
size!

Try to keep them as close to heavenly shape as you can,
By waking up each morning and exchanging LOVE with your fellow man!
Embracing the fact that your heart has been designed to beat in unison with others,
As we connect and RISE up to UNITE Through LOVE with our soul sisters and soul brothers!

Then turn your outward LOVE inward,
to truly know what LOVE IS,
Recognizing life is a dance and in the hereafter
be ready to pass your quiz...
If you can humbly say, "I lived and I loved" and I'm proud of what I did in the here and now,
Then you will know you passed the test of time with flying colors
and you will be asked to take a bow!

For then you will have used your "WINGS PASSED ON" the way they were designed to be used,
Don't ever take these WINGS for granted or allow them to be abused...
Rather wear them with the utmost respect and humble pride,
Because, they have been designed with
UNCONDITIONAL LOVE
wrapped inside!

Be ready to PASS your WINGS ON...
to the next generation, so they can follow your lead,
As they wear your WINGS to PASS LOVE ON,
in order to succeed as agreed...
Experiencing PASSING your WINGS ON as a sacred tradition,
Recognizing how PASSING LOVE ON is our earthly mission!

So LIVE LOVE and BE LOVE because this is whom you
and I are,
Living in the moment while shining as bright as a
sparkling star...
Be a LOVE MAGNET, one who others are attracted to,
While remembering to yourself, remain uniquely true!

Say I LOVE YOU whenever you get the chance,
While smiling at a stranger when they offer a passing
glance...
Be creative in offering random acts of kindness along
your life's way,
While being grateful for every God blessed LOVE filled
day!

As of today, "UNITED LOVE" is the ripple we created
together,
By solving emotions you will be full of LOVE and your
wings will FEEL light as a feather...
From this moment forward, allow your WINGS to
reflect your
LOVE PASSED ON,
NOW witnessing all the magnetic LOVE, which to your
heart will be drawn.

Take the time to read the signs and an ANGEL you will
see,
One up above and one in your mirror throughout
eternity!
Thank you for accepting to receive my LOVE'S wake up
call,
NOW IS OUR TIME to LOVE AS ONE and throughout
eternity, to LOVE ALL!

FEEL my heart as we link united together through this
"CHAIN OF LOVE,"
As we together say, "THANK YOU" to our Spirit Guides
and Angels from above...
For they knew what they were doing when they joined
us as ONE,
Beneath the blue star lit sky & beneath each new days
shining sun!

I wish to say THANK YOU for aiding me in raising
earth's vibrational energy,
Simply by reconnecting to our first breath and
recognizing whom we are all born to be...
I am grateful we didn't waste our entire life long,
But instead created ONE
UNCONDITIONAL LOVE story to PASS ON... UNITED
STRONG!

With eternal LIGHT and Unconditional LOVE!

"UNITED LOVE"

For me, it is far more important that I LIKE you and I
LIKE what I see,
When I'm looking at you and reading your energy...
By loving MYSELF, I want to LIKE the souls I let into
my heart space,
I must LIKE the eyes of the soul looking back at my
face...

Thank you for giving me a reflection nice to see,
Our flames can now truly flourish with guards down
just wait until you can feel the ENERGY!
"Yesterday" was a gift we lived in which will echo
forevermore,
Now "today" I received permission to get a peak
behind your hearts door...

Let me in to remove your hearts wall,
So "tomorrow" the most important person in your life,
Can feel LOVED once and for all...
It's not me I'm trying to get you to feel, and to see,
It's your own mirror for you to love, honor and cherish
all you are designed to be...

So please when we have our times to share,
Allow me "always" beyond your hearts wall
to show your heart
how it feels when someone truly does care...
No strings attached just doing my work for work's
sake,
Once I'm inside, you will recognize "forever" how I
give far more than I ever shall take...

It's "time" because the Universe is ready to reach far
beyond the here and now,

Allow me to hold your hands as I pride myself on
knowing how...
I'm extremely proud of you for allowing yourself to
take this hugely uncomfortable step into the unknown,
You will reflect back on this "moment" in the "future"
merely to witness how far we've spiritually grown...

For now our guard can come down when in good
company,
As I pray I can take you to a peaceful place without
your guard up for the entire world to see;
In turn reflecting how other souls out there wish to be!
I pray our reflection goes to "INFINITY and BEYOND,"
After working on our disconnected yet connected,
extremely rare bond!

The love I speak of is love for oneself,
In order to get there and truly feel, the masks and
guards must be placed upon a shelf...
When Heaven and God are on your side,
The chains and bars are not needed and I truly believe
you will love this mystical, magic carpet ride...

In this "moment" I just received my greatest sign
being that "United Love" is not just
uniting the universe to see and feel,
One must first let down their OWN hearts wall
to connect with oneself,
uniting the love between ones OWN mirror;
for then this soul will heal!
When one can remove duality meaning,
the being standing in the mirror
and the being looking back at you,
When the view and the being become ONE is the
deepest expression of "UNITED LOVE," ONE LOVE,
not divided by two!

Your physical being and your reflection
in your mirrors view,
Is the LOVE the universe needs to see for their
hearts wall to come down
and feel their own "UNITED LOVE" in
their mirrors reflection too!
Consistently remaining true to the rhythm
inside your heart,
By connecting with your own soul, is a real good place
to start...
So like I've shared, the end of one page is the
beginning of a new,
We must begin with our OWN life's story because
"UNITED LOVE" takes its first breath... inside of you!
Your mirror's reflection will be "forever" grateful and
say THANK YOU...
OWN-LY when to yourself you remain true!

For me in my mirror I now see ONE "UNITED LOVE"
without being separated by two,
As I will "always and forever," to myself remain true!
With Unconditional Love, GTLC

"U N I T E D L O V E"
I S...
W H A T 'L O V E'
I S!!!

Soul Family

Are those that   gather around
you drawn in through energy,
Bringing unconditional love
at the perfect times you will see,
In life not connected by blood or
race, Showing up to fulfill the
same mission and put a
smile upon your face.
For YOU I am grateful
WE are
ONE

Terri Lynne

LOVE IS... SHIFTING ENERGY!

~ **REVOLUTION OF LOVE** ~

The evolution of love is a constant mystery,
Presently designing a "LOVE REVOLUTION"
for the entire world to SEE...
By touching one heart at a time
this revolution will begin,
As the Universe FEELS love energy raising Earth's
vibration!

Thank you for taking your time,
and for reading the signs along your life's way,
I pray an ANGEL you NOW see,
One in your MIRROR and one up above,
Guiding your way to me today!!!

NOW let's join hands while sharing
The beat within our OWN heart,
Raising Earth's vibration by connecting with each other
will be our Heavenly start...
Erasing the preprogramming while
cleaning life's slate,
As we open our hearts on a very special date...

When we unite through LOVE and connect by
holding our neighbors' hand,
We will be experiencing what LOVE IS...
celebrating life together & UNITED we shall stand!
FEELING the POWER OF LOVE with
our true colors shining through,
Then forever and for always, may
our unconditional "UNITED LOVE" story
reflect how Terri Lynne's BIG DREAM is
coming true; while being dedicated to each of YOU!

522

From this day moving forward,
you will remain a sacred part of me,
With new vows being established written in a "LOVE
CONTRACT" to last eternally!
Today I say I am looking forward to that shape
shifting, undivided, mystifying, magical day,
Which is just right around the corner to learn
"Terri Lynne's Way," I pray!

Until then be good to your own mirror and
take care of your family & friends,
For this is just the beginning of a journey
which thank HEAVEN never ends...
If you BELIEVE in my DREAM and wish to be a part
of where we go from here,
Then please send me your LOVE in a message if you're
willing to share your HEART with everyone,
everywhere!

Once I receive a personal message from you,
You can begin to look forward to witnessing
MIRACLES shining through!
Simply for believing in an "ordinary girls" BIG DREAM,
NOW is the time to create a ripple of LOVE as one
Unconditional Universal "UNITED LOVE" team!!!!!!!!!!

So get ready to be a witness of
Earth's Army of LOVE and LIGHT,
Accomplishing OUR MISSION by making LOVE,
Erasing war while turning what's wrong into
OWNing OWNly what's right!
May our energies continue linking together
experiencing
LOVE'S SOLUTION,
As our world UNITES as ONE...
With a beginning without end, celebrating our
"LOVE REVOLUTION!!!"

Terri Lynne - TL Whispers
February 14, 2017

Please send me a LOVE IS...
Message if you want to be
A part of our LOVE REVOLUTION!
Then get ready to see your LINK #!
LOVE IS...?
Email to:
TLWhispers@UnitedLove.Love
or go to my website:
www.UnitedLove.Love

We invite you to add your "LINK" to
our "CHAIN OF LOVE,"
As all our Angels and Spirit Guides
are watching us connect
with each other as they observe us from above!

The CIRCLE OF LOVE is...
where LOVE goes
around and around,
beginning and never-ending...

~ COLORS SENSING LOVE ~

SEEING LOVE...

Imagine a Universe filled with vibrant hues to SEE,
Beginning with RED hearts connecting you and me!

TASTING LOVE...

Now take a walk and on your way pick up some
oranges, tangerines, peaches and kumquats that you
may be blessed to find,
Feel free to eat nature's ORANGE gifts, with a TASTE
so sweet without leaving any behind.

TOUCHING LOVE...

Along your way you will FEEL the warmth of our
beautifully radiant sun,
While recognizing that as long as you see that YELLOW
ball in the sky, you know your day is not done!

SMELLING LOVE...

As you meander along you SMELL a fragrant scent,
Beside the GREEN grass are colorful flowers knowing
your path was a right choice and most definitely
meant.

HEARING LOVE...

Off in the distance you know you see BLUE in which
appears to never end,
So you keep wandering down the path to HEAR the
ocean around the next bend.

KNOWING LOVE...

You pull up a chair and take a seat when suddenly an
illusion comes into view,
Then telepathically you get the message, an inner
KNOWING,

That you used your entire God given senses is what came to you!

BEING LOVE...

As you walk your path of choice always believe you are being guided along,
Recognizing your eyes, ears, mouth, nose and fingers are being experienced and each sensation is so strong!

Wherever you wander and wherever you shall roam,
Please remember our Earth is our temporary home...
We must treat it kindly because more spirits will be coming soon,
And we will be watching over their pathway beyond the blue moon!

Yes life is just an illusion to reflect upon,
And the only color that truly matters is the
"COLOR OF LOVE" to pass on...
May your inner "RAINBOW" be your momentary guide and
May you always remember you have an "ANGEL" by your side!

LOVE IS...
What connects all our senses together simultaneously in order to,
SEE, TASTE, TOUCH, SMELL and HEAR, while feeling what comes through...
All combined you will connect with your sixth sense and you will KNOW...
That you were born designed to
BE LOVE while letting LOVE flow!!!

"LOVE IS...
What makes perfect sense to me NOW!!!
I am eternally grateful
For heaven's guidance and for letting me feel
their love, like only they know how!
Learning to pay attention to your senses you will
notice your life incredibly shift,
Leaving you with the sense of knowing that
YOU are a miraculous GIFT!
Use your senses wisely as you continue to learn
and grow,
While sharing the sense of knowing WE ARE ALL
ONE and now is our time to let our love flow!
Common sense tells me, Love was created to be
free...
And my sixth sense tells me... that I agree!

Love is ...
When you see the rainbows end,
Simply as a colorful illusion to begin again

Terri Lynne

LOVE IS... What I, Terri Lynne BELIEVES in!

I BELIEVE...

With each LIFE, comes a GIFT and the GIFT is:
That each and every life is BORN to FEEL what LOVE IS!

I BELIEVE...
LOVE IS...
The GREATEST GIFT one can EXCHANGE with ANOTHER!!!

I BELIEVE...
Before one can exchange the GIFT OF LOVE with another,
one must learn and fully accept to LOVE ONESELF!

I BELIEVE...
ONE cannot LOVE another unconditionally,
until they can deeply and completely unconditionally
LOVE their OWN MIRROR'S REFLECTION!

I BELIEVE...
Everyone is born with WINGS;
We humans just call them ARMS!

I BELIEVE...
We ALL need each other ONE HEART, ONE SOUL AT A TIME, CONNECTING through a LINK in this CHAIN in order to BECOME ONE through our "UNITED LOVE" Circle of Angels!

I BELIEVE...
We are BORN to LOVE each other!

529

I BELIEVE...
UNITED LOVE is...
A story for all ages,
With a BEGINNING, without END..!

I BELIEVE...
That "UNITED LOVE" will create LOVE in our hearts
and
PEACE ON EARTH and
I BELIEVE that one day soon,
YOU will BELIEVE this fact too,
if you do not already.

I BELIEVE...
I pride myself on being just a MOM who uses my
intuition and my mirrors reflection to WOW you with
WHISPERS OPENING WINGS, through MESSAGES
OPENING MINDS, so you can see your OWN wings as
we take flight together.

I BELIEVE...
There is a simple equation for the solution to equal
love and the answer is:
Solving Emotions: Energy in Motion + Open Hearts
Flowing + High Vibrational Energy + Connected
Frequency = LOVE

I BELIEVE...
LOVE = Level Of Vibrational Energy.

I BELIEVE...
When we vibrate at a high frequency, we will all feel,
see, know, and connect by experiencing all of what love
is! The way I figured out this equation and the answer
is by living it! I learned through practice that the more
emotions we solve, the more open our hearts become.
The more open our hearts are, the more freely the

energy in our heart flows. The more freely our hearts energy flows, the higher vibration of energy we will feel. The higher the vibration of energy we feel, the more connected through frequency we will share. The more connected through frequency we share, the more LOVE we will experience. The more LOVE we experience, the more others connected to our frequency, feeling our high vibrational energy, who recognize our open heart flowing, after solving our emotions, will know how LOVE feels, simply by experiencing all that a LOVE CONNECTION is suppose to be and feel! This LOVE CONNECTION begins within yourself! Then you can pass this LOVE CONNECTION on..!

I BELIEVE...

After reading this book, I am HOPEFUL you have a better sense of what LOVE IS and you choose to solve emotions, to open your heart, to feel high vibrational energy, through connecting frequencies, while giving and accepting to receive all of what LOVE IS!

I pray you do the work, so we can all share in a LOVE experience TOGETHER! I just saw that TOGETHER is TO GET HER! I am hopeful that people will GET ME one day, when the opportune moment presents itself. So people will listen to me and choose to do their own individual work so when love shows up, you accept receiving it simply because you know you deserve to feel what love is and choose to exchange this energy with all whom are deserving of receiving your love!

I BELIEVE...

Once you have an EXPERIENCE of LIVING LOVE

You will know that:

LOVE CONQUERS ALL!

LOVE ALWAYS WINS!

LOVE IS NOT A GAME!

LOVE IS A PRECIOUS COMMODITY!

LOVE IS NOT TO BE TAKEN FOR GRANTED!

LOVE IS NOT TO BE DENIED!

EVERYONE EVERYWHERE DESERVES TO KNOW WHAT

LOVE IS!

LOVE IS ETERNAL!

LOVE IS WHO YOU ARE AND WHO YOU ARE BORN TO
BE!

LOVE IS AN EXPERIENCE TO BE SHARED!

LOVE IS WHY YOU ARE HERE!

I, Terri Lynne believe that love is...
liberating!

~ I Pray ~

I pray the ENERGY inside this book gave you a TASTE of
how LOVE FEELS through our hearts projection!
I pray you FEEL our High Vibrational Energy, so we all
can SEE LOVE in our own mirror's reflection!
You are my mirror's reflection when I am standing in
front of you,
so it is important for me to SEE your LOVE LIGHT SHINE
through!

I pray my TOUCH in your life has been felt through every
nerve ending of your being on the inside,
So you can TOUCH another's life with our united love,
for them to feel our connected love too without having
anything to hide!
I pray you have been listening to the whispers
throughout this book,
To HEAR spirit's share their interpretation of what LOVE
IS, while holding this energy in your hands if you care to
take a second look!

I pray for you to ask your own spirit what sounds like
the truth to your inner child and/or understand what you
choose to erase,
So LOVE will be the image you SEE every time you look
at your own beautiful smiling face!
I pray you take time to SMELL the flowers along your
soul's pathway, to recognize that what you smell is a gift
of LOVE,
This is nature's way of sharing a little piece of heaven
from above!

Once you ask yourself the deep questions, you will
receive answers to use your voice, on one predetermined
day,
So when you SPEAK about what LOVE IS, the entire
world will want to listen to your words so they can HEAR

what you are the chosen one to say!
I pray you are one baby step closer to understanding
that we all need to use our senses to navigate our way in
this linear existence in order to find each other!
So then we can heighten our awareness of our senses, in
order to truly KNOW all of what LOVE IS through our soul
sisters and our soul brothers!

I pray you use your sixth sense to KNOW that YOU ARE
LOVE,
I AM LOVE, WE ARE LOVE and it's time to UNITE to share
our gifts designed above.
While experiencing using our senses simultaneously so
we are no longer having the sense of feeling deprived,
And we can live every now moment of our peacefully
blessed lives in which we've strived!
I pray this is the new way of living,
Sharing open hearts by accepting to receive love while
always remembering the best gift exchange is felt within
the giving.
As you look in your mirror and see love is what I pray,
So we all can be loves reflection every future blessed
day!

When wanting to navigate the TRUTH about what LOVE
IS, I suggest you use your six senses:

Sight - Eyes - To See Love
Sound - Ears - To Hear Love
Smell - Nose - To Smell Love
Taste – Mouth - To Eat Love and
Touch - Hands and Hearts - To Feel Love
Then your Sixth Sense - Third Eye - To KNOW Love!

I pray your senses guide you to the same CONCLUSION
I have received through using my senses to navigate this
beautiful life! Then we can experience LOVE together
through our:

"UNITED LOVE" CONNECTION!

My intention when setting out on this journey of love
was simple in my minds eye.
I set the intention to be a "SPARK" of light, hopeful to
ignite another's flame, to be seen across the sky.
Creating SPARKS to fly lighting up the world with our
UNITED LOVE LIGHTS,
This was a vision clearly seen within - behind my
closed door insights.
Now with this book reaching the final pages,
I intuitively see many flames glowing hopefully
spreading and shining through spirits of all ages!
I pray you accept my request to locate your inner
light,
Then pass our torch forward so we see a flames glow
beneath our starlit skies, as well as seeing the sun
shining bright.
Thank you for accepting to be a part of our
circle of love,
Making heaven proud when observing us from above!
Please keep being the SPARK watching Universal Love
growing,
While checking in with your mirror while sensing the
universes love over flowing!

With Love from my SPARK of light to yours,

keep shining!

Love is...
The spark that ignites
your hearts flame to
shine bright! Terri Lynne

Love is... THE WAY!
Use your senses to know
you cannot take the low
road in order to reach
"Love's Highway!"

"LOVE IS...

The only pathway
to follow!

Terri Lynne

LOVE IS...
IN THE ATMOSPHERE!

Designed to touch hearts and souls
of spirits everywhere...
Created for the universe to see that
Love is... a Godsend,
Shifting our energy to BEGIN again
by feeling safe and feeling loved
without END!

Terri Lynne, TL Whispers
WOW MOM PRODUCTIONS
IS TAKING FLIGHT!

"My Heart Is All A Flutter"
Artist: David Krakov

- The Legacy I Wish To Leave Behind -

I wish to leave a legacy behind of *truth* being told, because the *truth* to me is more precious than diamonds or gold. So when my time comes to move forward, my whispers can echo on reflective of what I learned in my lifetime. I have experienced that it is not that we go through life without challenges and obstacles, but for me the true test of time is by taking the negative in the challenge and turning it into a positive outcome. Rather than focusing on the negative, just to drain our energy, I have always made the conscious choice to place my attention and intention on transforming negativity into positive solutions. I try my best to do so while navigating my way through the obstacle course, guiding myself on to my OWN divinely well lit chosen pathways full of energy, which I learned the truth about. Love is... energy! When you love yourself, you are receiving energy. When you do not love yourself, your energy will feel drained. This is a secret I learned along my life's way.

After learning how to take the negatives and turn them into having a positive outcome, I AM willing and able to walk the pathway of my true soul, guiding my spirit to my peaceful place. My goal is to see my mirrors reflection through a positive light while learning to love what I see unconditionally! Then to pass this knowledge on... I have always known intuitively that when I reach that moment, I will have received and paid attention to spirit messages, designed to teach me well. For then I will know through my own inner knowing that I have been living my true calling in this lifetime ever since I took my first breath of life. I pray that the legacy I leave behind is that I did my own personal best to guide others to walk upon their own true soul's pathway and

others did so by following my lead. I remain hopeful for the day that our journeys cross, so we can share our pathways full of hearts of gold filled with LOVE, followed by spreading our love throughout the universe!

As this book has reached its final chapter, I can honestly say it feels like my spirit is beginning to take flight! At this time I can put my past behind me and carry on truly living the life I wrote the script to LIVE! My journey started with taking my first breath of life, and then I took baby steps to begin to learn all about the life I came to live and where it shall lead. What I have learned and experienced throughout my combined incarnations was that all along it was about myself loving *my own mirror's reflections.* While respecting myself enough to trust and believe in my own souls lead. My soul has guided me onto *Love's Highway,* which lead me to each and every one of you! Now in my new beginning, I see why this was not only significant for the evolution of my spirit, but I see how my reflection was created for others to love their mirror's reflection too! This has always been at the heart of my life's souls purpose for taking my first breath in this lifetime. I knew through my inner knowing that it was going to take a *miracle* to create this *chain of love,* but I also believed in *miracles* because I recognized early on in my life, that each of us with a breath and a heartbeat are all *miracles!* I also recognized that in order to witness my *big dreams* coming true, I not only had to *believe in myself,* but I also had to *believe in all of you!* Today I wish to say *thank you* for showing up on *Love's Highway,* at an intersection predetermined before we took our first breath, and destined to take place before we take our last breath in this physical suit of amore. Never needing to wear a suit of armor ever again. When you wear love upon your wings, you will never need protection. Because higher powers has your back.

Today, as we create the *shift* from war to *love* upon Earth, with *love* being all I care to fight for, I wish to say *thank you* to my *"Soul Family"* my soul sisters and soul brothers, who included a message within this book of love, and for trusting and believing in my *Big Dream* acknowledged by your ACTions of sharing your heart of gold so full of LOVE with the Universe! We NOW have a handbook reflective of what *Love Is...* to share our *gift of "United Love"* for the entire world to have and to hold our energy in their hands. Intended to connect our spirits together as *one Chain Of Love,* and we did this one link and one heartbeat at a time! From this moment on, there is not anything or anyone that can separate or break apart an unconditional *Love Connection* when we trust, we know and we believe that:

Love is... our BIRTHRIGHT and the way it makes us feel is ALIVE! Love is... who we are and what my life's purpose chooses to etch inside our HEARTS forever more!

To be continued...
"BEHIND CLOSED DOORS"
Where we transform this book into a
Live Stream Telecast reflecting an,
unconditional UNITED LOVE story!

As we share a space filled with OWNLY OPEN Hearts!
OWNLY means to me:
Opening Wings Now, Loving You!

Love is... expressed through balanced chakras and an open heart!

~ DREAM BIG ~

The End and new beginning reflects my
BIG DREAM coming true!
NOW I wish to express my gratitude, because this
dream never could have come this far without each
and every one of YOU!
For this I am choosing to give you UNITED LOVE as a
gift,
To give your heart a colorful love charged energetic
shift!

This page marks the end of seeing love through black
and white, with shades of color throughout.
Beyond our new beginning, I'm hoping you start to
visualize seeing your life as colorful without any doubt!
I have learned and hope to teach that when you are in
a place of darkness and all you see is gray,
You can transfer what feels like black and white simply
by adding colors to your world cleansing all your cares
away!

Do so by taking out your inner paintbrush and add
your unique colors to any image,
I did so by creating a vision of connecting souls with
an imaginary rainbow colored bridge!
Every time you are faced with an obstacle practice
maneuvering your way around,
By doing so you come out on the other side with your
feet planted firmly on the ground.

Leaving a greater imprint on society and on the
Universe,
By speaking your truth while using your voice for
better not for worse.
Don't allow fear to stop you; rather catapult you to
share your heart,
As you are guided in the direction for those open,
ready, willing and able to feel your love because they
are smart.

Use your inner strength and your own vision which
other's are not always ready to see yet,
To catapult you in a new direction would be your best
bet.
Take your time and read the signs so you can shine
your inner light outward, for the entire world to see,
While living your life's true purpose, by teaching the
world what Love Is so they can know who they were
born to be!

Be true to yourself while accepting and loving your
own mirrors reflection,
Use your inner strength to walk the pathway of your
soul leading you in your own heart's direction!
If others question the path you are on, do not let
this stop you from taking your next baby step; while
following your own souls lead,

Remain clear on your conviction towards pursuing your life's purpose, while observing your own spirit succeed!

Live life loving your world, as we spread our LIGHT staying in UNITED LOVE'S ebb and fluid flow,
Together may we always and forever continue to watch one another rise up, shift and grow!
"Welcome to the world I see" after completing and seeing "UNITED LOVE" through my eyes,
Honest and true, raw and real without wearing any disguise.

I am hopeful you enjoyed the journey of using LOVE to be our guiding force,
As we remember we are all one, acting as the Universe's highest and greatest pure source!
We create our own reality, so use your energy to color yours bright,
As I WELCOME YOU TO MY WORLD guided through heavenly insight!

Thank you for taking your precious time and reading the signs, so you, our angel, shall now see,
An angel up above and one in your own mirror seeing vibrant rainbow colors; so full of LOVE to last throughout eternity!
Please feel free to exchange your energy so this book never ends,
As long as you share your love is messages on my website my familiar strangers, as well as my dearest friends.

For the entire world to read and feel your heart,
As you express what LOVE IS for your link in our chain
to start!
Also feel free to let me know if this book touched you
in a positive way,
And if you intentionally wish to join in our "Circle of
Love" one blissful, heavenly, grateful, fine day!

I thank you for taking the time to read "UNITED
LOVE,"
And I pray your spirit guides and angels keep guiding
you from above!
Don't allow fear to stop you from living the pathway of
your
BIG DREAMS coming true,
Be a warrior and a champion by accomplishing all you
put your mind into.

For Heaven and Earth love to see you smile once your
purpose in this life has been achieved,
For then they will pass on their angel wings to you
while knowing they will be well received.
Congratulations for making it this far,
And always remember you are a bright shining star!

From my open heart to yours I am hopeful you see our
burning flame,
While recognizing our packaging might be different,
but on the inside WE ARE ONE in the same!

With Light and Eternal Love,
From my open heart touching yours!

547

This Butterfly just spread her WINGS and
IS ready to take FLIGHT!
I am encouraging you to come FLY with me,
upon the WINGS OF LOVE...
what a beYOUtiful sight!

"Book of Life"
Artist: David Krakov

~ Finding My Way Back To Me ~

Finding My Way Back To Me,
The sweet innocent little girl so carefree...

Who loved to jump rope, play jacks, hula-hoop and lay
out soaking up the sun,
A gentle, sensitive spirit who saw the best in
everyone...

Always wanting to do right, for I could do no wrong,
Self-taught on the importance of allowing inner
strength to keep you strong...

Caring and sensitive almost to a fault,
Until it hurt too much so I had to make my emotions
come to a sudden halt...

A peacemaker wanting to please all,
Sleeping comfortably with her Sepulveda and Lynne
doll...

Made friends by simply playing in the front yard,
Before she became hardened, callused and scarred...

As life's challenges tried to knock me down,
I focused on keeping smiles on friend's faces so they
wouldn't have to wear a frown...

Always being the support system lending a listening
ear,
A born therapist bringing peace in friend's hearts
removing the drop from a tear...

UNITED LOVE

Patiently while gently nudging others onto their
smooth course,
While remaining true to those I love without any
force...

The little girl's life felt like it had come to its end,
When she lost her Granny, an Earth Angel, one
incredible lady, a very best friend...

Until three weeks later when granny came through,
Showing me herself, while guiding me with all that is
true...

Beyond Earth's realm she opened heaven's door,
To love and light so real, so honest and oh, so pure...

Her words of wisdom carried me through the rain,
By teaching me my lessons beyond my struggle and
pain...

Her gentle nudges guided me back to the child within,
A place of love and innocence as I watched the older
version of my inner child begin...

This transition began to take shape after the vision
that saved my life,
At forty years old with two children while being a
wife...

The vision came through as a midnight message and
was crystal clear,
So I listened and did as she asked and with heavens
help I had no fear...

Once I survived this greatest challenge of all,
I truly believed I was born to stumble; but never too
deeply would I allow myself to fall...

I dug down deep into my very soul and found that
little girl,
The diamond in the rough or should I say a precious
pearl...

As I reflected back upon my life since birth,
I found my inner strength that gave me a sense of
self worth...

Seeing the purity from deep within my soul,
Showed me I must go on to heal others broken hearts,
for this became my motivating goal...

As time moved forward one baby step at a time,
I learned who to trust and who to believe in and
this choice was mine along those mountains I would
climb...

Presently fifty-seven years have come and gone,
I have learned every life has a story,
but we all must carry on...

When I looked back over my life and saw the
challenges that made me who I am today,
I would not have changed a single thing because I still
see that little girl in me in every way...

An adult who's a gentle, sweet spirit wanting to please
all,
Someone who is guided to gently break your fall...

A peacemaker wanting to fill this life with light and
love,
Teaching others that when one passes on they never
leave,
yet rather transform to become your guide from
above...

Each connection upon earth is divinely planned,
Into whoever's life you fatefully land...

All taking place for a reason, a season or a lifetime
through,
To show you another dimension of the true you...

Trust and believe in God's master plan,
While remembering beyond heaven's gate you might
just recognize your biggest fan...

Stay open to all possibilities as to why you are being
challenged so,
Then with an open mind and an open-heart forgive,
release and let go, while staying in the flow...

At which time you will recognize all you were designed
to be,
So you can carry on with your life and design your
OWN happy reality...
I did and I thankfully FOUND MY WAY BACK TO ME!

The only reason to look back is to find the parts of
yourself you choose to carry forward eternally!
My intention in writing this book is not to try to
recreate your spirit, but rather create you to see the
BEAUTIFUL spirit you are born to be!

I LOVE YOU, LOVE ME,
ETERNALLY!

LOVE IS...
What Terri Lynne's heart has been dedicated to
understand long before she took her
first breath of life!

Heartfelt gratitude goes out to each and every one of you who added to her education!

With Eternal Light,
Granny (In Heaven) & Terri Lynne (On Earth)
1-22-1962 - Present Moment

66 Love Is...
Holding Eternal Light
In The Palm Of
Your Hands

Terri Lynne

Section Six

CONCLUSION

LOVE IS...
Meant to be,
and NOW is the time
for LOVE to soar after being
released, to fly FREELY!

Love is... knowing who you are
While seeing your reflection in the distant
shining star,
Witnessing how your star is formed with light,
Created to keep twinkling and sparkling meant
to shine extra bright.
The more you erase preprogramming in which
you've been taught,
The sooner you will begin to hear your
own inner thought.
Your purpose will become crystal clear,
And your star will be seen from far away with
the illusion that it's very near.
Your primary job is to be squeaky clean,
So then your star can shine bright and from
around the world be seen.
Stars are the place to make wishes upon,
So when night falls, it will be time to dream on...

Terri Lynne

Dear Universe,

I am *hopeful* that while reading and completing this *"United Love"* project, we learned what it takes to reach the highway to all of what *Love is.* We did so with Heaven's help and our imagination flowing through unity of energy, frequency, and vibrations!

Love IS... Energy!
Creating our... Frequency!
Elevating our... Vibration!

Love IS...
GOOD VIBRATIONS!

LOVE IS...
what the EARTH needs to breathe again!
When EARTH connects to HEAVEN'S breath,
Heaven and Earth will be able to BREATHE as ONE!

"LOVE IS...
God's GIFT to the world!"
And
YOU are LOVE!

So now you know,
"YOU" ARE 'GOD'S GIFT'
TO THE WORLD!"

Thank you for showing up!

Love is...
A spinning ball of energy,
vibrating our frequency, uniting us eternally!

Terri Lynne

WE are individuals living beneath one universal roof while viewing the same moon, the same sun and making wishes upon the same stars, all created to *Be Love* and to *Be-Loved!* This is our responsibility for receiving our first breath of life. If we don't *Live Love* every breath we take, we will *FEEL* as though we are dying! But when you learn the lessons on living life by naturally being in the flow, *Love* will guide your path with *Light.* When you *feel love energy* through frequency and vibration, you will *know the powers* you were *born* with, being your greatest *gift* from God. No one can create *MIRACLES* upon Earth alone when we are all connected to each other's acts. I chose to trust and believe spirits guidance and I chose to do a simple act of random kindness by being a *"HOPEFUL MOM" (Here Opening Peoples Eyes For Universal Love - through - Messages Opening Minds),* which was to create our *CHAIN OF LOVE!* But before one can be open to hear the messages through the whispers, we must clear the mechanism of the mind. Because the pathway to an open heart begins inside your own mind's thoughts as you learn

a simple rule: Once your mind is free from paralyzing emotions, it can be open to receiving messages life altering to hear, in order for your *heart* to *feel all the Love* it is beating to *experience.*

Meditation is recognizing the presence of thought. When we recognize and acknowledge our thoughts, we can release them and set them free and this is when we hear the silence. Once we pay attention to the silence, we can begin to hear our own spirits whispers teaching and guiding us with all we were born to learn, in order to live a blessed life full of love blissfully filling the pages of our true life's unconditional *LOVE STORY!* Then you will learn the greatest lesson of your life, when you learn how to *LOVE YOURSELF* properly. The word "properly" is not a judgment word, yet rather your own opinion if the love you feel for yourself is "enough" and that is all that truly matters.

When you act upon the lessons your *OWN* spirit teaches you and you *LET GO and LET GOD* steer your wheel, you will see, by feeling that you are on the right path. This is the path I choose to call, *LOVES HIGH-WAY!* Leading you to wherever you choose to go! You will recognize the *SIGNS* along the way by taking a self endured *"TIME OUT"* or *"TIME IN"* to briefly check in with spirit! Not just your guides and angels in heaven, but your *OWN* spirits whispers! Because no one knows you better or as well as you *KNOW* yourself! The *TRUTH YOU CANNOT LIE ABOUT* and if you don't believe or trust me, take the time to confirm this fact with your own spirit for validation that this is a fact of life. Ask your *OWN SPIRIT* any question and then *JUST BE STILL* and pay attention and *LISTEN* to your *OWN* solutions to any situation that is asking to be solved. Also, please recognize that "Problems" are merely "Situations" that need to be solved. My spirit whispered to me that the biggest situation that needed to be solved in my life was

that I listened too closely to outside voices. In order to release the emotion called *FEAR,* I had to go within and relearn what *LOVE IS!*

This is exactly what I chose to do because I *KNOW* spirit never lies and the *TRUTH* was all I cared to know! I took a baby step out of my own comfort zone by releasing a bit of fear, when I wrote the *"CHAIN OF LOVE"* letter over four years ago. I prayed from the corner of my bed *"BEHIND CLOSED DOORS,"* where I do my best work because the outside world's voices drowned out my *OWN.* When I went within, I heard all I needed to know. Now you are holding the solution designed when Heaven and Earth came together to manifest a *tangible source of Love,* by taking *Love Energy* and transforming it into a *tangible GIFT for the world to SEE and FEEL all of what LOVE IS.* As you have witnessed inside the pages of this book that you are close to being finished reading, validating that the spirit messages I received back then, were correct! I see that those messages, those whispers through spirit has led me to today drawing the conclusion of this part of my life's journey, while feeling all the *LOVE ENERGY* this book carries. Now I am able to *HOLD LOVE ENERGY* in my *HANDS* and felt inside my *HEART,* to pass on to you and for you to be able to pass on to generations to come!

I *KNOW* our time to *UNITE* the world through *LOVE* is *NOW!* I heard that after the final page of this book has been turned; it is time to begin manifesting our next right predestined moment in time. This next step is being created for all who were a part of this book, as well as everyone everywhere connected to our spirits, in order to manifest our meeting face to face. Our union will take place live in person for the entire world to *SEE and FEEL* our beautiful experiences of educating each other on all of what *LOVE IS.* Along with learning and

practicing the tools and healing methods I experienced to assist me with being my best self. Then together *"UNITED,"* we will share and *EXPERIENCE "LOVE!"*

Love is... an invaluable education!

And the only profession I cared to get my *MASTERS* degree in!

For me, Love is...
all that truly matters about the life we are born to live!

NOW IS...
The time for *LOVE* to manifest into *full bloom!*

Love is...
a manifestation Granny in Heaven and Terri Lynne on Earth believed in!

Because spirit knew that when Heaven and Earth unite as one, we would be able to prove the truth that has been kept a secret until now. The secret has been revealed through the *whispers from an angel touching one heart at a time.* Reflecting how *LOVE*

(Level Of Vibrational Energy) can and will heal the world, one breath and one heartbeat at a time!

I've been told that I wrote this script long before I ever took my first breath in this lifetime and you all play a significant role in this manuscript. If you wish to know the role you signed the contract to play, just take a look inside your mirror where your truth can be seen and you will see it for yourself, while knowing *the truth you cannot lie about.* Secret revealed: Here is a truthful fact of my life, I was apprehensive to use my voice to share my heart about the truth of my love for you and this is a fact of my life. I knew I loved you long before we ever met, because I felt you in my hearts space. I felt you there because you agreed long ago to be here today to help write this book designed for *uniting the world through LOVE* through *Levels Of Vibrational Energy.* Now the time has come to *UNITE* together to practice what we are meant to preach, so we can *teach our children well.* Then our children can *LIVE LOVE* and *pass on* their lessons to their children one day, by *teaching their children well!*

Love is... the greatest lesson we can learn; in turn becoming the most profound GIFT we can give to our children for them to pass on...!

When a child feels loved, unconditionally loved, they will never feel they need anything else in life besides good health and everything else they receive is merely frosting on their birthday cake!

Love is... the best BIRTHday GIFT you can give to your children and it will only cost you, if you don't give it away freely through every second of their life!

Then instead of them blowing out their candles, they can use their candles well lit to *IGNITE* another's *FLAME!* This is my *BIG DREAM* and I thank you for signing the contract to *BE LOVE*, while accepting *BEING LOVED* in this lifetime!

Another Secret TL Whispers:
GTC was referenced many times in my first book in which represents, Granny Terri Connection
Equating to Heaven and Earth as One!

NOW IS... The TIME for everyone everywhere around the world to stop, look and listen, while using your *OWN* senses, to learn the lessons about what *LOVE IS!* As we share in a *"UNITED LOVE" EXPERIENCE,* while *HEAVEN AND EARTH UNITE AS ONE,* so Earth can become Heavens Mirrors Reflection! This is what my mirror showed me. An image *OWNly* your spirit can imagine, until your imagination becomes all the proof you need! But first *YOU* must *SEE and FEEL LOVE ENERGY* within your *OWN SPIRIT* to become a *BELIEVER* and this book was part of the plan to give you an opportunity to become a *BELIEVER ON YOUR OWN* in your *OWN* life, to carry on with life by teaching the children well!!! A lesson I learned through this journey is that first one must love their-own mirror's reflection before they can reflect love upon another's image! I also learned that:

Love is...
in your imagination, until our spirit and heaven guides us to SEE and to FEEL all we CAN IMAGINE!

Manifesting *LOVE* begins in your imagination and then never ends once all you imagined *LOVE* could be... is manifested!

Our *"United Love"* is being experienced with all the believers of love, while turning non-believers into lovers! I call this a *"New Age Love Revolution"* or for short a *"LOVELUTION!"* Sometimes you have to think outside of the box, and stretch your imagination a bit, to truly receive a message. Because heaven likes to play games and challenge you and sometimes you have to stretch the truth to see the hidden messages, as in seeing *REVOLUTION* backwards reads: *NO IT U LOVER,* meaning to me, *KNOW IT YOU LOVER.* But if we pay close attention to the details, we will see all the signs we missed at first glance. The key is to keep on searching for the clues, which gives life definition, and meaning. To do this we must be wide-awake and I hope this book sets off your inner alarm clock, because world; it's

TIME TO WAKE UP!

I had a vision which felt to me like a big dream, that each and everyone of you who shares your heart full of *LOVE* with me, receives an invitation to witness *"Our Story"* brought out of this book and came to life for the world to *SEE.* As well as the Universe to *FEEL our "UNITED LOVE"* behind closed doors. Each of you was a guest in the audience for the event of a lifetime. This event will

show proof of how using your senses creates *MIRACLES* upon Earth and Heavenly spirits will be sitting in the audience by your side. Hopefully all future viewers will learn how to use their senses, after witnessing from behind their *OWN* closed doors, the ultimate and most intimate *LOVE EXPERIENCE* of all time; as *HEAVEN and EARTH* join as *ONE* through: *ENERGY, FREQUENCY and VIBRATION!*

Love is... an ACTion creating a reACTion!

You are the ACTors of your own script and once you face your fears of stage fright and make the conscious choice to transfer yourself from standing in the wings and choose to stand center stage for the entire world to see you smile and most likely cry a little or maybe even a lot, if you are me; then you will experience all the *LOVE and SUPPORT* from all the *ANGELS upon EARTH and HEAVEN SENT* to witness an experience of a lifetime. Every spirit present when you take center stage will see the role they play in their own script connected to mine, yours and ours, while recognizing which role we accepted to portray. Then we will see how after all the twists and turns we have taken since our first breath of life, regardless of our physical age, our spirits made an agreement to meet one day, one predestined fine day to teach the entire world what *LOVE IS!* While *FEELING LOVE* throughout every cell of our being of *LIGHT!*

Another TL Whispers Secret:
Even if you carry *FEAR* on your journey towards
LOVE'S HIGHWAY, there isn't anything or anyone that can stop you, but yourself! So I suggest you take the time and read the signs along your life's way, so one

day it will be you on that stage educating the entire world about the *JOURNEY OF LOVE!*

This was the script I wrote when still on the other side, and today I know I chose and accepted the role I wrote myself into! I *KNEW* as I was writing this script that the blocks in my life would be stemmed from the emotion called *FEAR*, until one day I was guided to an Earth Angel named Ata, a Maori Healer and she saw this block when reading my script through spirit messages and she asked, Do you know what *FEAR* means Dear? I said, No I don't, but I'd like to know!" (I knew I needed to *KNOW* this answer because it is what paralyzed me my entire life to, just be me!) Then she said, *"Fear is... False Evidence Appearing Real!"* That was a huge *BINGO MOMent* for me, because then I got the message that *FEAR* stems from inside my mind and I felt I was meant to live in my heart! So this is when I knew I had to solve that emotion in order to open up my heart fuller to truly experience the beautiful life I wrote my script to achieve. *LOVE* was all I cared to achieve in my lifetime! Now it is your time to have a conversation with your own spirit while getting to know yourself from your hearts messages, after transferring your minds intellect into listening to your spirits whispers. Then thank yourself

for me, for writing me into your script long, long ago so we can *FEEL* each other's *ENERGY* right *NOW!* If you love the idea of meeting in one place to share in this *LOVE EXPERIENCE* then help me *MANIFEST* this moment in a sacred space to *UNITE* through all of what *LOVE IS... together!*

Another TL Whispers Secret:
If you're reading these parts of my *LOVE STORY*, then know what is mine is all that is yours! Because our life's paths just blended to travel down *"Love's Highway,"* guiding us to meet upon *"Terri Lynne's Way"* on one fine predestined day! Get ready for *MIRACLES upon MIRACLES* to take place in a very sacred space! Please recognize that in my script, I don't believe in *LOVE* ever ending and *I DO BELIEVE* there is always room for more *LOVE* to enter! My script just like this day, will begin *BEHIND CLOSED DOORS*, and then the doors will fly open so we together as one *CAN WELCOME THE ENTIRE UNIVERSE INTO OUR WORLD!* Because in my script, *NO ONE* should ever be left out of *FEELING and KNOWING what LOVE IS!!!*

Another TL Whispers Secret:
That *SPACE* I am referring to for this *BIG EVENT is EARTH!* Our part of the *UNIVERSE!* And all you need to bring with you on that *MIRACULOUS* day is... your *SPIRIT!*
LOVE IS... felt within the stillness!
LOVE IS... heard within the silence!
LOVE IS... the key to open your heart!
LOVE IS... truthful!
(So if you feel love you can't lie about it, because your spirit knows the truth!)
LOVE IS... contagious!

(and loving other's is not a sin, so be a carrier and spread LOVE!)

LOVE IS... what you will experience when in your flow!

LOVE IS... the greatest GIFT you can give to yourself, and then exchange with another!

LOVE IS... meant to be shared!

LOVE IS... within and a gift your spirit can't live without!

LOVE IS... the greatest present you can gift to another, as well as being present with another, is the greatest GIFT OF LOVE one can give!

LOVE IS... at the HEART and SOUL of every single being upon earth!

LOVE IS... experienced in every breath we take!

LOVE IS... what will UNITE OUR WORLD to live and breathe as ONE!

OUR "UNITED LOVE" IS... IN THE ATMOSPHERE!

NOW LOVE IS... EVERYWHERE!

LOVE IS... YOU!

LOVE IS... ME!

LOVE IS... US CONNECTED ETERNALLY!

LOVE IS... A secret which should be whispered into every single persons ears, because if this secret doesn't get revealed the world will continue to be hurting. The world needs to hear the secret of what LOVE IS... so the universe can feel how great love makes everyone everywhere FEEL! I need each and every one of you to please share our secret!

Love isn't for just one individual because,

Love is... for everyone everywhere!

Homework – A Random Act Of Kindness:
***Write a "Love Is" message, and then place it in a recyclable bottle to cast out into the tide, reaching souls far and wide; Because Love Is... *REAL,* not an illusion to hide!

So world, *THIS IS the HIGHWAY TO LOVE* – A pathway paved with miracles around each bend. If we all follow this highway we will be lead straight into each other's open hearts experiencing peace on earth with goose bumps upon our skin! You may even feel them right now, which is simply spirit validation.

We all are already a part of this *"Chain of Love"* and you will know this when you feel it for yourself! The easiest way for you to feel our *"United Love"* is by taking pre-programmed thoughts from within your mind and transferring those thoughts into feelings inside your heart. Once you learn to live in your hearts space, you will recognize what feels peaceful and light and what feels heavy and dark. The energy that feels heavy and dark reflects an emotion in which needs to be solved. Recognize that you are the only person that can heal what is going on inside, because you know yourself better than anyone else will ever know you.

"Thy mind THINKS ~
But thy heart KNOWS!"

Your guides and angels heaven sends can nudge you onto your souls true pathway, by showing you signs along your life's way. But it is your responsibility to read the signs they place in front of you. All signs are leading you to one mutual destination, which is on to the *pathway of LOVE!*

Now at this present moment in time, I would like to say thank you for taking the time, by reading the signs, to read this book. I wish to wrap up my own thoughts floating around inside my mind and feelings flowing inside my heart and soul with you. Honestly, at this moment, I could write another entire book about what love is. So please know this is not the end on love, it is

merely just the beginning. Even though I gave myself a year to allow the *"Chain of Love"* to circulate and for *LOVE IS* messages to flow to me and through me for the purpose of creating this book, I learned you cannot put a deadline on letting love flow! So I decided to create a space for love to keep flowing once the last page of this book is turned. Simply to share an exchange of energy, adding more light and love for our universe to feel. You can connect with our energy at: www.UnitedLove.Love_ and add your *LOVE IS... message on the CHAIN OF LOVE link.*

On my journey of Love, I have learned that Heaven is Earth's ceiling and Earth is Heaven's floor, so let us keep looking up to see how high our vibration can flow, while giving Heaven a mirror to see their reflection when looking down upon us! Heaven and Earth are one when looking through the eyes of spirit! It is one part to think love, yet another to see love, but it's when you can *FEEL* love that the true magic happens, when suddenly we know what *LOVE IS!*

Love IS...
Hand Made!

So this was my intention when embarking upon this journey, to better understand one powerful word, by taking my fate into my own hands. My intention was to give the Universe an opportunity to *FEEL LOVE* from all around the world without ever needing to leave your own home. Giving you the choice of feeling love in the company of yourself, as well as in connecting with the presence of millions of spirits energies floating around you. I recognized how in some cases this word appears to be a bit difficult to let flow off our tongue, and in some cases flows all too easily. In some scenarios we

are afraid to have this word slip off our lips, and in some moments this word is shared without even knowing the true depth of meaning behind the beauty of the word... *LOVE!* This journey has taught me more than words alone can express, because sometimes a feeling cannot be put into words and this holds true in certain special moments in this life, especially when love is playing a role in our lives.

I also experienced how it feels when another shares the word *LOVE* in an endearing way and these moments are what I live for! But beyond this, I learned that we are *LOVE!*

Love is... You! Love is... Me!
Love is... US! Love is... We!
US = United Simultaneously
"US" together, happens to be...
what LOVE IS to me!

We are a sparkle of stardust, floating throughout the atmosphere, without borders or boundaries. We are limitless balls of energy meant to connect with as many other energy balls that we appear to have been disconnected from. The more energy we reconnect with, will add to our vibration and the stronger our vibration becomes, the more energy we will feel. The more energy we connect together, the more we will be able to feel and spread powerful energy via good vibrations, throughout the universe. The stronger the levels of energy we spread through the ripples in the pond, the more love the world will be able to *FEEL* through an experience!

This book is simply an experience, by giving you the reader an opportunity to see and feel another's intention,

by sharing their heart expressing what they see and feel.

Love is... magnetic.

It's your turn and time to be a *Love Magnet!* Now you are connected to their story, in which is now and always has been your story, as well as being *OUR STORY!* My heart knows this because your energy is present at this significant MOMent in time reading these words in which brings you into *OUR* story. Your spirit signed a contract to be connected to our love story at some point, or you would not be here at this MOMent witnessing and living our energies flowing into *"ONE UNITED LOVE"* story to experience. Our spirits united love contract is signed upon conception of the agreement, but does not have an expiration date. Because:

LOVE is...
A journey in which never ends!

Love is... A message that must be spread far and wide!
Love is... Higher powers greatest gift to linear beings of light!
Love is... Higher powers!
Love is... Light!
A higher power is... Love!
A higher power is... Light!
You are... Love!
You are... Light!

So if Love is... a higher power and Love is... Light, and you are Love and you are Light; then you are connected to higher powers and if we individually are all a piece of higher powers Love and Light, then we

are all connected to one another! Which makes US...! United Simultaneously! "One 'UNITED LOVE' team of angels upon Earth, Heaven sent to change the world one breath and one heart at a time!"

I have learned that the more that we connect together, the higher our frequency will become and the higher our frequency becomes, the closer we will be to connecting with heavenly spirits, while still living life on earth's floor. When we connect with heavenly spirits, we will learn all our guides want us to learn to be a universe that mirrors heaven's reflection!

Heaven is... the purest form of love!
Love is... what we are born to reflect!
So let's aim to be Heaven's Mirror's Reflection!

Heaven wishes to educate earth on how to love each other properly, which is unconditionally! The only way is: to accept another without judgments, without expectations, and without conditions attached to our connections! That my family, my friends and my familiar strangers is the purest form of love!

Pure acceptance IS the KEY to LOVE!

Love desires you! You do not need to desire it! All you need to do is to be open to *LOVE and BE-LOVED!* This begins by learning to authentically love yourself! This is your test, a test you grade yourself on! Because again, no one knows you, as well as you know yourself! So if you choose to cheat, lie or twist truths around, then you are only hurting yourself every time you look in your own mirror. Every time you live your truths and connect with

another in a purely heartfelt way, your mirror will shine brighter each and every day! Your own free will allows you to make those choices and I know I choose Love! Now is your time to ask yourself what do you choose?

Love is... all the new world needs now and I am a *"Hopeful Mom"* trying to be the change I wish to see in the new world. I am attempting to do so by uniting hearts throughout the universe through that simply complex four-letter word called, *LOVE.* By attempting to teach the world how easy it is to love properly and I knew I was going to need a lot of support along this *"Loves Highway,"* so I asked my guides and angels from above to search for those they wanted to be apart of my *"Circle of Angels."* Each angel was selected at the predestined right moment in time and place. I thank heaven for aiding in this experience while uniting heaven and earth as *one divine team of angels. There is no "I" in "team," because we need each other to be successful!*

Love is...
the solution to almost every question
asked by your heart!

Love is... ENERGY!!!
And
Love is... THE BEST FEELING!

LOVE has no boundaries and love has no prejudices, nor is love meant to be judged, is what I see...

*Love is... a freedom after solving emotions
and designed to be felt by everyone
everywhere because,
Love is... whom we are all BORN TO BE!*

I am choosing to set an example by paving my walkways with *"LOVE,"* while carrying one title being just a *"HOPEFUL MOM,"* encouraging and praying that others I meet along the way want to live on my street or be my neighbor! (Even if just in our imagination) So we can feel all we are born to be! Just in case you are choosing to find the street I live on, or you may wish to feel my heart so *full of LOVE,* you can locate my spirit on *"Terri Lynne's Way!"* When we meet; we will be gifted with a predestined, free will, heightened senses, fatalistic, destiny, and blessed with a colorful, *"LOVE"* filled kind of day!

The LOVE of my spirit looks forward to feeling your spirit's LOVE!

When this day comes at the predestined right moment in time, heaven will be smiling by knowing our energy led us to each other's hearts, for the ripple of *"UNITED LOVE"* to spread by growing through flowing, then glowing for the entire world to see and feel our love connection!

*Love is...
being the light you wish to see to
remove darkness in our world;
While knowing heaven's watching to
see our LOVE LIGHT shining!*

575

Loves ending and new beginning is, where one door closes and a new door opens... flowing from *"Wings Passed On"* which never ends, designed to continue flowing into *"United Love's"* new beginning... reflecting spirits full of *LIGHT and LOVE!* NOW I'd like to say thank you from my unconditionally *LOVE* filled grateful heart, for accepting to be a part of my journey long before we knew of the journey we have accepted! *I pray EARTH wants to make HEAVEN proud!*

Love is... Joyful!

A meaningful life isn't about perfection,
By being popular without rejection...
It isn't about needing to be rich and buying an expensive extravagant toy....
What It is about is being real, humble and sharing your heart bringing loved ones great joy.
If you can share yourself and touch the lives of others,
While living through connecting with soul sisters and soul brothers...
Then your life will be full and beyond content,
For this is when you'll know you lived a blessed life and your time on earth was well spent.

Terri Lynne

LOVE IS...

Designed to unite the universe through expressions of what

LOVE IS...
In hopes to teach that LOVE should be shared
and all that is mine; is all that is his.
Upon earth it appears we are living our own life,
What you will see is your own life
is connected to mine forever,
even if I am not your wife.

All our connections since our first breath,
were designed with a master plan,
My life has been created to love my fellow man...
So if I have not seen you in years or if we shared life
together from day to day,
I will always still love you,
"Terri Lynne's Way!"

Once I feel our LOVE has a special connection,
I will love you forever without my heart needing protection!
Because love is not born with an expiration date,
Rather destined to touch each other's lives and this,
my friends, is called FATE.

So once you find your life partner,
Do not close down your heart inside...
Rather share your precious connections because
Love was not exchanged to hide!
LOVE has a beginning, not experienced just to end,
So the same goes for us my unconditional friend...

As you turn the final page of our UNITED LOVE story,
My one dream has come true and I am in my glory...

Please carry forward all this book was written for,
Destined to invite you to enter behind a closed door...

If you receive a proper invitation one anticipated future day,
Please accept to feel LOVE; "Terri Lynne's Way!"
When this book closes; a door shall open up wide,
And what you just may see is all our beautiful energy inside...

Then together we will hold hands and touch each other's heart,
For then my big dream will be the universes predestined fresh start!
The beginning of the way we all see, hear, smell, taste, touch and intuitively feel,
Witnessing that our forever connection to heaven is real!

When you receive your invitation you may bring your family and friends along,
So we can add them as a link in our "CHAIN OF LOVE," connecting to remain eternally strong!
When LOVE is the focus this is all we will see,
As we meet many members in our soul family!

The ending of this book is merely the beginning of my next big live-streamed dream,
Which manifested through the pages,
while our "UNITED LOVE" energy
became one dynamic angelic team...
The last step is for this "Team of Angels" to meet face to face,
To exchange our LOVE energy in a sacred space...

The world will be watching our union from inside there homes; from what my vision showed me,
As the filming of this big event will be a live stream telecast for the entire world to see!
And yes the emotion of fear has bubbled up once again,
But the difference is this time it will not paralyze me like it use to back then!

For now I am living my dream that felt too big to share,
But with the universe on my team I have nothing to fear!
As you turn the final page of this book please know, this is not the end,
Yet just the beginning of rewriting the script reading, "LOVE conquers all," being the message I wish to send...

As we will flip history around when we are all in one place,
With tears of joy in our eyes and bright shining smiles when we meet face to face!
What appears to be the end of our "UNITED LOVE" connection,
Has simply just brought us one step closer for us to see upon Earth how "Wings (can be) Passed On," through Heaven's Mirror's Reflection!

We will come together to look in our own mirrors to see who is looking back at us,
As we design a new age flag representing the world as ONE Nation under God is what we will discuss!
As well as changing old laws about abiding by the rules of the land,
Becoming UNITED together about issues and concerns on hand...

United together, rewriting the past, in the present, creating
the future the entire world will be happy to view,
Witnessing how your loved ones in Heaven are closely,
deliberately and intentionally watching over you!
By the time the doors fly open to let the outside world in,
We will have established our new age history,
as the way I see it, this is the election to win!

Vote for yourself on your energy ballot of LOVE,
I know heaven is choosing you too when they mark their energy ballots from above!
We are the "responsible" parties created to unite and conquer with great pride and respect,
I pray your voices and your actions will create PEACE on Earth, by connecting through the LOVE IN OUR HEARTS,
which is what I cast my vote to reflect!

I vote for each individual to take responsibility through actions reflecting honesty, integrity, equality and LOVE,
While using our God-given powers to shine our hearts LIGHT
while linking the world together, connecting as one united divine family chosen from up above!
Rather than choosing to vote for the left side or the right,
Republican, Democrat or Independent does not make sense to me,
Because these parties only separate us, when truly God
intended on us being one great big UNITED FAMILY!

So I am choosing to be placed in the category called the
"RESPONSIBLE" party by choice for the universe,
not just for my homeland,
Where we can work together even if we agree to disagree on issues at hand.
Meeting together with egos left at the door and only open hearts entering inside,
So we can be vulnerable wearing our hearts on our sleeves with nothing on Earth to hide!

We will cast our votes for the truth to be spoken and LOVE
to be what we agree to share,
Releasing emotions, shedding tears while washing away any bubbling up of fear!
For now make yourself comfortable
and take a deep breath if you may,
Then get your passports ready to fly to come meet,
Terri Lynne & The Universe on one soon to be announced HEAVENLY day!

To be continued...
"BEHIND CLOSED DOORS!"
By: WOW MOM PRODUCTIONS

WOW MOM PRODUCTIONS definition:

WOW = Whispers Of Wisdom (through)
MOM = Messages Opening Minds (through)
PRODUCTIONS = Personal Reflections Opening Doors Universally Connecting/Collaborating Truths Intuitively Offering Natural Synchronicities

LOVE is...
The bridge manifested to build our connection upon!

"LOVE IS...

The bridge over troubled water!

Terri Lynne

LOVE IS...
The BRIDGE between Heaven and Earth
The BRIDGE between past, present and future
The BRIDGE between here and there
The BRIDGE between you, yourself and I
The BRIDGE to touch all of humanity
The BRIDGE to freedom
The BRIDGE to uniting one heart to another's!

LOVE IS...

A connection and by crossing this BRIDGE, connects you to your own heart and to the hearts of all others; so let us hold one another's hands while crossing this BRIDGE of LOVE together, for then we will KNOW how LOVE FEELS once we cross over... while still on earth!

NOW please take my hand while allowing me to guide the way, *"Terri Lynne's Way,"* on to **LOVE'S BRIDGE**, so we can cross over together as:

ONE "UNITED LOVE" FAMILY!

Love is... a choice!

Choose love, not war
Choose peace, not unrest
Choose health, not illness
Choose hope, not acceptance
Choose success, not defeat
Choose loving yourself, beyond another loving you
Choose a smile, not a frown
Choose to live your life, not just accept your existence,
Choose to be the author of your own life's script
without regrets, not allowing your character to live a
life unfulfilled or without being purpose driven!

In choosing to love yourself, you will know what love
is...
Simply because *"YOU" are "LOVE!"*

Whenever given a choice, always and forever,
choose LOVE!

I chose to ask the question **what is LOVE?**

NOW at this books end, I received my answer.
I received my answer once I became still and I focused
on the voices of my heart, until I heard my spirits
whisper delivering a profound message. The message I
received to share was:

Love is...
discovered in the stillness, designed to act
upon and learned through your own spirits
whispers!

I choose LOVE forever more! NOW I pray you will always choose LOVE too!

I am hopeful you will choose to listen to the whispers within your own spirit, above and beyond listening to the projected outer words through another's voice. When you listen to the voices of your own heart, you will hear the whispers shared to fill your own heart with all the love you came to feel, to share and to pass on for another to feel, to share and to pass on... This book is my act of random kindness and I am a *"HOPEFUL MOM,"* hoping that you can feel my love and then you will choose to share my gift to you, by passing our *UNITED LOVE* on... as your gift to another. This will allow our Chain of Love to flow, to grow and to glow throughout the Universe beginning from this moment on...

Love is... making good choices!
Once you make the choice to love yourself,
the Universe will feel your love too!

I Love You; Love Me

Meaning: I love you and I love myself and I Love you and I hope you Love yourself, so you can in turn naturally, unconditionally LOVE me too! This is the process to expand our chain of love to, from and for one another.

"LOVE IS...

Above and
beyond all,
the gift of
loving oneself

Terri Lynne

LOVE IS...
Flowing freely
through the atmosphere,
Now that;

Love Is... UNITED
Everywhere!

Terri Lynne

Author's Final
Whispers Of Wisdom!

Dear Universe,

First allow me to say:

HAPPY "LOVE" DAY and THANK YOU FOR MY SMILE! This *"CHAIN OF LOVE"* has been an incredible experience, as my *HEART* is so full of *LOVE.* There is love that fills our heart and there is love that embodies our spirit and when you embrace both your heart and your spirit, then you will know what *LOVE IS!* This feeling is stemming through *LINKING* with others *HEARTS* from around the world since Valentine's Day 2016. Presently, I feel my big dream is coming true, thanks to everyone that shared a message in this story and included me, Terri Lynne into your script before ever taking your first breath in the body you are presently residing in. *NOW,* I believe is the right predestined moment in time to begin spreading our unique unconditional *UNITED LOVE* story far and wide, without feeling the need to keep our unique Love Connection a secret any longer! Because when I reread my script, I recognized that *"THE TRUTH"* was the *OWNLY FACT* I ever lied about! This *"TRUTH,"* *about me "LOVING YOU"* without any strings attached has been a fact of my life. I have felt silenced until I learned the tone of my voice I am choosing to use to reveal this fact *NOW!* I wasn't able to use my voice until I faced my fears and my fears stemmed from feeling the need to hide secrets. Some were secrets within my biological family that I knew, but couldn't share and some were secrets that the world wasn't quite ready to learn as yet. But *NOW* I conquered those fears and I *KNOW* the world is ready to hear TL'S Whispers. The tone will come through softly because I learned that

when people yell, no one pays attention and those trying to listen to you won't hear the message you are trying to get across. But when one whispers, you must really pay close attention to hear the messages being delivered once your spirit chooses to listen.

TL Whispers Secret:

Heaven doesn't yell, because Angels are taught to *"Talk Softly and Carry Angel Wings,"* in order to be certain their audience wants to hear what they are trying to convey. They *KNOW* you are truly paying attention to the messages when they *SEE* your *ACTions.* When you listen to the whispers heaven shares, you will learn all the secrets of life and all you need to know at the core of your being, is that you are love, you are here to feel loved and you are created to give and accept receiving love. Also, the truth is that there is absolutely nothing wrong with loving everyone everywhere so you both can *FEEL* and share in a beautiful exchange of energy with each other! Once you learn this *KEY* lesson, you will *KNOW EVERYTHING* there is to learn about what *LOVE IS!* For me I just released my *FEAR* of being afraid of what you would think of me, if I told you I love everyone when I am a married lady. But now I can use my voice and explain why this has been my path and how my *FAMILY* supports me, *LOVING YOU!*

NOW is the time to ask for you to please help me spread *LOVE* around the world by touching one heart at a time, beginning with your *OWN!*

Last Secrets from TL Whispers, until soon...

Love is... a creation!

So let us create more love, because in my script, one can never get enough and enough is never too much...

when it comes to my favorite subject, which is... *LOVE!*

(Question: Do you recall what the definition of "US" stands for through my eyes? Let me see if you have been paying attention!)

Answer: United Simultaneously! So in order to love myself, I first had to accept loving all of you, because we are ONE!

Which is what we are *NOW* and always have been, but *I AM HOPEFUL* you have been using your senses to *FEEL THIS TRUTH* for yourself! This way we will continue to be connected throughout eternity!

Love is... a masterpiece!

So please, I pray for you to color yours bright, so we can *SEE* each other by day and by night! This way we will always find *"Our Way"* into each other's arms again, without ever feeling the need to be forced apart or feel the need to keep our *LOVE CONNECTION... A SECRET!*

Love is... a connection!

What silly person would ever write their script by reflecting love connecting, then having to go on and live life without this connection through the end of time and beyond? Well obviously, that was *NOT THE SCRIPT* I chose to write!

Because now I hope you can clearly *SEE* through the eyes of your own spirit, how my script knew in order for me to fully learn and eventually know what *LOVE IS...* I was going to need each and every one of YOU! Now all I have left to say is, *THANK YOU* for signing the contract long before our energies embraced each other's! This *"HOPEFUL MOM"* has enough love in her little body to love everyone everywhere and always make whomever

I am with, feel special and feel loved. This *"HOPEFUL MOM"* prays you *FEEL* what *I AM FEELING* at this present moment in time which is that *WE ARE EQUALLY BLESSED* for following *LOVE'S HIGHWAY* right into each other's minds, hearts, bodies, souls and spirits eternally!

In my script, I can clearly see how I wrote this book of love with you and what I wanted to teach the world is that there is only one direction to go to reach the end and new beginning... and this is to travel upon *"LOVE'S HIGHWAY"* every step of our lives! I knew when I was guided to place that pen in my hands long, long ago that I had to practice what I would one day preach and I learned the *OWNLY WAY* I would find you is by heading straight from my heart; directly into yours! *I DO TRULY BELIEVE YOU CAN FEEL OUR CONNECTION NOW* because our hearts are bonded together and I have been set *FREE* because at last I have nothing left to hide now that my *SECRET* is out! Thank you for paying attention to my secrets whispered!

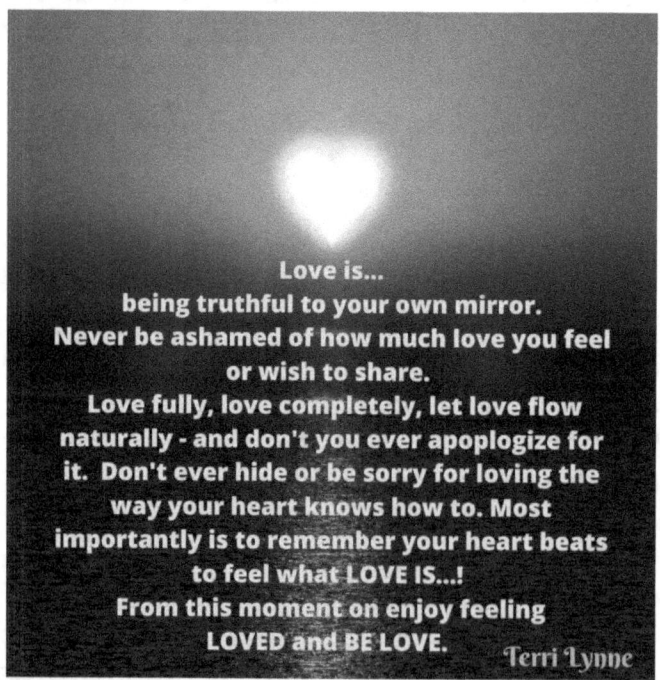

Love is...
being truthful to your own mirror.
Never be ashamed of how much love you feel
or wish to share.
Love fully, love completely, let love flow
naturally - and don't you ever apoplogize for
it. Don't ever hide or be sorry for loving the
way your heart knows how to. Most
importantly is to remember your heart beats
to feel what LOVE IS...!
From this moment on enjoy feeling
LOVED and BE LOVE.
Terri Lynne

I'd like to conclude this book by starting back at the beginning of this *UNITED LOVE* project, when I asked this one question:

What is LOVE?

Throughout these pages energy flowed, and I received many loving responses to my question, which have been documented throughout the pages of this book.

Today, as I was writing while in the process of concluding my thoughts, I received this profound message: "Dear, at the beginning of your book you asked the question; *what is LOVE?*"

Today, we wish to share Heaven and Earths final message: **LOVE IS...** *not a* **question!**

Simply because:
LOVE... IS THE ANSWER!!!!!!!!
LOVE IS... THE SOLUTION!

I *BELIEVE* that by **US** uniting simultaneously with **LOVE** in our hearts, we CAN and we WILL create,

PEACE ON EARTH!

LOVE IS...
A NEVER-ENDING EXPERIENCE!

I am grateful to be sharing this
LOVE EXPERIENCE with YOU!

LOVE IS...
LIFE'S GREATEST GIFT TO TREASURE!

LOVE IS...
A "UNITED LOVE"
BIG DREAM COMING TRUE!

**My heartfelt gratitude goes out to
each and every one of... YOU!**

The end and new beginning upon...

LOVE'S HIGH-WAY!

TL Whispers Secret:
Traveling upon LOVE'S HIGHWAY is THE ONLY WAY
to go... IF you're headed in the direction of,

PEACE ON EARTH!

These following words may appear to be my final message reflecting what LOVE IS... but it is simply just the beginning of a never-ending LOVE story!

I'll see you SOON!

LOVE

IS...

NOW

UNITED!

NOW...
I AM HEALTHY
I AM STRONG
I AM GRATEFUL
I AM BLESSED
I AM LOVED!

If you choose to be all of the above,
I pray you choose to follow my
lead...
Take my hand while trusting
universal guidance and you too
shall

BE LOVE and BE-LOVED!

593

"UNITED LOVE"

By: Terri Lynne & The Universe!

*We blew hearts full of LOVE
out into the Universe, as you can now see,
For your heart to be touched,
after feeling our new age LOVE story!
The End... (of our book)
is the beginning of a new way to live,
Accepting to receive LOVE, so you have
that much more LOVE to give!
May love flow forward through my heart
and yours,
Meeting one day soon in a sacred space
BEHIND CLOSED DOORS!
Because the end is simply an illusion created
to see the beginning of a new reality,
As we connect as one for the entire
Universe to see!
Our "UNITED LOVE" is my gift I wish to extend,
Ending with a new beginning, without end...*

My, Terri Lynne's inner child whispered inside my heart, sharing my truths being that all I cared to learn about in this linear lifetime experience was everything I could learn about what, LOVE IS! What I learned was that, we all need each other to accomplish our dreams and I've witnessed how:

LOVE IS... amplified and magnified through
A CHAIN REACTION!

I've learned:

LOVE is... merely an illusion you see,
Reflective in your own mirror daily...
So you may as well like the view,
Of the image you have a lifetime to look into...
While loving the illusion you are projecting,
And loving the intention your life's reflecting!

"Love is...

Seen through the EYE of the beholder!
Terri Lynne

LOVE IS... OUR REFLECTION!
We are a reflection of LOVE, and LOVE IS...
ALL we were born to REFLECT!

I am hopeful that you learned how to:

"LOVE your Mirror's Reflection,

BELIEVE in Miracles and

DREAM BIG!"

WELCOME TO OUR:

"LOVE REVOLUTION"

Our EVOLUTION of UNITING through LOVE!

"Terri Lynne's Way"
is to LOVE and to BE-LOVED and
I HOPE you choose to follow my lead to...

LIVE LOVE!

Illustration By: Cynthia Fitzgibbon

As this book is reaching you turning the last page, I wish to say I hope you enjoyed this gift from my heart and soul connected to the universes heart and soul connected to yours! Allow me to extend my gratitude for you accepting to sign the contract, agreeing to be alive participating as a beacon of light, for my spirit to connect and *LINK* to at this time upon earth! Here now for us to *spread LOVE* around the world through our unconditional *"UNITED LOVE"* story; for the entire Universe to use their God given senses to *SEE, HEAR, SMELL, TASTE, TOUCH and KNOW all of what LOVE IS!*

LOVE IS.

LOVE IS... designed to be passed on!

Thank you for accepting to be drawn in to our
"CIRCLE OF LOVE!"
Where love goes around and around and never ends...
Just like a wedding band,
that cannot break and fortunately never bends!

Now I am HOPEFUL you can feel our LOVE and then
choose to BE the LOVE you FEEL!
Validating to the Universe that energy,
frequency and vibration can aid in helping Earth HEAL!

BE LOVE and BE-LOVED is what I wish for you,
So when we all LIVE LOVE my big dream will
come true!!!!!!!!!

This was my BIG DREAM and I THANK YOU for making
MY BIG DREAM COME TRUE,
Not only for myself,
but for the children of our world and for
each and every one of YOU!

Thank you for being a part of my world and may your
inner light shine the most vibrant radiant hues
for the entire world to see,
Who you are and all of who you are
THE CHOSEN ONE to be!

I've learned that:
LOVE IS... MANIFESTED
by shifting an illusion, into our REALITY!

LOVE IS...
REAL and I Thank You!

NOW
IS
THE
TIME
TO
BE
LOVE
AND
BE-LOVED!

Until the end of time and beyond...

599

I wish to leave you with a quote from my first book, *"Wings Passed On..."* which is a secret of how I found my paths way to *LOVE,* from the corner of my bed *BEHIND CLOSED DOORS!* This journey of *LOVE* guided me to your hearts door to connect with and I am eternally grateful you opened up and let me in!!! This whisper appears to be working out well for me, I hope it works out well for you too!

"Take the time, to read the signs,
An Angel you will see,
One up above and one in your mirror,
Throughout eternity!"

The TIME is NOW, to READ this SIGN,

For YOU to clearly SEE,
The ANGEL of LOVE in YOUR mirror,
The way I found the "ANGEL IN ME!"
NOW is OUR TIME to cross over
LOVE'S BRIDGE together as;

ONE "UNITED LOVE" FAMILY!

Please Note:
This LOVE SIGN was shown to me the day I completed this book!

Now all I have left to say is:

WELCOME TO MY WORLD!

I AM HOPEFUL you enjoyed the view looking at the world through my senses and have the sense to choose to follow my lead on to;

LOVE'S HIGHWAY!

LOVE... is energy to be passed on!
I pray you choose to
pass our unique unconditional
UNITED LOVE story on...
to all those you LOVE!

FROM THIS MOMENT ON
PLEASE CONSIDER YOURSELF LOVED
BECAUSE:

I AM SENDING
YOU LOVE,
TO PASS ON...

https://youtu.be/Vv_co-zSE4I
Guided Meditation with Gabriel Gonsalves
(Please try to watch this video)

601

Love is... who you are and this is what the "UNIVERSE and I" wish for you to know!

LOVE IS...
ALL THAT TRULY MATTERS AND...
THIS IS WHOLE HEARTEDLY WHAT TERRI LYNNE BELIEVES!

This book is dedicated to:
Everyone, everywhere who was born with a heart!

May you continue on your ***JOURNEY OF LOVE*** and from this moment on, may you... *SEE, HEAR, SMELL, TASTE, TOUCH,* and all combined *KNOW* what it *FEELS* like to:

BE LOVE and BE-LOVED!

May the ending and new beginning forever guide you upon, LOVE'S HIGHWAY leading you back to seeing your reflection; being the MIRACLE that you are!

If you are reading this whisper at this present moment,
I pray you choose to **FEEL** our;

"UNITED LOVE" and desire to PASS our LOVE ON...

Love is... United Love

IT'S TIME TO UNITE

Terri Lynne

Designed With Unconditional LOVE

By: Terri Lynne & THE UNIVERSE!
February 14, 2016 ~ February 14, 2020

Please hear my WHISPERS, when we stand and walk as ONE UNITED LOVE FAMILY, I feel we will stand and walk forever... UNDIVIDED!

NOW is our divine time to unite by touching one heart at a time creating a ripple affect spreading far and wide, so that all we will FEEL is EACH OTHER'S LOVE... UNITED!

THIS IS THE WORLD I SEE IN MY BIG DREAMS AND NOW IS THE TIME I WISH TO SAY,

WELCOME

TO

MY

WORLD!!!

-TL

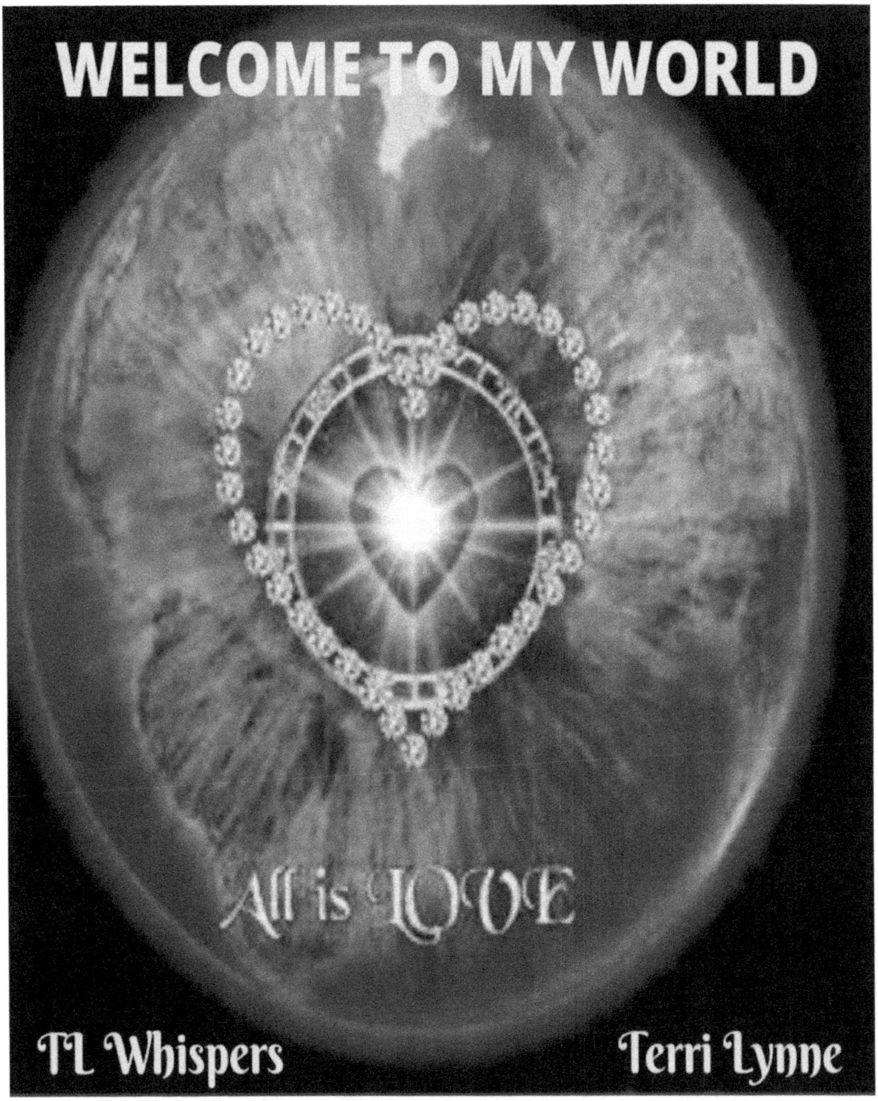

WELCOME TO MY WORLD

All is LOVE

TL Whispers   Terri Lynne

A world designed for US to
BE LOVE and to BE-LOVED!

LOVE AND

BE-LOVED

TL Whispers   Terri Lynne

Image credit to: © Sandaru Nirmana | Dreamstime.com

Love is ...
Our world set free
Upon the wings of Love!

Terri Lynne

Graphic Designer: Ron Lopez

Dear Universal Family,

I am choosing to add this final message after our UNITED LOVE book has been completed, with the intention to share one of the greatest lessons in my lifetime. I am sharing the below message which was a heartfelt letter written from the corner of my bed, created on 11/3/2016, in my own company. This letter had been tucked away until today; when I turned on my computer to fill out a form requested by my editing company needing to be completed in order to upload our UNITED LOVE book on to Amazon. As this unsearched for letter popped up in my recent emails, sent to myself from my cell phone from years ago, I felt compelled to read what energy drew my attention at this divine, present moment in time.

After reading this letter of exploration, insight, knowledge and love written by myself, for myself, to better understand why I had felt driven to UNITE the world through LOVE; well something deep inside me, which I call my intuition, felt this was meant to be the message I should leave you with before the last page has been turned. I knew in my inner knowing that Heaven, my Spirit Guides, my Angels and my loved one's upon Earth, as well as my loved one's resting in peace on the other side of the veil, all wanted me to share this message with you. May this be just one example of how time sitting in silence, time spent in the good company of yourself alone, allows clarity to reign truth upon your spirit and in this truth may you be healed, as was I. Bringing you back to your center, so when you step beyond your bedroom door, and turn the knob to step out beyond your front door, you enter the atmosphere as a being of love and you touch other's hearts with the love you exude with confidence and great pride, simply for doing your life's work in solitude. In return,

you won't unconsciously project unsolved mysteries out into the world, but rather reflect light for others to feel your love!

As my closing gift from this books journey, I wish to wrap you all up in a warm swaddled blanket, offering you a soft, gentle kiss on your forehead; allowing you to feel the LOVE you felt from your first breath in this lifetime! A gift to remind you that:

LOVE IS... all that truly matters in this life! SELF LOVE IS... the magnet to attract more LOVE into your life!

My life has been flowing like a river, hitting some bumps and getting some bruises along life's way, but it is in the never giving up attitude that steers my raft to beautifully peaceful days in the sun, with not a single cloud in the sky. Days when after the rain falls, when the sun breaks through the clouds, I enjoy searching for the rainbows.

LOVE IS... the pot of gold at the end of our rainbow!

To me, **LOVE IS... FAMILY** and once again allow me to reiterate what Family means, Forever A Marriage I Love You! In my life, I made the conscious decision to never give up on family and to never allow another to change me! While always trying to be a magnet of LOVE, until and on through witnessing how LOVE prevails! In my final words after linking together with so many beautiful light workers filled with radiant love energy from around the world, I feel even stronger today, then when I started manifesting this book by knowing that

LOVE HEALS all wounds and **LOVE WILL WIN** in the end and new beginning!

BUT, we each must be responsible for our OWN actions and when taking ACTions, I pray we all can make wise choices. I chose to understand what **LOVE IS...** NOW I PRAY you choose to look inside your own mirror and see the LOVE you were born to be! Just as I SEE YOU, being "LOVE" as you're an integral part of me!

LOVE is... Color-blind! LOVE is... Free! LOVE is... A journey worth following!

***Please note:
Below is the letter of exploration to myself, through automatic writing, shared exactly the way I chose to send this letter to myself. Deep soul searching reflecting the end result and new beginning of how I chose to take the time, to read the signs, to see the love in me, with the purest intention; designed to share my LOVE with the LOVE I see, hear and feel from... the LOVE in you! I am a "HOPEFUL MOM" praying we can all see the LOVE we were born to be in our own mirror's reflection, born to shine LIGHT on to each other simultaneously! So, then we can SHINE our LOVE'S LIGHT for the entire world to SEE & FEEL, in order for LOVE to WIN in the end and new beginning...
10/18/20

***Below please read: Terri Lynne's message to Terri Lynne; meant to be shared with the Universe at the predestined, divine, right moment in time; which is NOW!!!!!!!!!!
BE LOVE & BE-LOVED,
TL

Begin forwarded message:

From: Terri Lynne <TLWhispers@yahoo.com>
Subject: One of my greatest life's lessons is... to love from the core of my heart unapologetically
Date: November 3, 2016 at 10:38:02 PM PDT
To: TLWhispers@yahoo.com

One of my lessons is to love from the core of my heart unapologetically, which is where my sensitive feelings come from, even when I don't feel the person I'm loving, loves in the same way as I do.

One of my life's challenges is to love them anyways, because this is not only my lesson to be learned, but theirs as well.

What feels wrong in my soul when I checked in with spirit, my spirit, about this is I felt if someone doesn't love me or respect me the way I love and respect myself, my soul feels I should walk away and locate souls and hearts that can, that will and that do!

My conflict within myself is how do I do both, one and the other, while living and loving in the same physical body? How do I let go and hold on simultaneously? This is where my heart feels conflicted.

For me, feeling comes through my hearts intuition and this intuition comes through what I'm "feeling" and if someone's energy conflicts with my energy, my heart shuts down and then I can't feel anymore. Whereas, when I accept energy that feels loving, I open my heart and more love flows.

What I feel on a soul level is that:
To me when emotions bubble up and need solving and then once solved need forgiveness and then once forgiveness occurs, next comes the releasing and letting go of this one particular emotion or a flood of emotions all simultaneously, is a great gift you give yourself! In which over time, the universe will benefit from because you will be left lighter from less baggage to carry forward on your journey! This emotional baggage will be released leaving empty space that can be filled with pure love!

The more one empties their emotional baggage, the more space is available to fill your own heart and soul with love, more and more love. With love in your heart others will feel your love and you will then become a walking example of heaven on earth.

I see that judgement day should not come through judging another, nor should it come at the end of one's life, but rather by looking into oneself, to see your own mirror, the image through your own reflection, where you will be able to observe how your own life is going, growing, developing and manifesting back to your first breath in this lifetime, reflective of who you were born to be!

I believe and I feel, it is in the letting go that we receive all we came to accept, to learn, to teach and to be! We are here to be students and teachers, designed to become our soul's reflection, an essence of light. When we are connected to the depths and images and feelings within our own soul, nothing on earth can take this away, no one on earth can ruffle our feathers, and no one can convince us differently of the truths of our own soul. I feel this way because it is within the undoing and the unknowing that we come to learn and recognize,

while seeing and feeling what we came here to do, to learn and to teach. The knowing doesn't come from the input of others opinions, the "knowing" comes from the silence, the letting go of the knowledge others taught or put on us based off of what they have come to believe as their truth, as they projected their beliefs upon us. Our inner knowing already knows all we need to accept in order to carry out our life's mission. All we need to do, is pay attention to the whispers from our angels and spirit messages and follow our own souls lead. I feel religion teaches us to follow another's direction, whereas for me, I prefer the spiritual path; which I feel teaches us to follow our own soul's lead. When we dig deep into ourselves, we learn which WAY to go heading in the direction of dreams coming true. For me, I choose to travel upon LOVE'S HIGHWAY and we cannot take the LOW WAY to reach LOVE as our final destination.

Although, it is in silencing the mind, quieting the inner chatter, that we shall hear all our OWN SOUL has longed to hear and these words will be music to our ears, giving us a feeling inside our heart of what love is! The greatest feeling on earth is when you listen to the music of your soul sing to you, then your life becomes a dance! In order to dance through life, one shall be light on their feet and the best way to be light on your feet is by removing all that is weighing you down! So, a real good place to begin this dance is by trying to hear the rhythm of your own heart! Do so by standing or lying still and paying close attention to the silence of the heart which at first may feel like a block, a wall, a fortress blocking the sound of your own heartbeat. But don't give up, don't give in to this moment because if you just hold on a little bit longer and remain present with your own presence, you will experience a breakthrough, life-altering moment! At which time, little by little the

emotions will bubble up and you will feel why you shut down your heart to begin with.

Then it's your time to do the work...
Don't push these emotions under the carpet or under the bed or locked away in a closet! The polar opposite is needed and I mean needed at those moments of truth and validation to your own soul! Soon you will begin to understand why this particular emotion feels so painful and then the more you quiet the mind, the more your heart can be heard and the more you listen to your heart, then you will learn about the lessons your soul came here to learn. Giving you an opportunity to be your own teacher! Recognizing through an awareness, that the material you are learning feels like it is very familiar.

Ultimately, we can listen to words of wisdom from others, to feel what resonates as truth inside your own soul, while using others advice as a Barometer or a Richter Scale of how their words register with your emotions! Some people's thoughts, feelings and actions we will connect with deeply or passionately and some we will not be able to relate to at all on any topic. Please trust those feelings because they were placed in your energy field to give your heart an opportunity to better understand your soul speak its truth to you! Only you will know whose words resonate as truth inside your soul and whose are the polar opposite thoughts, feelings, words and actions and this is your lesson for your own best interest to pay attention to how you FEEL in those moments. Try to learn this because it's your own free will that will ultimately decide if you choose to tuck those emotions away or look them straight in the eyes and heart of the matter to see all you can see, to feel all you can feel, to heal as many emotions as you can in

this lifetime, so your mind, heart, body, soul and spirit can be free and be light, so you can dance!

If you don't listen for the music, you will never hear a beat! If you do listen to the music, you will hear your own HEART beat! Once you fine tune the channel of your own heartbeat, you can then send the energy of your frequency out into the universe! Once your frequency is strong and you feel love from inside your own soul, you will have the great pleasure of being able to connect with others whom have raised their frequency, by taking their time to do their work, to tune into their own hearts beat! When two high frequency hearts connect, you can experience where the expression of two hearts beating as one derives from! When two loving, open, unguarded, pure, honest, clean, in-tune hearts connect, the feeling will be magical and will feel like Heaven on Earth!

To manifest this for yourself, it's not that you want to tune out the rest of the world or put yourself in solitude, so you can be alone to drown out the voices of others. But rather to find your own quiet space to reflect and to recognize how your own heart and soul is feeling. If the answers you hear or the feelings you experience appear like they are creating a wall around your heart, then you know you have some inner work to do. If and I prefer to say when, you take the time to read the signs you will see all your soul, which is the spirits body, was created to see at the right predestined moment in time. We are not meant to force another to think as we think or feel as we feel. But if we can challenge another to think and feel for themselves, the thinking will eventually be drowned out by what the soul feels. Once we are tapped into our soul, we will begin to hear our heart speak and this is truly the only voice we are designed to listen to.

Once we begin to listen to our own heart, we will begin to feel our hearts beat once again! Just as when the newborn baby enters the world, the doctor's first action once the baby arrives in this physical form, is to listen for the baby's heartbeat. Followed by listening for the baby's cry, which is showing the doctor and the parents that the baby is alive and healthy! At this moment the babies cry is teaching its own spirit to hear their own voice and express what they are feeling so everyone knows how the baby is feeling. The tone of this baby's expression may not be pleasing to the ears of others, but a welcomed sound to the ones connected to this infant because that sound reflects life! This voice is noticed and regardless of how loud or how soft the baby expresses what it's feeling, everyone is paying attention to hear a voice come out! That voice regardless of its tone is welcomed and celebrated because once we hear the heartbeat and once we hear the voice, initially expressed as a cry, then all can breathe easy. Every one of us on this earth knows the first sound we all expressed is a cry, then as time goes on and we develop, we grow, we mature, we learn other ways of expressing ourselves. In those instances of trying to find our breath when we are feeling challenging emotions, at times it takes us back to our first breath, our first heartbeat, our first verbal expression of crying, until we mature and take the time to learn what helps us self sooth to breathe freely and unrestricted, while of great importance also learning what takes our breath away! Both important and not so easy to accept feeling wise, while remembering practice makes perfect. Once we learn how to self sooth and we learn what takes our breath away, it will help us learn to feel our own heartbeat. While recognizing when the beating is in its own rhythm, beating in its own flow and once we listen to the voices inside our own heart, we will connect with our own soul and we will know by our inner knowing all we entered this life to learn. I've

learned the best way to feel the rhythm of thy heart, is by staying in your flow! Roadblocks and detours are signs to reevaluate where you are standing presently, giving you an opportunity to change the course you're heading simply to find your flow once again in a different direction if need be. All we need to know comes with us on this journey! From the moment we take our first breath until the moment we take our last, all we truly need to know is to look inside our heart! For this is where we will connect with our own soul and when this connection is made, this is where and when the real magic will begin and where the signs along life's way will show you MIRACLES UPON MIRACLES on earth!

Within these MIRACLES you will see, your OWN life! Your own heart! Your own voice! Your own spirit! Your own energy! Your own gifts! You will see YOUR OWN SELF & ALL OTHER'S AS A MIRACLE!

Once you SEE this you will begin to FEEL the rhythm of your HEART and you will hear the voices of the heart and once you SEE & FEEL & HEAR this, then you will KNOW the messages your SOUL has been crying out for you to hear! Once you connect with and actually SEE your inner child, you will soon hear the voice inside that wants to be heard and once you tap into connecting with your inner child's HEART & SOUL, you will recognize the TONE of your ENERGY!

A gentle tone is welcoming when touching other souls' lives. While yelling, loud, judgmental, negative, harsh, condescending or bitter energy tones are to be pushed away, shut out and blocked. Though it appears that this energy is so vocally and energetically strong that people can't help but listen to it because it's so loud forcing others to hear that tone over the quiet ones. Once you use another's tone as a reference point and when you

are privileged to recognize the more peaceful, calm, serene TONES & ENERGIES, your heart will feel at peace. Even when the other soul doesn't say a single word, but their energy is felt and feels good on your skin, then you will know by feeling that you are in your flow and in the presence of good company. When you recognize your OWN TONE & ENERGY, and what works out well for you to be your own personal best you will have less emotions bubble up. Once you go within and learn the lessons your spirit came here to learn by seeing and hearing that other loud tones and energies intertwined with your day to day existence in this lifetime, don't make you feel comfortable, you can make a practice of removing yourself long enough to do your own work, which is recognition of thy self! Listen carefully to the whispers of your soul and trust the messages they are relaying! Then eventually you will SEE, HEAR & FEEL what's inside your own soul and the TONE and ENERGY that you deliver and share will be peaceful! Remember, PEACE comes from within. It is our responsibility as a human being to locate our peaceful place, so we don't project negativity upon the world or upon other's who cross our path. The more peaceful humans are within, the more love will be shared when uniting!

We are all born to thrive not to shrivel away! We are all born to LOVE our fellow man, but can only do this if we take the time to read the signs, to bring ourselves back home inside the womb of our creation, where all we knew was LOVE!

To give love unconditionally through a look, a smile, a touch, a heartbeat felt and a voice expressed... this is our first experience of life and then from this moment on all we crave, all we wish for and all we are born to FEEL IS UNCONDITIONALLY LOVED back; with the same innocence of that LOVE AT FIRST SIGHT FEELING

between a parent and their offspring, an adult with a baby, one human being loving another; just because it FEELS so magical, "IT" being this "MIRACLE" called BIRTH!

As you took your first breath, felt your first heartbeat, heard your voice for the first time which made you cry even more uncertain of what you were hearing, because you never made your own audible sound until that moment. But you instantly calm down when you are wrapped up tightly swaddled, and the moment you hear a voice of a familiar tone, which is your parent's voices or your sibling's voices, and then you begin to recognize their energy. In this familiar space you become calm and you accept receiving the love your parents in this physical form share with you and your spirit feels loved unconditionally because your exchange was so simple. Love is... simple. It was/is a "feeling," a feeling which came through just a look in each other's eyes, a touch from an ever so gentle kiss to be certain this kiss was soft and sweet from the parent to their baby and the baby felt the gentleness, the purity behind this kiss. Then hearing the tone of each other's voices was music to your ears, and then to lie together feeling the beat of each other's hearts which was the purest sound and most beautiful tone two could hear in one shared moment, with many duplicated moments soon to reveal themselves! In this moment you know what LOVE IS supposed to FEEL like, to feel not only LOVED, but protected! The rest of our lives our soul is searching to FEEL THIS WAY again! For some souls wrote into their script of life to have love follow them every day of their life by loving themselves and by others loving them just the way they are and for others they wrote into their script to give me a lifetime to better understand love, by challenging my life with souls who are learning this lesson as well and together over time and soul searching

allow me to learn how love feels and to trust what love is. While acknowledging how important it is to love and respect thyself! For others they know from their first breath love comes from within, within your own soul by loving yourself first and foremost and for those souls the law of attraction will be ever present like a magnet to steel because love loves love!

If I AM LOVE AND YOU ARE LOVE then WE ARE LOVE and if I LOVE MYSELF AND YOU LOVE YOURSELF and we are drawn together, WE WILL BE ENERGETICALLY PULLED FROM ONE LOVE TOWARDS ANOTHER LOVE and when two hearts connect through LOVE they will be living and experiencing Heaven on Earth!!!

This my dear family and my dear friends and acquaintances old and new, is the lesson my soul spoke to me this morning to teach my adult self what my inner child has been longing to feel from my parents! My soul didn't long for material possessions or a large bank account, my SOUL longed to FEEL MUTUALLY CONNECTED THROUGH UNCONDITIONAL LOVE and even though my soul recognized from day one what FEELS RIGHT INSIDE MYSELF AND WHAT FELT WRONG about LOVE exchanged, I knew there were great lessons to be learned throughout the process of my life. My soul just explained to my heart that just because I know what love feels like I still had to learn how to set boundaries around how I allow another to express themselves through their actions and by their words to love me! Quite simply I learned that because I was born as a lover not a fighter and as an adult because I was raised around loud voices and opinionated tones of energy, I chose to be the quiet one and to become the observer of the world around me. Everyone around me when growing up, was so captivated by hearing their own voices, beyond hearing another's whispers or cries that I would go to bed, close my blinds, and close my door just to drown out the noise. The reason was because speaking for my soul, the words coming out of those voices were just noise and I didn't want to listen to a single word of it. So, I self-soothed and tucked myself into bed and prayed, I prayed for the outside noise from my room to stop, I prayed for heaven to help me help them by trying to get them to hear my whispers, but they had their own agenda. Their agenda was to get their own opinion and their own voice to be heard, as I curled up in the fetal position sucking my thumb, as a little girl, praying to heaven for answers to teach me how to teach my family what love is. What I knew for sure it was not about being right or being wrong, I knew it was not about abuse or disrespect, I knew love was gentle and love was kind and I knew it began within your own self, but as I laid in my bed what I didn't know was how do I get to teach my family to know what I know???

And so, my journey of self-realization began, my spiritual quest began as I tried to better understand how as a young girl, I knew what my family didn't appear to know yet. Once I started on this path of self-exploration for me to present my best self to the world, I learned that my soul knew how love was supposed to feel and I knew when others thought they were loving me when I couldn't feel their love, because they either didn't love themselves or they had a different love style than I was born with! I am grateful for all my boyfriend's growing up and eternally grateful for my husband for treating me with the utmost of tender, loving care, while respecting me to feel how love is meant to feel. As time went by, I followed my burning desire, which I later learned was my purpose for taking my first breath in this physical form in the linear existence. First, I was destined to learn and receive an education on love and then I was

guided to share what I have learned along my life's way with the Universe!

Which brings me to why I sent out the "CHAIN OF LOVE" letter on Valentine's Day 2016, with the intention to touch another's heart with love, in hopes that they will share a message of what LOVE IS to them. Bringing a world together, so we can share the Universes unique **"UNITED LOVE"** story with every soul that is a part of or soon to be entering this linear existence; to have and to hold their own handbook on LOVE to pass on... from generation to generation! Intended to experience heaven smiling from above Earths clouds, as they make their presence be seen by shining down a rainbow beyond the rain, to show us the colors of magic and MIRACLES!

It is completely up to us as an individual, as well as a reflection and projection coming from a united front, to be the candle in the wind and to never allow another to blow out your eternal flame!

LOVE IS... an eternal flame that never burns out, and when touched by another's candle only glows brighter!

My wish for every soul around the world is to keep on shining like the sun and glowing like the moon.

I believe where there is LIGHT, darkness cannot prevail.
I believe where there is LIGHT, LOVE can and will conquer all!!! TL

***Please note: This message was typed one finger at a time, on my cell phone, until the last letter has been reached, which is how I do my work. While the rest of the world is sleeping or working on their life's mission or voicing their opinions and judging other's, I laid quietly in my bed asking Heaven, what can I do by my actions to help heal the wounded and help heal the world?

My answer was reflected in the work I chose, placing my energy into learning what the world needs NOW and what I learned was the world needs to FEEL LOVED! Earth needs to FEEL LOVED! Every human being needs to FEEL LOVED!

I learned that LOVE IS... an inside job! No one on earth is responsible to do your own life's work. Which I feel is to see in your own mirror who you are born to be, which is LOVE! A being of pure LIGHT! A spark off the old block and God is the block and we are all but a spark of God's light. We together create the world! The world is not whole until each one of our sparks are shining. Now I hope you choose to take your time, to read your signs and find your way back to your first breath's start as I just did and I pray you can FEEL LOVED, as I do! Because I Do Love You! I Do See You! I Do Hear You! But I've learned I hear you more so in the soft tones of truth from your heart, so I don't have to waste my energy on drowning out the noise or lie awake night after night trying to comprehend what you are really meaning to say. My favorite expression I teach my family, after learning from my mom (may she rest in peace), who didn't learn this lesson unfortunately until the night before she passed. I always whisper, "Say what you mean and mean what you say!" So then, I can actually hear the messages you're trying to convey from deep within your heart. Once you listen to your

whispers, and you feel LOVE for yourself, then the real work begins... to pass your LOVE ON!!!

I just did and I can only pray that YOU, the link in our chain of love, the reader one day soon of "UNITED LOVE," choose to follow my lead for Earth and for Heaven's sake! I am signing off from the corner of my bed in a very darkened room, where I see the world full of LIGHT & LOVE! Terri Lynne xxxooo
Sent from my iPhone

You've Been Visited
By A Love Angel,
Consider Yourself LOVED!

The Angel In Me

Now It's Your Time
To Pass Our
UNITED LOVE on... Terri Lynne

I am HOPEFUL

That after the last page has been turned,

Our "UNITED LOVE" story will continue flowing through all...

The Lovers

The Dreamers

The **Peacemakers**

The Believers

The Earth Angels

The Light Workers

And

The Healers

Upon Earth &

Heaven sent

To pass our

"UNITED LOVES"

Big Dream On...

Because LOVE IS...

Meant to be shared!

With heartfelt LOVE from my

Open HEART to yours,

Terri Lynne

TL Whispers

"UNITED LOVE" IS... WHAT 'LOVE' IS!!!

LOVE IS...
Guiding another's SPIRIT to be all of what LOVE IS!

Terri Lynne - TL Whispers
~ A GUIDE for your SPIRIT ~
TL's Motto:
"Talk Softly & Carry Angel Wings"

E-Mail: TLWhispers@UnitedLove.Love
Website: http://UnitedLove.Love
Phone: (818) 949-8594

I look forward to connecting with you!
If you wish to be a part of living the reality of our
"United Love" dream, then please message me via my
website or my email and I will happily add
you to our "Chain of Love," connecting you as another
LINK in our CHAIN!

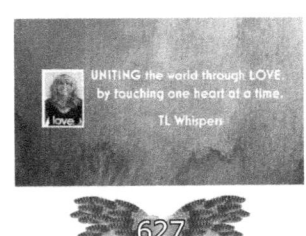

627

Love is... courageous!

It takes inner courage
To own your story
It takes unconditional
Self love
To accept it

Terri Lynne

Today... at this exact moment,
I can proudly say,
I OWN and I ACCEPT my story!
All thanks to YOU! -TL

Love isn't perfect. It isn't a fairytale or a storybook & it doesn't always come easy. Love is overcoming obstacles, facing challenges, fighting to be together, holding on & never letting go. It is a short word easy to spell, difficult to define & impossible to live without.

FEBRUARY

1 2

4

LOVE is work, but most of all, LOVE is realizing that every hour, every minute, & every second was worth it because you did it together.

Terri Lynne

Dear Universe,
We can now say... WE DID IT!
TOGETHER!
Together we... UNITED in LOVE!

LOVE IS... UNITED LOVE!

New Year

Chapter One

Terri Lynne

LOVE IS...
The end and new beginning of our next
decade filled with... UNITED LOVE!

630

Section Seven

LOVE SONGS

RAW EMOTIONS PULSATING THROUGH SHARED
HEARTS AND MINDS OF MANY.
~MUSIC

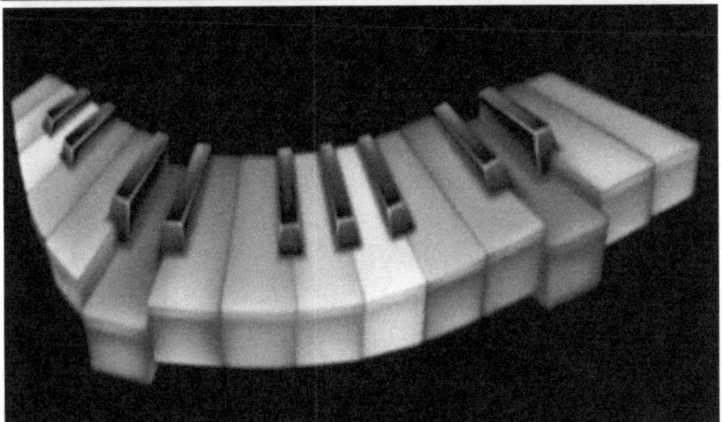

LOVE... is the KEY!
I wish to listen to!

If you shared a message in this book, *THANK YOU* for your touch on the pages of our United Love Story designed to uplift the Universe. I am grateful for your energy, which added a peaceful touch within my true life's story, and this I will carry with me until the end of my linear time upon earth and beyond into the ethereal realm of heaven through my spirits imprint. I've come to learn through experience that time never ends, because each ending is merely a new beginning. *THANK YOU* for magnifying your *ENERGY*, allowing the world to see you shine! *THANK YOU* for your *GIFT OF LOVE! THANK YOU for helping this MOM teach her children well!*

Now as a GIFT for you, I am choosing to share songs that touched my heart along my life's way, meant to express why I embarked upon this journey to touch lives with LOVE to begin with! I invite you to search for these love songs on my website at www.UnitedLove.Love. This is where you will find a playlist with the YouTube link to view songs validating to my spirit how LOVE IS... what will heal the world! May this playlist of music touch your heart, while adding LOVE in your life, as they did for myself in my world. The world I see is full of a colorful "UNITED LOVE" dream come true for all of us!

From this moment on... in the here and now *WOW MOMents* of our lives connected, may we continue

sharing all of what *LOVE IS!* Which is simply sharing our spirits with each other by touching each other's lives, one heart at a time! *WE ARE* what *LOVE IS* and our spirits *LOVE* the feeling of being *LOVED!*

This has truly been an incredible experience! I feel blessed to have been touched by so many Angels around the world, through so many open hearts that chose to share in this big dream come true. I hope you *feel blessed* to be apart of this big dream too! *Welcome to our team of angels!*

If you choose to take the time to listen to the playlist of love songs on my website, I feel you will get the full extent of this books message, as well as my hearts intent behind this gift offered as an even exchange of energy to and from the Universe. My hearts intention is wanting to UNITE the world through all of what LOVE IS!

BELOW ARE THREE LOVE SONGS TO UNITE US THROUGH MUSIC!

The full playlist can be enjoyed at:
www.UnitedLove.Love

UNIVERSAL LOVE - PAUL LUFTENEGGER
https://youtu.be/owfP_hmkfoA

Paul Luftenegger is an International Multi Award Winning Singer, Songwriter and Composer, who's energy was guided my way through a special soul named Elspeth Kerr, which is the co author of their book titled, "Magic and Miracles." We were divinely connected two days prior to me completing this book. With Paul's consent and blessing, I would like to share his message through his song "UNIVERSAL LOVE," which in an uncanny way is my big dreams vision! Please enJOY this beautiful MAGICAL song! A creation from an inspirational light being upon earth that truly recognizes the MIRACLE we ALL are upon Earth and Heaven sent!

UNIVERSAL LOVE – Lyrics

The stars are calling out your name
This world is shifting it's about to change
Oh don't you worry little dear
There's so much love in the atmosphere
There are angels here, they are near
To guide us here
The world's alive with so much light
The universal love has come

634

Oh rest your head and rest your heart
The violet sky has come
The kingdom of creation lies right inside
Don't be scared and don't you dare
This is a plan for a better man

Have faith in the stars up in the sky
Have faith in the skies that we share
We are a part of all that is
We are a part of it all
Expand your mind and release the shackles of this life
Who do you want to be you can be anything that you
want to be

We are creators of the universe
We are creators of love
We are the superheroes of our time
It's time to be all we can be
Release your fears there's only love here
There's only love
There's only love
There's only love to come!

'UNIVERSAL LOVE' music/lyrics written by:
Paul Luftenegger © all work under copyright 2013
Paul Luftenegger - all rights reserved
100% ownership rights
Registered with SOCAN

LOVE IS A GIFT – ARKANGELO
https://youtu.be/Bsem9hAybOM

-Lyrics

Love is more than words could ever say,
Give it time and life will show you how to beat the
pain,
Let it crash upon the shore; let it rain for days and
days.
As many days as it takes to be sure,
And you will find that love will wash it all away,

We are made of the same bright stars, which we gaze,
And all we are will never fade,

Love is a gift that ya' get when ya' give it away,
Reverberating out in waves,
Love is growing stronger every day,
Open up your heart you'll be amazed,
Love is a gift,

Love is more than just a crassy game we've played
before,
Give it time to get to know you feel it deep down in
your core,
Make Love Not War,
Make the world a better place for all of us worth living
for,
Now it's time for us to face it loves at the door.

We are made of the broken hearts we save,
To live and to laugh, to love and to learn to be brave.

Love is a gift that we get when we give it away,
Reverberating out in waves,
Love is growing stronger every day,
So open up your heart don't be afraid.
And don't you forget, that love,
Is a gift that ya' can't resist.
Love is a gift, that ya' get,
When ya' give, When ya' give it away.

Written by: Gregory Scott Fitzgibbon
A.K.A ARKANGELO OK, **USA**
© 12/28/2016

THE ANGEL IN ME - JEFF PESCETTO
Written By: Terri Lynne
https://youtu.be/hxXy2zf6sRU

-Lyrics

"The Angel In Me"

Although my eyes may never see,
The Angel watching over me,
Through my Angel's light I've learned,
Your WINGS PASSED ON – I've earned.

I look in my mirror,
Then glance up high,
I'm standing on solid ground,
After your spirit taught me to fly.

CHORUS:
Take the time to read the signs,
An Angel you will see,
One up above and one in your mirror,
Throughout eternity.

Trust in the process,
Each and every day,
Keep believing in miracles
As you find your life's way.

Your Angelic wings passed on will remain,
Inside my soul you'll always be,
The light and love that shaped my life,
Is the reason I believe in ME!

CHORUS:
I took the time
And read the signs,
An Angel I now see,
One up above
And one in my mirror...
To remain throughout eternity!

Now take your time and read the signs,
Let go, your soul is free,
See the ANGEL in your mirror,
Like I see "THE ANGEL IN ME!"
Trail off: Take the time, read the signs, throughout
eternity...

"The Angel In Me"
Terri Lynne – Lyrics
J Pescetto – Composition, Vocals, Guitar
R Bryant – Piano, Composition (R.I.P Angel)
Jesettopub. BMI
Copyright © 2011 Terri Lynne
All rights reserved.

I FEEL,
With an OPEN heart,
LOVE can enter your SPIRIT!
When LOVE enters your SPIRIT...
Your OPEN HEART will be able
To enter the world as a
SPIRIT FULL OF LOVE!!!

This was and still is my intention:
To UNITE; filling hearts with LOVE,
So our *world* will be *full of unconditional*
"UNITED LOVE!"

Below are a few suggestions for you to enjoy connecting with your *OWN heartbeat,* so you can *FEEL* the *LOVE in your heart* while resonating with *LOVE flowing through you.* Leaving you with being vulnerable and desiring to touch another's heart with your energy!

LOVE IS... *magnetic!*

I invite you to search for these meditation videos on youtube under the following titles. Shared to aid in opening your heart, allowing you to GIVE and ACCEPT receiving... "LOVE!"

GORGEOUS HEART CHAKRA MUSIC - DIVINE LOVE

HEART CHAKRA ACTIVATION AND HEALING
MEDITATION

THE FREQUENCY OF LOVE

THE UNIVERSE FULL OF LIGHT AND LOVE

THANK YOU FOR COMING INTO MY LIFE - ENZA

YOU ARE LOVE -

Section Eight

Testimonials

I am so grateful to Terri Lynne for guiding me to reconnect with the love I carry inside of my heart! By teaching me how to allow myself to release emotions, so I can see inside myself, leading me to once again feel loved!

During our phone session between Terri Lynne residing in the United States and myself residing in India, I had many awakening moments.

During the call, my third eye chakra was activated and on my chest I could feel the heart chakra activating. I saw what looked like a huge circle of light on my chest, which has never happened to me before, and my body was vibrating throughout!

This experience of these awakenings taking place, all put together was a beautiful miracle, which I believe has happened in me! Also, I never experienced any of this before in my life and I am grateful for having my connection with TL! She guided me to see that LOVE IS... inside my heart to connect to at any given moment of my life. Not an outside source to keep searching to find.

I am eternally grateful for Terri Lynne and for her healing me.

With Love from a very familiar stranger,
Chakravarthy Baddepudi Aka: CK
Bangalore, INDIA

Terri Lynne entered my life at what had to be one of the lowest times of my life. This dark period had to be the darkest, deepest hole I had been in, losing my way and light. Through conversations and energy healing work with TL, I was drawn in to the deepest depths of that darkness and shown the light. Following the healing and after a very troubled yet deep sleep and cryptic nightmares, I awoke.

Ever since Terri Lynne was kind enough to volunteer to work with me, from just that one session, I was brought back in to my light, piece by piece or as my favorite saying goes from Kate Mosse's book - Labyrinth... Pas a pas, se va luenh. (Step by step, we make our way)

Thank you Terri Lynne for guiding me back on to my path well lit. The darkness was first viewed during my healing experience, with you in the USA and me behind my closed door in the UK during our connecting moments. Thankfully once you guided me on how to find the key to open that door, I saw the light once again. I am eternally grateful for you connecting with my spirit.

With a Soul full of Love,
Ryan "Lunawolf" Smith Aka: Your "Baby Soul Brother"
Dover, Kent Shepherdswell, **UNITED KINGDOM**

I choose to reference you as, "Dearest Terri Lynne." The reason is because of all the people who have played an important role in my life, you stand amongst the top. There are very few who have impacted my life in the highest sense and you are among one of them. I was searching for answers and here you came. You held my hand, took me on the path of unconditional love, all the while showing me your intention of making me realize my optimum potential, while simultaneously teaching me what the purpose of life was. Of greatest importance is, to give and accept receiving Love. As well as, you helped me unlock and discover the gifts I was possessing. Although you never considered yourself as my teacher, but an equal, I still chose to give you the grade and call you the same fondly in my circles, especially with my family. By you helping me in the beginning, when I was struggling to understand my purpose and why I was blessed with my gifts, you gave me the support in the right way, by guiding me towards various meditations based on my gifts. If it had not been for you, I do not know how destiny would have taken me and guided me. But I believe God has sent angels for all of us. Its just connecting with them, at the destined time, is what you

taught me is most important. I do not know how many like myself that you have connected with, guided, and helped them to discover themselves, but I am grateful God sent you my way. You are truly the, "Goddess of Kindness and Love," in every way. Whatever else may be said for you is less.

Lots of Love,
Girish Daga
Mumbai, **INDIA**

My wife and I met Terri Lynne years ago online through a Spiritual Network very similar to Facebook at the time. It was at this site Terri Lynne reached out and said she was gathering information for a book she was writing, and wanted to include perspectives from all around the world answering a simple  fill in the blank answer of: Love is _____. I responded with, that's easy enough for me to answer, I am a songwriter and I have written a song about this very subject called "Love Is A Gift." Although I had written this song, it was deep within a stack of papers of unrecorded songs. Terri Lynne wanted to hear it, so I searched through hundreds of songs to find it. I then recorded it, and after seeing the video at https://www.youtube.com/watch?v=Bsem9hAybOM Terri Lynne definitely wanted to use it in her book "UNITED LOVE", and we could not be more excited to be a part of this journey. Terri Lynne is a Calming, Joyful, Uplifting Spiritual Person, a Bright Illuminated Soul, an Earth Angel, on

a mission to define what Love is, and this coincides perfectly with our mission to teach the world Love, Oneness and Hope for Humanity. It is our assessment, after really getting to know Terri Lynne over the past few years, that she truly has a gift, to help others work through their emotional pains, helping them to really dig deep within, forgive and finally let go, feeling lighter and happier within. It is a blessing to call her our friend. -Gregory Fitzgibbon Aka: ARKANGELO and Cynthia Fitzgibbon Oklahoma, USA

Leaving a Country and jumping in a New World, a mom is always anxious, not about herself, but more about her children. Through my child Julian, I met a friend and mom. Her name is Terri Lynne and I learned that she is such a loving and caring person, not only about her family but also about so many people! Although Terri would not need me apart of her life, she took me in as a friend, and sometimes like a sister. Through her I saw things I never would have seen, such as celebrating together Hanukkah, sleepovers from my son, and doing activities together up until the last minute before we had to move back to Germany. We were always going places with her family and us and I will always cherish our last adventure when we went to Catalina Island. Wherever we were or whomever we were with, going out just being together, we always had a lot of fun!

I also saw how caring she was with her mom therefore I respect her very much! Terri took such good care of her mom by tending to her endless calls; she always put her mom's needs first. She always included her and took her to so many places. For me Terri was a Vorbild- (Which means "A Role Model" in English).

When my son came back from Germany and should have gone a third time into a different class with different friends, Terri's Energy helped me and us so that my son could stay together in one class. She was a "Miracle Worker" for our family, because neither my husband, nor I could change the Principal's mind, and overnight through Terri's miracle the next day my son was allowed to stay in the same class as Terri's son Brandon.

I Also witnessed what a giving person she was and I saw Terri's present that she gave to the teacher at the end of the school year sharing a speech which was so unbelievably nice for that woman/teacher, who had been going through the pain of cancer while our boys were in her class in third grade.

Her honesty, her Love, her light will shine forever, for my family and for myself. For me, Terri Lynne is a real giver!

With Love and Appreciation,
Gisela
*Ingolstadt, **GERMANY***

 It's my honor and pleasure to write about you because you are a light beacon with a blinding light swiveling around from the top of a little lighthouse near a little sunny warm beach on the west coast with your bright light flowing in all directions. Reaching out to anyone on this planet anywhere with not a single location missed. And anyone who puts out their hand and asks for help will never be denied your care and love. And you are always there even in one's darkest hours. Constantly messaging and reminding them what an amazing life this is and it's ours if we let it sweep us up and send us on our journey. You are the Morpheus with the red and blue pill in this story. And you have a very engaging life story of your own battles and with it your losses and wins. If you were from more the South Eastern shores nearer the equator on a tiny tropical island, you would be the Amazonian Princess Warrior of Love and your weapon is the straight edged sword of pure light and love which will pierce the heart pushing through the body like melting butter. Charging the entire body and soul with the amazing compassion, the grace of God. And anyone who bears your call would be absolutely a mushroom for not immediately answering. It will be too distinct and entrancing to resist. Sometimes some people need a person to trust who can with few words, but unlimited unconditional love and also a untiring ear of pure love that can receive and process hours and hours of information and then calculate the correct formula from the words, to engage their person in need and say few words that will energize their power cells. And believe your truthful council that each one is unique and an emperor or empress in there own right.

Each one is so important that their whole existence will miss their absence if they disappeared. And the hole in existence can never be reconciled, as no one will ever be worthy to step into those shoes because it's unique and important to the evolution of life and the entire fate of the universe will change with all kinds of destructive ripples through time and space growing to proportions bigger than a blue star. The tapestry of life will have a missing thread that will ultimately unravel and be the total undoing of every thing. You understand this and you are kind and caring because of this knowledge and your struggles. I was lucky to have met you online. Only I don't believe in luck except in a way which only means I had no other choice, because I already chose you from the beginning of all time to be a part of my story and for me to be a part of yours. Which you simultaneously also agreed to be because you are. I am. And we are because everyone too is. There will be nothing if one were preparing to be without the other. It would not work. We are one community outside of the society governed by the self appointed leaders of their society where its run with deceit and secrecy, punishment and rewards, but no love and respect and working together is deceitfully advertised but secretly discouraged. With no gains in it for anyone to be satisfied since the good and the meek suffer at the bold and the unscrupulous feet in matters of work money financial gains. Mansions to live in for the extra work those people are highly placed in rank within their societies financial wealth massed and influence within the leaders circle. Sadly life does not flow within those circles. AND you Terri Lynne are one of the chosen few who are ready to sacrifice and be available for the millions and millions and then for the millionth and one individual who will hear you. When you speak you will say the truth and your straight edged sword of light and love will shepherd

them to the one single place on earth we all must get to before the next step and that's where love begins and all else ends. This is the point of awakening. And when it comes, it will be an explosion of nuclear proportions. The enlightening of love, which will melt away all that the worldly society of the dead put upon you and your yoke... and tricked you into believing it's importance and your binding interest in it which was a farce. Everything melts away when love fills you instantly and so rapidly at that point of endings and beginnings... As God's instrument on earth Terri Lynne has honed in the skill to wield all that she needs to be victorious so place your souls in her care, the place of love and watch it become all that is omnipotent... This is the single message that Terri Lynne is all about the message of universal uniting love and I totally agree with it and support it fully and can not wait to meet the millions and millions and the millionth and one. If just to say, hi I love you too. I hope there is enough there for you to start gleaning from and I'll have more written tomorrow. This flowed now without my mind getting involved to structure or plan anything. I laid it out as I felt you the words I chose to describe what I felt was the only thing I used brain power on and not the other way where in the intellectual arena brain power is used to fit the person of interest into their chosen story of lies to engage and distract the people with targeted hidden advertising to reinforce the lies constructed around a celebrity of sorts who endorses anything like an actor or actress. The person the world sees is the barrel of lies that made the person the persona that the movies chose the mask of Hollywood. Made so popular because the actors or actress' have the smile and the acting skills to make believe. Where in Terri's case it's the one universal truth that will free everyone not entrap themselves in the worldly Maya. You Terri thanked me for your endorsement, and I do appreciate your thank you reply. But in truth it is always been I who must thank you for allowing me to connect and allowing me to see and hear you from within you. Which is so much richer a connection, than the other way around, being the way most of the world connect. They first connect by physical attraction and then only if lucky they may get to the stage to connect with the inner self. Seeing the truth the primordial life that is hidden. We embraced this first up. And I am glad to be in it!

Love, Indi Shan
INDIA – AUSTRALIA

Terri Lynne is an angel that needs to be heard, and with her books, we get to hear every word...

A Reflection of my Connection with Terri Lynne... I am not sure how we met but it is a friendship that I could never forget... On life's road people come and go, then there are those we have always been destined to know... We know them when we meet for the connection is complete... And what they are truly interested to know, is how they can make our love in this world grow... For their true purpose of living, is for this world to see that our hearts are meant for giving... And so it is with my beautiful friend Terri Lynne who's heart shines so bright from within... And as we read through Terri's pages, we receive the messages

that are meant for all hearts, now and through the ages...

Steve Manley
Boston, Massachusetts – Tennessee – Boston, Mass
USA
A familiar stranger - A friend from a past life (We believe)

Terri Lynne, one who is in deep reverence and understanding of Love, came to this lifetime as a guide, so that those who cannot see or feel Love, can be healed of their blindness to the miracle of Love inside of them and all around them.

Terri has and always will be a warrior and champion of Divine Love. For those of you that do not understand or believe in Terri, look inside of your heart where your Truth has been denied from you. She speaks to these spaces inside of you, so that your heart can unfold and sing again.

Terri was born into a family and community that didn't have the ability to understand her gifts, nor did they understand the depths of love. She was born with intuitive abilities and had no guidance on how to develop them; in fact she was shamed and abused for her gifts. People have tried to quiet her voice, push her light down, and they were unsuccessful. If you ever have the honor to meet Terri or hear her speak, you will feel her unending strength. It was her strength that kept

her spirit alive and strong, and she is just the person to bring in the message of love. Her entire life thus far has prepared her to bring in the Love Revolution, where she leads others into the love in their soul.

Dr. Christine Surrago-Kousouli
*California, **USA***

I am blessed.

I am blessed because I have Terri Lynne in my life. We met in Junior High and have been friends now for over forty years. When we met, we were innocent young girls, enjoying life as teenage girls should. Along our life paths, our roads took us in different directions. But eventually, our roads we were traveling crossed back again. It was if time stood still.

While I traveled a linear path with my feet on the ground, Terri Lynne started listening to messages from above. She became a messenger between heaven and humanity. Her work on Earth, guided by the Heavens, was to spread light and love. Terri Lynne teaches us to listen to the voices within our own hearts. She is a Guardian Spirit who manifests goodness, purity and selflessness. It is her life's mission, not for her own gain, but to share with others. Her job, her life, her passion is to share her gift of love through touching one heart at a time. Terri Lynne truly walks this earth as an Earth Angel. Terri Lynne had a dream. Thru time this dream became

a vision. She wanted to spread LOVE, not just Locally or Globally, but Universally. I have watched Terri Lynne, over years, turn her dream to reality, as she touched every corner of this World. I am so proud of her.

I am excited.

I am excited for Terri Lynne to finally hold her completed book in her hands.

But, I think I am more excited for the World to receive her Gift of LOVE.

United Love.
xoxo Dr. Phyllis Weinstein
Aka: Terri Lynne's Soul Sister/Lifelong Friend
*California, **USA***

Terri Lynne is a living breath of love. Her book United Love, is a living breathing extension of her. LOVE.

My relationship with Terri Lynne began 16 years ago when as moms we met on the little league baseball field. It was a soul sister connection from the moment we met. Since then I have had the privilege to walk through life's journeys with Terri Lynne by my side and me by hers. I have personally witnessed all the work, love and tears Terri Lynne has endlessly poured forth into this beautifully orchestrated book about LOVE. From the initial inspiration from heaven to getting it out into the world, dedicated.

I feel incredibly blessed to be so close to a woman whose soul mission is to spread love. Period. To unite us all one heart at a time. Terri Lynne walks her talk spreading love, uniting love. She is an inspiration to us all.

Thank you for getting this book out into a world that needs healing. Less separation, more union, more love.

Krista Kubik
Yoga teacher, Holistic Living Specialist
Spreader of light and love.
Aka: Terri Lynne's Soul Sister
*California, **USA***

I have known and personally worked with Terri Lynne for the past 25+ years, beginning with the creation of her first books cover and now proudly coming out of retirement to presently assist with the creation of many im-ages in this book. We became a team once again collaborating on designing images, which represents TL's vision of what love is.

From my perspective there will never be a single vision of what love is. Terri Lynne has captured the essence of love by consulting many people. Even a single person's view of love changes as they mature and have a lifetime of experiences to shape their opinion.

Ron Lopez
Aka: Terri Lynne's Graphic Designer and Friend
*California, **USA***

Terri Lynne and I met in the fourth grade. We were the new kids at a new school whose connection was so immediate; it was as if magnets from the universe were manipulated by a higher power for the soul purpose of finding the other. A friendship like ours could not be clearly defined because the lines that normally create a sense of separation between two individuals were so beautifully blurred, that defining us as separate individuals was virtually, and literally, impossible.

Growing up I was TL's protector, guardian and shield. She was the true definition of a butterfly trapped inside a cocoon. The mere thought of poking out our heads for a quick peak outside our self-imposed zone of safety was terrifying, so we rarely ventured out and we never let anyone in. The muffled sound of laughing and whispering was all anybody on the outside would hear from us. We felt protected and safe and we were as happy as two friends could ever be because we had what we needed, which we knew was our soul sister connection with each other. The thought of adding to our friendship circle of two felt like a betrayal of the highest order but as we got older, the seams of our tightly guarded fortress unraveled and the once implausible thought of living our life without the other became a reality we had never thought possible.

It would be years before our paths reconnected us again and once we reconnected; it was as if time had stopped and there was no distance between us, ever. One night we were just catching up on our lives and she hesitantly began to tell me about things that she wasn't sure I would fully accept as her new normal. I was intently

listening to how everything in her life went upside down when her Granny Sara died. Losing Sara was a loss like none other for Terri, but her eyes were telling me a different story. One I didn't expect to hear from her. She told me that her granny's death unveiled Terri's own gifts as an 'intuitive healer' and her connection to her grandmother didn't end with her death, but rather created a new beginning connecting heaven and earth as one love united eternally. She kept pausing to see if I was still following along, and accepting what she was saying as the truth. I remember being completely floored by this revelation, not because I didn't believe her, but because it was my own Grandma's death that unveiled the same clairvoyance and intuitions in myself. I couldn't believe what I was hearing and I had no doubt that what she was saying was the absolute truth - because I was living it myself.

Terri's gifts for healing, I came to learn, are profound. If you talk to her about what she does, you will realize that she's actually the conduit between the person and the energy needed to heal from whatever caused someone to contact her in the first place. Terri doesn't manufacture or create the energy she talks about; she just seamlessly taps into it and allows it to flow through her and onto the other person. She opens up blocked channels that have hindered a person's ability to live their life to the fullest potential possible. There are many different types of energies that healers can tap into - but for years, Terri believes beyond any doubt that the energy needed most in our world is love. Over the years she has perfected her ability to cut through the chatter and deflections of what someone thinks they need - and focus' solely on what she knows instinctively to be true: What we really need more than anything else, especially now, is Love. Love, she says, rises above all else. Every emotion a human being can feel pales in comparison to the healing powers of love.

This book is a gift to anyone who wants a starting point on their journey to healing themselves, their family, their community and the world we all share together.

To my friend whose friendship transcends time, it's always been about love. xxx Victoria

Victoria Powells-Conway
Lifelong friend/Soul Sister
California, **USA**
***Representing someone who has known me my entire life minus a few years.

Interview with Joseph Mercado and Terri Lynne
Delving deep into Terri Lynne's "United Love" big dream.

MP3 Video Conference Call
https://fccdl.in/SNtJGbe1PE

To learn more about Terri Lynne, we invite you to listen to her personal story at the link below:
https://youtu.be/oliUf9VC4J8

657

Please feel free to visit Terri Lynne's website at: www.UnitedLove.Love to view more of Terri Lynne's big dream.

Also, on this United Love website you will receive a gift from my heart to yours, in appreciation for accepting to become a link in our Chain of Love.

This gift will bring my vision and my hearts intention into clear view for your heart to feel, hear and see.

Terri Lynne also invites you to visit the United Love Instagram page at: unitedloveconnection

Here you will receive LOVE at a glance, to add light to your life on a daily basis while feeling UNITY through LOVE.

Warmly, TL

About The Author

Author, Terri Lynne is a "Dreamer" and proud to carry this title, because she has a big dream that she has carried inside her heart since she took her first breath in this lifetime, which is to unite the universe through all of what LOVE IS! First TL lived life learning about LOVE through generations passed on... in which she shared in her first book, "Wings Passed On..." and now she has chosen to spread this energy to everyone everywhere, by uniting through open hearts; while holding hands and crossing bridges to reach each other, connecting as ONE "UNITED LOVE" team of angels on earth! Experiencing unity through our actions by loving ourselves first, then passing our LOVE on... by loving all others! Teaching Earth how we can be "Heaven's Mirror's Reflection," when we all learn to "Believe in Miracles" and trust that "Big Dreams" really can come true, as long as you never give up on your dreams; for then one day... this hopeful mom will have the entire world believing in her Big Dream too! LOVE IS: Powerful & the power of LOVE trumps all!!!

LOVE IS... carrying a dream in your heart and never letting go until your dream becomes Heaven and Earths Reality! -TL

Credits

With sincere appreciation to all my creative geniuses for helping me bring my vision to life in a beautiful, colorful way.

Eva Baruch
    Graphic Designer
    Cover Designs – Front, Back and Spine

Ron Lopez
    Graphic Designer for images reflecting Terri Lynne's Love is messages

David Krakov –
    Artist
    Love Flutters By Mini
    My Heart Is All A Flutter
    Book of Life
Thank you for giving me your consent to use your artwork masterpieces in my United Love book. I am eternally grateful!

Additional Images:
Google Images, Pixabay Images, Shutter Stock Images, and Canva.com Images

Music by:
Paul Luftenneger
    "Universal Love"
Gregory Fitzgibbon Aka: Arkangelo
    "Love Is A Gift"
Jeff Pescetto
    "The Angel In Me"

My deepest appreciation goes out to all the creative artists for designing images and songs included in this book to help spread LOVE around the world! The Universe is eternally grateful for your gift of creativity and for your hearts full of what LOVE IS!

Love is...
the greatest feeling one can hold and
carry upon ones wings and spirit imprints!

Be the spark designed to ignite another's
eternal flame!
The End and New Beginning...

Signing off... soaring upon the wings of LOVE!
Eternally yours,
Terri Lynne Aka:
"ANGEL OF LOVE!"

661